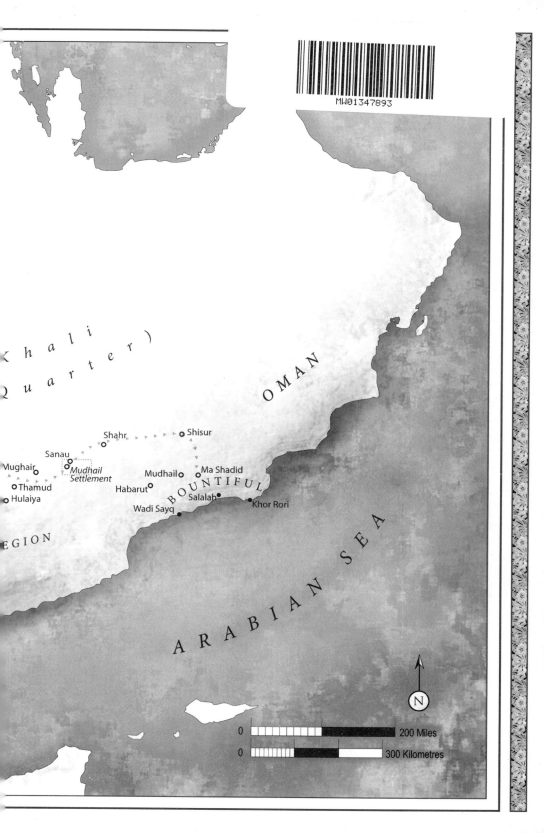

OUT OF JERUSALEM

—VOLUME TWO—

A LIGHT IN THE WILDERNESS

OTHER BOOKS AND AUDIO BOOKS
BY H. B. MOORE:

Out of Jerusalem: Of Goodly Parents

OUT OF JERUSALEM

─✦─ VOLUME TWO ─✦─

A LIGHT IN THE WILDERNESS

a novel by

H. B. MOORE

Covenant Communications, Inc.

Cover image *Lehi Traveling Near the Red Sea* © Gary E. Smith

Cover design copyrighted 2005 by Covenant Communications, Inc.

Published by Covenant Communications, Inc.
American Fork, Utah

Copyright © 2005 by H. B. Moore

All rights reserved. No part of this book may be reproduced in any format or in any medium without the written permission of the publisher, Covenant Communications, Inc., P.O. Box 416, American Fork, UT 84003. This work is not an official publication of The Church of Jesus Christ of Latter-day Saints. The views expressed within this work are the sole responsibility of the author and do not necessarily reflect the position of The Church of Jesus Christ of Latter-day Saints, Covenant Communications, Inc., or any other entity.

This is a work of fiction. The characters, names, incidents, places, and dialogue are products of the author's imagination, and are not to be construed as real.

Printed in Canada
First Printing: September 2005

11 10 09 08 07 06 05   10 9 8 7 6 5 4 3 2 1

ISBN 1-19156-943-5

Dedicated to my husband, Chris.
May our own journey continue with faith.

Acknowledgments

Words cannot express my appreciation for my husband's support in writing this second volume. There are only so many ways to say "thank you," so I hope this dedication will suffice. And my gratitude for my sweet children—Kaelin, Kara, Dana, and Rose, who at six months old kept me company during many early morning hours of writing—is endless.

My parents, Kent and Gayle Brown, have added authenticity to the manuscript through their perceptive and careful reading. This venture would not have come to fruition if it weren't for their encouragement and the expertise of my father. A thousand thanks.

My gratitude also extends to my father-in-law, Lester Moore, for his insightful review and tremendous support.

Special thanks goes to my critique group for their sacrifice of time and willingness to work with my deadline—LuAnn Staheli, Stephanni Hicken, Annette Lyon, Jeff Savage, Lynda Keith, and Michelle Holmes.

My appreciation extends to Amy Finnegan for her intuitive review and Dave LeFevre, whose evaluation helped fine-tune several historical details.

In addition, the staff at Covenant has been truly generous and wonderful to work with, namely Christian Sorensen for his proficient editing.

Finally, heart-felt appreciation goes to Karen, Loree, KD, Linda, and Jean for their friendship and support in my day-to-day life as a mother and a writer.

PREFACE

A Light in the Wilderness, the second volume in the Out of Jerusalem series, continues the saga of Lehi and Ishmael's families on their journey through the wilderness. In volume one, *Of Goodly Parents,* the prophet Lehi was commanded by the Lord to take his family and flee Jerusalem. Once they were settled in the wilderness, Lehi's sons returned to Jerusalem to retrieve the brass plates at the Lord's request. Then, a second time, Lehi's sons were commanded to go to their homeland and bring Ishmael's family into the wilderness. The daughters of Ishmael each married a son of Lehi. Paralleling 1 Nephi 1–16, volume one concluded soon after the broken bow incident in chapter sixteen.

From the moment Lehi and his family left Jerusalem to the time they reached the land of Bountiful, they spent eight years sojourning in the desert. Research indicates that it would have taken a caravan approximately four months to travel the 2,200 miles along the incense trail from Jerusalem to the estimated location of the land of Bountiful. Thus, the questions arise: Why did it take Lehi and his family eight years to sojourn in the wilderness and what happened during that time?

Further research was required beyond the few verses found in 1 Nephi 17. To *sojourn* not only means to travel or journey, but it also denotes servitude. In the Old Testament, the verb to *sojourn* applies to servile relationships (Ex. 12:48–49; Lev. 16:29; 17:8; etc.). David Daube, historian and expert in ancient law, expounds, "throughout the Old Testament the verb definitely has the connotation 'to live as a subject'—be it as resident alien, hireling, slave or inferior wife" (*The Exodus Pattern in the Bible,* 24). In the Book of Mormon this meaning may be twofold in the sense that Nephi could have meant they were refugees under the protection of their God or that they were strangers living under the protection of another. Book of Mormon scholar S. Kent Brown theorizes that Lehi's family may have entered into a servile relationship with nomads in the Arabian Desert (*From Jerusalem to Zarahemla,* 55–59).

Hints of the family's possible challenges appear throughout the Book of Mormon in references to "battle" and "bondage" (Alma 9:22), "enemies" (Omni 1:6; Alma 9:10), and being "smitten with . . . sore afflictions" (Mosiah 1:17). Just before Lehi's death, he urged his sons to "shake off the awful chains," possibly relating their spiritual salvation to the servitude they experienced (2 Ne. 1:13).

Another hint comes later when Lehi blesses his youngest son, Joseph, and refers to the time spent in the wilderness as "the days of [his] greatest sorrow" (2 Ne. 3:1). In addition, Alma the Younger offers this valuable morsel: "[God] has also brought our fathers out of the land of Jerusalem; and he has also . . . delivered them out of bondage and captivity" (Alma 36:29).

Other clues pertaining to the possible events in the wilderness are found in the histories of southern Arabia, which outline the presence of inhospitable tribes from antiquity to the recent past. Traveling between the territories controlled by warring and bloodthirsty tribes would have been a challenge for Lehi's family. Bargaining and negotiating for safe passage and protection would have been perilous. As a result, the women toiled and suffered all things in such a way that it may have been better had they died before leaving Jerusalem (1 Ne. 17:20).

This second volume covers thirteen verses from 1 Nephi 16:33 through 17:6. Because there was so little scriptural information to rely on, I spent a great deal of time researching works written by well-respected explorers of Arabia such as Wilfred Thesiger, Charles Doughty, and Bertram Thomas. Various Book of Mormon scholars, including George Potter, Richard Wellington, Warren Aston, S. Kent Brown, Lynn Hilton, and David Seely, were among the appreciated authors whose works offered insights.

Of important note, the journey Lehi's family took from Nahom was "nearly eastward" (1 Ne. 17:1) until they reached western Oman where their journey would have turned south. Some of the terrain covered would have been rocky and mountainous, and encounters with hostile tribes may have caused the travelers to deviate from a direct eastward journey through present-day Yemen. Without question, water would have been paramount to the family's survival. Thus, the route I have portrayed in the book follows a pattern of water sources including wells, springs, or rain runoff.

It is my hope that the readers will continue to enjoy this fictional interpretation of the inspirational story of Lehi and Ishmael's families and come to understand the types of sacrifices made by prophets of God and their children on our behalf.

Enjoy the journey!

FAMILY CHART

Lehi & Sariah—Lineage of Manasseh
    Laman [m. Anah]
    Lemuel [m. Puah]
    Samuel [m. Tamar]
    Nephi [m. Isaabel]
    Elisheba
    Dinah

Ishmael & Bashemath—Lineage of Ephraim
    Raamah [m. Leah, deceased]
        Tiras
    Heth [m. Zillah]
        Jochebed
    Rebeka [m. Zoram]
    Anah [m. Laman]
    Puah [m. Lemuel]
    Tamar [m. Sam]
    Isaabel [m. Nephi]

Zoram [m. Rebeka]

CHAPTER 1

*Now faith is the substance of things hoped for,
the evidence of things not seen.*
(Hebrews 11:1)

Gusts of wind danced on the arid oasis of Bishah, erasing the footprints from Nephi's triumphant return to camp. Like fallen dates, black tents dotted the landscape, housing the sleeping family members of Lehi and Ishmael. In the center of camp, tendrils of smoke curled toward the sky from the morning fire as Sariah placed atim wood onto the crackling flames.

A short distance away, Nephi knelt next to the rough altar in the pale light. Before him lay the Liahona, which had found a temporary home in front of the mound of stones. Bowing his head, Nephi began to pray. "O Lord, through Thy mercies we have been blessed with food. Harmony exists among the family members, for which I am grateful. O Father, Thou knowest all our needs. Please ease the suffering of my father-in-law, Ishmael. Let us know Thy will, O God. Amen."

Footsteps approached. Nephi turned and saw a slight figure coming toward him. Gratitude flooded through him. It was his wife, Isaabel, and although she was young, she had already brought a quiet strength beyond her years to their marriage.

"I've interrupted you," Isaabel said when she stopped beside him.

"I am finished." Nephi rose to his feet and took her hand. "How is your father?"

Isaabel pulled away and stared past him, her dark eyes rimmed in red. "His coughing brings up blood."

Wincing, Nephi touched the hair that curled against her forehead, wishing he could erase the agony etched in her copper complexion. "Is your mother with him?"

Isaabel brought her gaze to meet Nephi's. "She's been crying since dawn."

Nephi closed his eyes briefly, feeling a lump form in his throat. "And you, my Isa, how are you?"

Isaabel covered her face with her hands, all resolve melting.

Nephi pulled her trembling body into his embrace. He glanced at the cloudless sky, blinking his own tears away. "My father and I will give him a blessing," he said in a thick voice. "I'll find him and meet you at your father's tent."

After a few moments, Isaabel began to relax. She raised her face to Nephi's. "Thank you."

Nephi wiped away the tears that stained Isaabel's cheeks with his turban, then kissed her forehead. Isaabel turned and walked back to the camp.

After watching her go, Nephi faced the altar again. "Please, Lord, let Ishmael find comfort and healing," he whispered. Tears filled his eyes as he thought about his father-in-law. The faithfulness of the man was almost beyond comprehension—following Lehi's family into the wilderness without hesitation, bringing his daughters and sons, risking his own failing health. Nephi glanced at the Liahona against the base of the altar. To his amazement, words began forming on the brass ball, something that had never happened without the presence of Lehi.

Nephi knelt in the soft sand, staring at the words—a command—for his family to leave the oasis Bishah. Nephi clasped his hands together and raised his eyes to the heavens. "O Lord of my righteousness, hear my prayer. Lift up the light of

Thy countenance upon us. Have mercy on Ishmael and bless him with strength to travel so that we may obey Thy commandments." A sensation of warmth grew within Nephi's bosom, giving him the knowledge that the Lord was mindful of Ishmael.

The sound of approaching footsteps caused Nephi to conclude his prayer. He looked up to see his father, Lehi, at his side.

Lehi placed a hand on his shoulder. Words were not needed.

Covering Lehi's hand with his own, Nephi studied his father. Since the day Nephi had returned to camp bearing the slain animals, spirits had run high amid the combined families of Lehi and Ishmael. Lehi's determination had waxed stronger than ever, his faith solidified.

Although Ishmael's illness brought Lehi grief, Nephi saw that his father's expression appeared lighter, and the wrinkles etched in his face had diminished. "Father, look," Nephi said, pointing at the Liahona.

Lehi crouched to read the words. He was silent for several moments, then said, "It is for the best. We must move before food grows scarce." Rising, he scanned the shimmering terrain to the south. "May God keep us." He motioned with his hand to Nephi. "Come, we have a devout man who needs a blessing before the journey."

Nephi rose and joined his father on the short walk back to camp. The rest of the family members were just beginning to stir with the new day. A couple of the women busied themselves around the fire, preparing for the morning meal. As Nephi and Lehi approached Ishmael's tent, Isaabel stepped out and greeted them, then held the flap so they could pass through.

It took a moment for Nephi's eyes to adjust to the dimness within the tent. Ishmael was propped in a near-sitting position against several bedrolls. Once a jovial and well-proportioned man, Ishmael's gaunt figure formed only a remnant of the presence he once commanded. The physical change was unsettling to Nephi, but the faith and conviction in Ishmael's eyes remained constant.

Ishmael raised his hand in weak acknowledgement. "Welcome," he said in a strained voice. Then his face contorted, and his hand flew to his mouth. He doubled over in pain as great coughs wracked his chest.

His wife, Bashemath, held a cloth to his mouth and stroked his back. Bashemath's graying hair was well hidden beneath her mantle, her skin brown and weathered. Though her eyes were swollen with anguish, her stout hands worked deftly as she cared for her husband. When the coughing subsided, Ishmael leaned back, his energy spent. Bashemath gently wiped the blood from his lips and chin, then drew respectfully away and sat against the far side of the tent.

Nephi stepped over Ishmael and knelt on one side with Lehi opposite him. They placed their hands on Ishmael's head, and Lehi began to pray in a low voice. The words were not those of healing, Nephi noticed, but of comfort. He felt the urge to cry out and plead for Ishmael to recover his full strength and live many years.

When Lehi concluded the prayer, Ishmael opened his damp eyes. Nephi took his tremulous hand and steadied it with his own.

"We have been commanded to continue our journey," Lehi told Ishmael. "The Lord will keep you as only He is able."

Ishmael nodded. Suddenly a high-pitched wail interrupted the quiet of the tent.

"My husband is in no condition to move. Can't you see it will kill him?" Bashemath cried, collapsing to her knees with a sob.

Lehi turned to look at her, his face grave. "We must follow the Lord's commandments, for it is He who sustains our lives."

Ishmael pressed Nephi's hand. Nephi met the ailing man's eyes and smiled. Ishmael once again had chosen to follow the Lord's prophet in faith. "He understands," Nephi said.

Bashemath stared at the men with disdain. "He's delirious." She wrung her hands together.

Ishmael raised himself on an elbow, triggering another wracking cough.

"Don't—" Bashemath began, her eyes widening. She started to move to his side.

But her husband held up a hand, his expression determined. He waited to catch his breath. "Prepare—our—things," he wheezed.

Nephi rose to his feet, marveling at his father-in-law's endurance, and joined Isaabel outside. By the time they reached their own tent, word had spread quickly, and provisions were already being loaded. Ishmael's sons, Raamah and Heth, were burying the fire pit with sand. Heth's wife, Zillah, sat with their three-year-old daughter, Jochebed, so she would not get in the way of preparations. When Nephi and Isaabel had finished packing and loading their tent and supplies, they separated to help each of their parents.

On the way to Lehi's tent, Nephi passed his two sisters, Elisheba and Dinah, who were letting Raamah's six-year-old son, Tiras, chase them. When Dinah spotted Nephi, she ran up to him. "Are we going to the promised land now?" she asked, sliding her hand into Nephi's.

Nephi smiled at his youngest sister as they walked hand in hand. Her long lashes fluttered against her curved cheeks as she grinned up at him. Even at the age of eleven, she was still full of childlike exuberance. "Every time we travel, we draw closer to the land of promise," Nephi said.

"Do you think there will be other girls my age?" Dinah asked, her black eyes growing serious.

"If the Lord guides other families to the promised land, then there will surely be more children for you to be friends with."

Dinah considered his answer. "I wish we were already there."

Nephi squeezed her hand. "Me too."

They soon reached Lehi's tent, where Sariah was pulling stakes from the ground. The roundness of her stomach made the task of bending seem arduous. With a pang, Nephi noticed the dark spots on her hands, the only real sign of his mother's forty years in age.

"Rest, Mother. We can finish here," Nephi said, kneeling beside her and taking a stake from her hand.

Sariah turned and shielded her eyes from the rising sun. Beads of perspiration dotted her forehead, emphasizing faint lines in her skin. A lock of dark brown hair, still free from gray, had fallen over her shoulder. "Good morning, Nephi." She stretched her back. "Thank you. Perhaps I'd better rest for a while."

Lehi emerged from the tent, carrying a bedroll. "This is the last of it."

Seeing Nephi, he said, "I'll bring the camels to be loaded. I do not want Mother working more than necessary."

Grateful that his father was willing to aid with the women's work, Nephi instructed Dinah to finish removing the stakes, then together they folded the tent.

"I cannot wait until Mother's baby is born." Dinah's cheerful manner penetrated through Nephi's thoughts.

Nephi glanced at her across the tent. "You will be a great help." Inwardly he was relieved that his mother would also have Bashemath and her daughters to attend her during the birth. He secured the rolled tent with a lashing.

"When is Isaabel going to have a baby?" Dinah asked.

Nephi felt his face grow warm. "I don't know." He lifted one end of the tent and dragged it to the waiting camels.

Dinah kept pace. "Rebeka's going to have one, so why not Isaabel?"

"Only the Lord knows such things." Nephi turned and looked at his sister. "Now go see if Mother needs anything else."

Dinah smiled and scurried off through the sand, unaware of the feelings she had stirred in Nephi.

When his parents' provisions were secured on the camels, Nephi scanned the camp. Only a few other camels were loaded. He sighed, knowing that his father would want to leave as soon as possible. Two tents were still erect, and Laman and Lemuel were nowhere to be seen.

Nephi saw his older brother, who was in his usual good spirits, approach. Although Sam's round face had grown thinner since living in the wilderness, his sense of humor remained intact. And the mop of hair on his head was curlier than ever.

"There you are," Sam said as he neared. "I think we need to give our other brothers a gentle nudge." His eyes twinkled as his mouth widened into a mischievous grin.

"Sure." Nephi held back a smile. "Lead the way."

When Nephi and Sam reached the two tents, they hesitated, listening. But there was no sign of movement or conversation.

"I'll take this one," Sam whispered, pointing at the closest one. Nephi nodded and moved noiselessly toward the other one.

With a few swift actions, both tents were unstaked. The brothers stood back, watching the panels cave inward.

Shouts erupted from within the goat-hair walls and several grunts could be heard. After some wild movements, Laman struggled out of the opening. When he saw his younger brothers laughing, his face turned from red to purple. "You!" He scrambled to his feet, but he was too late. Sam and Nephi fled the scene, clutching their sides in laughter.

Lemuel emerged from his collapsed tent. "What's going on here?"

Laman's handsome face twisted as he scowled at his brother. "Looks like we're leaving again. Go fetch the good camels." Behind him, Anah finally emerged. Laman turned to his wife. "Prepare our things to be loaded. I'm going to eat."

Anah stared after her husband as he walked away.

* * *

Isaabel moistened her father's forehead with a damp cloth. His breathing was rapid, but his body relaxed as he lay on a rug in the warming sand. She hummed as her mother and sisters finished loading their camels. Nearby she saw Rebeka stagger forward and empty the contents of her stomach. Her oldest sister had been with child a few months, but she still looked like a reed. If it were possible, Rebeka had grown thinner than before.

Rising quickly, Isaabel hurried to her sister. "Come and sit by Father. I'll finish your chores."

Relief stretched across Rebeka's face. "You sound like Zoram."

Isaabel led her gently to their father's side. "You have a good husband. I'll tell him where you are."

Nodding, Rebeka settled next to their father, taking his hand in hers.

Isaabel then left to find Zoram. On the way, she neared two of her sisters, Anah and Puah, who were just finishing their preparations. Their husbands, Laman and Lemuel, were nowhere in sight. Without even turning around, Isaabel knew that the two brothers would be sitting around the fire, lingering over their morning meal, while everyone else worked.

"How's Father?" Anah asked.

"He's determined to travel," Isaabel answered.

A shadow passed over Anah's face. "Is he feeling any better?"

With hesitation, Isaabel answered, "Lehi and Nephi gave him a blessing . . . It calmed him a great deal."

Puah's brow creased in apprehension. "He needs a room with clay walls and a good bed. We should never have come into the wilderness."

Chewing her lip, Isaabel decided that now wasn't the time to argue with her sisters. She too desired her father's well being, but there was nothing they could do. After their experience with the broken bow, she knew that following the Lord's commandments came before any physical illness or discomfort. It was perplexing to Isaabel that her sisters could seem so grateful one moment and so angry the next. "If Father grows worse, I'm certain Lehi will stop."

Puah snorted and turned away.

Anah's eyes grew moist. "How much more can he endure?" she asked.

Isaabel stepped forward and touched her older sister's arm. "At least we're not on our hands and knees like Rebeka."

A small smile escaped Anah's lips. "Isa, you are impossible to complain to."

Relieved at her sister's change in countenance, Isaabel sighed. "I'd better see if Zoram needs anything since Rebeka is too weak to help." She walked to where her brother-in-law battled a cantankerous camel. Zoram's pockmarked face glistened with sweat.

"Steady, boy," Zoram commanded as he tried to calm the beast.

Isaabel reached up and stroked the camel's neck. She offered a date to the groaning animal, which finally dropped to its knees and settled in the sand.

Zoram looked sideways at her. "I was just going to do that." He bent and picked up a bundle then lashed it onto the reclining camel's back. "Have you seen my wife?"

"She's keeping Father company," Isaabel said. "I don't think she's feeling well."

"Of course she isn't, even though she insists she's fine." Worry crossed Zoram's face as he secured the rope. "I've never met a more stubborn woman than Rebeka. If it's the only thing I accomplish today, she's going to be riding the camel, whether she agrees to or not."

"It looks like you are ready to go," Isaabel said, scratching the camel's head. "I'll let Rebeka know you're packed." She dropped her hand and moved away.

The camel lunged forward as it struggled to its feet. When it almost tipped off balance, Zoram cursed. His face reddened. "I'm sorry, I—"

Isaabel waved him off and walked away, no longer able to contain her smile. Though Zoram had never been outspoken in his beliefs about God, she could sense his strong faith. He was friendly with everyone and rarely took sides in any argument.

As she continued to walk, Isaabel passed Lehi and Sariah's vacant campsite. Something glinted in the sand, catching her eye. She bent and picked it up. It was a gold hoop earring, probably Sariah's. Staring at the gleaming metal, Isaabel was surprised to feel her eyes well with emotion. Sometimes the nostalgic feelings for home caught her unaware. But she kept her longings to herself, knowing that if she spoke about them, she'd only dwell on them more.

Raising her head, Isaabel inspected the busy camp for Nephi. Soon she saw him working in tandem with Sam as they loaded Tamar's bedroll and tent onto a camel. The brothers were laughing about something while Tamar stood nearby, hands on her hips. Obviously she didn't find their joke amusing.

Watching her new husband made her heart swell with humility. When she had believed she would never see Nephi or his family again, she had almost given up hope. Then came the trial of the marriage contracts. Laman had made his intentions toward her clear, and she had lived each day in fear that she would be given to a man who only regarded her with lust in his heart. But who was she to think that she was worthy of Nephi?

Her chin trembled as the memories resurfaced. Nephi had loved her and left the betrothal decision to the Lord. Waves of gratitude filled her soul as she realized the blessing the Lord had granted her. A young, inexperienced girl to become the wife of a man like Nephi—a man who had seen visions from God, who would be the leader of his family someday. She closed her eyes, offering a prayer of appreciation for the miracles in her life.

With Nephi by her side, she could endure her father's illness, her sisters' complaints, and her fear of the unknown journey before them.

An urgent voice broke through her thoughts. "Hurry, Isa. We're ready."

She raised her head and saw Tamar coming toward her.

"What are you doing? Sleeping like a mule?" Tamar asked.

Isaabel moved forward so her sister couldn't see her eyes and quickly displayed the earring she'd found. "I discovered this in the sand."

"It must be one of Sariah's," Tamar said.

"That's what I thought." Isaabel cleared her throat. "What were Nephi and Sam laughing about?"

Pursing her lips, Tamar remained silent.

Isaabel linked her arm through her sister's. "Come now, tell me. I won't laugh."

"I told them to make their older brothers help their wives more. But they seemed to think it was a great accomplishment that Laman and Lemuel were even awake." Tamar sighed with frustration.

Isaabel squeezed her sister's arm. "I agree with you, but we need to let Nephi and Sam handle it. We don't want to cause a rift with our sisters."

Although Tamar didn't answer, Isaabel knew that she herself wouldn't try to interfere with the brothers' relationship again unless it was a matter of Nephi's safety. She had decided to leave the arguments for Nephi to deal with. Anah and Puah were disenchanted at times with their husbands' behaviors, but their marriages were their own affair. Isaabel wondered if what little faith her sisters had in God was sometimes drowned out by their husbands' complaints and the hardships they continued to experience. She sighed inwardly, knowing that ultimately her sisters would be responsible for their own choices, regardless of the path their husbands took.

When they reached Tamar and Sam's camel, nearly all the camp was ready to leave. Lehi stood at the front of the caravan, giving instructions to Laman about the formation they would travel in.

Sariah sat upon her camel in the middle of the procession, her face pale but her head held high. Isaabel moved to her side and handed her the earring, receiving a grateful smile in return.

Lehi held up his arms for silence. As the conversations faded, he said, "As you know, the Lord has instructed us to move forward again. We will do so in faith. We have much to be grateful for and will continue to keep the commandments so that we may be guided by the word of God through the Liahona."

CHAPTER 2

*For this child I prayed; and the Lord
hath given me my petition which I asked of him.*
(1 Samuel 1:27)

Lehi noticed Sariah gripping her camel's neck, which caused it to let out a groan of protest. He moved to her side and touched her hand. Just then, her face twisted with pain. "Please give me Thy strength, O Lord, to endure this well," she muttered.

"We will stop now," Lehi said.

Perspiration bathing her face, Sariah looked at him. "There is no water here," she said, the desperation evident in her voice.

"Your time has arrived," Lehi said in an even tone, trying to conceal the alarm he felt. "We can delay no longer."

As the group came to a halt, the women rushed forward to help Sariah from her camel. She cradled her abdomen as her breathing shortened. Speaking in a soft voice, Isaabel grasped Sariah's shoulders as another convulsion escalated. "We'll have you settled soon."

Sariah was lowered to the ground onto a rug. When she opened her eyes briefly, Bashemath held a cup near her face. "Take a drink, dear," she urged.

Raising her head, Sariah sipped the lukewarm shrub tea. Seeing that the women had taken Sariah into their care, Lehi stepped away as they erected the birthing tent, which would block the heat of the sun. As he turned his back and started to walk away, he heard her familiar voice cry out, "Have mercy, O Lord."

The words of his wife pained him to the core. Once he reached the proper distance required between a birthing mother and her husband, Lehi stopped and paced. According to practice, it was essential that his wife have enough water for cleansing the baby and herself. But the concern of where to get the needed water only momentarily overruled Lehi's true worry—the baby was coming earlier than expected, and Sariah's life was at risk. He glanced away from where Sariah was stationed to where the others were setting up camp—a respectable distance from the birthing tent.

Lehi strode to where Nephi and Sam unloaded the camels. "Mother needs water."

Nephi paused in his work and wiped his brow. "Should we continue on until we find some?"

"We don't know how far it may be," Lehi said. "You and Sam travel back to the oasis we came across yesterday and fetch water from its well."

Laman appeared behind Nephi. "Sam and Nephi aren't going anywhere," he said harshly. His eyes were bloodshot, and his mouth twitched.

Looking at his oldest son in surprise, Lehi began, "But—"

"*But*," Laman mocked. "Mother should not be going through this. Not here." He spat on the ground, and his eyes narrowed. "She should be in a comfortable home with a midwife to attend."

Lehi stared at his son, recognizing the rage that was about to spill forth.

"It is not right, Father." Laman clenched his hands. "A man of God such as you should have felt more compassion for his own wife. *You* are to blame for this."

"Laman, arguing will not help your mother." Lehi raised his voice, speaking in measured tones.

"I am not finished, Father." Raising his fist, Laman shook it toward Lehi. "Lemuel and I will go and fetch the water, but only because Mother is in dire need." His gaze settled on Nephi. "We don't need someone who will stop and pray every few paces along the way."

Nephi stepped forward, his mouth opening in protest.

But Laman had already turned away. He began jerking goatskin bags from the pile of provisions that Nephi and Sam had just unloaded. He whistled, and Lemuel rushed over. "Come. We are going back to the well for water."

Without comment, Lemuel followed his brother's lead, and soon he and Laman were merely a dust cloud in the distance.

* * *

Isaabel entered the small tent. The air was somewhat humid from Sariah's heavy breathing in the close quarters. Isaabel had come to help with the birthing process but felt anxious for the events about to take place. Though she'd never attended a birth, she hoped she could be of service.

Bashemath hummed while dabbing Sariah's forehead with a damp cloth. She turned to see who'd entered. "Not you, Isaabel," she said. "Bring Rebeka."

Noticing the perspiration upon her mother's brow, Isaabel said, "But Rebeka is too weak."

Bashemath wrinkled her nose. "I was never so helpless when I was with child." She studied her youngest daughter for a moment. "What about Anah or Puah?"

"Laman and Lemuel left to find water, so they are unloading by themselves," Isaabel said, knowing her sisters set up by themselves regardless of their husbands' whereabouts.

"I guess you'll do," Bashemath said with reluctance.

A moan came from Sariah.

Isaabel swallowed hard against the rising fear. Seeing her mother-in-law in such a state distressed her.

"Take this cloth and wet it every few moments," Bashemath instructed, pointing to a nearly empty goatskin bag. "Be mindful of how much water you use. This is the last of it." She shifted her position, scooped a mint leaf paste from a clay bowl, and began to rub it onto Sariah's legs.

The aroma of mint filled the tent, and Isaabel inhaled deeply, hoping the scent would calm her. "Does that help with the pain?" she asked her mother.

Bashemath grimaced and shook her head. "The pain will be the same, but the mint leaves are meant to soothe. It stimulates the blood flow for mother and child."

Isaabel took the cloth and moistened it from the goatskin, then gently dabbed Sariah's hairline. Sariah's eyes were closed and tears stained her cheeks. Her parched mouth moved in rhythmic motion as she repeated the same words over and over. Isaabel leaned closer to hear.

"Thy will be done," Sariah whispered.

"Are you all right, Sariah?" Isaabel asked, but her mother-in-law continued muttering. Isaabel straightened and stared at her mother. "Do you understand what she's saying?"

"It means nothing," Bashemath said without looking up. "The pain has made her incoherent."

"But her words are so disheartening," Isaabel said, worry sounding in her voice. "Do you think she'll be all right?"

Bashemath stopped rubbing Sariah's leg and looked at her daughter with reproach. Then her face softened. "Childbirth is what women must endure. Sariah is strong and has borne six healthy children already. Remain calm and have faith." She touched Isaabel's arm.

Isaabel looked at the lined hand upon her arm. Her mother rarely showed affection. The long fingers and strong knuckles resembled her own, though aged in appearance. In her mother's hand she saw her own future reflected—a future of hard work and caring for children. Although her mother's unsympathetic nature often caused Isaabel sorrow, she saw that the love and caring came not through her mother's eyes, but through her hands—and deeds.

Bashemath withdrew her touch and continued to rub Sariah's legs. For a moment, Isaabel had felt akin to her mother. As she remoistened the cloth and blotted the perspiration from Sariah's face, Isaabel vowed that if she gave birth to a daughter, she would never make her feel less for being female.

Suddenly a cry erupted from Sariah. Isaabel, her pulse beating wildly, looked at her mother.

"It is time," Bashemath said in an unhurried tone.

Panic rose in Isaabel's chest. She silently prayed for her own strength.

Bashemath's steady voice set Isaabel into action. "First, we will help Sariah to a kneeling position. Then you must brace yourself against her so that she may use you for support."

Isaabel started to lift Sariah when her mother said, "Wait until the next pain passes."

A moment later, Sariah cried out again, and her eyes flew open. She seemed to focus on something on the tent ceiling, her gaze clouded. Her cries grew louder, forming incomprehensible words that sounded somewhat like a prayer chant.

A tear escaped Isaabel's eye as she tried to stave off her emotion.

"Now," Bashemath said, taking hold of Sariah's right side. Together they heaved Sariah forward until she was kneeling.

* * *

Lehi watched the northwestern horizon as his eyes strained in the gathering darkness. Cries could be heard coming from Sariah's tent. He moistened his dry lips against the gathering wind and closed his eyes. "Please make haste," he whispered to the empty sky. Laman and Lemuel should be on their way back, and he hoped they would arrive soon with the water. He felt the wrenching in his stomach grow. What if the primitive conditions proved too much for Sariah and their newborn? She was older than most childbearing women, and desert travel made giving birth an even greater risk.

He sensed someone approaching. Opening his eyes, he saw Nephi. Lehi embraced his youngest son with fierceness, his body trembling beneath Nephi's solid frame.

"Mother should bring forth the babe soon," Lehi said thickly. "Her life is in the Lord's hands now." He pulled away from Nephi but continued to grip his arm, as if to draw strength from the youth of his son.

"Father," Nephi began, then fell silent. Words eluded both men as they stood together, waiting. With each cry from Sariah, their hearts grew heavier.

After some time, Lehi noticed movement on the horizon. He let out a sigh of relief. "They're coming."

Nephi raised his head. Laman and Lemuel were still small figures in the distance, but their camels rapidly approached.

"We must act with haste," Lehi said.

When Laman and Lemuel neared, Laman climbed off his camel, passed by Lehi without so much as a glance, and walked toward the birthing tent.

* * *

Once Laman reached the tent, he stood outside, hesitating. The sounds inside were muffled, periodically pierced with his mother's cries. He gritted his teeth together as his chest heaved, not only from exhaustion, but from anger.

Now hearing his mother's pitiful cries, he regretted his recent harsh words to his wife. She too would likely experience childbirth in the wilderness if the family didn't reach the promised land soon. Only the day before, she had told him of her suspicions. He contemplated stopping at the next oasis and informing the family that he and Anah would join them after the birth. Another cry interrupted his thoughts and set him into action.

"I've brought the water, Mother."

Fully expecting Bashemath to appear, he was taken aback when Isaabel exited the tent. Although she was Nephi's wife, Laman couldn't help but notice how her beauty had matured. Remembering how he'd made his intentions toward Isaabel known before their marriages, the hairs on his neck bristled at the memory of Nephi getting his choice of bride in the end. Isaabel's eyes were filled with anxiety. She stopped when she saw Laman. But without wasting a moment, she grabbed the goatskin bags from his outstretched hands.

Laman felt his throat constrict. "Isaabel, I—"

"There's no time for words." Her eyes settled upon his face, her surprise evident. "Send one of my sisters to help."

He nodded curtly and left.

* * *

As soon as Laman departed, Isaabel reentered the shelter. Bashemath motioned for her to help support Sariah. *Please,* Isaabel thought, *let this be over with soon. Spare this woman further agony.*

When Anah joined Isaabel and Bashemath in the birthing tent, Sariah was heaving with exhaustion. Anah took her mother's place in supporting Sariah on her right side, and Bashemath crouched in position to receive the baby.

"The babe is coming," Bashemath said. "Take a deep breath and push again."

With great effort Sariah complied.

"Again!" Bashemath called. A smile lit her face. "Once more!"

Sariah strained, letting a shattering cry escape.

"You've done it!"

Isaabel and Anah struggled to support Sariah's sagging form. Isaabel blinked against hot tears and saw that Anah and her mother were also crying. Sariah's breath came in deep gasps.

The miracle of life had transpired.

Isaabel stared in fascination at the tiny being squirming in Bashemath's arms—the reddened body, the dark matted hair, the scrunched face. The baby let out a loud cry. Anah began to wash the child with water.

"It's a son," Bashemath announced proudly.

Sariah gave a joyful wail. "Heaven be thanked."

Isaabel looked at Sariah's fatigued, yet radiant face. Her hair, damp from exertion, clung to her neck and brow. Her mother-in-law seemed oblivious to everything else but her son.

"Tell the others," Bashemath said to Isaabel. "We'll finish in here." When Isaabel hesitated, Bashemath continued, "Go now and spread the good news."

Isaabel stumbled out of the tent, realizing her own hair was soaked and lay in curly tendrils about her face and neck. The fresh air pricked her skin and caused her to gasp for breath. Her arms and back hurt from supporting Sariah, but her heart danced with song.

Lehi was the first to meet her. "You have a son," Isaabel cried out.

"And Sariah?"

"She's well. They're both well," Isaabel said, nearly laughing.

Lehi grabbed her shoulders and kissed her forehead. "Thank you." He sank to his knees and rocked back and forth, praying.

A joyous shout arose among the gathering family members when they heard the announcement. Isaabel found Nephi in the throng of celebration. Nephi grabbed her hand, pulling her next to him. She embraced him happily.

Drawing Isaabel away from the commotion, Nephi said, "Thank you for helping my mother."

Isaabel grinned, feeling as if her feet floated above the ground. "Life is truly a miracle."

He brought his hand to her face, tracing her cheek. "You must be tired."

"I am, but I feel wonderful," Isaabel said, awe in her voice. "It's like nothing I've ever experienced." Nephi drew her close, and Isaabel felt his heart pounding. She wondered what it would be like to have a life growing inside of her, then, with sudden realization, said a prayer that she would be able to endure the things Sariah just had.

CHAPTER 3

If a woman have conceived seed, and born a man child: then she shall be unclean seven days; according to the days of the separation for her infirmity shall she be unclean.
(Leviticus 12:2)

Lehi stepped inside the tent where Sariah lay nursing their newborn. The canvas enclosure was still quite warm, but the women had removed all evidence of the delivery.

Sariah held out her hand, and Lehi sat next to her. He took his wife's hand and stroked her calloused fingers. "Another son," he murmured, watching the tiny being suckle hungrily. "He's greedy already."

Smiling, Sariah removed the child from her breast. "He will grow strong like his brothers." She handed the infant to Lehi.

He took the child in his arms and was welcomed with a yawn. Lehi chuckled. "He is tired from his journey." Lehi's eyes glistened as he examined his son's perfect form. "We will call him Jacob."

"This will be the first Jacob in our family lineage," Sariah said.

"Ah. You forget, dear wife. We are descended from Joseph of Egypt, whose father was Jacob—father of the twelve tribes of Israel."

Sariah reached out and touched the infant's rosy cheek. "Jacob," she said softly, "a worthy name for a son born to a prophet of God."

"Then it shall be so." Lehi leaned over and kissed Sariah. "You need your rest. I'll send Bashemath to tend to the child."

"No," Sariah said. "Bashemath needs to care for her husband. Send one of our daughters, perhaps Elisheba."

Lehi nodded and kissed his wife and child again. He left the tent, welcoming the cool night air, his heart full with gratitude. It was well past midnight, but the family had started cooking the celebration meal. Though the meat wouldn't be as plentiful at their other meals, spirits were high.

Approaching the main camp, Lehi felt his concern return. They had stopped in a desolate area without vegetation to indicate water beneath the surface. With Sariah unable to travel for a few days, someone would have to fetch more water for the camp.

After sending Elisheba to help Sariah, Lehi paused at the door of Ishmael's shelter. All was quiet within. He continued to his own tent and went inside where Nephi waited.

"Father," Nephi said, rising. "How is Mother?"

"Very well," Lehi said.

"And my little brother?"

Lehi smiled. "Strong and healthy. He will be called Jacob."

"Jacob, Father of Joseph," Nephi mused.

"Yes." Lehi settled onto a mat, pleased with his son's knowledge. "Bring the brass plates. I would like to read over Jacob's history again."

"Won't you join in the celebrations?" Nephi asked.

"Not yet." Lehi's eyes seemed to darken with worry. "Tomorrow we will present a peace offering to the Lord. After that, we will need to bring water into the camp until Mother's days of purifying are over."

"But that won't be for seven more days," Nephi said, staring at Lehi. "And with no water here . . ." His voice trailed off. But Lehi didn't answer, so Nephi crossed to the back of the tent to get the brass plates.

When Nephi returned, Lehi found the story of Jacob's birth and began to read in a low voice. "And the Lord said unto her, Two nations are in thy womb, and two manner of people shall be separated from thy bowels; and the one people shall be stronger than the other people; and the elder shall serve the younger."

As Lehi read, the noise of the family's celebration seemed to dim with each verse.

"And after that came his brother out, and his hand took hold on Esau's heel; and his name was called Jacob . . . And the boys grew . . . and Jacob was a plain man, dwelling in tents."

"From the beginning, the Lord knew what would happen to each boy," Nephi said.

Lehi looked at Nephi, feeling the impact of the sacred words in his heart. "Our Jacob has a great name to emulate. It is my prayer he will follow the Lord in righteousness." He placed a hand on his son's shoulder and felt the burden of having two sons who struggled with their faith lighten somewhat.

"We have much to be thankful for this night," Nephi said, his eyes misting. "The Liahona continues to direct us, Mother and Jacob are safe, and we have food to eat."

Rising slowly, Lehi crossed to the door, his jaw set firm. "You are right, my son. Let us join in the celebrations."

* * *

Nephi woke in the stillness of the morning as Isaabel slept peacefully next to him. Due to the previous night's celebration, he knew the rest of the camp wouldn't rouse until later in the morning. Stepping around his wife so as not to disturb her, he slipped out of the tent. A short distance from camp he saw Lehi stacking rocks for an altar. He was surprised that his father hadn't come to enlist his help.

Moving toward Lehi, Nephi raised his hand in greeting. His father met him with a grateful nod.

"I didn't want to disturb your rest," Lehi said, as Nephi joined him.

Nephi hefted a rock from the ground, a slight smile playing on his lips. "That hasn't stopped you in the past."

Lehi chuckled.

Together they worked in companionable silence for a few minutes. Nephi lifted the rocks, and Lehi directed him where they should be placed. "What will the offering be?" Nephi eventually asked.

"I heard some wild goats in the distance this morning. You and Sam should be able to locate them."

When the makeshift altar was completed, Nephi left to wake Sam. He called softly from outside Sam's tent.

A tousled head appeared through the flap. "Is your head full of sand?" Sam asked, stifling a yawn.

Nephi grinned. "It's a beautiful morning. Let's go catch a goat."

The head disappeared, and Nephi heard a groan escape from his brother. A moment later, Sam emerged, sleepy-eyed but dressed. "Let me predict. It's for the peace offering."

"You sound like Laman," Nephi teased.

Sam snorted. "Just because I'd appreciate a little more sleep?" He followed Nephi through the camp.

"Jacob will appreciate the gesture."

Sam stopped. "Jacob, eh? Already the tent dweller. Very fitting."

Nephi laughed out loud, then covered his mouth, not wanting to wake anyone else. "Don't let on to Father how much you remember from the brass plates. You'll be replacing me soon."

"Never," Sam said with a grin. "You won't have to worry about me trying to take over the leadership of *this* family—although my wife would probably enjoy giving me plenty of advice."

Nephi suddenly had an image of Tamar standing with her hands on her hips. "Those daughters of Ishmael aren't the most demure females, are they?"

"I, for one, wouldn't have it any other way." Sam started to whistle, obviously not the least bothered by Tamar's strong opinions.

When they had passed the altar, Nephi slowed. "Father said he heard the goats this morning, so they can't be too far away." He looked beyond the first grouping of boulders and shrubs where the early light bounced off the rocky landscape—colors of yellow and orange blending in brilliance. He inhaled deeply, the morning air crisp and invigorating.

A movement on the horizon caught both of their attention. Something was out there, but it was too large to be a goat.

"Should we get the bow?" Sam asked.

Nephi shook his head and continued to walk toward the figure. After a few moments, he said, "It's Laman."

"Is he trying to catch a goat too?"

Nephi smiled at the comment, but his glance told Sam to remain quiet.

When they neared their older brother, Sam spoke first. "Awake early?"

Laman glowered and was about to pass by when Nephi asked, "What's wrong?"

With his eyes focused straight ahead, Laman paused. "What *isn't* wrong?" His voice was low and harsh.

Nephi felt a knot form in his stomach. Laman hadn't been enjoying a morning of quiet reflection. Seeing the swollen skin beneath Laman's eyes and the haggard lines throughout his face, Nephi knew Laman had most likely been awake all night, brooding. And nothing good could come of that. Nephi felt the hairs on his neck rise as his own anger started to surface.

Thankfully, Sam interjected. "Tell us what's bothering you."

Laman's gaze focused on his younger brothers. "What's *not* bothering me?" he asked. After a brief hesitation, he said, "Anah is with child."

Sam reached a hand out in congratulations, but Laman ignored the gesture.

"My wife will not bear children in this forsaken wilderness," he hissed, turning to Nephi, his eyes narrow. "You may sacrifice a whole herd of animals to your God in thanksgiving for our new brother, but it will not bring us water or a decent home. Someday, when your precious Isaabel is with child, you'll finally understand."

Nephi felt as if the sword of Laban had passed through his heart. His brother's words had uncovered his own hidden fear.

Laman brushed past them and was gone before Sam or Nephi could respond. Nephi felt a slow throb begin in his temples. The land suddenly looked dreary and the sky dull.

Sam placed a hand on Nephi's arm. "It might be somewhat easier if we were living in Jerusalem. But childbearing is a risk all women must take," he said. "Our wives are strong, and the Lord will watch over them."

Nephi turned to Sam and gripped his shoulder. Never before had he been so thankful for his brother's understanding.

When Nephi and Sam returned to camp with a struggling wild goat they had chased down and caught, most of the family had gathered around the altar. Noticeably missing were Laman, Anah, Ishmael, Sariah, and the baby. Lehi greeted his sons and took the goat, then commenced the peace offering ceremony.

"O Lord our God," Lehi said. "We have brought forth this goat without blemish as an offering of peace."

Nephi handed his father a dagger. With a single motion, Lehi laid his hand upon the goat's head and slit its throat. After the blood drained into a bowl, Nephi and Sam sprinkled the goat blood around the altar.

With a knife, Lehi carefully removed the fat from the animal and started a fire with flint. Then he burned the goat's fat upon the altar. "O Lord, we are gathered in the spirit of thanksgiving and rejoicing. And we give Thee all the fat of the peace offering. This reminds us that throughout our generations and all our dwellings we shall eat neither fat nor blood."

Isabel moved next to Nephi, and they exchanged smiles. She poured some sand into his hands, which he used to clean the bloodstains on his fingers. Then they bowed their heads as the concluding prayer was said by Lehi.

When the ceremony ended, the family started to move away to begin their daily chores.

A voice cut through the commotion. "Lehi!"

Everyone stopped and looked in the direction it was coming from. Sariah stood outside her tent, and in her arms she cradled her new son. Lehi took several steps forward. "Sariah?"

She started walking toward the group. "Lehi!" she said again.

Lehi rushed forward to meet her. "Wait, I'll come to you." Several family members hurried alongside Lehi, curious about Sariah.

When Lehi reached Sariah, he stopped and asked, "What is it?" He took the baby from her arms and removed the folded fabric, peering at Jacob's face. "Is the baby all right?"

"He's fine. Why are we not loading the camels?" Sariah asked, waving toward the hobbled animals.

"We will wait until the days of your uncleanliness are over before we take up our journey," Lehi said. The baby started to fuss, and Lehi rocked him. "By then you will be stronger for travel."

Sariah scanned the family members who had come to listen, then let her steady gaze settle on Lehi. "There is no water here. It is not fit that we should tarry any longer in such desolation."

"But your fragile condition doesn't permit—" Lehi began.

"The Lord has given me strength to bear this child in the wilderness." She took the infant from Lehi. "He will give me strength to ride upon a camel."

10.07% 11-21-05

CHAPTER 4

And when the days of her purifying are fulfilled, for a son, or for a daughter, she shall bring a lamb of the first year for a burnt offering.
(LEVITICUS 12:6)

Over a month had passed since the birth of Jacob. His circumcision had taken place on the eighth day after Sariah had delivered, followed by a short naming ceremony. Now they moved through a desolate stretch of land, but with the direction of the Liahona, they were guided to the more fertile parts of the wilderness. Once the family reached the next oasis, they would be able to camp and rest for a while.

Isaabel kept a close watch on Sariah. She marveled at the strength her mother-in-law showed traveling under such conditions. Elisheba and Dinah walked next to Sariah. They often quarreled over whose turn it was to hold the baby. Isaabel smiled as she thought how soon there would be plenty of babies for everyone to hold.

Anah had recently announced that she was with child, and Rebeka's belly had become full beneath her tunic. After Rebeka's nausea had passed, she had no trouble eating food equal to any man's portion.

Isaabel turned her head to see her husband riding next to Lehi, deep in conversation. Their morning meetings had grown in length, and when Isaabel asked Nephi the reason, he said he would tell her when the time was right.

Laughter erupted behind her. Without looking, she recognized Laman's deep bellow cutting through the wind. Relief filled her as she thought about their encounter a few days before.

At the last oasis, Isaabel and her sisters had been tending to her father when she exited his tent. Laman had been waiting outside for Anah, she assumed. But when she had walked past him he called to her.

"Isa," he had said.

She turned in surprise and glanced warily at the tent door. Anah could appear any moment. "Yes?" she asked.

He looked quickly around, then moved toward her. "I'm sorry."

Isaabel couldn't have been more shocked, but she tried not to show it. "Sorry for what?"

"For everything," Laman said. When Isaabel didn't respond, he continued. "I'm sorry that you women have to endure this harsh wilderness. I'm sorry Nephi and I quarrel so often, and . . ."

Isaabel felt her heart pounding beneath her chest. The man before her wasn't the Laman she knew. This man was contrite and his demeanor soft. "Yes?" she prompted, gently this time.

"I'm sorry for ever making you feel uncomfortable around me." For a moment, Laman had held her eyes, his gaze sincere, then he turned abruptly and strode away.

Isaabel had stared at his retreating figure. An apology from Laman? It was hard to believe, but then maybe his heart had changed. Joy spread through her as she thought how happy Nephi and his father would be if Laman were truly penitent. The journey would be easier for everyone.

Though it had been several days since Laman's apology, Isaabel hadn't said anything to Nephi yet. She shook her head at the memory as she walked and decided to tell Nephi tonight.

He would be glad to hear the news. She wondered if Nephi had also noticed that Laman's manner had been more kindhearted toward his wife since they announced she was with child.

Tamar moved to Isaabel's side and linked arms. "Who's next?"

"What?" Isaabel asked, her senses coming into focus. Thoughts of Laman fled her mind as she looked at Tamar. Isaabel noticed her sister was wearing the goat hair socks she'd woven for her, which protected her feet against the burning sand.

"Rebeka and Anah are with child," Tamar said in a hushed voice. "It's your turn next."

Isaabel glanced around to make sure no one could hear. "You're the older sister." She jabbed Tamar in the ribs. "Tell me, have you experienced the symptoms yet?"

Instead of continuing the jest, Tamar's face grew serious. "I think the coming babies are the only thing keeping Father alive."

Isaabel swallowed deeply, trying to quell her rising dread. "To see his grandchildren?"

Tamar nodded. The two sisters continued to walk arm in arm in silence, their feet warm against the sand.

A short time later, the terrain began changing. Rocks protruded from the ground, making the travel more difficult, yet the desert grass became more abundant, decorating the land. Palm trees loomed in the distance, and a few frankincense trees were scattered about, indicating water beneath the dry wadi bed.

"It's an oasis," Elisheba exclaimed for everyone to hear.

Ahead of Isaabel and Tamar, Lehi chuckled. "So it is, and not a day too soon."

"What does he mean?" Isaabel whispered to Tamar when she heard Lehi's words.

"Sariah's days of purification are over. She can now make her burnt offering and sin offering and be cleansed."

When the family reached the small oasis, they settled beneath the shade provided by groups of palms. Laman and Lemuel drew water from the well for the camels. Nephi and Sam constructed the altar for their mother's offerings. Two young birds had also been caught, one to be used for each offering.

Lehi, dressed in his finest robe, approached the altar, while Elisheba stood to the side, holding young Jacob. Sariah knelt before the altar with the birds in her hands. Lehi bowed his head and after a brief pause, offered a prayer. When he finished, he took the birds from his wife, one to represent the burnt offering, the other to represent the sin offering.

With the sacrifice of the birds, the atonement was made, and Lehi pronounced Sariah clean.

Sariah embraced her family members. When she reached Isaabel, she said, "I would like to visit your mother."

Isaabel smiled, grateful that now Sariah would be able to visit throughout the camp again. Sariah left Jacob with Elisheba, and Isaabel led her to Bashemath's tent, which was set apart several paces from the others.

Stopping outside of the tent, Isaabel listened for a moment, but found the perimeter quiet. She called softly to Bashemath.

The woman's head appeared through the tent door. The tired lines seemed to fade against Bashemath's face when she saw her visitors. "Come in," she said in an eager voice.

Sariah and Isaabel stepped inside, taking in the threadbare rugs spread on the ground and disjointed seams of the tent walls. Isaabel was struck with the evidence of how little time her mother had to spend repairing rugs and goatskins since tending to her father.

"How is he?" Sariah asked.

"Not good today," Bashemath said. "He hasn't been sleeping well either. But I'm glad you came."

Isaabel followed Sariah's gaze to see the figure in the corner where, although the sun was beating through the fabric of the tent, Ishmael was covered in rugs. "Is he too hot?" Sariah asked.

Bashemath shook her head. "He complains of the cold, so I keep him covered."

Nodding, Sariah murmured in sympathy.

Bashemath led them to a small area partitioned off from the rest of the tent. "Sit. I'm pleased Isaabel has brought you to see me. I don't have much to offer, but I do have a little tea left over. It's the last of the mint."

With appreciation, Isaabel and Sariah accepted a cup.

"Thank you," Sariah said. "It's wonderful to move about the camp again."

"Your son is strong and healthy?" Bashemath asked.

"Yes, thank you for your concern," Sariah said.

"He looks like Sam," Isaabel interjected.

A smile lit Bashemath's face. Isaabel was content to see her mother look happy, especially since there hadn't been much to rejoice about of late.

"Rebeka seems to be faring well," Sariah said.

Bashemath nodded, a flicker of unease in her expression. "It's always hard to know with the first child." Her gaze strayed to Isaabel, then dropped as she picked at the threads of the rug beneath her with calloused fingers. Isaabel looked away and brought the teacup to her lips.

Sariah joined Isaabel and sipped her mint tea in silence. After a moment, Sariah finally said, "We have enough experience between the two of us to help her through it. And now that Isaabel has gained practice—"

Suddenly, Bashemath leaned forward and spoke in an urgent whisper. "How much longer, Sariah, until we reach this promised land? It is all he talks about," she said, her eyes flitting in Ishmael's direction. "Every time I complain, he tells me that we must press forward, regardless of what happens."

Isaabel looked intently at her mother and saw tears in her eyes. "We have come so far already. It can't be much longer," Isaabel suggested.

"Ishmael says that if he dies . . ." Bashemath's voice broke. "I should continue with your family."

Placing a hand on Bashemath's arm, Sariah spoke. "Of course. Our families are bound, and we will stay together no matter what."

Bashemath gripped Sariah's other arm. "I am so afraid."

"God speaks to us through the Liahona, guiding us, leading us. We can't go wrong as long as we have faith," Sariah said.

Drawing away, Bashemath wiped her eyes. "I know. But I'm not as strong as Ishmael. If he—" Her voice faltered. "If anything happens to my husband, I don't know if I could live without him." Fresh tears fell.

Sariah took Bashemath's and Isaabel's hands and closed her eyes, whispering a soft prayer. Isaabel lowered her gaze and wondered herself if she could continue to live without her husband.

*　*　*

Nephi watched his mother and Isaabel exit Ishmael's tent and part ways. By the way Sariah hurried past without looking at him, he knew she was upset. He was about to follow Isaabel when Elisheba ran up to him.

"Nephi," she said, her breathing heavy from running. "Our brothers want to see you. *Now.*"

"Why?" Nephi asked, already moving in their direction.

"They think we are being followed by raiders," Elisheba said in a half-whisper.

He hesitated, almost unbelieving, but Nephi had heard such stories before. Bands of marauders followed smaller caravans, then robbed them in the middle of the night. Without another word, Nephi left Elisheba and hurried to where his brothers stood underneath a group of palms.

Zoram was speaking rapidly to the men, and when he saw Nephi, he motioned for him to join them. "We must continue as if we don't sense anything unusual. They may even be spying on us right now."

Several heads turned and looked around.

"No," Zoram said. "Don't look for them."

The nervous attention focused back on Zoram.

"How is it you know so much about the raiders' habits?" Lemuel asked, his voice skeptical.

"Working for Laban, one hears tales of the perils in the wilderness," Zoram said.

Lemuel snickered and made a face at Laman.

Zoram saw the interchange. "You don't understand," he pressed. "The Bedus who engage in this type of raid consider their profession honorable. If they die in a raid, they become a legend among their people. Day after day, they lie in wait until they see any smoke, dust, or other evidence of people traveling, then they attack."

Laman listened with interest, Lemuel following suit. Nephi folded his arms across his chest, his jaw set firm.

"The title *haramy*, or robber, is one of the most sought after honors by these desert youth," Zoram said.

Sam cleared his throat, visibly paled by the information. "So we are to become a young man's trophy."

"Not if we stop them," Zoram said.

Laman punched an arm over his head. "That's more like it."

Raamah and Heth laughed and flexed their fingers. "We'll teach them a lesson," Raamah said with a grin.

"Slow down," Nephi said, stepping forward. All eyes focused on him. "How many raiders are there, Zoram?"

Zoram let out a short breath. "I'd guess about a dozen at the most. They travel in small groups, scavenging off the land as they go. They will have a leader who commands them. He is the one we must identify. If we capture him, the others will lose courage."

"We can each handle two," Lemuel interjected.

"Of course," Nephi said then frowned, "we must protect the sword of Laban, the Liahona, and the brass plates. They are essential for our survival."

"He's right," Lemuel agreed. "Unless they are only looking for a few extra bedrolls and an old tent."

Chuckles erupted among the men.

Zoram hesitated for a moment. "That's where you are wrong." He glanced at the men then looked away. "Our women would be the most treasured prizes for these desert plunderers."

CHAPTER 5

Therefore my persecutors shall stumble, and they shall not prevail.
(JEREMIAH 20:11)

"Did you see that?" Zoram whispered.

Nephi squinted into the afternoon sun and adjusted his elbows against the rocky slope they were crouched on. "Where?"

"There!" Zoram pointed to a group of bushes on the next hill.

Nephi then saw the slight movement of a head covered in an earth-colored turban. As Nephi's eyes grew accustomed to the shape, he suddenly noticed another head, then another. "A whole group of them are hidden," he said, astounded.

"Yes." Zoram let out a low sigh. "They are very patient to remain in one place. As soon as the smoke from our fire tonight dies out, they will begin to move into action."

Nephi felt his pulse quicken. "Do you think they know we are watching them?"

"Possibly. Another sign of experienced raiders. If they do, they are giving no indication. They will know to expect a counterattack and will come prepared with daggers ready," Zoram said.

Nephi stiffened but continued to stare hard at the distant figures. "They won't settle for just stealing property?"

"No," Zoram said. "Engaging in battle will only elevate their status."

"But they can't get away so fast on foot."

"Their horses or camels are likely a short distance out. When dark falls, they'll retrieve them and move closer to our camp," Zoram said.

Nephi let the words sink in. He had seen the promised land in his vision and knew they would arrive there eventually. But a seed of concern arose as he tried to remember if his vision of the promised land had included the entire family.

Zoram broke through his thoughts. "We must return and put our plan together."

The two men slithered backward down the slope until they were out of sight from the other hillside. Then they were able to move more freely toward camp. "We are indebted to you, Zoram, for your knowledge about such things," Nephi said.

Zoram slowed his pace. "They are not things that I wish to know, but when I was sold as a servant to Laban, I learned to keep my eyes open and ears tuned."

Nephi stared at the man he'd brought out of Jerusalem. "I didn't know you had been sold. By whom?" When Zoram remained silent, Nephi said, "I'm sorry. I didn't mean to ask such a bold question."

"It's all right," Zoram said. "I haven't talked about it before, to anyone."

"Not even Rebeka?"

Zoram shook his head. "She knows a few things, but not the whole story."

Nephi waited for him to continue as their walking slowed.

"My father was a foolish man and dug our family into a pit of debt. My learning was cut short when I reached the age of ten. After that, I worked long days just to help with the food. I never married because we were too impoverished to provide the bride's mohar, and I was twenty-five when my father passed away. My mother was devastated to be left a penniless widow. I was all she had." Zoram paused and looked in the distance.

"How did you come to work for Laban?" Nephi asked.

"It was not by choice." Zoram snorted. "It started with my mother, who even in her forties was a beautiful woman. Her hands were nimble like a younger woman's, and her beauty was legendary in our village. She wove intricate, original designs used in women's fine clothing. One of Laban's concubines owned a garment made by my mother. He was interested in having a new robe for himself and one day came to seek her services."

Closing his eyes, Nephi tried to imagine Laban, in all his decadence, entering a home as humble as Zoram's must have been.

"That was the last time I ever saw my mother," Zoram said.

Nephi snapped his head around and stared at him. "What happened?"

"When Laban realized the dire straits my mother was in, he saw an opportunity. Recognizing her incredible talent—and no doubt her beauty—he offered to relieve her of all debt. In exchange for me serving in his house and my mother's unending services, she was provided with a decent living, and I could start paying down my father's debt. Two years later, I was informed that she had died."

"I'm sorry," Nephi said, trying to imagine what Zoram had experienced. "So you continued working for Laban after her passing?"

Zoram kicked a rock out of their path. "I had no choice. The contract was for five years. I spent my time learning the dialects I heard from visiting dignitaries and listening to their stories of travel. I had two left to serve before you came."

"And now here you are, in the wilderness, fearing for your life," Nephi said.

"There's no other place I'd rather be." Zoram stopped walking and placed a hand on Nephi's shoulder. "I have a beautiful wife, a new family, and my faith in God has been restored. A man can die happy with good fortune such as that."

They arrived at camp just as the family was gathering inside Lehi's tent for his final instructions. "With the appearance of these raiders, we need to formulate a plan for protecting our valuables," Lehi said to the family members surrounding him.

"Perhaps our *valuables* such as the sword of Laban and the brass plates could be used to buy protection," Laman said.

"These raiders won't settle for just a few trinkets and some bags of seed," Zoram said.

"He's right," Nephi said. "The women must be protected."

"Yes," Lehi said. "The women will stay together in this tent, out of harm's way. And if . . . the men should lose power over the raiders, the women must flee, along with the valuables." He paused, glancing at Sariah.

Sariah clutched her baby tightly. "We will not be able to carry the valuables," she said.

"You are right," Lehi agreed. "We must bury them."

"But," Laman protested, "if they are buried, how will we buy our way out of an attack?"

"If we lose the Liahona, the seed, and the brass plates, we will surely perish, with or without raiders," Lehi said. "I will appoint two men and their wives to be in charge of hiding the valuables each time we camp and each time we encounter others in the future." He scanned the group, his gaze settling on Zoram.

Laman interrupted. "Zoram's wife is too weak to dig."

Lehi brought his gaze sharply to Laman. "Then Rebeka will stand as a shield while her husband digs. And," he looked around the group again, "Sam and Tamar will be the second couple."

Folding his arms across his chest, Laman scowled. "The ground is too rocky here to dig deep enough."

With a sigh, Lehi said, "I will let Sam and Zoram decide on the best method of concealment. Every place we stop will present a new challenge."

Laman, his mouth set in a tight line, looked away from his father and locked eyes with Nephi. "If we are to bury the valuables, let's hope that our manpower is greater than the desert raiders'."

* * *

"You must stay with the others," Nephi said, nudging Isaabel toward his father's tent.

Isaabel's dark eyes flashed at her husband. "I don't want you to leave."

Nephi took her hand and led her to the entrance. "The raiders will continue to follow us if we keep moving. Zoram said we only need to capture the leader."

"What are you going to do with him?" Isaabel asked, her voice rising.

"Just scare him," Nephi said. He bent and kissed her forehead. "Go now, and keep the women calm."

Isaabel finally relented, knowing the others would expect it of her. But inside, she felt panic building. Entering the tent, Isaabel found her sisters huddled together in conversation. "What if they reach the tents?" Anah was saying.

Puah pulled her mantle tightly about her. "We will have to defend ourselves."

"Or flee before they get here," Anah suggested. The women nodded, favoring fleeing to fighting.

"I'll keep watch," Elisheba said. The older women looked at her.

"You're too young for such a task. We don't want to risk being discovered," Anah said.

Elisheba's cheeks reddened. "I'm nearly fourteen, only a year younger than Isaabel."

Anah didn't look convinced.

"I'll go with her," Isaabel offered.

Anah turned and studied her youngest sister. "All right. But you must move quickly and let no one see you. If our men are losing ground, return to the tent and warn us. If you are caught . . ."

"They won't catch us," Elisheba said with defiance.

Anah ignored her and continued, "If you are caught, you'll be a tribesman's concubine or wife."

Elisheba gasped. "They wouldn't—"

"Yes," Isaabel said. "They would."

As darkness fell over the oasis, the level of anticipation grew in the tent. Isaabel crouched near the entrance, lost in her own thoughts. Tamar sat by her at one point and tried to start a conversation, but soon gave up. Anah, Puah, Rebeka, and Heth's wife, Zillah, stayed together, with Elisheba and Dinah settled next to Sariah. Even Ishmael had been brought into the tent, and Bashemath remained by his side.

"Isaabel."

Isaabel blinked and turned toward the voice. Sariah took her hands and pressed a trinket box into them.

"What's this for?" Isaabel asked, looking down at the ornate container that held all of Sariah's inherited jewelry.

"I had Nephi bring it to me," Sariah whispered. "Do you still have the key I gave you?"

Isaabel nodded. "Of course."

"Good. Take it with you when you go. I'd rather the jewels save my family's lives than adorn their bodies." Sariah patted Isaabel's shoulder and moved away.

Isaabel fingered the key hanging from the chain around her neck. She squeezed her eyes shut, imagining herself begging for Nephi's life to be spared again as she did when Laman and Lemuel had bound Nephi and left him to be devoured by wild beasts in the wilderness. But this time it would be against a group of savage raiders. Her palms began to sweat as she tightened her grip on Sariah's trinket box. *Oh Lord*, she prayed silently, *please protect us this night. We've come so far and have maintained our faith in Thee. Spare us from harm if it be Thy will.*

If only she could feel Nephi's arms about her, strong and reassuring.

"It's time, Isa," Anah said.

Isaabel looked up and saw Anah and Elisheba standing over her. A quiet sob came from the corner of the tent. Isaabel glanced in its direction and saw her mother hovering over her father's limp form, muttering to herself. With a pang, Isaabel realized that with her father's weakened condition, it would be impossible for him to flee with the women. And, she knew her mother would never leave his side.

Standing, Isaabel grabbed Elisheba's hand, and together they crept out of Lehi's tent.

"What are you carrying?" Elisheba whispered.

"Shh," Isaabel hissed. "Don't make a sound."

They proceeded forward stealthily, moving from tent to tent until they reached the outskirts of the camp. By then their eyes had grown accustomed to the night.

Isaabel put a hand on Elisheba's arm and pulled her down into a crouching position next to a tent positioned on the edge of the camp's perimeter. Wordlessly, she pointed in the distance. Elisheba squinted to see what Isaabel was pointing out, then nodded. They could barely make out the forms of their brothers lying in wait on the ground next to a stand of palms.

Tapping Elisheba's arm, Isaabel pointed another direction where a second group of men noiselessly closed in on the camp. They were still some distance away, but their identities were unmistakable.

Elisheba covered her mouth to stifle a gasp.

Isaabel nudged her with a warning glare. She felt Elisheba grip her arm in fear, her breathing coming fast.

It seemed that time froze as Isaabel and Elisheba watched the raiders draw closer to their brothers. The marauders were half-naked, their waists wrapped in brightly colored cloth that reflected in the moonlight. Isaabel found herself holding her breath for long intervals. Then suddenly, the men dropped to the ground. They must have sensed danger. But after a short time, they rose and continued moving forward.

A loud cry erupted. Isaabel flinched, and Elisheba let out her own cry. Isaabel clamped her hand over the girl's mouth.

Beneath the moonlight, they watched Laman, Nephi, Raamah, and the other men rush forward and form a barrier between the raiders and the camp. Shouts rose in the air as arguing commenced. One of the men stepped forward, holding a long dagger in his hand. The leader.

The two groups of men inched closer and closer to each other, the tension building.

"If you value your lives, you will leave us," Laman shouted.

The raiders merely sneered at their opponents. One laughed out loud and shouted something in their dialect. The others joined in the laughter.

Lehi's voice rose over the commotion as he spoke their language. At first, the raiders seemed astounded at hearing their own dialect from a group of foreigners. Then they began to talk amongst themselves until the leader spoke in harsh tones to Lehi. Lemuel and Sam pushed their way in front of their father.

"You've made your choice," Laman shouted. He lunged forward at the tribe leader, who ducked and rolled away. Laman landed with a thud and emitted a loud groan. The other tribesmen scoffed.

Lemuel lowered his head and stampeded into the leader, who fell backward, stunned. The laughter faded as shouts rose up. As the leader rose and regained his balance, Nephi and Sam dove onto him, pinning him to the ground face first.

Laman waved his knife in the air. "One more step and I cut his throat." He grabbed the leader's hair and yanked his head backward. The knife grazed the man's neck, drawing blood.

The raiders stepped backward, and one even fled the scene. Then, suddenly, mayhem broke out. The men attacked.

From their hiding place, Isaabel and Elisheba clung to each other. "Let's run back to the tent," Elisheba said, her voice quiet but full of panic.

Just then, Isaabel saw Nephi struck to the ground. "No," she screamed. "We have to help." She tried to run to the men, but Elisheba held her back.

"Stop! You'll get killed," Elisheba shouted through her hysterics.

Two raiders broke free from the fighting mob and ran straight toward them.

"Run!" Isaabel screamed and pushed Elisheba away. But Elisheba stood rooted in fear.

The tribesmen lunged for the women and caught them before they could flee. Isaabel felt herself being half-dragged across the ground, a knife held to her chest. She gasped for air and struggled against the powerful arms.

"Nephi," Isaabel cried, hoping he would hear her. The man covered her mouth and nose with his sweaty hand. She could hear Elisheba's screams and tried to look around for her, but Elisheba had not been led in the same direction.

When the tribesman shouted something, several of the fighting men stopped and turned.

"Isaabel!" It was Nephi. Desperate to make her captor release her, she lifted the trinket box into sight.

The raider knocked the box from her hand, its contents spilling onto the ground. The prize he'd already captured was greater than the jewels in the dust.

Suddenly, Nephi was running toward her with two raiders in pursuit. Isaabel barely had a chance to see his eyes flashing before she felt herself thrown to the ground. She pulled her knees up to her chest and covered her head while she listened to the fighting. They were all around her, but she was afraid to move. She watched as Nephi spun around and confronted two raiders at the same time. With one swift movement, he had them both on the ground. Then from behind, another raider pounced on top of Nephi's back.

"Watch out!" Isaabel tried to shout, but all that came from her throat was a rasping croak.

Nephi twisted beneath his attacker and managed to thwart the blows. Each sickening thud echoed in Isaabel's stomach. *I must help him,* she thought.

Isaabel raised herself to her knees and began to crawl toward Nephi.

"Mashi! Mashi!" someone shouted.

Isaabel felt a sharp jab to her side, and she caved to the ground. Squeezing her eyes shut, she cried out, "Nephi!"

Men rushed past her, yelling, "Run!"

Isaabel opened her eyes and saw Raamah standing a few paces away. In his hands he held the severed arm of a raider. He screamed over and over, "Your leader is dead!"

The raiders scattered, and Isaabel searched the area for Nephi. She moved to her knees and crawled toward a figure lying in the dirt. "Nephi?" she called as she grew closer.

He turned his head and partially opened his swollen eyes. "Isaabel." Blood dripped from a wound on his temple, and his lip was split and inflamed.

Isaabel flung herself toward him. "Are you all right?"

Nephi groaned, trying to sit up. He gingerly touched the wound on his head then reached out to Isaabel. "Why did you come here? You could have been killed."

Isaabel clung to him, her tears wetting his chest. Then she remembered. "Elisheba."

"She came too?"

Isaabel rose to her feet and started calling for her. She saw Raamah bending over Elisheba's still form on the ground. "Is she all right?"

Nephi joined Isaabel at Elisheba's side while Raamah finished inspecting for injuries.

Then Raamah lifted Elisheba. "She'll be fine. I discovered her just in time." His pained gaze looked past Isaabel and settled on Nephi. "The leader was trying to ravage your sister."

"So you cut off his arm," Nephi said.

Raamah nodded curtly. "No one touches her." Then he turned away, carrying Elisheba in his arms.

CHAPTER 6

And, behold, this day I am going the way of all the earth.
(Joshua 23:14)

The family had gathered together inside Lehi's tent. Ishmael lay propped up against some rugs, his weakness evident but his expression determined. The various injuries from the encounter with the desert men had been tended to. Raamah sat a short distance away from Elisheba, who stayed huddled next to Sariah. His gaze kept returning to Elisheba's face.

Lehi stood before the group, and the hushed voices ceased. His complexion was sallow and his eyes rimmed in red. In his hands, he gripped his myrtle staff as if depending on its support to control his emotion.

"Our camp has been sullied by robbers who care not for our lives. Blood has been shed in defense of our families and possessions. And," Lehi's voice cracked as he looked at, Elisheba, "the virtue of our women has been threatened."

Heads nodded in unison, and tears rolled down several faces. Raamah tore his gaze from Elisheba and looked at Lehi.

"Attacks on unsuspecting travelers are common in this part of the desert, and we may not have seen the last of them," Lehi continued. "Tonight we are weary and need rest. In the morning, we will vacate this camp before the raiders gather more men to seek their revenge. Our life is in God's hands. We must pray that the Liahona will lead us away from further harm."

"Where was the Liahona yesterday when the raiders were tracking us?" Raamah asked. The question, directed to Lehi, was greeted with silence. A few family members shifted uncomfortably. "We are to expect that the Liahona will keep us safe?" Raamah's voice rose. "Where was the Liahona when your daughter was being attacked by a marauder? Where was God when the leader dragged Elisheba by her hair? I am the one who fought him. I don't see God's hand in that."

Lehi tightened his grip on his staff.

"Without God's protection, we would have not discovered the raiders or had time to develop a plan," Nephi countered, unwilling to allow the others to berate his father.

Raamah rose, his eyes blazing through Nephi's. "Believe what you will, Nephi. But Zoram was the one who discovered the tribesmen, not the Liahona. *We* developed the plan, not the Liahona."

"Have you forgotten that the Liahona has guided us to the more fertile parts of the wilderness?" Nephi asked.

"Fertile?" Laman spoke from the other side of the tent. "Compared to what?"

A sharp intake of breath came from Sariah.

Laman stepped out of the shadows. "Is fertile defined by scant water supply and barely enough meat to survive on?"

Folding his arms against his chest, Raamah nodded. "Laman's right. However each of us chooses to interpret our situation, the facts are the same." He glanced around at the family members. "I know what it's like to lose someone dear. I'm about to lose my father, and now Elisheba was almost lost."

Ishmael made a feeble attempt to rise, but Bashemath restrained him.

Staring at Raamah, Elisheba gripped her mother's arm.

Lehi's shoulders sagged in sorrow. "Elisheba is safe tonight because of the Lord's protection—"

"If God had been protecting us, we wouldn't have had to face those raiders in the first place," Raamah spat out. He crossed to the tent door, took one more look at Elisheba, then disappeared.

Laman moved toward the exit to follow Raamah, but Lehi's voice stopped him. "We leave at sunrise."

Laman nodded and left, Lemuel close behind.

* * *

Isaabel and Elisheba trudged through the sand, walking arm in arm toward the sunrise. If anyone had slept the night before, it was minimal. The camels had been loaded before dawn, and the family moved out just as the first trickle of sunlight poured over the horizon.

For the first few miles, little was said between the two women. Isaabel waited for Elisheba to speak when she was ready. The ground began to grow increasingly rocky, and the family picked their way slowly through the difficult terrain as it sloped upward.

"Your brother is a brave man," Elisheba said at last.

Isaabel chose her words carefully. "Raamah cares a good deal for you."

Elisheba glanced away, a slow burn creeping up her neck. "He would have done the same for anyone else."

"No," Isaabel said, lightly squeezing Elisheba's arm. "I don't think it was by mere chance that he reached you before any of your brothers. It was as if he sensed what was happening."

Elisheba gazed into the distance, not responding.

"Although Raamah won't admit it, I believe he was led by God's Spirit to find you and do what needed to be done to protect you," Isaabel said. "We are blessed, Elisheba. You must never forget that."

A slight smile crossed Elisheba's face. "You are so much like Nephi. Even as a young girl, I knew there was something different about him."

"How so?" Isaabel asked.

"It's as if the world somehow becomes brighter and more alive when he is around," Elisheba said. "But now," her voice faltered, "the hardships seem to outweigh any happiness."

"I know that we are living under unusual circumstances, but hardships naturally increase as we grow older."

Elisheba frowned. "In the past year I've known so many hardships."

"Yes," Isaabel agreed. "So have we all."

"Tell me what Raamah's wife was like."

Isaabel suppressed her surprise, then she had to stop herself from grinning. So Elisheba *was* interested in Raamah. "She was very quiet and seemed frail even before she was with child." Isaabel cast a sideways glance at Elisheba. "Nothing like yourself."

Elisheba's mouth opened to speak, but Isaabel continued. "It was an arranged marriage, of course. With Raamah being the eldest and set to inherit my father's land one day, he had several brides to choose from. When he told my father he was interested in Leah, we were all surprised because she was so different from our mother. They married, and he brought her home to live, but I could tell she was never quite happy. I rarely saw her smile, and she never joined in any of our conversations. Then she died in childbirth. Raamah did not marry again. He stayed busy with Father's land and seemed content. He had a son to carry his name and didn't appear to want anything more." She paused and took a deep breath. "Until now."

Elisheba's face turned an unmistakable red. "I don't think—"

"I suspected it some time ago," Isaabel broke in. "Last night just confirmed it."

Several emotions seemed to flit across Elisheba's brow. "He sees me as a child—as a playmate for his son."

Isaabel sighed, realizing Elisheba's doubts mirrored the kind she had once held about Nephi. "Perhaps he'll be more plain about his feelings someday. Then you'll understand for yourself."

"Was that how it was with you and Nephi?" Elisheba asked.

Isaabel nodded. "I denied it even more than you."

A fresh grin erupted on Elisheba's face, and she spontaneously kissed Isaabel's cheek.

A short distance ahead, Isaabel saw Nephi. "I'll be back," she said, and left to catch up with her husband.

"Has the Liahona given instructions today?" Isaabel asked Nephi as she joined his side.

"Let's ask Father," Nephi said, and led his camel toward his father. "What does the Liahona say?"

Lehi wiped perspiration from his brow with his turban. "Nothing yet." He gazed ahead at the boulder-strewn pass they were about to cross.

With a sigh, Isaabel glanced at the sullen family members traveling behind them.

Nephi continued speaking to his father, "Raamah was out of character last night. I wish that Laman and Lemuel hadn't left after he spoke."

Lehi seemed to stiffen, but his voice was gentle. "Fear commanded Raamah's words." He turned his neck and looked at his son's profile. "Raamah has grown close to Laman and Lemuel. Naturally, the three of them would support one another."

"Do you think something will evolve between Raamah and Elisheba?" Nephi asked.

Trying to hide her smile, Isaabel glanced at Lehi to gauge his reaction, but Lehi didn't show any surprise at the question. "Considering our situation, it would be favorable."

Isaabel wondered what Nephi thought about his sister marrying a man who was beginning to be just as defiant as his older brothers.

"The Liahona has a new message," Lehi suddenly said. He removed the covering from the brass ball that he carried. "It says we are to camp in the next valley." He replaced the Liahona in his baggage, and they continued moving forward.

Just then, Lehi, Nephi, and Isaabel crested the top of the slope they'd been climbing. They stopped in amazement and stared at the valley spread before them. Pastures and farmlands crisscrossed each other, dotted with encampments of structures and tents. Grazing flocks roamed the hillsides and terrain below. The other family members arrived one by one and stopped to look at the sight.

"A valley," Lehi said, looking at the pointers on the Liahona. "We've arrived." With trepidation, they began the descent along the wadi.

Raamah caught up to them, his face red with exertion. "It's my father," he said. "He's fainted."

Turning, Isaabel saw Ishmael slumped over the back of his camel. Lehi released the reins of the animal he led and rushed to Ishmael's side, the others trailing. Standing beside Ishmael's mount, Bashemath quietly cried. Isaabel clung to her mother and stared in dismay at her father's limp form.

The men brought Ishmael down from his camel and laid him upon a rug on the ground as the family assembled silently around them. Lehi bent over him and placed a hand against his chest. Ishmael was still breathing, though in shallow breaths.

"He's still with us. We need to set up camp quickly and make him comfortable." Lehi's gaze settled on Nephi. "Bring the Liahona."

"No," Raamah said through gritted teeth. "My father's life is more important than what that thing says."

Lehi looked at Ishmael's eldest son, his face weary. "The Liahona has already instructed us to dwell in this valley."

Raamah's demeanor relaxed, and he nodded at Nephi.

Nephi crossed to Lehi's camel and fetched the brass instrument. When he rejoined the family, he said, "We are instructed to make camp on this side of the valley."

Rising, Lehi stood and scanned the south end of the valley where they stood. Isaabel followed his gaze and saw that smoke curled from many of the encampments.

"Let's hope our neighbors are friendly," Lehi said. He pointed to a cluster of date palms several hundred paces away. "We will set up over there." Eyes followed Lehi's outstretched hand, and the family fell into immediate action.

Isaabel watched as Raamah, Heth, Nephi, and Sam carried her father to the designated location and placed him beneath a swaying palm. Five paces south of the palm, Zoram began to dig and soon had the valuables hidden away. A stiff breeze had started, stirring the hot air and bringing relief. Bashemath stationed herself next to her husband and took his hand while Isaabel and her sisters quickly erected a shelter to surround their ailing father. When Ishmael was settled, Raamah and Heth joined them.

Taking a few steps back, Isaabel and her sisters moved away to allow their brothers to sit close to him. Raamah took his father's hand and pressed it gently.

After some time, Ishmael stirred from his state of unconsciousness. Isaabel brought her hand to her heart. "Mother," she said, "he's moving!"

With a cry of relief, Bashemath moved to his side.

Ishmael reached out his other hand although his eyes stayed closed. "My children," he whispered.

"We are all here, Father," Heth said.

Isaabel linked arms with Tamar and Puah as they strained to hear their father's words.

A grimace crossed Ishmael's face briefly. Then he relaxed and asked, "Where are we?"

"We've stopped to rest near a fertile valley," Raamah said.

Ishmael nodded slightly, then increased his grip on his son's hands. "This is the place where I shall be buried."

Isaabel felt as if a great weight pressed against her heart. Her mother let out a sob, and Isaabel found herself holding back her own. Raamah and Heth began to protest.

"My sons, my daughters," Ishmael said again.

They fell silent, listening.

"My time has drawn nigh, and I must speak to you."

Tamar and Isaabel glanced at each other with apprehension.

"The Lord God has brought us into this wilderness so that we may escape the great destruction of Jerusalem. Had we not followed my cousin's family, we would have perished with the others," Ishmael said. His eyes opened, and he raised his gaze to his daughters' faces, then it gradually settled on his sons.

Isaabel felt the blood start to drain from her face as a knot formed in her stomach. Her forehead prickled with sweat. She'd heard her father speak these words before, but now they were said with finality. She saw a tear trickle down her mother's cheek and became aware of the absolute sorrow her mother must be experiencing.

"Before I go down unto my grave, I want a promise from my children."

Time seemed to hold its breath as Isaabel heard those words. With the absence of their father from the family, it would be up to her oldest brother to implement Ishmael's wishes.

His eyes rolling upward, Ishmael continued. "I want each of you to promise that you will follow Lehi to the promised land and establish a new life." He paused and licked his cracked lips. "Raamah, keep the family together."

"Yes, Father," Raamah whispered. He leaned forward and kissed both of his father's cheeks. Before Raamah drew away, Ishmael clasped his hand.

"My son, remember the words of Jacob, our forefather. 'And let my name be named on them, and the name of my fathers

Abraham and Isaac; and let them grow into a multitude in the midst of the earth.'" Ishmael paused. "We are of the lineage of Ephraim, and by marrying into Lehi's family, who are of the lineage of Manasseh, two branches of Joseph's family are united." He turned his gaze toward his other children. "Do not let this union divide."

Ishmael dropped his hold on Raamah and looked up at the sky, staring blankly as if his words had drained all his strength. Heth moved toward him and kissed each cheek. Rebeka followed suit, then Anah, Puah, and Tamar.

Finally, Isaabel took her turn by his side, placing her hand over Ishmael's cool fingers.

"Ah, my little Isa," Ishmael said, focusing on her face. "Who would have thought my time would come so soon?" He breathed in with labored effort. "I will miss you."

Isaabel bent over her father, inhaling his familiar fragrance as she kissed his leathery cheek for the last time. She forced herself to pull away from him, knowing her mother waited.

As Isaabel drew away, her father held out a trembling hand. "Bashemath."

With a soft moan, Bashemath clung to Ishmael's chest, her sobs muffled against him.

"Dearest Bashemath," Ishmael said, raising his hand and stroking his wife's cheek. His breathing grew labored and Isaabel held her breath as her father searched for his next gulp of air.

"Breathe," Bashemath whispered. "Just breathe."

The moments stretched out, each second passing agonizingly slow.

Suddenly Bashemath let out a wail. "He grows cold," she cried and began to rub Ishmael's hands furiously. "Bring me more rugs."

A scurry of activity surrounded Isaabel. She could not make her feet move. Her sisters brought the rugs, and Raamah knelt beside Bashemath and covered their father's body with an additional layer.

"We must get him warm," Bashemath said, her voice frantic.

Raamah placed a hand on their mother's shoulder. "He's dying, Mother."

With a sob, Bashemath collapsed onto her husband.

Isaabel bowed her head. And then Ishmael took a final shallow breath, his chest growing still as his spirit departed.

CHAPTER 7

To every thing there is a season, and a time to every purpose under the heaven: A time to be born, and a time to die.
(ECCLESIASTES 3:1–2)

From a distance, Nephi heard the wailing fill the valley. He felt like a dagger had pierced his soul—Ishmael had died. A great and faithful man had given his life in pursuit of the promised land. Nephi sank to his knees as if a chain had pulled him down. It was too difficult to comprehend, to accept that Ishmael was gone. But the high-pitched cries were unmistakable.

"Oh, Isa," he whispered. She was among the mourners, and the men could only listen to the women lament while their own grief was kept quiet. Nephi wanted to run to her, comfort her, but he knew that he could not be included in the women's mourning rites.

He saw a lone figure walking in the direction of Ishmael's family and recognized it as his father. Instinctively, Nephi tried to rise, but he was rooted to the earth. His body felt heavy, his limbs like iron ore.

"Father," he said, his voice guttural, but Lehi didn't seem to hear him.

Nephi hung his head. His chest expanded, and he felt a dizziness claim him. He put his hands out in front of him to catch his fall, but he landed on the ground, his face planted in the sand. Nephi moaned and turned over. With great effort, he was able to sit up. He brushed the sand from his face and blinked against the offending granules. Still, the tears did not come.

"Nephi," a voice sounded above him.

Nephi looked up to see his father. Lehi knelt beside him.

"You've heard about Ishmael, then?"

"Yes," Nephi said. "As soon as I heard the wails, I knew."

Lehi nodded and put an arm about Nephi's shoulders. After a moment, he said, "A local man told me this place is called Nahom."

"Nahom?" Nephi asked. With a nod from Lehi, he continued, "Perhaps Nahom will turn out to be a place of comfort."

"Or a place to be comforted," Lehi said, his expression somber. "Ishmael . . ." But his voice lost strength.

"Yes," Nephi said.

They sat together for a few moments before they saw Sariah, Elisheba, and Dinah join the group of women.

A slow agony crept through Nephi. With his father-in-law's death, a patriarch had been lost, but most importantly, one whom he had loved. He felt his father's shoulders quivering. Nephi looked at Lehi, who had removed his arm and bowed his head, his hands clasped together.

"O God," Lehi whispered, "please give our family Thy strength and comfort." His voice was low and filled with anguish. "We have followed Thy commandments and have relied on Thee for all our needs."

Nephi felt his throat swell with sorrow as he listened to his father's prayer.

"We are filled with grief, O Lord," Lehi continued. "We have lost a cousin, a father . . . a husband. But we know Thy will has been done. Give us . . . the ability to accept it . . ." His words faltered.

After a moment, Nephi said, "Amen." He opened his eyes and saw that his father was staring straight ahead, his expression set firm.

"We must find a proper place to bury him," Lehi said.

Nephi nodded, amazed at his father's newfound strength. He scanned the landscape surrounding them, wondering how they were going to tell the women that their father would be buried in the wilderness.

"Come. Let's see if Raamah and Heth will accompany us to meet with the tribal leader. We need to make an agreement when choosing a location," Lehi said.

Nephi knew better than to question his father's judgment, but he wondered if Raamah and Heth would be ready to discuss such details.

They left their resting place and crossed to where Raamah and Heth sat a respectable distance from the mourning women. Nephi spotted Isaabel among her sisters. The women formed a circle, kneeling on the earth, as they swayed in tandem. Their wails were piteous to listen to, but the way they rent their clothing made Nephi's heart ache.

When Raamah saw Lehi and Nephi approaching, he rose unsteadily to his feet.

"Our hearts are filled with sorrow . . . " Lehi started to say.

The expression on Raamah's face was one of shock and anguish. He fell into Lehi's open arms, hushed sobs wracking his frame.

Next to them, Heth's face was a mask of stone, his eyes empty. It was as if the death of his father hadn't happened and by sheer will, Heth could prevent it. He turned from Raamah's open grief and started to walk away.

"Heth," Nephi cried out. But the call was ignored, and Heth continued walking.

Raamah pulled away from Lehi. "Leave my brother. He will find his way back."

The men gazed at Heth's retreating figure, looking vulnerable and alone.

"We must go to the local tribe and ask where we can bury your father," Lehi said, his voice breaking into their thoughts.

Raamah brought his focus back to Lehi, a white line forming above his lip. "We are to bury him here?" He stared incredulously at Lehi. "In the *wilderness?*"

"Raamah," Lehi said, placing a hand on Raamah's shoulder. "I know it is difficult—"

"*Difficult?* It's unbearable, unthinkable . . . It is *shameful* that my father has to be buried here." His voice rose, choked with emotion. "He should be buried in the land of his birth, *not here.* Not in this wasteland filled with nomads and scorpions."

"I too," Lehi said, "wish your father would have lived to see the promised land."

"The promised land?" Raamah spat out. "Is that all you can think about? My father believed in your promised land, and for whatever reason, he believed in *you.* And now . . ." He hesitated, searching for the words. "He is gone. Forever."

A movement from behind made them all turn. Anah had broken away from the women, with Puah close behind. Her face was streaked with tears and her hands were outstretched toward Lehi. "Because of you, we have been led to perish in this land. My father was blinded by your dreams, and now he has paid with his life."

Puah joined her sister's side, eyes wild. "Had we remained in Jerusalem, our father would still be alive." She clung to Anah's arm for support. "The Lord has forsaken us."

"If you are a prophet of God, why did you not heal our father?" Anah sobbed.

Sariah ran to the weeping women and pulled them into her arms. They clung to her, as Sariah's own red-rimmed eyes met Lehi's gaze. "We must prepare the body for burial," she said.

Lehi nodded. "We will attend to the other arrangements."

The women stumbled away and joined the others. If possible, their wailing seemed to grow louder.

"Raamah," Lehi said, turning back to the men. "When you are ready . . ."

Letting out a heavy sigh, Raamah said, "I am ready."

Lehi led the way, as the three men skirted the edge of the valley eastward until they arrived at the first tribal settlement. Several children ran to greet them as they drew closer. They spoke rapidly, and Lehi answered their questions with patience.

"Take us to your leader," Lehi said.

Almost as soon as he had spoken, a group of men formed at the edge of the camp. The man in the center, dressed in a dark robe and scarlet turban, was the obvious leader. His eyes were wary, but beneath the cool exterior Lehi sensed a warmth.

"I am Lehi of Jerusalem. One of our family members has died," Lehi said in the local tongue, which was similar to other languages he had learned as a merchant.

The man's expression didn't change. "I am Khali . . . Is there disease in your family?"

"No," Lehi said. "He was far along in years and had been ailing for some time."

The leader's demeanor softened. "Who is this person?"

Raamah stepped forward and spoke in a halting southern dialect. "He is my father." His words were awkward, yet deliberate. "He was a great man—many children. We want to give him a good burial where he will be at peace."

The leader nodded. "I understand." He looked at the bedraggled travelers. "I know a place where the body won't be bothered. And when your family moves on," he paused, "he will be left in peace."

Raamah bowed slightly, relief evident on his face. "Thank you."

"The site is of value to us," continued the man.

Raamah glanced at Lehi and Nephi, worry in his eyes. Lehi spread his hands wide, indicating that he had nothing to give.

But Nephi stepped forward. "What is your price?"

The leader settled his gaze on the young man before him. "Gold."

"How much?" Nephi asked.

Khali surveyed the men for a moment before answering. "Enough to adorn my youngest wife."

Nephi nodded almost imperceptibly, his brow furrowed. "It will not be easy. We are not carrying anything of value."

Lehi turned to Khali with a bow. "We will see what we can gather."

The tribal leader returned the bow, his eyes shifting from Lehi to Nephi, then settling on Raamah.

Raamah bowed, his jaw set firm. As Lehi and Nephi turned to leave, he moved to Nephi's side. "You have gold?" he blurted, then pursed his lips together.

"Our family might be able to come up with something."

"I thought you had nothing," Raamah said. "Weren't your father's valuables stolen by Laban?"

"Yes," Nephi said. "But not my mother's."

Raamah stopped and stared after Nephi's retreating figure. "Maybe my father was right about Lehi, Sariah, and Nephi," he muttered to himself.

When they reached camp, Nephi went immediately to Bashemath's tent. "Mother," Nephi said. Sariah sat close to Bashemath in the tent, her mantle draped loosely about her. Several tears had already appeared in Bashemath's clothing, signifying her grief.

"We've been offered a private burial place for Ishmael," Nephi said. "And we have been given a price."

"I suspected," Sariah said, withdrawing a trinket box from beneath her robe. "I had Isaabel bring it just before you arrived."

Bashemath reached out a trembling hand and touched the box.

"How did you guess?" Nephi asked, staring at the intricate carvings.

"I couldn't be more proud than to give this up for a great man such as Ishmael." She rose and handed the box to Nephi.

"We won't need all of it," Nephi said. "A few of the pieces of jewelry should be enough."

Sariah obliged and selected two solid bracelets and a gold ring.

Bashemath watched the interchange, her eyes moist. With trembling hands she began to remove some of her own jewelry, but Sariah stopped her. "Keep the mohar from your husband. It's all you have left."

"Thank you," Bashemath whispered, her voice full of emotion.

"You're welcome," Sariah said.

"I'll be going then," Nephi said, his eyes meeting Bashemath's with grateful acknowledgment.

Nephi exited his mother's tent to find Raamah. "I have the price for the burial site."

"Your mother's jewelry?" Raamah asked.

Nephi nodded.

When Raamah started to object, Nephi put his hand on his arm. "It was my mother's wish. Now let's hurry before Khali changes his mind about the negotiation," Nephi said.

Raamah's eyes widened. "I was afraid of that possibility."

When Lehi joined them, the men returned to Khali's settlement.

As they stood on the outskirts, waiting for the Minaean leader to arrive, Raamah turned to Lehi and Nephi. "Thank you. My family will appreciate your efforts in assuring my father is properly buried."

Nephi felt a spring of hope form in his chest, knowing how difficult it must have been for Raamah to speak those words. "Your father was an honorable man," he said, "and I will sorely miss him."

Next to him, Lehi said, "I consider your family to be a part of our own."

Raamah nodded gruffly, his face twisting with emotion.

Khali arrived with his men. "You've brought the gold," he stated, though his eyebrows were raised in question.

Stepping forward, Lehi hesitated before responding. "The agreement still stands?"

Khali bowed respectfully, his eyes lit with desire. "Of course."

Nephi joined his father, his mother's jewelry concealed in his robe from the tribal members. "Our treasure and property were stolen. The only valuables we have left are from my mother's mohar."

The leader furrowed his brow and studied Nephi's face. When he determined that the young man was telling the truth, he squatted on the ground and indicated for Nephi to join him.

Nephi obliged and withdrew the pieces of jewelry from his robe. In his mother's tent, the items had appeared precious and lustrous. But against the dark hands of the tribesman, they looked frail and inferior. Nephi found himself holding his breath, waiting for the leader's reaction.

In his hand, Khali turned over the bracelets one by one. Then he took the ring and inspected it closely. He handed it to one of his guards who promptly bit down on the gold and pronounced it authentic.

For several more moments, Khali studied the jewelry then rose to his feet and started speaking to his men in their rapid dialect, too rapid for Nephi to follow. Nephi's pulse quickened as he realized that neither he nor Raamah were armed. What if they decided that the gold wasn't enough?

"It is a deal," the leader said finally.

Relief filled Nephi.

Khali bowed. "My men will show you where you can bury your father."

Raamah and Lehi both returned the bow. Raamah expressed many thanks in Hebrew, which Khali waved away. "Show them the place," he told his guards. Then he turned back to his settlement, whistling softly as he walked away.

The Minaean guards stepped forward, their eyes not as welcoming as their leader's had been. They silently passed Nephi and led the way to a rocky cleft at the edge of the valley. The men stood before the burial site with reverence. On the way back to camp, Raamah clapped Nephi on the shoulder and thanked him again.

Later that night, as Nephi sat hunched before the smoking embers of the fire, Heth appeared. Nephi rose to greet him, but Heth ignored him and crouched, spreading his palms toward the fading warmth.

"We were able to purchase a burial site for your father," Nephi said after a while.

Heth merely continued to stare straight ahead, his eyes unseeing.

After a few silent moments, Nephi returned to his tent, leaving Heth to his thoughts. But sleep eluded Nephi, and he watched the changing shadows until the first light arrived.

At dawn, the family gathered together. The women led the funeral procession, ashes streaked on their faces, their wailing voices rising and falling every few steps. Zillah played the psaltery, keeping rhythm with the wailing. The men lifted the shrouded body of Ishmael on a bier and followed the women to the burial place. Lehi walked in front of the men, a prayer shawl covering his shoulders.

Once they reached the site by the rocky cleft, the women fell silent.

From his vantage point, Nephi watched Isaabel, who was shrouded in a black veil. As Lehi prayed over Ishmael's grave, arms raised, Nephi felt comforted. But even with Ishmael's death, he knew the Lord would continue to protect them under his father's guidance. Nonetheless, fresh tears formed in his eyes as he watched his wife. Then another wave washed over him—a wave of grief. Grief for his wife's sorrow, her family's loss, and Ishmael's suffering the past several months all combined with disquiet over his sisters-in-law's angst so recently displayed.

When Lehi concluded his prayer, Isaabel and the women started their wailing again. Soon it was time to move away from the burial site so that the men could finish their task. Isaabel clung to Tamar as they walked back to camp, beating her chest and crying loudly.

After the women left, Raamah and Heth covered Ishmael's enshrouded body with stones. Then they constructed a formation of rocks and earth to create a mounded tomb, following the instructions given to them by Khali, while the other men bowed their heads in respect.

* * *

A week later, on the final day of mourning, the women removed their black sackcloth clothing and washed the ashes from their faces. Nephi found Isaabel inside their tent, dabbing at the streaks of dried blood on her cheeks and forehead. The rawness of her skin from the itchy goat hair was a painful reminder of the grief she had endured. He touched her shoulder softly after sitting next to her.

She turned and looked at him with luminous eyes. "I feel like I should stay in mourning."

Nephi took the damp cloth from her and tended to the facial wounds caused by her renting. "Your father would want you to heal your grief."

Isaabel's eyes filled with tears. "After all he suffered—all we've suffered—to journey this far and have him die . . ."

Pulling his wife into his arms, Nephi whispered, "Your father put the Lord first. For that he was blessed. He led his family away from destruction." To Nephi's surprise, Isaabel stiffened.

"Oh, Nephi," she whispered. "What else will we have to face before we reach the promised land?"

Nephi stroked her hair and held her tight. He had wondered the same thing.

Throughout the next several days, Nephi noticed Isaabel spent more and more time with her sisters. Bashemath was rarely seen outside her tent, and Isaabel and her sisters spent a great deal of their days inside.

One evening after the men had eaten and the women were about to begin their meal, Bashemath exited her tent and strode to the fire. Sariah rushed to meet her. "Come and join us for supper," she said.

But Bashemath brushed her off. She walked to Lehi, who was speaking with Sam, and stopped before them.

"Bashemath, it's good to see you," Lehi said. "Has your health improved?"

"*My* health? You're worried about *me*? My husband is lying on the hard ground, entombed by rocks. He's the one you should have been worried about." She glared at the family members who had stopped their conversations to listen. "Ishmael would have never hurt any of you, nor caused any one discomfort. Yet Lehi was so determined to travel that Ishmael wasn't able to recover from his last bout of illness. And now . . ." She settled her gaze once again on Lehi. "The prophet asks how *my* health is."

"Bashemath," Lehi said, putting out his hand.

"Don't try to hush me," she retorted, vehemence in her eyes. "If I told you how poorly I feel, you'd take it upon yourself to make us all travel again."

Sariah fidgeted where she stood. "Lehi didn't mean—" she began.

"Look at your own baby, Sariah. Why does your son have to be born in such a desolate place and not with the comforts your other children had? Is Jacob less of a person? Does he deserve no privilege?" She drew in a breath. "I have two daughters . . ." Her voice rose. "Two daughters who will give birth in this forsaken land if we do not return to Jerusalem."

Seated near the fire, Rebeka lowered her head into her hands.

Anah and Puah joined their mother's side, eyes flashing.

"We have had no meat for days," Bashemath said.

"The men are planning a hunt in the morning," Nephi said, crossing to join Lehi.

"You," Bashemath said, "are just like your father."

Nephi felt as if he had been slapped. "Ishmael was a father to me too," he said, his voice cracking. He glanced at Isaabel, seated next to Rebeka. She was looking at the ground and didn't respond.

"I'm sorry, Nephi," Bashemath said, looking anything but sorrowful. "I supported my husband and believed in your father, but no longer. I have two grandchildren on the way and will not risk losing them for some . . . *dream* . . . that you and your father had of a promised land."

Rebeka rose and walked with her head held high, joining her mother and sisters. Her eyes were moist, and her chin trembled. "My mother is right. Our journey in the wilderness has been nothing more than wanderings. In Jerusalem, we had a home and a father. Here we have neither. And now—" Her voice broke. "My child will never know his grandfather." Sobs spilled from her, and Bashemath took Rebeka into her arms.

"What will we tell our children when they are born?" Anah asked, her eyes blurring. "That their grandfather gave up his life for this?" She waved her arm in a circle. "He traded his life for his family to suffer hunger, thirst, and fatigue?"

"Haven't we endured enough, Lehi?" Bashemath broke in. She clung to her daughters and started to wail.

Nephi stepped toward Isaabel to comfort her, but she embraced Rebeka and wailed along with the women. He looked at his mother helplessly, seeing despair written on her face. Nephi followed her gaze. His father had started walking away from the camp, shoulders hunched, head down. He made a forlorn figure, robes billowing behind him as he retreated from the family. Nephi knew his father had left to plead with the Lord.

CHAPTER 8

They also that erred in spirit shall come to understanding, and they that murmured shall learn doctrine.
(ISAIAH 29:24)

"I have spoken to Khali, leader of the neighboring Minaean settlement. He has offered seed for planting if we are willing to pay him with one-third of our crop," Lehi said. He stood before the family members in their first council since Ishmael's death. The traditional mourning period of seven days had ended weeks before.

"The ground is fertile enough to farm, but we will have to carry water here—that is why the locals have not used it," Lehi said. "But the Lord doesn't want us to use the seeds and grain we brought from Jerusalem. We will cultivate barley, which has been grown successfully here."

Nephi sat close to Isaabel. He had been concerned about her sullen behavior since Ishmael's death, which made him relieved that his father wanted to dwell in Nahom for a period of time. The family would thrive on routine and comfort in this part of the desert.

Laman, who sat across from Nephi, caught his eye. The look on his face was disapproving. Nephi glanced away, letting out a slow breath. His brother didn't understand that their father was trying to make life easier on the women. Rebeka was advancing toward her time for delivery, and Laman's own wife, Anah, would benefit from less traveling.

He looked at Lemuel, who stared past him with glassy eyes. Nephi had already suspected that Laman and Lemuel had been bartering for date palm wine. He wondered what they had traded for it.

Lehi's voice continued. "We will organize labor teams, and the women will only work during the morning."

Suddenly Laman rose to his feet. "Is *this* the promised land, then?"

Lemuel rose next to his brother, somewhat unsteadily, and pointed to the settlements in the valley. "It looks like someone already chose the best land."

Laman snickered at his brother's comment. On the other side of the circle, Raamah and Heth joined in the exchange.

Turning toward his sons, Lehi raised his hand for silence. "We will tarry in Nahom until the Lord instructs us otherwise."

"Or until Nephi tells us otherwise . . ." Laman muttered.

"The Liahona—" Lehi began.

"The Liahona guided us to a burial ground," Laman finished. "And now are we to farm someone else's land?"

Isaabel shifted next to Nephi. He glanced at her profile, trying to read her thoughts. Her expression seemed passive, but her eyelids were lowered so it was difficult to guess her mind.

Lehi answered the question. "Our lives are in the Lord's hands, and until he instructs us to continue our journey, we will remain in Nahom and farm to provide food for our families."

Nephi looked at Raamah, whose head was bent in conversation with Heth. There were no more objections, so Lehi adjourned the meeting.

Later that afternoon, Lehi took his sons to meet with Khali.

Sam and Nephi walked behind their brothers as they followed their father. Nephi glanced at Sam, who was being unusually quiet. Several paces ahead, Laman and Lemuel were deep in conversation.

"Are you all right?" Nephi finally ventured.

Sam looked at Nephi as if he didn't hear the question. "What?"

"You look troubled."

Breathing a sigh, Sam shook his head. "I don't know how to say this . . ." his voice trailed off.

Nephi felt a familiar uneasiness creep into his stomach. "You can trust me."

"It's not about trust," Sam said, avoiding Nephi's gaze. "It's about your wife."

"What about her?" Nephi's unease turned to dread. What could Sam possibly know about Isaabel that he didn't?

"Isaabel has been talking with Anah and Puah." The words came in a rush as if Sam was relieved to get it over with.

Nephi arched his eyebrows, not understanding Sam's trepidation. "And?"

Sam slowed his pace, letting the distance increase between them and the others. "Their husbands have also been party to these talks," he said in a low voice.

"Laman and Lemuel?" Nephi whispered, staring ahead at the backs of his older brothers. "What have they been discussing?"

With a shrug, Sam said, "I don't know. That's why I didn't say anything before, because I hoped it was harmless."

At those words, Nephi knew that no conversations between Laman and Isaabel without his presence could be harmless. "Has Isaabel confided in Tamar?"

"No." Sam looked at Nephi with regret. "They haven't spoken much since Ishmael died."

Nephi clenched his jaw. Isaabel hadn't spoken to him much either.

Ahead of him, the others had stopped. Nephi could see that Khali was already on his way to meet the group. Apparently the

Minaean had been expecting them. Laman stepped forward with Lehi and the negotiations began. All the while, Nephi watched the interchange with a sinking heart as he thought about the conversation that he would soon have with Isaabel.

* * *

Elisheba often took long walks along the edges of the nearby settlement. She enjoyed talking with Minaean children, learning some of their dialect and teaching them Hebrew. Once in a while, her sister accompanied her, but mostly she walked alone. She found herself thinking about what Isaabel had said to her before they reached Nahom. Not only about Raamah caring for her, but that he had been led by the Spirit and not recognized it.

It was puzzling how differently her brothers reacted to their challenges in the wilderness. She had watched Sam and Nephi work and toil all day with little complaint, except for what was said in good humor. In contrast, Laman and Lemuel only worked as much as necessary and grumbled incessantly, often breaking out in fierce arguments.

Raamah and his brother, Heth, spent the majority of their time with Laman and Lemuel. And it seemed that for the last few months, Raamah's beliefs supported those of her eldest brothers'. Elisheba kicked at a stone on the ground. She was skirting an encampment and could see the children playing in the field.

If she were Raamah's wife, she would have to support him, no matter what he believed, even if it went against her own father.

Wife? She smiled at the thought, then felt a twinge of anxiety in her chest. Raamah was a full-grown man with a son and had been married before. She was merely a girl—how could she make a man such as Raamah content?

Without realizing it, Elisheba had climbed the steep terrain near Ishmael's burial site. She stopped with hushed reverence, thinking about the kind man who continued to be mourned by the entire family. A small stone tumbled past her. Startled, she looked up and saw Raamah rising to his feet. It looked as if he had been kneeling before his father's place of rest.

Elisheba found her eyes locked with Raamah's—his full of grief. Her cheeks grew warm under his open gaze. She felt her own heart twist in pain as Raamah's sorrow seemed to pour into her. Opening her mouth, she tried to speak, but the words caught.

She took a step backward and turned away in embarrassment. The ground beneath her appeared to give way, and she stumbled into a bush. Reaching for the prickly branches, she tried awkwardly to regain her balance.

A firm hand grasped her elbow and steadied her. "Here, let me help you," Raamah said. His voice was gentle.

"Thank you," Elisheba managed to say. She kept her eyes lowered, not daring to look at him at such a close distance. She tried to pull away, but Raamah's hand remained tightly on her arm.

With reluctance, Elisheba raised her gaze to meet his. Raamah was not a handsome man—his features were too angular. But something about his manner entranced her. "I'm sorry I disturbed you."

Raamah shook his head. "You don't need to apologize." He fell silent and stared past her.

Elisheba looked down at his hand still on her arm. She felt her pulse quicken, and she suddenly wished she were in the comforting confines of the camp. It was one thing to imagine an encounter with Raamah, but another to experience it. "Do you come here often?" she asked, then felt her face redden at the thoughtless question.

Raamah brought his gaze back to Elisheba's. "Every day," he said sounding far away.

"I will take care not to disturb you again." Elisheba's heart sank. If only she had been paying attention to where she was walking.

"No," Raamah said. He relaxed his grip but continued to hold her arm. "You didn't disturb me." His eyes seemed to focus on her, the grief dissipating. "I'm glad to see you. We have much to discuss."

Elisheba raised her eyebrows, wondering what he meant. They saw each other every day.

"You are nearly ready," he said.

Feeling confused, Elisheba asked, "For what?"

Raamah's face filled with amusement—dispelling the grief that had been there just moments before.

Elisheba was taken aback. Was something funny?

He released her elbow, letting his hand brush down her arm until he held her hand in his. "To marry."

Elisheba stared at him, trying to understand his meaning. Was he offering marriage? Her breath caught at the thought, and hope flooded her being. "Marry . . ." she said, her voice trailing off as Raamah drew her hand to his lips.

The tingling sensation caused her to jerk her hand away. Instantly she regretted her actions. *I am like a child,* she realized.

He threw back his head and laughed. "That's what I like about you, Elisheba." His gaze tender, he continued to smile. "You are still naïve. To any other woman, my words would have been obvious."

She lowered her eyes. He had called her naïve. Now she knew he thought her a child.

Raamah tilted her chin upward. "Elisheba, I have watched you for many months. I could not bear the thought of anything happening to you. That is why I so fiercely fought the raider who was attacking you."

Elisheba moved backward, away from his touch. Images of that violent night came to her mind and made her shudder. Her life was indebted to Raamah, and all she could think about was whether or not he had intentions of proposing. Shame engulfed her as she realized she'd never thanked him. "I never had a chance to thank you for saving me that night," she said. "I owe you my life . . . and virtue."

Raamah remained silent for a moment.

She finally raised her eyes to meet his. The look Raamah gave her was so intense and enveloping that Elisheba felt she somehow belonged to him. Perhaps he would propose. Her heart pounded fiercely at the possibility, and she wondered if he could hear it.

"You're welcome," Raamah said softly. "My father . . ."

Elisheba saw Raamah's eyes search for words. She wished that she could do something to heal his pain and was surprised when he moved away abruptly, his expression hardened.

"You must return before your family misses you," Raamah said.

Confused, Elisheba took a few steps backward, baffled by Raamah's change in conversation. She turned and hurried down the slope. She sensed Raamah's gaze following her. He had seemed so tender one moment, but in that last instant, he looked anything but gentle. She had caused him to slay another in her defense, and now, she had just interrupted his grieving. Tears stung her eyes as she hastened back to camp.

* * *

Isaabel sat in Anah's tent. Nephi had fallen asleep early, and she crept out as soon as she could. It was comforting to be able to talk to her sisters about their father. Her mother silently wallowed in her grief and avoided any conversation of him now, and Tamar had moved on to her normal routine. But with Anah and Puah, Isaabel could discuss the emptiness that she still felt.

Once in a while, Laman and Lemuel had joined them, but Isaabel usually made an excuse to leave soon after. The men talked about returning to Jerusalem, but Isaabel remained quiet during those conversations. She knew her duty was to stay with Nephi, no matter the hardships—though she hadn't expected to lose her father in the process. It helped her sleep better at night to unload her heartache to her sisters.

She felt sad that she'd pushed Nephi away so much, but she hoped he understood. She felt confident that when she was through healing, things would return as they were before—with her husband and the Lord.

"Tomorrow we'll go together to Father's burial site," Puah said.

"I would like that," Anah said. "I haven't been there since we buried him, and I didn't want to go there alone."

Isaabel and Puah both reached for Anah's hands. "We'll stay together," Isaabel said.

"If only our father was still alive." Tears rolled down Puah's cheeks. "We shouldn't have come into the wilderness."

Isaabel sighed. They had had this conversation many times since her mother's outburst in front of the family. Nothing she said had seemed to help. Even through her grief, she realized the futility of the comment. "We can't go back now."

Anah raised her head with a sniff, looking directly at Isaabel. "It's time you knew, Isaabel. We've already made a plan."

Isaabel felt her pulse quicken, combined with a sense of dismay. "A plan?"

Anah spoke earnestly. "We are returning to Jerusalem." Before Isaabel could remonstrate, Anah continued. "We know Nephi won't come, but we couldn't bear to be separated from you. You will be taken care of by our husbands, and they have promised to support you as a sister. Heth will bring his family, and Raamah wants Elisheba to journey with us as well. We know that Lehi and Nephi will try to stop us, so we'll leave during the night. By the time the others awake, it will be too late."

Isaabel was at a loss for words.

Puah touched Isaabel's shoulder. "You cannot tell anyone. Not even Tamar. We'll leave the night after Rebeka gives birth." She winked. "The camp will be in an uproar, and when everyone is asleep after the celebration, we'll make our escape."

The tent walls seemed stifling. Isaabel tried to take a deep breath. "You want me to leave my husband?"

"I know it sounds difficult, Isa, but it's the only way we can have a proper home again. Once you have a chance to think about it, you'll agree."

Isaabel nodded numbly, feeling her head grow light. "I need some air," she said. She rose and pushed through the tent opening. The night air hit her with full force, and after walking a few paces, she fell to her knees, her stomach protesting.

After the wave passed, Isaabel felt her mind clear. What her sisters had proposed was mad. The devastation her husband and father-in-law would feel was incomprehensible. She rose to her feet with new determination—she had let her mourning carry her too far, and now she needed to set her sisters on the right path.

She was about to reenter Anah's tent when a low whistle sounded behind her. Someone took her arm and pulled her back from the entrance. When she turned, half-expecting to see Nephi, she gasped.

"Shhh," Laman whispered, his eyes glittering in the moonlight. "Having another discussion with my wife?"

Isaabel's head felt rooted in place, and her mouth wouldn't open. The last time she'd been alone with Laman was when he'd apologized to her. But tonight there was no sign of remorse on his face.

"You look pale," Laman said, his eyes soaking in her features. "Have you heard of the plan then?"

Isaabel nodded and pulled her arm away, which earned her another smile.

"Ever the tigress, I see," he hissed. "Well, are you coming with us back to Jerusalem?"

"No," Isaabel said, a little too loudly. She clapped her hand over her mouth.

"Ah." Laman chuckled quietly. "I see that you have not been properly persuaded, Isaabel." He leaned close, his voice barely audible. "And did they tell you what will happen if you do not join us?"

Isaabel shook her head, feeling her skin prickle with fear. "What?" she asked in a whisper.

"I will kill Nephi."

Isaabel stumbled blindly to her tent, the words of Laman echoing in her mind. To kill one's own brother was almost unimaginable. Her greatest fear had grown to fruition in the past few moments. In her heart, she knew that Laman was serious about killing Nephi. She hesitated outside her tent, trying to calm her breathing, when a new concern developed. Would she have to sacrifice her own happiness and freedom for Nephi's life?

Yes. She sank to the ground, and tears dotted the sand beneath her. Nephi's life was more important than her happiness. And for that reason, she must not reveal anything to her husband, for surely he wouldn't allow her to return to Jerusalem with the others.

The silence in the camp was the only confidante for her torrid thoughts. Isaabel wished she could wake Nephi and warn him, but as she entered the tent, she knew his life would be in danger if she did. He lay on his side, facing away from her. She positioned herself a short distance away so as not to disturb his sleep. He would be leaving early in the morning for a hunting trip. Crops had been planted, but in the meantime, meat was needed. With her back turned toward him, Isaabel bit her lip against the emotion welling within her. Her father was gone, and now she was faced with losing her husband. She squeezed her eyes shut against the hot tears of despair.

CHAPTER 9

Thou shalt fear the Lord thy God; him shalt thou serve, and to him shalt thou cleave, and swear by his name.
(Deuteronomy 10:20)

Next to Isaabel, Nephi kept his breathing steady and refrained from turning over to look at his wife. He sensed she was still awake. She'd been gone for some time, and he'd almost risen to look for her. Sam had been right. Isaabel's grief over Ishmael's death had driven her away from him, and now she turned to others for comfort—her sisters, Anah and Puah, and possibly also Laman and Lemuel.

His brothers and their wives had grown more vocal in their complaining the past week. Nephi could feel an undercurrent of unrest among the family members. And this time it wasn't just Laman and Lemuel with Ishmael's sons following behind. The women continued to murmur openly against Lehi. Isaabel hadn't said anything to him, but her eyes were expressionless when he talked to her. She gave him only short replies to his questions.

Anger sprouted inside him. Nephi clenched his teeth together as if he could will it away. His eyes began to sting. It made him feel even more irritated when he felt anger toward his brothers. He felt helpless as he contemplated his weaknesses.

Why could he not reach out to his wife, and why could he not have more influence over his brothers?

Frustrated, he turned over and stared at the back of Isaabel's head. How he longed for the unity to return, the security, the love. He reached out and lightly touched her hair that spilled across her shoulders. If she was still awake, she didn't respond to his touch. She was his, and yet he felt she dwelt somewhere else.

With a disgruntled sigh, Nephi rose and pulled his cloak around him. He would not find his answers inside the tent. Stepping out into the night, he moved along the moonlit ground through the sleeping camp.

Some distance away, he knelt on the ground and pled for peace. Peace among the family members. Peace to accept Ishmael's death. Peace for Isaabel. Peace in his own heart.

* * *

Sam finished with his hunting preparations before dawn. A short distance away, Zoram exited his tent. Sam raised his hand in greeting and was met with a tired smile.

Zoram crossed to Sam. "How long will we be gone this time?" he asked.

Sam noticed the dark circles under Zoram's eyes. "Only a day or two. Will Rebeka be all right?"

"Of course. She'll be taken care of if her time comes while we are away. And she thinks it will be a few weeks yet," Zoram said.

Sam nodded, his gaze still focused on Zoram's troubled face. "Is something bothering you?"

Hesitating, Zoram met Sam's gaze. "All is not well."

"What do you mean?" Sam asked, surprised at the response.

"Within the camp," he lowered his voice, "something is not right."

Sam felt a slow twist in his stomach. He wondered how much Zoram really knew. Had Zoram talked with Laman and Lemuel? "Nephi and I have felt concerned too."

"What did Nephi say?" Zoram asked sharply.

Again, Sam was surprised. "Only that he is uneasy." He didn't think he should talk to Zoram about Nephi's distress.

"Rebeka told me that Isaabel and Tamar aren't speaking."

"Yes," Sam said. "It's true." He looked away, knowing that the two sisters not speaking was the least of it. He paused, then said, "It has been since the death of Ishmael."

"The women of Ishmael's family continue to blame Lehi and Nephi for their father's death," Zoram said simply.

Sam arched a brow. "Unfortunately, you're right. Where does Rebeka stand?"

"She has mourned greatly, but with a child growing within her, she feels gratitude also." Zoram paused. "Though sometimes I fear Rebeka will take her sisters' side if any trouble comes from it."

"I was concerned about Tamar too. But she has assured me that she supports Lehi," Sam said, hoping that it would be true. *But if Isaabel should turn against her own husband, who is a man of God . . .*

"Nephi's coming," Zoram said, interrupting Sam's thoughts.

Sam turned and looked at the approaching figure walking toward them. "Nephi," he whispered.

As Nephi drew closer, Sam could see that he had dark circles under his eyes. His face was pale and drawn, and his hands hung limp at his side.

"Are you ill?" Sam asked. He'd never seen Nephi look so dejected.

Nephi halted in front of the two men, and they waited for him to explain. "I have been praying through the night for my anger to leave," he said in a hoarse voice.

Zoram and Sam stared at him, not knowing what to say.

"Exhaustion has calmed my spirit, but my anger has weakened me. I am no good to protect our father now," Nephi continued.

"Protect him from what?" Sam blurted out.

"From our brothers and Ishmael's sons," Nephi said. "Their murmuring has increased, and the women support them. I fear for the outcome. Sam, you need to remain behind in our father's tent, if only to act as a watchman."

"But—" Sam started.

"If I leave to hunt with Zoram, perhaps some of the adverse feelings will be defused," Nephi said, staring past them. "And perhaps . . . my wife will notice my absence and rejoice when I return."

The pain emerging from Nephi pierced Sam's heart.

Zoram nodded. "As you wish, Nephi. When should we leave?"

"Now," Nephi said. "I do not wish to return to my tent."

* * *

Morning came too soon. Isaabel opened her eyes with reluctance, feeling a cold emptiness within her tent. Nephi had not returned and had most likely left for the hunt, she realized. When he had reached out to her last night, she should have responded. But she knew if she had, she would have confessed Laman's words and all would have been lost.

Isabel rose and dressed in the chilly air, pulling her mantle over her inner tunic. No doubt the morning fire had been started and her sisters would be chatting around it, awaiting her company. With a sinking heart, she knew what had to be done. She hesitated before exiting the tent, realizing she hadn't offered her morning prayer. "It's not *my* will, O Lord," she whispered. Disapproval filled the tent, as if the tent itself knew she was making the wrong choice. With defiance, she said out loud, "I must do this, if only to preserve Nephi's life." Then she stepped into the early light.

Just as she predicted, Isaabel found Anah and Puah sitting by the fire. The rest of the women hadn't stirred, and breakfast was still some time away. Anah reclined against a rolled mat, trying to find a comfortable position to support her back. Puah drew circles in the sand with her finger. When Isaabel approached, they both looked up with apprehension.

Anah spoke first. "We hope we didn't drive you away last night, Isa."

Isaabel sat next to them, holding her hands out to the fire's warmth. She waited a moment before responding. "I saw Laman outside the tent. He made the plan clear."

Anah and Puah glanced at each other.

"Clear enough so that I know what my answer must be," Isaabel said. She looked at her sisters with a steady gaze. "I will return to Jerusalem with you."

"Wonderful," a male voice said.

Isaabel turned to see Laman standing behind her. She started to rise, her face flushed.

"Sit with us a while, little sister," Laman said, his eyes glittering. "We are happy that you have chosen so wisely." He sprawled before the crackling fire, winking at her. "We knew you would agree to our plan."

Feeling awkward, Isaabel resumed her position. Just then, Lemuel joined the circle.

"A fine morning, brother," Laman said to Lemuel. "With Nephi and the others gone hunting, we can talk freely of our plans."

"Is she joining us?" Lemuel asked, tilting his head toward Isaabel.

"Yes," Laman said with a grin. "We must make preparations in secret so as not to arouse suspicion from Father."

"Now?" Lemuel asked.

Laman looked at the women in the circle. "We will be leaving tonight."

Isaabel brought her hand to her chest. "But I thought—"

"With Nephi gone for at least two days, there is no better time to put distance between us," Laman said.

Lemuel chuckled. "Again, the eldest brother—and rightful leader—is clever." He turned to his wife. "You heard him, go and prepare our things. Be discreet."

Puah's face drained of color, yet she rose obediently, Anah following. Isaabel watched them leave, a hard lump forming in her throat.

Trying to conceal her anxiety, Isaabel stood, hoping that the conversation with Nephi's brothers was over. But Laman rose and moved to her side, his satisfied gaze settling on her. "Don't be afraid, Isa. I'll take care of you."

Isaabel lowered her head and moved away. She tried to walk away from them at a casual pace. Once she was out of Laman and Lemuel's sight, she started to run, her tears obscuring her steps. She reached her tent and pushed her way inside, searching for any sign that Nephi hadn't left. Bursting out of the tent, she scanned the camp, hoping that for some reason he was still preparing for the hunt.

But he was gone.

She picked up her skirts and ran along the perimeter of the camp, searching, though she didn't dare call out his name. At last she reached the far end, and in the distance she could see two camels traveling with men upon them.

"Nephi," she said with anguish. But she knew she could never catch up with them, that they would never hear her no matter how she screamed.

Sinking to the earth, Isaabel hung her head in despair. She had made the wrong choice. She should have told her husband about Laman's plot. And now, because of her mistake, she would never see him again.

* * *

Laman had watched Isaabel's retreating figure. She seemed such a fragile creature on the outside, but within, she was made of steel. To not warn her own husband of danger was a testament to him that she would be a survivor on the return trip to Jerusalem. While Anah was busy with childbearing and the upcoming baby, Isaabel would make a good second wife.

It was not unheard of to take a second wife—Jerusalem had become infiltrated with the practice. And, according to custom, if something happened to Nephi, it would be his duty as the eldest brother. He tried to suppress the grin spreading to his face; he didn't want Lemuel, who sat next to him, prying into his thoughts. Even in the extreme climate and bleak conditions of desert living, Isaabel had somehow managed to maintain her beauty.

Suddenly, Laman let out a low sigh as his pleasant thoughts became tainted with doubt. What if Isaabel hadn't told Nephi about their plans because she was stubborn and afraid? What if it was because she loved him more than she loved herself?

A cloud of discontent settled over him. Marrying a woman who loved another man so deeply wouldn't be satisfying. The thought that Isaabel's heart would always be with Nephi, even if they were separated, angered Laman. But he would find a way to change Isaabel's mind. Somehow.

"Go find Raamah and Heth," Laman practically shouted at Lemuel.

Lemuel jumped at the harsh command. He rose and left quickly.

Alone at last, Laman mused over the last conclusion. Isaabel would never stop loving Nephi, unless . . . he was dead. And Lehi would have to die too—then no one could remind Isaabel of her precious husband. As he sat waiting for Lemuel and the others to return, he formulated a new plan, one that would be more satisfying for everyone involved.

A sound to his left brought Laman's focus back to the present. Lemuel, Raamah, and Heth had arrived. Laman rose to greet them. "Follow me."

Once they were gathered beneath a group of palms away from the camp, Laman outlined his plan. "Since Ishmael's death, Nephi desires to become the leader of both families."

Raamah's face drew into a slight frown.

"And my father supports Nephi," Laman continued. "Our brother has lied to us. He pretends that angels have spoken to him, giving him the power to rule over us."

Nodding, Lemuel interrupted, "His 'promised land' does not exist."

"You're right," Laman agreed. "Nephi plans to lead us further into the wilderness and then become our king. If we do nothing, we will be his subjects. So you can see that abandoning the camp is no longer enough."

Raamah and Heth looked at each other with interest.

"We must make him pay for our misery and answer for what he has done," Laman said.

The men nodded in unison.

Laman paused, his next words carefully chosen. "He must make up for the loss of Ishmael's life."

Eyes wide, Lemuel stared at his brother. "What do you mean?"

"I think you all know what I mean. Before we leave for Jerusalem, we will kill Nephi . . ." Laman waited for the words to take effect before continuing, ". . . with the very sword that Nephi used to cut off Laban's head." His stomach shook with silent laughter, but his face remained serious. "Unfortunately, our father must also die. It is the only way. And on our way back to Jerusalem, the brass plates will be useful in bartering. The curious ball might buy us another camel . . . Sam and Zoram will follow when they see they have no other choice."

The men listened in astounded silence as Laman outlined his plan.

CHAPTER 10

And all these things were done in secret.
(Moses 5:30)

Sam sat with his parents in their tent. A cheery fire had been built, and a pot of shrub tea neared boiling. Sam's baby brother, Jacob, thrived. Sam held the infant and smiled into his sober eyes. "He looks like his sisters."

Sariah nodded happily. "He'll grow into a beautiful boy."

"Look at how long his lashes are," Sam said with admiration. "Like a camel's."

Lehi reached for the child, and Sam handed him over. "You're right," Lehi said. "It is fitting that he should resemble a desert animal."

"This is going too far," Sariah said in mock exasperation. "Give me the poor child." Just then, Jacob let out a cry. Sariah shook her head. "See, he knows you are comparing him to a camel."

Lehi reluctantly handed the child to Sariah, who took him to the other section of the tent to nurse him to sleep.

Turning to Sam, Lehi said, "Now tell me what troubles you, son."

Not surprised at his father's astuteness, Sam said, "To be honest, I'm not quite sure. It's more of a feeling than anything that has happened. Nephi thought I should stay with you instead of going on the hunt." He hesitated. "There's been talk in the family."

"I'm grateful that you stayed, and yes, I know there have been complaints," Lehi said. "The death of Ishmael has been hard on us all. With time, our pain will soften."

"It's more than that," Sam said. "Some in the family have let their wounds fester."

Lehi stroked his beard. "Perhaps you're right. When Nephi and Zoram return, we'll call the family together in counsel."

"Father," Sam spoke louder than he intended to. Lehi looked at him, an eyebrow arched. "There is talk of returning to Jerusalem."

A shadow passed over Lehi's face, leaving his coloring ashen. "It is a thorn that remains in my side. Why Laman and Lemuel do not make an effort to understand the Lord's teachings, I do not know. But their efforts to lead others away with them grieves me."

Sam shifted in his place, suddenly feeling uncomfortable as his father continued.

"They have witnessed the miracles just as we have. When Ishmael brought his family into the wilderness, when Nephi made a bow and found food, the Liahona, the birth of Jacob . . . Why can they not believe in the promised land?" Lehi's voice rose in anguish. "Day and night, I pray for all of my children that they may have faith in the Lord. Still Laman and Lemuel's hearts are hardened. Why will they not partake of the fruit?"

Sam fingered a broken thread on his robe. He could not answer his father's questions. There were times when he thought his older brothers had sincerely repented, only to see them fall back into old complaints. "Perhaps once we reach the promised land and they see it for themselves, they'll believe." As soon as he said it, Sam knew it wasn't true.

Lehi hung his head and closed his eyes briefly. For a moment, Sam wondered if his father had fallen asleep. Then

Lehi raised his head and spoke. "Do you not understand? We will not make it to the promised land if we are not righteous."

Sam felt the skin on his arms prickle as the gravity of the situation settled into his heart.

"The Liahona has remained silent since Ishmael's death," Lehi continued. "Until our family is unified in faith, we will not progress."

Tearing the frayed thread from his robe, Sam realized that it was time that he and Tamar intervened. It would be the last thing his brothers would expect. And, tonight, for reasons he did not understand yet, Sam felt he should relocate the buried valuables.

* * *

Isaabel stepped outside her mother's tent, leaving Rebeka to sit with their mother during the morning meal. Bashemath was still weak with grief over the loss of her husband and rarely set foot outside her quarters; instead, she let her daughters bring her food. Since Rebeka was too great with child to work in the field, she spent the days by her mother's side.

Locating a palm frond, Isaabel began to sweep the sand from the rear panels when she heard voices coming from within the tent. She paused to listen when her name was mentioned.

"Have you seen Isaabel?" Anah asked.

"She was just here with Rebeka," Bashemath said.

"Oh?" Puah said. "We've been looking for her since early this morning." A pause. "Mother, are you all right?"

Bashemath spoke in a soft voice. "If your father hadn't endured so many afflictions in the wilderness, he would be alive today. We should not have come. Now I am nothing without my husband."

Anah spoke next. "We know, Mother. Very soon we will do something about our situation."

Outside the tent walls, Isaabel felt her heart begin to pound as she listened for her mother's response. She placed the palm frond on the ground, intending to leave.

"So we are near the promised land?" Bashemath asked, hope in her voice.

"No," Puah said. "That is why we are planning to return to Jerusalem."

Tangible silence permeated the tent.

"After all this, we are to return to Jerusalem?" Bashemath finally asked. "How can Lehi afflict us so?"

"It is not Lehi's decision," Anah clarified. "Our husbands are leaving without Lehi and those who support him. We are returning to Jerusalem without their knowledge."

A short pause followed.

"What does Nephi say about this plan?" Bashemath asked.

"Oh, Mother. Nephi may proclaim to be our leader, but Laman is the true one," Anah said. "Nephi has no knowledge of this plan, or he would try to stop us."

"What about Isaabel? You expect her to leave her husband?"

"She's agreed to our plan," Puah said. "She knows that in order to survive, she must come with us."

Isaabel brought her hand to her chest, covering her pounding heart.

"Everything will be provided for you, Mother. Don't worry about when and where. We will collect you when the time is at hand," Anah explained.

"And Tamar? Is she leaving her husband too?" Bashemath asked.

Puah answered. "She doesn't know of our plans yet. We hope she will choose to join us."

"I cannot leave any of my children behind," Bashemath said in a trembling voice. "Isaabel, come inside."

Hearing her mother's call, Isaabel moved alongside the tent and entered the main entrance. She was met by surprised stares from her sisters.

"Well," Bashemath said, "don't just stand there listening. Is this all true?"

* * *

From the opposite side of the field, Elisheba sensed Raamah watching her. Each time she lifted her head, he turned his focus back to his digging. The women were seeding where the men had prepared holes. Elisheba could see Raamah grip his sharp stick and with steady strokes open the surprisingly rich soil. She relished the feel of moist earth beneath her bare feet. Although the climate was hot and dry, the Minaeans had developed methods to channel the runoff from the rain for irrigation.

She glanced again at Raamah, her slight but strong frame bending in rhythm as she moved down the rows of overturned earth, carefully dropping seeds. It was a fair distraction from the words she had heard Anah and Puah speak earlier that day over the morning fire. They had not realized she was listening, or if they had, they didn't seem to care. Their bitter complaints still resounded in her ears. *I don't know why our father believed that Lehi was a prophet of God. If he was 'chosen,' then why would we be allowed to live in such primitive conditions? There is no reason for us to remain here with Lehi now.*

Elisheba knew that Ishmael had never wavered in his beliefs. From the first time her brothers entered Ishmael's home and set out their proposal to the moment of his last breath, Ishmael believed that Lehi was a prophet of God. Thoughts continued to pour into Elisheba's head, some convoluted.

Watching Raamah, Elisheba knew that she would be miserable if Raamah returned to Jerusalem. Isaabel had told her about Raamah's deathbed promise to his father to continue on to the promised land. With all her heart, Elisheba hoped that Raamah would keep that promise, not only because it would prove his honor but because it would mean there was a chance. *Chance for marriage?* The thought caused bumps to form on her arms. *If only I knew how he felt about me.*

Her chin tingled as she recalled Raamah's touch when she met him at Ishmael's burial site. She scolded her memory when the image of Raamah's grief-filled eyes surfaced. Like a mother nurturing her child, Elisheba yearned to ease his pain. Lost in thought, she realized that Raamah had straightened and was looking at her. A faint smile crept to his lips. Elisheba felt her neck grow warm, and she quickly looked down. His gaze had been so open and kind. Perhaps he had forgotten her earlier intrusion. *Which path would his grief take him? Bitterness or peace?* Elisheba shuddered to think of how quickly anger could consume Raamah and add fuel to the rebellion that had begun among the other family members.

* * *

Nephi took careful aim at the gazelle. Just before he released the arrow, he lost his grip. "Ow!" he muttered. "That's the second time."

"Watch this," Zoram whispered beside him, taking aim at another gazelle several paces away. With one swift motion he let the arrow sail through the air. At the last second, the gazelle bolted.

"Let's move to the other side of the hill," Nephi said. He started walking without waiting for Zoram to gather his things.

Once Zoram caught up, Nephi motioned for him to crouch. "Over there," he whispered. "In the brush."

Zoram narrowed his eyes against the glare of the sun. "I don't see anything."

With deft precision, Nephi raised his bow and stretched it taut. The arrow skimmed through the air.

"I think you hit it—"

"No," Nephi said, "there it goes." A scraggly ibex leaped from the cluster of underbrush and sprang away. Its fur hung in patches, and one horn was broken.

"If there's one, there are probably twenty," Zoram said.

"It's a young male, probably separated from its group. In this heat, the animal was only looking for a bit of shade," Nephi said. "I don't think it will lead us to more."

With a frustrated sigh, Zoram said, "With our luck, we'll be returning tomorrow with a few grouse. Is this where the Liahona directed us to hunt?"

Nephi shook his head. "The Liahona hasn't given instructions since Ishmael's death."

They waited in silence, each searching for any other sign of life besides the pesky insects that insisted on occupying their sweaty arms.

Zoram let out a low sigh. "I wish there were a way to dissolve the contention within the family." When Nephi didn't answer, Zoram looked at him. "Nephi?" The color from Nephi's face had drained, leaving his complexion a pasty yellow. "What is it?"

But Nephi didn't seem to hear him. Instead, he rose to his feet and headed toward the camels.

Zoram followed him. "Is something wrong?"

His eyes wide and filled with worry, Nephi met Zoram's gaze. "We must return immediately to camp."

"Why?" Zoram asked.

"The Spirit has warned me," Nephi said. "My father's life is in danger."

With Nephi's words, Zoram felt a sudden urgency envelop him. Without further questioning, he sprinted to the camels.

Before they climbed onto the beasts, Nephi turned to Zoram. "Pray for a swift return. And that we will not be too late."

Zoram nodded. He climbed onto his camel and urged it forward, keeping pace with Nephi.

34.56% 11-22-15

CHAPTER 11

Forgive, I pray thee now, the trespass of thy brethren, and their sin; for they did unto thee evil.
(Genesis 50:17)

Isaabel moved along the perimeter of the camp. The light was just beginning to change, night smothering the day. Those who had worked in the fields were back at camp, and she could see smoke rising from the evening fire. Even at a distance, she could smell the meal cooking. Her stomach whined in loud complaint—she hadn't eaten all day. Beneath her chest, her heart pounded harder with each step that brought her closer to camp. Assuredly, Anah and Puah had noticed her absence. By their account, she should have been packing her things in preparation to leave.

But Isaabel's determination had lost its drive. Weakness had overtaken her, and she could no longer bear the thought of leaving Nephi. It seemed too fantastic that Laman would actually kill him—perhaps he had only made the threat in order to force her into action. She considered the other men in the family who would take Nephi's side: Sam, Zoram, and Lehi. She was unsure about her brothers, Raamah and Heth. She had little hope in Heth, even though he had tried to dissuade Laman and Lemuel when they had bound Nephi just outside of Jerusalem. And Raamah . . . he was unpredictable.

She was just a few paces away now from Lehi's tent when an angry shout stopped her in her tracks—Laman's voice. Isabel felt every part of her body stiffen as she sensed something terrible going on. Slowly, she moved around the tent until she came into view of the scene.

The setting was one that mirrored her worst dreams—dreams that rendered her exhausted and trembling upon awakening. Laman stood near the entrance of the tent, his arm gripping Lehi's body close to him. In one hand, he held a knife in the air, waving it above him. Lehi's eyes were closed, his hands limp in defeat. Sariah sat crumpled on the ground, clutching her crying infant while Elisheba and Dinah clung to her robes.

Nearby, Sam was restrained by Lemuel and Raamah. Heth stood in front of the group of women, who watched the exchange with fearful eyes. The only sounds were Jacob's cries and Laman's harsh voice.

"Because of our father's support, Nephi has gained too much power over us," Laman said. "Nephi claims that angels have spoken to him, commanding him to be our ruler. Our younger brother is cunning and desires that we continue farther into the wilderness, so there is no hope of return."

Although they looked frightened, the women behind Heth nodded. Only Tamar stood apart from the others, rocking back and forth slightly, her mouth forming unspoken words. She moved her head and met Isaabel's gaze. Tamar's eyes flickered in acknowledgment, but her expression was accusing.

Isaabel felt her heart sink, knowing that Tamar thought she'd had a hand in this—and perhaps she had. But now she wished she had told Nephi everything. Then he wouldn't have left to go hunting.

Laman didn't notice Isaabel standing at the side of the tent. His voice escalated in anger. "Nephi will make himself king over us. King! In this desolate place, we are doomed to live with our younger brother as our ruler." He paused, then pointed his knife in Anah's direction. "Here is my wife, carrying our child who should inherit the birthright from *me*. As the eldest son, the birthright falls to me, whether or not the angels approve."

Lemuel let out a short chuckle, which was quickly silenced by a single look from Laman.

"Our younger brother believes that a land of promise has been prepared for us and that it's choice above all other lands. How could this be so? How could another land be more choice than Jerusalem?" He paused, jabbing his knife into the air again. "I'll tell you how—through a clever plan that will rob us of our natural birthright. For thousands of years the birthright has been passed from fathers to the eldest sons." Laman's gaze fell upon Sam. "What right does Nephi have to challenge this law, this tradition? We must hold sacred our way of life. If we don't uphold the traditions of our fathers and their fathers before them, all is for naught. We are spitting upon the graves of our ancestors."

A moan escaped Lehi's lips. Isaabel's stomach churned as she remembered when Laman had held a knife to Nephi's throat. Something had to be done. Isaabel caught Tamar's gaze once again. She couldn't bear it any longer. Without considering the consequences she rushed forward, stopping in front of Laman. "I beg you to spare Lehi's life."

A slow grin spread across Laman's face as he brought the blade to his father's throat. "I wondered when you would appear. It looks as if you have changed your mind about leaving with us."

"Please." Isaabel inhaled. "He has done nothing except follow the Lord's commandments."

"Ah, so you are now a prophetess?" Laman asked, his color darkening in displeasure. "It's too late for begging." With a swift kick, Laman sent her sprawling backward.

She landed hard on the ground, and a sudden burst of pain shot through her shoulders and neck. Behind her, the women gasped, but none rushed forward to help. Isaabel slowly moved to a sitting position. Baby Jacob's cries turned to whimpers, and everyone remained silent as they watched her. To her side, Lemuel stifled a laugh.

Isaabel shifted to her knees and with her head bowed said, "Laman, I'll do whatever you wish. Please spare the life of your father, and I will return with you to Jerusalem." She raised her eyes to meet his suspicious gaze. "If we leave now, we'll be gone before Nephi returns."

Laman's eyes hardened. "We will not leave before Nephi returns. After we are finished with my father, it will be Nephi's blood upon this blade."

Clenching her trembling hands together, Isaabel took several deep breaths. Frantic thoughts played through her mind as she tried to control her fright. "You promised if I went with you, my husband would not be harmed."

"I am not your precious Nephi who keeps promises no matter the consequences." Laman's mouth twitched with amusement. "A man has a right to change his mind, and under the circumstances, it is better to be rid of the adversary. I will not leave my wife's family behind to continue their suffering."

Isaabel inched forward, desperately hoping he would be persuaded. She noticed that Lehi's eyes had opened, and he watched her with wariness. Knowing this might be her last chance, she grabbed the hem of Laman's robe. "Please, Laman," she said. "Your desires will be obeyed. Release your father and take me instead. Let us leave those who want to stay here. I'll travel back to Jerusalem, and you'll be able to claim your inheritance."

"No one's returning to Jerusalem." It was Nephi's voice.

Everyone looked to the side of the tent where Nephi and Zoram had suddenly appeared.

Laman tightened his grip on Lehi. Isaabel felt her hands fall away from Laman's robe, a mixture of relief and fear encompassing her.

"Seize them!" Laman shouted.

Without hesitation, Raamah and Heth bared their knives and flew at Nephi and Zoram, while Lemuel continued to restrain Sam. After a fierce struggle and threats against Lehi, Raamah and Heth had the two men subdued at knifepoint.

"Now, Isaabel," Laman said, glancing at her. "We will see who your true master is."

Isaabel caught Nephi's gaze. His expression was mixed with anger and confusion. She wished she could explain to him what had happened. A cry from Rebeka sounded behind the women. "I . . . it's the baby . . ." She let out another cry.

"Silence her!" Laman said.

With those words, Zoram began to struggle fiercely beneath Heth's grip. Heth struck Zoram until he yielded.

"Rebeka's time has come," Bashemath said.

Laman spat on the ground. "Then take her away so we cannot hear."

Bashemath led the distressed Rebeka back to the tent, casting a furtive glance behind her. But Isaabel saw that her mother was too timid to ask for help.

The enmity among the family caused Rebeka's time to start. Isaabel's heart sank. An early delivery brought danger for the baby. She inched over to where her sisters sat, her gaze fixed on Nephi. By the expression on his face, Isaabel knew he was not going to give in to Laman easily.

"This is your plan, then, Laman?" Nephi asked through gritted teeth. "To take my wife and her sisters back to Jerusalem?"

Laman cast a steely gaze in his brother's direction. "Yes, when you and Father are dead, we will be free to obtain prosperity again."

Nephi met the threat with composure, though his eyes burned with anger. "You will fail."

His face twisting in disgust, Laman let out a grunt.

"If Father dies at your hand, you will be nothing," Nephi said. "You cannot claim your inheritance without him." He looked at Lemuel, Raamah, and Heth before continuing. "You will be cut off from your position in society. We are all you have in this world, Laman. Father's valuables have been stolen, his land overtaken, and his teachings rejected. And the sarim will be looking for Laban's killer and the man who took the brass plates."

Laman's eyes shifted from Nephi to the rest of the family. "See the lies he tells us? Jerusalem offers all of us a new beginning with comfort and peace—"

"The city of Jerusalem is marked for destruction," Nephi interrupted, his voice growing in strength. "You will be destroyed with it."

Please listen to Nephi, Isaabel thought.

Beneath Laman's strong grip, Lehi struggled to speak. "He is right." His voice came out in gasps. "The Lord has shown me the destruction of Jerusalem and its people. The Lord wants us to travel to the promised land . . . and prosper in our own right."

Laman smirked, tightening his grip on Lehi. "And with Nephi as our leader, all will be well. Is that what you believe, Father?" he asked with sarcasm. He looked directly at Raamah. "Only with Nephi's death will the birthright be restored." He nodded briefly. "Slay him."

Raamah brought the knife to Nephi's throat. Isaabel followed her brother's gaze and saw that it met with Elisheba's, who looked at him with a mixture of betrayal and hatred. *No,* Isaabel thought, *please do not believe my brother is capable of murder.* By the expression on Elisheba's face, Isaabel knew she believed just that. *It's time to put this to an end,* Isaabel thought desperately. Just as she was about to make another lunge at Laman's feet, Raamah lowered his arms and dropped the knife into the sand.

"Raamah!" Laman shouted. "What are you doing?"

Nephi stepped to the side, his hand automatically covering his throat.

"I will honor my promise to my father," Raamah said. "Although there's nowhere I'd rather be than home in Jerusalem right now, I swore to my father that I would follow Lehi to the promised land." He took a defiant step forward, his voice firm. "I am the leader of the family of Ishmael, and I will not murder those whom my father revered."

Laman staggered backward, Lehi still in his grip. "But we agreed," he said weakly, as if Raamah had physically hit him.

"Release your father," Raamah said. "It is no use, Laman." He turned to Heth. "In the name of our father, Ishmael, release Zoram," he commanded.

Heth glanced at Laman, then released Zoram, who immediately joined Nephi.

Lemuel tightened his hold on Sam, his eyes fixed on Laman.

"You see, Laman," Raamah said, as his gaze swept across the family members. "What Nephi said is true. If we return to Jerusalem, we will have nothing and be nothing. If we continue to the promised land, we will have land for our sons to inherit."

"But . . ." The dark rage on Laman's face multiplied. His grip on Lehi remained firm, but defeat had crept into his stance. "Your father wouldn't be dead if we hadn't come into the wilderness. How can you support those who led us here?"

Isabel exhaled. She knew the last thing Raamah desired was to make an enemy of Laman. In the past few weeks, Isabel had seen happiness in her brother, and she knew it was due to Elisheba. But now, with her brother's participation in Laman's plan, Raamah had caused Elisheba great pain and fear. She held her breath as Raamah took a step forward, meeting Laman's gaze.

"My sisters, my mother, and my brother and I will follow Lehi to the promised land. Do as you will, Laman, but leave us to our destiny," Raamah said.

Please Lord, Isaabel silently prayed. *Soften Laman's heart.*

Nephi and Zoram moved to Raamah's side, and Nephi placed a hand on Raamah's shoulder. Nephi's gaze moved to Lemuel, who still restrained Sam. "Let our brother go," he whispered.

Lemuel cast a furtive look at Laman.

Meeting his brother's gaze with fury, Laman cried out. "You are cowards, all of you." He released Lehi and thrust him toward Sariah. Lehi stumbled at Sariah's feet, and she and her daughters wrapped their arms about him.

"It is *your* decision, then," Laman ranted. "We will *all* rot in this forsaken land and watch our women and children suffer." Clenching his fists he shouted at Lemuel. "Release him!"

Lemuel dropped his hold on Sam. Tamar ran to Sam and clutched him in her arms.

Sobs of relief were heard among the women. *It is finished,* Isaabel realized, feeling her rapid breathing slow. She saw Nephi embrace his father and kiss his mother tenderly.

Isaabel rose and moved to Nephi, past the other family members. She took his arm. "Forgive me." Her eyes brimmed with tears. "Please, I didn't know this would happen."

Nephi turned from his mother and gazed at Isaabel. He guided Isaabel several steps away from the others, then faced her. "Tell me why," he said quietly, looking at her hand upon his arm.

"I . . . " Isaabel bit her lip. "I should have known Laman was lying. He threatened to kill you if I didn't go with them. So I agreed, but he tried to kill you anyway. I should have known the Lord would protect you—protect *us.*" She raised her eyes to meet his. "Oh, Nephi. How could I falter in my faith in you? In the Lord?" Isaabel let her hand drop from Nephi's arm, feeling as if her chest would burst with anguish. Her grief over her father and the plot against his life had created a gulf between them, but now she hoped Nephi could see that she was repentant.

"Of all the people to make secret plans with," Nephi whispered, "to promise Laman that you would return to Jerusalem with him . . . " His voice dropped off, unable to continue.

Isaabel brought her hands to her chest. "I would have done anything to spare your life or your father's, though I would put a blade in my own chest rather than live under Laman's dominion." She lowered her trembling hands and began to turn away.

Nephi pulled her toward him and drew her into his arms. Gripping her against his chest, he kissed the top of her head. "I know," he said. "I know."

Closing her eyes against the hot tears, Isaabel welcomed the touch of Nephi's clothing against her cheek. It had been too long since she'd sought comfort from him. The beating of his heart seemed to join hers in tandem. She knew she had been forgiven.

Nephi drew away and met Laman's eyes. Words did not need to be spoken, but Isaabel knew that Laman would leave her alone.

Finally, Laman dropped his stare and nodded toward Lemuel. "Let's go," he said gruffly.

As the two eldest brothers turned to leave, Lehi called for attention. "Wait!" he said. "The Lord wants us to gather for instruction from Him."

38.26% 11-22-05

CHAPTER 12

Behold, happy is the man whom God correcteth: therefore despise not thou the chastening of the Almighty.

(Job 5:17)

Laman turned and stared at Lehi. The shock on his face masked any feelings he may have felt at his father's words. "The Lord?"

Lehi opened his arms toward his oldest son. "Come."

Shaking his head in disbelief, Laman said, "Father, you have been sorely disillusioned."

Laman and Lemuel, it is expedient that you repent of your sins. My soul is grieved by your actions.

The voice seemed to be coming from above, yet it surrounded them, cutting their hearts. Lemuel reached for Laman to steady himself.

Lehi sank to his knees, bowing his head.

One by one each of the family members knelt with bowed heads as the voice continued.

Repent or you will perish in the wilderness.

It was the voice of the Lord speaking to them, and everyone could hear the words. Laman began to tremble. Lemuel slid to the ground, burying his face in his hands.

Because of the faithfulness of your father, I have commanded him to take his family and depart into the wilderness. Wo unto Jerusalem. Her abominations are great, and many shall perish by the sword, and many shall be carried captive into Babylon.

Laman clutched his robe in astonishment as the words consumed his soul. Terrible remorse filled his heart as the pain and anguish of his actions passed through him. "Have mercy," he whispered.

Bashemath stepped out of her tent, where Rebeka had stopped her cries. Seeing the family kneeling in their various places caused her to drop to her knees from where she stood.

The divine voice continued.

A grievous sin has been committed against your father and your brother. Ye must repent and transgress no more.

It was as if a dagger had pierced Laman's stomach, slowly twisting until he could no longer stand the pain. He cried out, clutching his middle. Every muscle in his body tensed as guilt pumped through his veins. "Forgive me," he gasped, forcing the words through his constricted throat.

A groan erupted from Lemuel. He shifted next to Laman, raising his head slightly, his face beaded with perspiration. "Forgive us, Lord . . . for our trespasses."

"We are at Thy mercy," Laman said, his voice full of agony. "Do with us what Thou wilt."

Then a tranquil feeling spread through Laman, making his skin tingle with gratitude. As the Lord counseled them to hearken unto their father, all anger and malice fled Laman's being and was replaced with love. The cold sweat was replaced with warm comfort, and he knew that they'd been forgiven.

Laman turned to Lemuel, who had tears streaming down his cheeks, and embraced him.

"My sons, the Lord has forgiven you," Lehi said.

They pulled apart and rose. "Forgive us," they both said, clinging to their father.

Nephi walked toward the group and was greeted with open arms. Soon the entire family had gathered around Laman and Lemuel, and they rejoiced together with full hearts.

* * *

"Rebeka!" Bashemath cried. She turned and rushed back to her tent.

Isaabel heard the cry and hurried after her. Caught up in the counsel from the Lord and the family's rejoicing, she'd forgotten about Rebeka's pains. The other women joined her in racing toward the tent.

"She's unconscious," Bashemath said when they entered. "Look how pale she is."

"We must make her comfortable," Sariah said in a firm tone. With the help of Bashemath, Sariah turned Rebeka onto her side and propped a folded rug against her back. Then she took Rebeka's wrist, feeling her pulse. "Her heart is strong."

"Heaven be thanked," Bashemath said.

"Bring water, now," Sariah told Isaabel.

Isaabel left immediately, calling Tamar to assist her. Soon she returned with a goatskin bag filled with water. "Tamar has gone to fetch more," she said.

"Thank you." Sariah nodded. "Bashemath, attend to Rebeka just as you did to me."

"Of course." Bashemath began to rub Rebeka's legs. "Isaabel, tell your sisters to prepare the birthing tent."

"Wait," Sariah said. "I don't think she should be moved."

Bashemath raised her eyes to meet Sariah's. "Why not?"

Sariah hesitated, then said, "We have what we need right here." Sariah glanced at Isaabel and motioned for her to follow her outside the tent.

Once outside, Sariah said quietly, "Go into my quarters and bring me the goatskin pouch hanging on the west side."

"Is she going to be all right?" Isaabel asked, her voice full of apprehension.

Sariah glanced away and sighed. "I'm afraid it's too early to tell." She placed a hand on Isaabel's arm. "Tell Nephi and Lehi to come. Rebeka is going to need a blessing."

"What should I tell Zoram?"

"I don't want Zoram to know about the blessing yet," Sariah said, "in case there is no cause for worry."

Isaabel left and walked quickly to Sariah's tent. She hesitated outside, calling out, "Is anyone in there?"

A curly head poked itself out of the opening. Dinah grinned at the visitor. "Did she have the baby yet?"

"Not yet," Isaabel said, trying to keep her voice calm. "I need to get something for your mother."

Dinah retreated into the tent, leading the way. Isaabel found a small measure of comfort in the familiar interior. Although the tent walls were made of the same goatskin panels as the other tents, there was something more luxurious about Sariah's. The rooms were sectioned off by curtains, and a small alcove had been created for Jacob. Elisheba, who was holding the child, rose to welcome Isaabel.

Jacob grinned in response to Isaabel's greeting. "He is so healthy and strong now," Isaabel commented.

"Yes," Elisheba said. "He does not lack in nourishment, nor will he let my mother forget to feed him. Jacob lets everyone know when his belly is empty."

Isaabel grasped the baby's dimpled hand, wonderment filling her as she thought about Rebeka carrying such a child within her. Rebeka. Worry panged her heart. "Your mother asked me to bring the goatskin pouch hanging on the west wall."

Elisheba followed Isaabel's gaze. "The tonic bag?"

"She needs it for Rebeka."

"Is Rebeka all right?" Elisheba asked, a slight frown turning down the corners of her mouth. "Mother rarely uses anything from the pouch, unless . . ."

"Your mother is very skilled with herbs, and I'm sure Rebeka will be fine," Isaabel said, trying to convince herself with her own words.

Dinah handed the bag to Isaabel. "Careful," Dinah said. "It has precious herbs and roots."

Isaabel took the bag and found it surprisingly heavy as she hoisted it over her shoulder. She left Sariah's tent, hoping that she wouldn't run into Zoram on the way.

She saw Nephi on the outskirts of camp in deep conversation with Sam. By the time she reached Nephi, she was out of breath.

"Isa," Nephi said as soon as he saw her.

"Rebeka needs a blessing," she blurted before he could ask any questions.

Nephi stiffened. "What's wrong?"

"I don't know," Isaabel said, fear beneath her voice. "Sariah didn't say."

"Let's go, Sam," Nephi said.

"She said to bring your father," Isaabel said.

Sam hesitated. "I'll go and fetch him."

As Sam left them, Isaabel couldn't help but feel awkward. "Nephi," she said. "I didn't mean—"

"I know you didn't," Nephi said, taking her hand. "Don't worry about Sam. Let's see how we can help Rebeka."

Isaabel waited for Nephi by the evening fire, long after the other family members had returned to their tents. When he approached, she sighed with relief, knowing that Bashemath and Anah were keeping vigil by Rebeka's side. Nephi settled next to her, and she nestled into his warmth. Together they watched the glowing embers fade.

"Do you think Rebeka will be all right?" Isaabel asked.

Nephi stretched his hands before the radiating heat—the hands that had joined with his father's in the recent blessing. "For all our sakes, I hope Rebeka and the baby will be fine.

When my father offered the blessing, I felt a peace come over me that she would be protected by the Lord."

Staring at the ground, Isaabel nodded. Even with the rejuvenation of her brothers-in-law's faith, she feared another tragedy would be a blow from which they might not recover. She shivered as she thought about Laman's angry words.

"I was so frightened, Nephi," Isaabel said softly.

Nephi kissed the top of her head and squeezed her shoulder with reassurance. "So was I, Isa . . ."

Sniffing back her tears, Isaabel sighed. "I don't know why I was so afraid to defy Laman and tell you the truth. I should have had more faith that the Lord would protect us."

"Shh," Nephi consoled. He drew away from Isaabel and looked her in the eyes. "We can always rely on the Lord. He will never abandon us." Gently, he traced her cheek. "I never want to feel apart from you again, Isaabel. You mean too much to me. You don't need to protect me from anything."

A slight smile framed Isaabel's face, bringing light to her eyes. It did seem odd that she didn't believe her husband could protect himself from his brothers. She touched his shoulder, moving her hand down his strong arm. Not only did her husband physically surpass his older brothers, but she now knew the Lord would never let him be killed while he had the Lord's work to do.

"I will not doubt again," Isaabel said, turning her gaze to the fire once again. "Laman and Lemuel seemed truly repentant."

"Yes," Nephi agreed. "It was a humbling experience for the whole family." He paused. "If it weren't for Raamah . . ."

"I am so proud of him," Isaabel said. "He has honored our father's wishes."

Nephi drew Isaabel close. "Ishmael was a noble man, and I am glad his wishes have been respected. I know my father is pleased to call Raamah his son, and Raamah has proved his loyalty."

* * *

Elisheba lay next to Dinah. Her heart still hammered, making sleep impossible. Raamah's words echoed in her mind. *My sisters, my mother, and my brother and I will follow Lehi to the promised land.*

She had been fearful that Raamah would carry out Laman's wishes. Instead, he had stood up to Laman and defied him. At that moment, Elisheba had gained a new respect for the man whom she had seen complain about conditions in the wilderness, support Laman and Lemuel in their beliefs, grieve over the loss of Ishmael, and agree to follow Laman's plan of escape. Raamah's heart had changed, and Elisheba hoped it would stay that way.

Do as you will, Laman, but leave us to our destiny, Raamah had said.

Elisheba sat up in the quiet tent. *Destiny.* What was her destiny? she wondered. Since that horrible night when the thief had attacked her and Raamah had come to her rescue, she'd let herself believe that perhaps Raamah had feelings for her. Nothing could make her more happy, but since their awkward meeting at Ishmael's tomb, she dared not hope. Although the events today had given her even more hope.

Her older brothers, Laman and Lemuel, were ill-tempered and dangerous—a result, she knew, that came from breaking the commandments. Although she thought they would never hurt her or Dinah, she was afraid of their outbursts. Then when Raamah stood against them with such power and force—it was a true testament of his devotion to her father. A sigh escaped her lips. Next to her, Dinah mumbled something in her sleep. Elisheba lay back down carefully. Raamah was a man of courage, a man who knew his mind and wasn't afraid to stand up for it. *But what does he think of me? Does he think I am just a young girl who likes to play games with his son? Will he ever see me as a woman? As a wife?*

He had said he would follow Lehi to the promised land, even if it meant splitting up the family. It was as if her father had become Raamah's father. Elisheba wrapped her arms around her torso and smiled. Finally her eyes grew heavy, and her thoughts turned into dreams.

* * *

Sam stepped out into the dissipating darkness. It would be some time before the others awoke. With the family reconciled and faith restored, he hoped the Lord would bless them with meat again. He trudged to his father's tent and listened outside. All was quiet. Since Nahom was a relatively safe place, Sam knew his father kept the Liahona nestled in his sleeping quarters instead of buried. He crept into the tent and gently roused his father.

Lehi woke with a start. "Sam? What is it?"

"I am leaving to hunt. But I need the guidance of the Liahona," Sam whispered.

Rising to a sitting position, Lehi gave a curt nod. "You have planned in advance as usual, Sam. With our family reconciled, the Lord will surely bless us with food." Lehi reached behind his bedroll and retrieved the director. "Let us pray first."

Sam bowed his head, listening to his father's supplicating words.

"Oh, Lord, our God. Hear our words and consider our supplication. We have suffered because of our disobedience, and we recognize Thy hand in all things. Have mercy on us, O God. Lead us, O Lord, in righteousness and provide us with our next location to hunt. Wilt Thou bless the righteous desires of our hearts and favor us in our need? We are ever Thy servants and will worship Thee as Thou commandeth."

When Lehi's prayer concluded, Sam looked eagerly at the Liahona. A tingling sensation spread through Sam's limbs as words appeared on the director.

"Just as I hoped," Lehi said. "The Liahona is functioning again." He paused as he read, then looked up. "Above the valley to the north, you will find the best place to hunt."

"Very well," Sam said. "I will rouse Nephi and the others."

"Wait," Lehi said. "There is more."

"What do you mean?" Sam asked.

"Nephi is to remain at camp." Lehi's brow furrowed as he gazed at the instrument. "There are no further instructions."

"Thank you, Father," Sam said. He stepped out of the tent, feeling lightness in his heart. It felt good to have the Lord instructing them again, and he felt renewed. He made his way toward Laman's tent, knowing his brother would not be pleased to be awakened so early. But once Laman heard about the instructions from the Liahona, he would not complain.

"Sam," a voice called.

He turned and saw Zoram approach. The haggard look on his face made his pointed chin seem even longer. Sam remembered Rebeka and the baby. "How is your wife doing?" he asked.

"I haven't heard yet," Zoram said. "I have circled the tent several times, but all is quiet within."

"They are sleeping then," Sam said. "That must be good news."

But the expression on Zoram's face belied his agitation. "Did you know that Nephi and Lehi gave her a blessing?"

Sam nodded, feeling reluctant. "I happened to be with Nephi when he was asked to administer."

Zoram's shoulders sagged. "They are trying not to worry me, I know. It's too early for the baby to come . . ." He placed a hand on Sam's arm. "What if . . . she . . ." His voice broke.

"I do not know much about the birthing process," Sam confided. "But my mother told me she labored for three days with me. And Jacob came early."

"But how early is too early?" Zoram's troubled gaze met Sam's.

"I don't know," Sam said. "We must continue to pray and have faith. And we must begin our next hunt. The Lord has spoken through the Liahona again."

"What did the Liahona say?" Zoram asked, a hint of hope in his voice.

"To head north."

Zoram looked past Sam, a far-off look in his eyes. "So we continue to be preserved. As a result, we will raise posterity unto the Lord."

Sam clapped the man on the shoulder. "That sounds better. Now help me wake the others so that we can begin the hunt and bring nourishment to your wife."

CHAPTER 13

Yea, and as often as my people repent will I forgive them their trespasses against me.
(Mosiah 26:30)

Isaabel slipped into the quiet tent. Bashemath lay curled in a bedroll next to her sleeping daughter, Rebeka. The skin on Rebeka's face glowed with pink tones, in contrast to the paleness of the night before.

Creeping to her sister's side, Isaabel carefully touched her sister's forehead.

Rebeka's eyes opened and blinked into focus. Slowly, a smile spread to her lips. "Hello Isa," she said.

"Hello," Isaabel said and kissed Rebeka's cheek. "How do you feel?"

"Hungry."

Stifling a giggle, Isaabel whispered, "Maybe I can do something about that."

"Put your hand here," Rebeka said, guiding Isaabel's hand to her enlarged abdomen.

Isaabel placed her hand on her sister's stomach. It was soft and fleshy, then suddenly it hardened. Rebeka drew a breath in sharply.

"Does it hurt?" Isaabel asked.

"Not like yesterday. Sariah prepared a poultice from halômut leaves, and it eased the pains," Rebeka said. Her face clouded. "What happened with Laman and the others after I left?"

Hesitating, Isaabel settled next to Rebeka. In a low voice, she said, "It was both awful and wonderful—awful because Laman and Lemuel had murder written in their eyes. Wonderful because Raamah stood up to them."

"Raamah?" Rebeka looked at her with surprise.

"He told Laman and Lemuel that our family would follow Lehi to the promised land. He said, 'Do as you will, Laman, but leave us to our destiny.'"

Rebeka brought her hand to her mouth. "What did Laman say?"

"He became very angry, but when he realized that Raamah had more influence than he over our family, Laman relented," Isaabel said. "But even more amazing, the Lord's voice came and spoke to all of us."

"I heard the voice," Rebeka said with reverence.

Nearby, Bashemath stirred. "Rebeka?" she called sleepily.

"I'm awake, Mother," Rebeka replied.

Bashemath sat up, suddenly alert. "Oh, my dear. How do you feel?"

"As I was just saying to Isaabel, hungry."

Bashemath looked from one daughter to the other and smiled in delight. For a moment, Isaabel caught the look of maternal love in her mother's expression. It was rare for Bashemath to show tender emotions, but at this moment, Isaabel could feel the affection surrounding them.

"I'll start boiling the barley," Bashemath said. "Some soft cereal is just what you need."

Anah entered the tent, her own belly grown round. Hearing what her mother said, she interrupted, "I've stoked the fire and will sit with Rebeka while you're out."

"Thank you," Bashemath said, gratitude in her eyes.

With a quick glance in Anah's direction, Isaabel followed her mother out the door. The smile Anah offered was open and guileless. Inwardly, Isaabel felt a peaceful feeling spread through her. Laman must have truly repented, and Anah's relaxed demeanor was evidence of that. She let out a slow breath as she walked with her mother to the fire pit. Tamar was crouched in front of the blaze, stirring barley in the cooking pan.

Isaabel hesitated, remembering how the events of the night before had been distressing for the whole family. She would never again take her relationship with Tamar for granted. It was too precious to be thrown away over hurt feelings. Tamar rose, and Isaabel met her gaze, knowing that she would have to make the first move.

Stepping forward, Isaabel embraced Tamar. "Forgive me?" she asked.

"Always," Tamar whispered.

After leaving Tamar, Isaabel had one more visit to make. She left the camp and walked toward the mountains. The terrain became steeper as Isaabel drew closer to her father's burial place. She had come alone to pay her respects to the man who had cherished her from birth. Each step seemed to echo in her once empty heart. She had found joy again in living. Reconciling with Nephi and Tamar had finally brought her peace, as had watching her brothers-in-law come to repentance.

She reached the rock pile that marked her father's burial and gently touched the outcroppings of stone. It was difficult to believe that her father's lifeless body lay beneath the stones. He would never speak, walk, or hold her again in this life.

"Father," she whispered. "Why did you have to leave us so soon?" As she said it, Isaabel realized she already knew the answer. By coming into the wilderness, Ishmael had sacrificed his physical health for the spiritual salvation of his entire family.

A tear broke free and cascaded down her cheek, splashing onto the tomb. It was all so clear now. Through her father's faith in the Lord, his posterity would reach the promised land and receive all the promised blessings. Isaabel closed her eyes, trying to picture her father in her mind—his once-broad shoulders, generous hands, light brown eyes beneath graying brows, curly beard streaked with white . . .

Taking a deep breath, Isaabel began to pray. She thanked the Lord for the protection and guidance their family had received. She thanked Him for her faithful husband and dear mother-in-law. Then she thanked the Lord for the growth she'd experienced through their trials. A year ago, she had been a young girl, consumed with the inconsequential things of life. Now, as a married woman, surviving day to day in the heart of the wilderness, she had come to value so much more. Her faith in the Lord was paramount to her well-being.

"Father," she said, opening her eyes and staring at the golden-colored rock. "We will follow your wishes." She stooped and kissed the stone, then turned away from the tomb.

* * *

A rocky cleft protruded above Sam's head. He reached out one hand and grasped the edge, pulling himself up with all his might. One last effort, and he climbed onto the ledge, his breath coming in short gasps. The others waited below. Raamah, Heth, Laman, and Lemuel all watched Sam's ascent. Sam craned his neck to scan the cliff above him. At close range, it was intimidating.

"Are you sure this is where the Minaean tribesman pointed?" Lemuel asked Laman.

"Yes, this is the eastern plateau," Laman assured him for the third time. He brushed away the dripping perspiration from his eyes. "Who's next?"

The men jostled each other. "Come on, Heth," Lemuel said. "You can climb with any goat."

Heth scoffed and tightened his leather belt. With a grunt, he began to scale the same course that Sam had moments before.

When he reached Sam's perch, he was panting hard. "I hope this is worth it," Heth said. "There'd better be a whole herd."

Next came Raamah, then Lemuel, and finally, Laman joined the group, out of breath from the steep climb. His sunburned nose and cheeks peeked through his wrapped turban. "Where did the Minaean see those gazelles? Surely it wasn't all the way up here."

"Shh," said Sam. Everyone froze as a pebble tumbled past them. "There's something up there."

Raamah raised his thick eyebrows, his mustache twitching in anticipation. "A wild goat?" he whispered.

Lemuel hooted with laughter. Instantly he was met with several stern "Shhs."

The seconds crept by as the men listened, straining to hear over their pounding hearts. The merciless rays of the sun beat upon their shoulders and backs, adding to the perspiration already soaking their tunics.

"I'm going up," Sam said, not able to stand the wait. No one else offered to join him. On his back, he carried Nephi's wooden bow, two arrows, and a goatskin sling of water.

"Careful," Heth whispered as Sam found his first foothold.

As Sam climbed, doubt crept into his mind. Although he had told his brothers about the directions given by the Liahona, they had insisted on coming here first. After all, it was on the way to the northern mountain. Sam mouthed a prayer. *O Lord, Thou hast directed our path once again, and we praise Thee for Thy guidance. Through this divergence, please multiply our efforts.*

Pausing to catch his breath, he squinted upward and found he was near the top. "Just a little farther," he whispered to himself. The next step sent more pebbles cascading past him, but he didn't dare look down to see if they hit anyone. One more hoist and he crested the mount.

It was just as he had pictured. A plateau of green grass spread before him. Limestone boulders and trees provided some shade for a herd of quietly grazing gazelle. There were dozens, possibly hundreds, of beasts roaming and foraging under the tranquil sky. Sam realized he was holding his breath, and when he let it out, he felt a grin involuntarily spread across his face. The landscape was like a gemstone hidden away in the desert—pure and untouched. A virgin oasis.

He moved toward the nearest boulder. Just one, he thought, then he would signal the others. Sam's mouth salivated as if he were seated at a king's feast. His family would grow strong again, and work in the fields would increase. The babies would be born healthy—there was enough meat here to sustain them for several months, if not longer. He couldn't wait to tell Nephi about the treasure he had just discovered.

Thwack.

For an instant, Sam felt nothing. Then the pain exploded through his head, spreading to his neck. Disbelief and confusion flashed through his mind before the physical reaction set in. A scream of pain pulsated from his stomach but was cut off as it reached his throat. Then another blow and Sam slumped to the ground, darkness engulfing him.

* * *

Laman stifled a yawn, covering the ebbing worry he felt running through his limbs. It had been too long since Sam had disappeared over the summit of the mount. Laman looked at the others. Raamah and Heth dozed where they sat, and Lemuel looked drowsy enough to join them any moment.

"Lemuel," Laman hissed.

Bringing his head up, Lemuel moved his bleary gaze to Laman.

"We should follow Sam."

"Let's just rest a while longer," Lemuel said, reluctant to begin the dangerous climb. "He's probably spotted some tracks and is following them."

Raamah grunted in his sleep, then began to smack his lips. Soon his eyes opened. "Thirsty," he muttered, withdrawing the pouch of water from his waistband. After a long guzzle, he eyed Laman. "How long has it been?"

"Too long," Laman replied. He saw alarm flicker in Raamah's eyes.

"We can't let him have all the fun. If the Minaeans were correct, there should be plenty of prizes for everyone, right?"

"It's not a dream," Heth said with a moan. "I really am sleeping on a cliff."

"That's because wild goats sleep on cliffs," Lemuel said with a chuckle. When no one joined his laughter, he fell silent.

"Let's go," Raamah said, nudging Heth. "Your dream is about to get a little more precarious."

Laman rose and stretched the stiffness from his body. His neck ached and his throat felt as if it had been scorched. He brought up the rear of the mountaineering group and was the last to reach the top. The sight was straight from heaven. As far as he could see was the color of lush green—a color he'd almost forgotten existed. The other men crouched together on a grassy knoll behind a large boulder, waiting for him to join them. Laman crossed over and asked, "Any sign of Sam?"

"No," Raamah hissed. He motioned for Laman to crouch. "Something's not right here."

Taking his place alongside the others, Laman peered across the landscape surrounding them. Trees dotted the meadow, and the drone of insects was heard. Raamah was right, Laman realized. Something was wrong.

"With such vegetation," Heth whispered, "You'd expect to see birds and animals."

Laman nodded. He agreed with Heth—it was *too* quiet.

"Maybe Sam scared them off," Lemuel said. "He probably took one shot and every beast fled." He chortled. "He's likely chasing them right now—trying to redeem his mistake."

Raamah put a firm hand on Lemuel, shushing him. "Look over there."

Laman's eyes followed Raamah's direction. Not far from where they had crested the mount was an area of grass that had been pulled up. *Had an animal dug into the ground?* Then something else caught his eye—a dark shape.

"We should have continued north," Laman muttered. "I'll go check it out." Leaving the shelter the boulder offered, Laman's instincts kicked in and he kept low to the ground. As he came closer to the dark object, his pulse quickened. It was Sam's goatskin bag. He picked it up and examined it, then was about to hold it up for the others to see, when he stopped in horror.

Beneath him, the grass was stained with blood—fresh blood.

Holding the goatskin bag, he rushed to where the other men waited.

"What is it?" Raamah asked immediately.

Laman took a deep breath, his heart pounding in his chest. "Sam's . . . Next to it, I found blood on the grass."

Raamah let out a low whistle.

"Maybe Sam killed a beast and dragged it out of sight for protection," Lemuel suggested.

No one responded. In their hearts they knew whose blood it was.

The stunned silence was finally broken by Laman's gruff voice. "We will not leave Sam, wherever he is, no matter what's happened." Everyone nodded anxiously. "Even if it means risking our own lives. We do not know what or who we are about to face." He looked at each man in the eye. "But we have to find him. Who's willing?"

"Aye," Heth and Lemuel both said.

Then Lemuel raised his hand. "Do you think one of us should fetch Nephi and Zoram?"

"No," Raamah said, his eyes flickering toward the sun. "We may already be too late." He removed the slingshot hanging from his waist and chose a pebble from his pouch. "Get your weapons ready and stay in a group."

"Wait," Heth interrupted. He licked his dry lips. "Let's offer a prayer."

Laman's mouth twitched with indecision as he stared at Heth. "All right. I'll say it." He removed his turban and bowed his head. "O Lord . . ." He paused, then continued in a halting voice. "We stumble because of our weaknesses . . . Thou hast forgiven us our wrongdoings and for that we turn ourselves to Thee. As a unified body, we supplicate Thee to spare our brother, Sam. Protect him . . . and . . . help us find him and bring him to safety." He opened an eye. "Amen."

"Amen," the men said heartily.

CHAPTER 14

And they were girded about after the manner of robbers; and they had a lamb-skin about their loins, and they were dyed in blood, and their heads were shorn.

(3 Nephi 4:7)

The sky was dark, the heat intense. It seemed to permeate from one location, causing every part of Sam's body to throb at once. The noise in his ears was deafening, like the howling of a violent sandstorm. Sand. His mouth was full of it, choking him, gagging him. He tried to rise, but somehow his body was too heavy to move. *Open your eyes,* he commanded himself. His mind raced as he tried to control his eyelids and force them open. The effort it required was too great, and he soon gave up. He sputtered and struggled to inhale a fresh breath of air, but the only thing that came in was more sand. *Just calm yourself and think.* An odor struck his senses, almost causing him to suffocate. It was the smell of something burning—and it was not an animal.

The chanting grew louder, pulsating, thumping. The sound closed in around him until he thought his head would burst. Then clawlike hands grabbed his forearms, and he felt himself being dragged. The pain of the rocks scraping off his skin was nothing compared to the pounding in his head.

A man chanted above him.

Through cracked eyelids, Sam could barely make out the form. At first he thought it was half-man, half-beast. As his eyes lost some blurriness, he saw that the tribesman wore the decapitated head of a gazelle. The man's skin glistened in the firelight, looking red and dark, as if he had covered himself in blood. The only clothing he wore was a cloth about his loins.

The chanting continued.

The man's movements were jerky and frantic. In his hand, he wielded a long, curved dagger. Then Sam noticed the others. They were adorned similarly and wore the heads of gazelles. He could see the black ridges of the curving horns, the white markings on the lifeless faces contrasting against the reddish brown fur, and the empty eye sockets of the animal's heads. The horns rose in sharp spikes, as if piercing the night sky above. Smoke billowed behind them, surrounding a skewer that rotated in the flames. The carcass on the skewer was unidentifiable.

Sam felt his stomach recoil in horror. Something told him it was human.

* * *

No more than a dozen paces away, Laman, Lemuel, Raamah, and Heth watched the terrifying events. They had crept through the brush, arriving at a clump of rocks that formed a hiding place between themselves and the heinous ceremony.

Laman had heard of such practices but had given little credence to the stories. *Cannibals,* he thought. The rumors of bloodthirsty tribes took on a new significance. By traveling to the mount for the hunt, they had taken themselves a fair distance from the place called Nahom and were no longer in the cultivated surroundings that offered protection.

This tribal group was unlike any they had ever encountered; the raiders who had attacked them earlier were gentle lambs compared to these men.

"What should we do?" Raamah's hot whisper sounded in Laman's ear.

Laman licked his parched lips, the hunger pangs in his stomach had long since been replaced by nausea. "Only the leader is armed with a dagger, at least from what I can see."

Raamah nodded beside him. "Sam looks too injured to fight. We have our own daggers for protection."

"We'll have to use the fire to our advantage," Laman said gravely. "If we attack from two sides, the surprise and confusion will be greater."

Heth joined the conversation. "Raamah and I will head to the left, and you and Lemuel go right."

The chanting rose in pitch, and the dancing became more frenzied.

"Our brother is about to be sacrificed," Laman said, his eyes wild with apprehension.

Words were no longer needed. Each man would follow his instincts in battling for Sam's life. Negotiations were not plausible, and time had run out.

With a lunge, Raamah and Heth leaped from their hiding place and sprinted toward the tribesman closest to Sam. Raamah dove into the man with the curved dagger, slamming his head against the tribesman's chest with a thud. They both landed on the ground, precariously close to the fire. Raamah wrestled the dagger from the man's grip and, with one swift blow, rendered him motionless.

Laman and Lemuel attacked from the rear, stunning the tribesmen. Using surprise to their advantage, they knocked several men into the fire. The tribesmen began to flee, yelping from painful burns as they went.

Lemuel reached Sam first and, grabbing his ankles, pulled him away from the action. Sam let out a groan.

"Sorry, brother," Lemuel said, and he left to help Laman fend off blows from an angry tribesman.

Laman glanced at Lemuel when he came to his aid. "Did you free Sam?"

"Yes," panted Lemuel.

"Watch out!" Heth shouted from across the fire.

The two brothers jumped out of the way just as an arrow sailed through the air past them.

"More are coming," Raamah cried. "Let's get out of here."

With the immediate tribal group subdued or fled, the brothers made a dash for the clump of boulders. Sam was stationed behind them, trying to untie his bands. "Here," Laman said urgently, "let me help." As he cut the ropes from Sam's wrists and ankles, his mind flashed back to a day many months before when Sam had been tied by Lemuel and Raamah—under *his* command.

"Sorry," Laman said, noticing the dried blood on Sam's head wound.

"Sorry?" Sam whispered. "No . . . thank you for saving my life." He brought his hand to his head and gingerly touched the site.

"Thank us later, *if* we get out of this." Laman's gaze fell on Sam's wound. "It's a severe one, but I think you'll live," he said, then turned toward the others. "Let's go!" he commanded. Looking back to Sam, he asked more gently, "Can you walk?"

"Of course," Sam said, rising to his feet with a grimace. "I'm right behind you."

Another arrow whizzed past the brothers.

"Follow me!" Laman cried out. The men hunched over and ran in a zigzagging fashion, narrowly escaping arrows and stones flying through the night air.

As the terrain grew steeper, Laman started to slow and scanned for protection. "We'll have to hide someplace," he called over his shoulder. "Then I'll try to scare them off with arrows of my own."

Sam began to object, but Raamah gripped his arm and pushed him forward. "These tribesmen know this land better than we do, so we'd better do what Laman says."

His head pounding, Laman stumbled forward, tripping against protruding rocks. Behind him, Raamah scrambled up the mountainside with Sam in tow. Laman wondered how they could possibly outlast the wiry desert men. The fate that they had narrowly escaped sent a shudder down his back. What if they hadn't found Sam in time?

Finally the landscape leveled, and Laman spotted a cave. "Over here," he said.

Following the men into the cave, Laman saw that they were well hidden inside the dank interior. "Listen for my signal when I return," he said.

Breathlessly, the four men nodded as they crowded together. As Laman left the cave, he could hear Sam's whispered prayers.

"Please, Lord," Sam pled. "Spare Laman's life. Bring him safely back to us."

Each of the men echoed, "Amen."

Laman began the descent down the hillside, using various bushes for cover. Although he couldn't hear anything, he knew that the tribesmen were still out there, searching. He tried to still his rapid breathing as he moved low to the ground. Suddenly an arrow sliced through the air, making contact with his right shoulder just as he ducked. The pain seared through his shoulder, at first stunning him with disbelief, then numbing him against all other feeling. He felt his legs buckle, and his body slid to the ground.

It is over, he decided. He would die. He was sure of it. By the time the others found him, he would have bled to death. *Ironic,* he thought, a thin smile creasing his mustache. He would be the first to meet his maker. After all the times he had made fun of Nephi's teachings and complained against his father's visions, *he* would be the one who would know firsthand what really happened on the way to heaven. *Or Sheol,* he reminded himself. Were the recent actions he had taken enough to redeem him?

"Anah," he whispered, his throat painfully dry. "Tell our unborn baby I'm sorry." He would never see his child. The circumstances that would surround his wife's first birth now seemed insignificant compared to what he was about to experience. As his wife would pass through the valley of death experiencing childbirth, he would dwell in it. Forever.

He stared, unblinking, at the tiny pricks of light dotting the black sky. If Nephi were in his place, would there be this unquenchable regret? *Nephi.* His brother had tried to warn him. Numerous times. *Hearken unto the word of God, and hold fast unto it, and you will never perish . . . There cannot any unclean thing enter into the kingdom of God . . . The righteous shall be lifted up at the last day.*

A warmth descended upon him, enveloping him like a soft bedroll. If this was death's hand, maybe it wouldn't turn out to be so dreadful. A faint tingling sensation spread through his cheek, as if someone were touching him . . .

Laman's eyes flew open. "Nephi?"

The familiar dark head nodded. "Try to relax. This will only take a second."

"How did you—?" Laman asked, struggling to rise.

"Shh, lie down. I'll tell you everything later." Nephi tied a leather strap, taken from his waist, around Laman's upper arm. Then with swift precision, he pulled the arrow from his brother's shoulder.

Involuntarily jerking, Laman gasped with pain.

Nephi pressed a wad of cloth against the gaping wound to stanch the flow of blood. Then he brought a flask of water to Laman's mouth. "Drink this."

Laman raised his head and took several gulps of the refreshing liquid. "Thank you," he whispered before he lay back, breathing a sigh of relief. "Is this heaven?"

A quiet chuckle sounded above him. "It's as close as you're going to get for now," Nephi said. "But the easy part is over. We need to find shelter as soon as possible. The tribesmen haven't given up yet."

"All right," Laman said, making an effort to rise. It felt as if the arrow was still lodged in his shoulder muscle. He clamped his jaw shut to keep from crying out.

Nephi helped Laman stand, then supported his weight as they started to move. "Faster," Nephi whispered. After several paces, he asked, "What happened to the others?"

"I hid them in a cave," Laman sputtered through uneven breaths.

"While you fought those devils by yourself?" Nephi asked, incredulous.

"Sam was hurt," Laman said. "I thought it would be best to separate—"

"Sam?" Nephi said, his tone worried. "What happened to Sam?"

They had reached a grouping of brush. "Rest . . . for a moment . . ." Laman panted.

Nephi helped Laman sit on the ground. "Tell me what happened to Sam."

"We made him divert from the Liahona's instructions. He climbed to the top of the mount first, but never returned. When we discovered he was missing, we followed his trail . . . or the trail of blood that was left."

Nephi stared at Laman, his face draining of color. "The tribesmen captured him?"

"Not just tribesmen—cannibals. And they were about to sacrifice him," Laman said. "That's when we caught up to them and attacked."

Following a deep sigh, Nephi fell quiet for a moment. "How bad is he?"

"No worse than me." Laman grimaced. "You didn't tell me how you happened to come out here."

"Remember Khali?" After Laman's nod, Nephi continued. "Father and I visited with him today, and when he learned of your whereabouts, he warned us about the outlying tribes. After we returned to camp, I couldn't shake the feeling that something was amiss."

He paused, listening to something. "I think we're being followed."

Together, they turned to look behind them. At first, they saw nothing, then Laman was able to make out a stationary shape that didn't blend with the moonlit landscape. He felt coldness spread through his limbs, but he couldn't tell if there was more than one from his angle. With Laman's shoulder injury, Nephi was the only one who could shoot an arrow. He nudged Nephi. "There. To the left."

Nephi followed Laman's direction, then he removed an arrow from his quiver and pulled the bow into taut position.

"Steady," Laman whispered.

Just as Nephi was about to release the bow, he hesitated. The form rose and cried out, "Wait!"

"Raamah?" Nephi said, lowering his bow and arrow.

"We're over here," Raamah whispered loudly, waving frantically.

Nephi helped guide Laman, and they joined Raamah, who led them to the secluded cave. Stepping into the enclosure, the men crouched in the pitch black. Laman tried to make out the faces within.

"Laman! Nephi!" It was Sam's voice.

Laman felt someone grab for him and pat his shoulder. "Everyone's still here?" he asked.

"Yes," Raamah replied. "We were growing fearful that you would not return."

"I wouldn't have if it weren't for Nephi. He pulled an arrow from my shoulder," Laman said into the blackness.

"Sam, are you all right?" Nephi whispered.

"Better now that I'm not meant for human sacrifice," he said. "What about you, Laman?"

"Good enough for now," Laman said. He shifted beside the rock he was leaning against. He wouldn't get much more comfortable under the circumstances.

"How did you find us?" It was Heth.

Nephi quickly explained the promptings that had led him to search for them and how the glow from the tribesmen's fire guided him to the proper location, where he eventually found Laman.

Lemuel spoke next. "How long do you think we should stay hidden?"

Raamah sat closest to the entrance, keeping watch. "It's going to be awhile."

The men settled into silence, fear still in their souls. Yet they were comforted to be together.

Laman closed his eyes against the musty cave air. His shoulder throbbed while painful pulses radiated down to his wrist. But he was alive. And Sam had been rescued. As he sank into a light slumber, he realized that God had answered his prayer.

* * *

Whether a great deal of time had passed, it was hard to guess, but the men knew they needed to make their escape. No outside sounds could be heard, and no words had been exchanged for some time. Nephi joined Raamah at the entrance of the cave and scouted for any signs of life. The air was silent and no movement among the rocks or undergrowth detected. Eventually, he signaled the others. One by one, they filed out, noiseless, except for their nervous breathing.

Laman, favoring his shoulder, moved into the front, leading the group in an uphill climb. No one seemed to be following them. Once they reached the plateau, they stopped and rested, catching their breath.

"It was here that I was captured," Sam whispered to Nephi. The herd of gazelles had long since fled, but the boulders stood ominous in the moonlight. Around them, the wind whistled faintly, creating just enough noise to thwart the sounds of the desert night.

"Should we run or proceed slowly?" Heth asked. The other men eyed the nearest boulder. Only one side was illuminated in the moonlight, the rest looked suspiciously dark.

"Whatever happens, stay together," Laman hissed. "Follow me." He leaped forward, holding his right arm in place, and sprinted to the first boulder, the others running close behind. After a few seconds of heart-hammering rest, they ran to the next outcropping of rock, then to the next.

Finally, they reached the far side of the plateau, bordering Nahom. Laman and Nephi moved to the edge, peering over the side of the mount. Below, they could see no sign of movement. "Let's signal the others," Laman said.

"Wait," Nephi said, placing a hand on Laman's arm. "I see something moving."

Next to Nephi, Laman drew his breath in sharply. Sure enough, several paces below them, a shadow moved. It was almost imperceptible at first, but as their eyes grew accustomed to the shape, it was obviously a man. "Do you think there's only one?" Laman asked.

"I can't tell yet."

The minutes passed slowly as Nephi and Laman waited to see the man's next movements. They didn't have to wait much longer. As the man climbed the mount, his face came into full view, lit by the moon.

"It's Zoram!" Nephi whispered.

Laman waved, trying to capture Zoram's attention. "Zoram, over here," he said, louder than he'd intended.

Zoram looked up and spotted Nephi and Laman and waved in response.

Turning, Nephi signaled Sam and the others that it was all right to come out of hiding. But he was an instant too early. Just as Sam and Raamah rose from their hiding places, they were attacked from all sides. Tribesmen poured from the surrounding boulders. Two of the painted men pounced on Laman, who was immediately restrained, his injured shoulder preventing him from matching the tribesmen in strength. Heth narrowly avoided a dagger thrust at his chest, then found himself in a headlock.

"Watch out!" Nephi shouted just as Raamah dodged a hurtling arrow. He scrambled to his feet and dove into the commotion, Lemuel beside him. Nephi tried to make his way to Sam, who had already felt the wrath of the fierce desert men. They were outnumbered, but Nephi knew their fate would be worse if they didn't free themselves from their attackers.

A shout reached Nephi's ears as he battled with a ferocious looking tribesman who was half his size, but agile and quick. The shouting grew louder, and Nephi thought he recognized the words. But he didn't have time to look at the source. Suddenly, the tribesmen began to cry out in terror, shrinking from Nephi and his brothers. Then they backed away and started running the opposite direction.

Turning, Nephi saw the cause of their fear. Standing at the edge of the plateau was Zoram with dozens of men from the Minaean tribe, bows and arrows poised to launch. Nephi's mouth dropped open. He and Lemuel had seen only Zoram climbing the mount, and now he had appeared with an army of reinforcements. The Minaeans jumped into the battle, fighting fiercely.

The tribesmen were outnumbered. Nephi ducked as arrows zinged past him, finding their enemy targets. Several men cried out in pain as they were struck. Many retreated from the center of battle and fled. Others fought until they saw that there was no hope of victory, then they too fled, dragging their injured away.

When the last of the tribesmen had disappeared into the night, Nephi crossed to Zoram. They embraced, careful to avoid each other's wounds. "How did you know?" Nephi asked.

"Your father told me, and Khali sent his best men." Zoram embraced the other men in the family, assessing the various injuries. "Come," he said, "these wounds need attention."

Nephi supported Sam as they descended the mount into the valley. Laman was helped by Raamah and Heth. Zoram thanked the Minaeans as they departed for their settlement. Then the men returned to their camp, where food, drink, and a joyous reunion awaited them.

CHAPTER 15

For whither thou goest, I will go; and where thou lodgest, I will lodge: thy people shall be my people, and thy God my God.
(Ruth 1:16)

One year later

Lehi sat alone in his tent as the early afternoon light streamed in through the flaps. A lazy fly droned above his head, looking for something more meaty than brass plates. Lehi's neck ached from leaning over the sacred records, but he was determined to finish the section he was reading. It touched him to know he was descended from Joseph of Egypt, the man who had found forgiveness in his heart for the brothers who had sold him into slavery. Joseph's father, Jacob, had grieved his whole life for the loss of his son, only to be reunited with him when Joseph had provided grain to the family in their time of starvation.

In the adjacent section of the tent, Lehi heard his own young son, Jacob, stir in his sleep. Sariah had put him down for a nap and left to prepare supper. With a calloused finger, Lehi traced the words from his ancestors. *And Joseph made ready his chariot, and went up to meet Israel his father, to Goshen, and presented himself unto him; and he fell on his neck, and wept on his neck a good while. And Israel said unto Joseph, Now let me die, since I have seen thy face, because thou art yet alive.*

Wiping a tear from his eye, Lehi continued to read about the Israelites settling in Goshen and the blessings Jacob gave his grandsons, Ephraim and Manasseh.

Then he came across the verses that he and Ishmael had studied together. *And Israel said unto Joseph, Behold, I die: but God shall be with you, and bring you again unto the land of your fathers.*

Upon Jacob's death, Joseph had his father's body embalmed. Later his remains were buried in Canaan, the land of his birth. Lehi clasped his hands together, wishing that he could have given Ishmael the same gift—a burial place in the promised land, their family's future. But with a sinking heart, he knew the time would come when the family would leave Nahom—and Ishmael—behind.

As if on cue, a cry erupted from his son.

Lehi rose to his feet and crossed the room to peek at Jacob. Sure enough, the little boy's eyes were open, and he was staring at the goatskin ceiling above.

"Jacob," Lehi said. His son turned his face toward the sound. When Jacob saw his father, his face broke into a timid smile. "Come here, son," Lehi said, crouching down and extending his arms.

The young lad toddled into his father's embrace. "Did you sleep well?" Lehi asked, tousling Jacob's curly hair. The boy took after Sam.

"Mum," Jacob replied somberly.

"You want your mother? I should have guessed," Lehi said. "Let's go find her."

***

With the meal finished and the younger children tucked in their bedrolls, the family gathered around the evening fire. Isaabel sat next to Nephi, watching Tamar cradle her belly.

Tamar leaned her head against her husband's shoulder. Her eyes were weary, but her countenance was at peace.

Isaabel had known this day was fast approaching. After the days of Puah's purification had ended and the appropriate burnt offerings made, it was only a matter of time before Lehi gathered the family in council. She gazed at baby Javan in Puah's arms, still a tiny bundle who slept peacefully—most of the time.

Since the announcement that Tamar was with child, Isaabel's longing for children of her own had increased. She and Tamar had always been close, shared so many experiences. She worried motherhood wouldn't be one of them. A sigh escaped, and Nephi's arm wrapped around her shoulders. His touch ignited the memory of the day she'd injured her ankle at the Valley of Lemuel when Nephi had tended to her injury. She had been so unsure of their relationship then, and now . . . her heart ached as the ability to bear a child continued to elude her. And now they would be leaving the safe dwelling of Nahom.

She hoped the family would be accepting of the next part of their journey. Her eyes met Tamar's, who sat across the fire. Knowing smiles were exchanged between the two sisters. They had already agreed that the sooner they began, the sooner they would reach the promised land. Family relationships had been serene since the incident with Sam and the cannibals, yet Isaabel wondered what reaction her mother would have at the forthcoming news.

"Family," Lehi said in a clear voice that stopped all conversations. "As you may know, we have gathered tonight under sober circumstances. Our stay in Nahom has been fruitful, in more ways than one." A few scattered chuckles were heard.

Lehi continued. "We have been blessed. Our women have borne healthy children, our crops have been successful, and we are of one heart."

Isaabel cast a sideways glance at Nephi, whose eyes were intent on Lehi.

"We recognize the one-year anniversary of our dear Ishmael's death. He is still missed and will always be so," Lehi said.

Isaabel couldn't help but look at her mother. Bashemath's face was grave, but it was evident she appreciated Lehi's tribute.

"And now . . ." Lehi paused. "We have been commanded to take up our journey again into the wilderness." A few family members looked surprised, but most just nodded their heads.

Lehi raised his hand for complete attention. "The Liahona has given us directions to travel nearly eastward from Nahom." His eyes scanned the faces before him. "Lemuel has assured me that Puah is fit enough to travel. And as our debts have been paid to Khali's tribe, tomorrow morning I would like to hold a tribute at Ishmael's burial site before we depart. His earthly body will be left behind, but his spirit will continue with us."

Gratitude replaced the weight on Isaabel's shoulders. She knew it would be difficult to leave Nahom, but Lehi's tribute would make the departure easier. From where she sat, Isaabel saw Bashemath bury her face in her hands. She was relieved that her mother didn't cry out or assail Lehi. The whole family had grown in spiritual matters over the past months, and all were stronger for it.

Isaabel focused once again on what Lehi was saying. "We shall prepare to leave in five days' time," he said.

Five days? Isaabel felt Nephi squeeze her shoulder.

"While the women prepare the provisions, the men will go on one final hunt before departing," Lehi said. "We will need all the dried meat we can carry."

* * *

Next to Isaabel, Nephi stiffened. There were many fertile parts in the desert, he knew, and the Liahona had been accurate in directing them. Yet the change of his father's tone alerted Nephi's senses. He glanced in Sam's direction, but his brother's gaze was lowered. Perhaps Sam picked up on Lehi's intonation too.

When the counsel concluded and the family members dispersed, Nephi turned to Isaabel. "I'll meet you at the tent soon, right after I talk with Sam."

Isaabel nodded, her eyes reflecting angst. "What is it?"

"Probably nothing," Nephi said, giving her a kiss on the cheek. "We'll discuss it later."

When Nephi located Sam, he was in hushed discussion with Zoram. By the looks of their rapid speech and exaggerated arm movements, it wasn't amiable. As Nephi drew near, Sam motioned for him to join the conversation. Zoram hesitated at the sight of Nephi.

"Zoram wants to know if Father has any idea of where the promised land is," Sam said.

"Certainly not in this desert," Nephi offered, "if that brings you any comfort."

Zoram's face darkened. "According to members of Khali's tribe, there is very little cultivation eastward."

"Nearly eastward," Nephi corrected.

Letting out a sigh of exasperation, Zoram said, "The exact direction isn't important. My point is that the only thing between us and the great sea is the High Sands."

Sam shuddered. "Sounds forbidding. I know we studied geography, but the High Sands don't sound familiar."

Nephi looked at his brother with amusement. "It's a desert, Sam."

"We are already *in* a desert," Sam said with frustration. "What do you call Nahom?" He waved his arms about him.

"Nahom has water, cultivation, peaceful tribes—for the most part—and food," Zoram interrupted. "Those tribesmen who captured you, Sam, were mild mannered compared to the warriors of the desert."

"Warriors?" Sam asked. "Warriors who fight for what? Sand?"

Zoram pursed his lips together, eyes blazing. "You'll see."

Nephi put a hand on each man's arm. "Let's have faith in the direction our father has been commanded to take. The Lord has protected us thus far. Why not against warriors, miles of sand, and no food?"

With a sigh, Sam said, "Nephi's right. What more could be out there that we haven't already experienced?"

Zoram's shoulders sagged. He turned and walked slowly away.

"Should I go after him?" Sam asked.

"No," said Nephi. "We all must struggle with our faith. He'll find his way back." Nephi stifled a yawn, trying to conceal the unease growing in his stomach. "Time to end the day. Good night, Sam."

"Good night, Nephi," Sam said.

On the way to his tent, the knot in Nephi's stomach persisted. Something in Zoram's words had caused him to worry.

* * *

The time of preparation passed, and the loading of the tents and provisions began. On the final morning in Nahom, Lehi went early to pay his respects to Khali. Farewells were made and promises given by the Minaean leader to protect the burial site of Ishmael. A gift of a gold bracelet was presented to Khali for his generosity.

"Thank you," Khali said in his dialect. "May your God protect you."

Lehi smiled at his friend. "You know we have the protection of our God."

"Of course," the tribal leader said, bowing. "And you will need that protection."

Raising his eyebrows with surprise, Lehi asked, "You know something of the land eastward?"

"Only secondhand," Khali said. He motioned to one of his tribesman. Soon three camels were brought to him, and Khali turned solemnly to Lehi. "The milk from these nursing camels will provide the sustenance your family will need as you travel through desolate land past Shabwah."

Lehi's eyes widened. A camel in milk was like a traveling oasis, and the meersy could be reserved for times of desperate need. "You would give up your own camels for my family?" he asked incredulously. "We have nothing to offer you in return."

With a tremulous smile, Khali placed a hand on his friend's shoulder. "That you have sufficient nourishment for your children and grandchildren is my reward." Khali touched his forehead. "My mind will know you will survive, and," he placed his hand over his heart, "my soul will be at peace. Go and prosper in your chosen land."

"The promised land," Lehi corrected, his own emotion building. "It is not too late to join us, my friend."

A grin spread under Khali's mustache. "My tribe is happy here. You go to your *promised land* and flourish."

Lehi studied the Minaean leader's face for a moment, then smiled. "May you live in peace," he said.

"May you go in peace," said the Minaean, kissing each of Lehi's cheeks.

Slowly, Lehi turned away and walked to the campsite where the rest of the family had assembled.

* * *

Lehi was the final one to take his place. He took the reins of the camel that Sariah sat upon holding Jacob. Lined up behind them were Nephi and Sam. The women were positioned in the center of the caravan, most on foot, with Laman and Raamah bringing up the rear. Laman rode upon the only horse in the group of camels, having bartered for it from a local Minaean.

"Aiyah," Lehi commanded the camel to begin moving, pulling on its reins. It began its sure, loping strides forward.

After several paces, Isaabel called out, "Wait! My mother!"

The others turned to see Bashemath fleeing from the moving caravan. "Mother," Isaabel cried out again, running toward her. Bashemath didn't turn but continued to dart across the sand. Isaabel's breath already came in short gasps, but she knew that she could outlast her mother. It was only a matter of time before she caught up.

Ahead of Isaabel, the black clothed figure slowed. *At last,* Isaabel thought, her legs burning from exertion, *she's stopping.* Then, in an instant, Bashemath crumpled to the ground like fallen ash.

Isaabel increased her speed until she reached her mother's side. She sank into the sand next to Bashemath. No sound came, no sobbing, no wailing. "Mother," Isaabel said as she stroked her mother's back.

Eventually, Bashemath raised her head. The expression on her face stung Isaabel's heart. It was one of desperation and grief so deep that Isaabel wondered if her mother had lost her senses.

She took her mother's hand. Bashemath stared past her with empty eyes. "Are you all right?" Isaabel whispered. After receiving no answer, she took the bewildered woman into her arms and rocked her, humming softly. Bashemath remained quiet like a comforted babe.

Squeezing her eyes shut against her own tears, Isaabel continued to rock and hum to her mother—blocking out the sight of the stark sand, the smell of perspiration, and the sound of buzzing insects. She knew the Lord would protect her father's burial place, but even that wouldn't be comforting to her mother.

A hand on Isaabel's shoulder brought her back. Nephi stood above her, holding the reins of a camel. Without a word, he helped Bashemath onto the back of the camel, then took Isaabel by the hand. Together they led the beast away from the waiting caravan toward the hillside where Ishmael was buried.

When they reached the tomb, Nephi brought the camel to a halt and urged the animal to its knees so that Bashemath could climb off. Then Isaabel and Nephi watched as Bashemath approached the stacked rocks to bid her final farewell to her beloved Ishmael.

CHAPTER 16

Yea, I will bless her, and she shall be a mother of nations; kings of people shall be of her.
(Genesis 17:16)

It was like a garden, a large and spacious field. And a river of water. *Just like Father's dream,* Nephi realized as he gazed at the valley below them. The family had been traveling for some time in an eastward direction from Nahom, and now they had arrived at another populated settlement.

Next to Nephi, Lehi stopped, looking from the pointers on the Liahona to the valley, then back again. Nephi placed a hand on his father's shoulder. "Does this look familiar?"

Turning, Lehi smiled. "You see it too?"

"Are we at the promised land?" Dinah asked, coming up from behind and slipping her hand into Lehi's.

Nephi chuckled at his little sister's question. "Not yet."

"What's that?" she asked, pointing to an immense mountainlike structure in the distance.

"A dam," Lehi said, amazement in his voice. "I've heard stories of this structure. We must be at Marib."

Nephi followed his father's and sister's gazes and stared at the face of the dam, which was supported by two towering piers, one on the north and one on the south. Between them, a mountain of dirt and rocks had been constructed, preserving the water runoff from the rainy season. A channel directed the water from the dam, creating the river that irrigated the valley.

Lehi picked up his staff and began to move forward. "Come, let us find a place to camp."

* * *

Isaabel watched her nephews and niece play together—or at least poke each other. Her brother-in-law, Jacob, was like a king among the youngsters. He was approaching his second birthday, and his stoutness matched his soberness. "No, no," she heard him tell Rebeka's eldest, Eve. The one-year-old pouted, her lower lip trembling, as her eyes welled with tears. It was evident that Eve had just put a handful of sand in her mouth.

Nearby, Rebeka, who was weaving a basket, saw the interchange and hurried to scoop up her daughter. "Jacob's right. You shouldn't eat the sand, dear. Let's go wash out your mouth." She carried Eve off as her whimpering turned to wailing.

Anah's son, Shem, observed the action through luminous eyes. At the tender age of ten months, he sat peacefully on a rug in the shade, content to watch his mother weave a mat from palm fronds.

"What's wrong with Eve?" Puah asked, joining the women. In her arms, she carried her infant son, Javan. She settled next to her mother, who offered to hold the sleeping baby. Puah's gaze scanned the women. "You look tired, Tamar," she said.

Tamar patted her round belly and sighed. "I look forward to my body returning to normal, but the whole birthing process worries me."

Bashemath clucked her tongue. "Dwelling in Nahom for so long, and now Marib, has brought strength to us all. There is nothing to fear," she said in her practical way.

Isaabel watched Tamar lower her gaze, knowing that her mother's comment was not comforting in the way that Tamar had wished. Isaabel put her stitching aside and rose, stretching her cramped legs. "I'd better return to the fields," she said to no one in particular.

Leaving the women and children, Isaabel passed Elisheba and Dinah. They had already finished their tasks for the day and were helping Sariah prepare the evening meal of goat meat and cooked barley, which they had purchased the day before. Sariah greeted Isaabel warmly. "Had your fill of crying children for the day?" Sariah asked.

Isaabel's smile contrasted with the twinge in her heart. "I haven't finished in the fields." She knew Sariah meant well, but there was nothing that Isaabel wanted more than to have her own child, crying or not. She waved good-bye and continued on her way to the plot of land that had been designated for the family.

Of course, Isaabel thought, with the misery she saw on Tamar's face, she could at least be grateful she was energetic and strong—strong enough to work in the fields every day. As if that was consolation for an empty womb. The men came into view when she neared the rows of barley—the whiskery-eared plants nodding with maturity. Nephi saw her approach and stopped what he was doing to meet her.

"Tired of women talk?" Nephi teased.

"We do much more than talk," Isaabel retorted. She turned and started walking to her place.

"Wait, Isa," Nephi called. He caught up to her and put his hand on her arm. "What's wrong?"

She tried to brush him off. She didn't want to cry in front of him. But Nephi wasn't deterred.

"Tell me what's bothering you," he said, watching her closely.

Isaabel bit her lip to keep it from trembling. "I'm just being selfish," she said. "A little hard work is all I need."

With a grunt, Nephi said, "You're the least selfish person in Marib."

"I should get started," she said, trying to move past him.

"Isaabel," Nephi said in such a way that it caused her to look at him. "Whenever you are around your sisters and their children, you come away despondent."

"How can I help it?" she asked, fighting the stinging in her eyes. "They've had no trouble having children . . . even your mother has little Jacob—"

"Are you still upset about last week?" Nephi asked, taking her hand.

"It's not just last week, when I dared to believe I was with child. Each moon I hope, only to be met with despair." Her voice cracked, and she looked at the ground, not wanting to see Nephi's expression. But the words were out and it was too late to take them back. After all their blessings, Nephi must think her ungrateful.

"Isaabel," he said softly, lifting her chin so that she had to meet his gaze. "I have seen our posterity."

Tears spilled onto her cheeks, and she tried to suppress the sob catching in her throat.

"Don't you understand?" Nephi asked. "We *will* have children. Maybe not this year or the next, but they will come. I know it."

"I just wish I could know *when*," Isaabel said, her chin quivering. "I told you I was selfish."

Nephi took her into his arms and held her firmly. "I know it is difficult for you to see your sisters bringing babies into the world. Although you haven't seen the things I have, you must have faith. Trust in the Lord, Isaabel. Trust Him to know what's best for you. For *us*."

"I'm trying to," she said, sniffling. "If my mother saw me now," a smile crept to her lips, "she'd tell me it was a blessing not to endure bearing children in the wilderness."

"When the time does come, Isaabel—and it will—your mother will be a great help to us both," Nephi said.

"That is true," agreed Isabel, pulling away from him. "Thank you for always acknowledging her strengths."

"You're welcome." Then a shadow darkened Nephi's brow. "I just hope everyone's strength continues once we leave this settlement."

"Has your father received instruction from the Liahona?"

"Not yet," Nephi said. "But I sense that after Tamar gives birth, our days in Marib will be few."

"Isaabel!"

Nephi and Isabel turned to see Dinah hurtling toward them. "Hurry! It's Tamar."

Without further explanation, Isabel picked up her skirts and ran toward camp to set up the birthing tent, leaving Nephi to notify Sam. As she neared Dinah, she said, "Where is Tamar?"

"She's in your mother's tent."

Both of them ran toward Bashemath's tent. Waiting outside was Elisheba, her eyes round. In her arms, she held the goatskin panels and pegs. "Our mothers are inside with Tamar. They want us to make haste with the birthing tent."

Isabel took part of the load from Elisheba's arms. She heard a groan coming from the inside of the tent. "Let's go."

Elisheba followed Isabel's lead as they passed through the center of the camp. "Where are my other sisters?" Isabel asked.

"I think they are resting with their children for the afternoon," Elisheba said. Her steps had slowed under the weight of the goatskin as they had reached the perimeter of the camp. Isabel spied a shady place.

"We're almost there," Isabel said, wishing that Anah or Puah would come and help. But she knew that their husbands wouldn't stop their labors to tend the children, regardless of the circumstance.

Once they had hammered in the pegs with a stone, Elisheba used the stake she had brought to erect the tent into formation. "Get the rugs and water," Isabel said. Her bodice was soaked with perspiration, and underneath her head covering, her hair was moist. She glanced at Elisheba, whose face was pink with exertion. "We'll both go," Isaabel said.

On the way back to camp, they met Dinah again. "Mother says Tamar's time is progressing very fast," she said, panting.

"All right. We must act with haste," Isaabel said. "Elisheba, you bring two goatskin bags of water. Dinah, fetch three or four rugs, and I'll go help move Tamar." The three parted ways, and Isaabel hurried to her mother's tent.

Entering the dim interior, Isaabel saw immediately that moving Tamar would be no easy task. Every few minutes, her body seized with another pain. Her tanned face looked pale against her dark mantle. Isaabel rushed to her sister's side, ignoring Bashemath's caution. Grabbing Tamar's hand, Isaabel said, "Are you all right?"

A touch on Isaabel's shoulder caused her to turn. It was Sariah. "She will not be able to walk to the birthing tent," she whispered. "She'll have to be carried."

Suddenly Isaabel understood. Sariah wanted her to do something that Bashemath would not approve of—something that went against all custom.

With a quick nod, Isaabel rose, reluctant to leave her sister so helpless yet anxious to get out of the tent.

The fresh air hit her like a welcome drink. She had to find Nephi and Sam immediately and without arousing anyone else's interest. In the distance, she could see the men still at work in the field. She'd already interrupted their work once today, but this was even more important.

Nephi spotted her first and had started to cross over when Isaabel saw him. She ran toward him almost at full tilt.

"Whoa, slow down," he said. "What's the matter?"

Trying to catch her breath, Isaabel stammered, "Tamar . . . needs help . . . you and Sam . . . must carry her to the birthing tent."

If Nephi was surprised at the request, he didn't show it. He simply said, "We'll be right there."

Isaabel stumbled back to camp, wishing she could remove her mantle and let the air dry the sweat soaking her body. According to custom, men weren't allowed to be around a woman in labor, lest they become contaminated by the birthing mother. The menstruant or laboring woman was not only considered impure, but she also contaminated others and those in her proximity.

By the time Isaabel reached Bashemath's tent, Nephi and Sam were close behind. Before they entered, Isaabel grabbed Nephi's arm. "Wait," she said. "Be careful no one sees."

Nephi said, "There are no Hebrew officials or sarim here to chastise us for helping a woman in labor."

Nodding, Isaabel followed Nephi inside the tent. Sam was already kneeling by his wife. Isaabel wasn't sure who looked more pale, Tamar or Sam.

Tamar's watery gaze met her husband's, then she closed her eyes as if relieved. The two men gingerly picked up Tamar and carried her through the tent door. At several points, they stopped when Tamar's pains wracked her body with force, but she told them through gritted teeth to keep moving.

Once Sam and Nephi placed Tamar on the rugs inside the birthing tent, the women were able to take over. Sariah had brought her pouch with various medicinal herbs, and by the time Tamar was settled, Sariah had begun to apply a poultice of dried juniper berries to Tamar's limbs. "This will ease the pain," she said.

* * *

Sam and Nephi stood outside the birthing tent. The wrenching in Sam's stomach increased with each moment. He was relieved that Tamar's time had finally come, but to see her in such a state . . .

Seeing the expression on Sam's face, Nephi placed a hand on his shoulder. "Are you all right?"

Jaw clenched, Sam looked away, wishing that there were a way he could help his wife.

"Come," Nephi said, guiding Sam away from the tent. They walked a short distance and stopped under a grouping of trees. The late afternoon sun had spent its heat, and now the cooler air began its creep along the land.

The men sat together in companionable silence for several moments. Finally, Sam said, "I'm about to be a father."

"Congratulations," Nephi said.

Sam's mouth tugged into a tight line. "If something happens to my wife . . ." He hung his head. "No child could replace her."

Tracing a circle in the sand beneath him, Nephi stared at the ground. "No, our wives cannot be replaced," he said, his voice sounding empty.

Sam glanced sharply at his brother, his own commiserating replaced by curiosity. "Is Isaabel . . ." he hesitated.

Nephi simply shook his head and continued drawing with his finger.

"We've been in the wilderness so long, I suppose I've let my fears grow stronger than my faith," Sam said.

Raising his eyes, Nephi looked at his older brother. "You are right. The Lord has his own timetable."

With Nephi's words, Sam knew they were talking about different things. Tamar had told him that Isaabel wished to have a child too. Yet seeing the pain and grief that labor brought to his wife, he envied Nephi not having to experience a wrenching heart. *No*, Sam thought, *I do not envy Nephi anything.* He just wished he could trust that Tamar would have a safe delivery.

"Are you ready to return to camp?" Nephi asked, breaking through Sam's reflection.

"I think I'll stay a while longer," Sam said. He watched Nephi rise and walk toward the main camp. Then he turned and looked at the structure which housed his wife and unborn child. From his position, he couldn't hear anything. All was quiet. *Too quiet.*

With Nephi gone, Sam suddenly felt very alone. His turban, which had soaked up his sweat just a short time before now, provided little protection from the strengthening breeze. The sand beneath him began to lift itself up, swirling about his feet. Sam squinted toward the sinking sun and saw that the light was rapidly fading—faster than normal. With a jolt, he realized a sand storm was on its way.

"Tamar," Sam said under his breath. The birthing tent would provide minimal protection against violent winds and blowing sand. By the time he rose to his feet, the wind had intensified. Sam started in the direction of Tamar's tent, shielding his face against the flying sand. He blinked rapidly against the granules stinging his eyes.

When he neared the tent, he knew the storm was too fierce to try to carry Tamar back to camp. They would have to wait it out.

"Sam!" came a voice from behind him. Sam turned and tried to make out the figure. "It's Nephi."

Sam reached out before him blindly, feeling for his brother through the swirling sand. Nephi grasped his arm firmly. "We must use our bodies to hold down the tent on each side," Nephi said.

With an imperceptible acknowledgement, Sam gripped Nephi's arm, and the two moved to the entramce of the tent.

"Isaabel," Nephi called out. A muffled voice responded from within. "We are here to secure the tent."

A head poked through the tent opening. It was Isaabel. "Come inside."

"We'll be able to hold the tent down better from the outside," Nephi said.

Isaabel paused, then quickly disappeared back inside the tent.

Sam heard a faint cry. "Did you hear that?" he asked Nephi, calling through the driving wind. "It sounded like Tamar."

Nephi didn't respond but tugged Sam along with him to the side of the tent. Both men sat against the goatskin panels, distributing their weight in order to secure the structure against the howling wind. Sam covered his face with his turban but was still able to feel the pelting sand through the cloth against his skin.

The cries coming from inside the tent blended with the howling pitch of the wind, making one indistinguishable from the other. Sam's lips began to move against the dryness in his mouth. What he wouldn't give for a calm day and a drink of water, but he knew that his sacrifice was small compared to what his wife was experiencing.

"O Lord, my God," Sam whispered. "In Thee do I put my trust." His head ached as he thought about Tamar. "Hear my prayer and have compassion on my wife."

Another cry sounded, or was it the high pitch of the wind? "O Lord, have mercy on her and let her deliver with strength." Sam continued, his tone rising. "Calm the winds and bring our hearts peace."

The wind seemed to lessen for a moment, then the momentum increased again. "Protect her, O God . . . Save her . . ." Sam's voice lost its strength and fell to a whisper. "I will remain faithful to Thee all my days . . ."

When Sam finished his verbal prayer, his pleadings continued in his heart. As the sky deepened with night, Sam burrowed within his robes, waiting for the storm to subside.

Hours later, cries echoed in his mind as Sam lay curled in a fetal position. *I must help Tamar,* he thought. He tried to move, to find the source of the cries, but his neck ached, and his body was as heavy as limestone, cold and stiff. Suddenly he opened his eyes. The cries he heard were not of his wife in agony, but of a child.

A baby.

Blinking, Sam slowly focused on the sky above. It was a brilliant blue, brighter than a gemstone. Turning his head to the side, he was met with an earful of sand—warm, quiet sand. The wind had stopped, and the only sound interrupting the morning was the crying of an infant.

Sam heaved himself to a sitting position. Nephi was gone, but his tracks were visible as they led away from the tent toward camp. Mounds of sand surrounded Sam, piled against the tent that he and Nephi had sustained through the night. He scrambled to his feet, his sore limbs no longer weighing him down.

"Tamar," he wheezed. His throat felt as if he'd swallowed the whole desert. Reaching the tent opening, Sam dug away some of the sand piled before the entrance. "Tamar," he said again, pushing through the flap. It took a moment for his eyes to adjust, and when they did, he found four women staring at him. Three were frowning, but one, the only one who mattered, was smiling.

"Sam, you're here," Tamar said. In her arms she held a bundle.

"Is that him?" Sam asked, ignoring all protocol.

"Her." Tamar corrected.

"A girl?" Sam asked. The grin that broke through his face matched Tamar's. "All *this* for a girl?"

Tamar laughed, delight in her voice. "When you're finished decorating the entrance, come see your new daughter."

Without further coercion, Sam moved to Tamar's side.

Bashemath cleared her throat. "The cleansing is not yet finished."

Whether Sam ignored the comment or didn't hear it, he took the baby in his arms before he could be restrained. He stared at the tiny red face and black hair with open elation. The fussing stopped, and the infant returned his gaze with innocence. "You are a tempest, that's what," Sam said. "Don't pretend you had nothing to do with last night."

Tamar placed a hand on her husband's arm, and Sam looked at her tenderly.

"I was worried about you," he said.

"I know," Tamar said in a soft voice. "Now we can enjoy the gift we have been given."

"Yes," Sam agreed, his eyes moist. "Our prayers have been answered." He paused, his expression growing amused. "And her name shall be Govad."

Tamar raised a brow. "Govad?"

"It's the word for *wind,* as used by the Persian tribes from the North," Sam said with a wink.

CHAPTER 17

Behold, all ye that kindle a fire, that compass yourselves about with sparks: walk in the light of your fire, and in the sparks that ye have kindled. This shall ye have of mine hand; ye shall lie down in sorrow.
(Isaiah 50:11)

After leaving Marib, the family continued in an easterly direction. They covered as much ground as possible each day, but water was sparse, making travel difficult.

Elisheba walked next to Dinah, who chattered incessantly. With a simple nod here or there, Elisheba let Dinah know that she was listening, although her thoughts were elsewhere.

Elisheba knew she went without water longer than she should many of the days. She would take a small drink and pass the goatskin on to one of the younger children, encouraging them to drink deeply. When the family did come across a well, she drank her fill, then tried to ignore the desperate thirst that increased with each subsequent step.

It had been nearly two days since the last water stop, and now Elisheba started to feel the effects of missing the portion she had given to Raamah's son, Tiras. As Dinah continued to talk, Elisheba stole a glance behind her where Tiras walked hand-in-hand with his father. The look on the young boy's face made her feel instantly contrite. Past the grittiness of her mouth and the burning in her throat and stomach, she could see that

Tiras fared worse. His thin legs dragged his feet with effort through the unforgiving sand.

Up ahead, Lehi slowed. Elisheba placed a hand on Dinah's arm, interrupting her flow of words. "We're stopping." Together they moved to where Lehi and several other family members had gathered. Palm trees in the distance gave evidence of another oasis.

Water, Elisheba thought. *Finally.* She felt faint just thinking about the first swallow. But she soon realized they had arrived at no common oasis. In the distance were buildings, several floors high, and surrounding the city was a fortification wall, complete with armed guards keeping watch.

"Let's approach," Lehi said.

Elisheba linked her arm through Dinah's, and they moved next to Sariah. Once they reached the entrance, Lehi presented a collection of spices they'd obtained in Marib to the guards, and the family was allowed to enter the city.

After speaking with Lehi, Sariah joined her daughters once again. "Shabwah," Sariah told them. "He says we are in Shabwah, the center of incense trading in this part of Arabia."

Elisheba couldn't help but stare at the buildings they passed. *Great and spacious buildings—as in Father's dream.* "Is that a temple?" she asked, pointing at the limestone structure before them.

Sariah nodded. "Shabwah is also a worship center."

When they reached the open marketplace, they were met with a flurry of merchants and traders. Animals loaded with frankincense from the East had stopped in Shabwah before continuing west. Frankincense of all qualities, ranging from white to dark yellow in color, was displayed on skins. Great sacks of salt had been stacked together, harvested from the salt mines surrounding the city. Off to one side, a line had formed at a well, where people drew water for themselves and their camels.

Elisheba saw that Isaabel and her sisters had secured a place in line to fetch water. "I'll go and wait with the other women,"

Elisheba told her mother, wishing that the few paces to the well didn't seem so far to walk.

The last thing Elisheba remembered was turning away from her mother and sister to walk toward the well.

Some time later, Elisheba awoke in cool darkness. She closed her eyes, then opened them again, trying to make sense of the shapes around her.

"She's awake," said a woman's voice close by.

Blinking hard, Elisheba turned her head, coming eye to eye with a wrinkled face.

The wrinkles grew deeper as the old woman smiled. "Welcome," she said.

Or at least that's what Elisheba thought she said. The woman's dialect sounded similar to what was spoken in other villages. She struggled to sit up, then felt the dizziness engulf her again.

"Rest," the woman said, placing a cool, dry hand on Elisheba's forehead.

Elisheba exhaled slowly and relaxed onto the rug beneath her. "Where am I?"

"My home—near the marketplace where I found you," the woman answered.

"Elisheba?" It was her mother. Relief flooded through her at the sound of the familiar voice.

Sariah came into view and knelt by her side, asking, "How do you feel?"

"Thirsty," Elisheba said.

"Drink this," her mother said gently, as she held a cup to Elisheba's mouth. "You fainted in the marketplace."

Elisheba swallowed carefully, feeling the cool tea slide down her parched throat. She remembered the market and all the commotion surrounding her. After several swallows, she rose to a sitting position.

"Your coloring has returned," Sariah said, touching her cheek.

Gradually, the tea revived Elisheba's parched body, helping her head clear. "I'm feeling much better," she said, looking at her aged hostess. "Thank you for the tea and the cool room to rest in. I had lost hope of feeling this refreshed . . . How can I repay you?"

The woman raised her thin eyebrows, creating deep crevices in her forehead. "Marry my son."

* * *

"Don't you even want to see what her son looks like?" Dinah asked Elisheba as the two sat in front of their tent watching the evening sun melt against the horizon.

Elisheba shook her head emphatically. That evening when her mother told Lehi what the old woman had said, he had chuckled in reply. With a sigh of relief, Elisheba had been relieved that her father hadn't seriously considered the offer. But now, as the two sisters sat on the edge of their encampment in Shabwah, Dinah's curiosity plagued her.

"Perhaps this is the promised land, and we'll live here," Dinah said, eyes glowing with excitement. "Did you see all that frankincense in the market? Mmm. I can still smell it."

"Dinah," Elisheba said sternly. "You must stop pestering Father about the promised land every time you see a palm tree."

"But they already have temples here and everything," Dinah protested.

"Not temples we can worship in," Elisheba said.

"We can build one—"

"Dinah!" Elisheba interrupted, feeling exasperated. "Maybe you should take your questions elsewhere."

"But you just said to stop asking Father." Dinah's eyes narrowed as her mouth formed a pout.

"I'm sorry," Elisheba said quickly. "It's just that I am still upset about the prospect of being married off to a strange man."

"He wouldn't be strange if you met him," Dinah said.

Elisheba tried to contain a groan. *Younger sisters.* What she wouldn't give to be so naïve again. Of course, Raamah had once called *her* naïve. What else had he said? *To any other woman my words would have been obvious.* Elisheba stole a glance in the direction of the men who sat gathered around the evening fire. Raamah was in conversation with one of her brothers. She found herself wondering if he had heard of the marriage proposal, and if so, what he thought of it.

* * *

Something doesn't feel right, Nephi thought. The family had left Shabwah a few days before and had stopped at a small clump of palms to rest. Nephi was appreciative when his father had announced at the evening meal that the family would be traveling during the night from now on, as the heat had become unbearable. But beneath Lehi's composed exterior, Nephi sensed that something other than the temperature was troubling his father.

The family rested at a small well along the incense trail. The trail itself was sparse in vegetation and limited in water. Fortunately, Laman had traded his horse in Shabwah for a camel since the stretches of sand started to grow in length. Nephi was grateful there were no other Bedu people to share the camp with, though he feared some might appear and claim the blighted spot.

When the families were settled in their separate areas for the evening, Nephi found his father by the smoldering fire. Lehi was bent over the plates of brass, reading them in the dimness of the firelight.

"What are you studying?" Nephi asked.

Lehi looked up from the text. "I had Sam unearth the plates so I could read about Moses tonight," he said. "Come, we'll read together."

Lehi ran his finger along the ancient text as he read. "And they thirsted not when he led them through the deserts: he caused the waters to flow out of the rock for them: he clave the rock also, and the waters gushed out."

Nephi nodded as his father read the familiar words of the prophet Isaiah. Studying the experiences of the prophets helped him understand how the Lord took care of His children. Nephi found himself reflecting on the journey of Moses, the prophet who led the children from the land of Egypt only to spend forty long years in the wilderness. *Forty years.* His mind tuned into the words that his father was reading aloud.

"Can a woman forget her sucking child, that she should not have compassion on the son of her womb? yea, they may forget, yet will I not forget thee. Behold, I have graven thee upon the palms of my hands; thy walls are continually before me." Rocking back on his heels, Lehi paused. "Those are some of my favorite verses."

Nephi agreed. He too had felt the power of the words written by Isaiah. "I watch the women with their children and the care and patience it takes to rear them. Our wives would protect the little ones with their lives. So," he hesitated, "it seems impossible that a mother could forget her child. And that is the point. As she does not, so the Lord does not."

"Your mother could never forget you or your siblings. When you and your brothers went to Jerusalem for the brass plates, your mother grew more agitated each day until even I could not console her."

"Knowing how much a mother loves her child, I find it interesting that according to the words of Isaiah, compared to the love of the Holy One of Israel for us, a mother's love for her child is minor," Nephi said.

Lehi stroked his beard in quiet thought, then said, "I would like you to share your thoughts on this scripture after the morning meal."

"Of course," Nephi replied. "Is there anything else you would like to discuss?"

Lehi looked like he wanted to add more, but then said, "No, I'd better put these plates back in their hiding place."

When Lehi left, Nephi's uneasy feeling didn't lessen. If anything, it increased. Rarely did his father ask him to address the family on spiritual matters—since the incident in Nahom, Lehi had minimized Nephi's involvement in teaching the others. Nephi knew that once they reached the promised land, it would be easier to fulfill the instructions given by the Lord about his leadership in the family. With their discontent about the hardships experienced in the wilderness, it was simpler to concentrate on the physical aspects of life and not continually preach to them about their salvation.

Nephi paced before the weakening fire. Although it would be left to die out on its own, in the morning, the embers could be used to stoke a new blaze.

"Nephi!"

He turned and saw his father hurrying toward him. "What is it?" Nephi asked.

"Douse the fire," Lehi said, urgency in his voice.

Alarmed, Nephi pushed dirt on top of the flames, creating smoldering smoke. Within a few moments, the smoke had dissipated, all hope of reusable embers gone with it. When Nephi looked at his father, Lehi was kneeling on the ground.

"Father?" Nephi asked, crossing to him. "What's wrong?"

"The Lord," Lehi said. "He has commanded us to no longer make fire."

"Not even for cooking?" Nephi asked, incredulous.

"He will make our meat sweet so that we will not have to cook it." Lehi paused to steady his voice. "He will be our light in the wilderness and will prepare the way for us."

"Then we will no longer make fire," Nephi said.

"And," Lehi continued, "we will eat our meat raw."

It was a long time before Nephi fell asleep. And when the sun stretched its grasp over the inhospitable land, he awoke to his mother's gentle touch.

"Why are you sleeping by the fire pit?" she asked, concern in her voice.

For an instant, Nephi wondered the same thing. Then the events of the night before became clear. "Father has received instruction that we are no longer to make fire."

Amusement leaped to Sariah's face. "Is that what you were dreaming about?"

"No, Mother," Nephi rose on one elbow. "It was no dream."

Sariah clucked her tongue and began to stack the few pieces of acacia kindling, but a strong hand on her arm made her pause.

"We will have to eat our meat raw," Nephi said.

Sariah met her son's gaze with bewilderment. "Are you sure?" she whispered.

"The Lord has made it known to Father."

"But . . ." Sariah straightened and scanned the tents, as if looking for Lehi. "The Law of Moses . . ."

"I know," Nephi interrupted. "We will continue to drain the blood from the meat before eating it."

Sariah's hand flew to her mouth, then the other hand to her stomach.

"Are you all right?" Nephi asked, placing an arm about his mother's shoulders.

She nodded and took a few steps away. "I will be," she gasped, then hurried toward her tent.

Nephi sighed as he watched his mother leave. He could only imagine what Isaabel would think, or her mother. Or Laman.

None too soon, the women began to emerge from their shelters. Isaabel reached him first. "Is your mother ill?" she asked immediately upon seeing that the fire wasn't lit.

By the time Nephi explained the situation, the rest of the women had gathered, staring at him dumbfounded. He was grateful when his father arrived on the scene. In his authoritative way, Lehi told the women about the direction he had received from the Liahona.

"It is for our own protection," Lehi said. "We are in a part of the desert that is inhabited with tribes who may take advantage of our family."

"Eating uncooked meat will make us ill," Anah exclaimed.

The other women joined her in the dispute, the noise rousing the men of the camp. Soon Lehi was surrounded by complaints coming from all sides.

Sariah joined the group, her mouth in a grim line. But Nephi could see that she supported her husband.

"You may say this is a hard thing to ask," Lehi said. "We must have faith that the Lord has our best interest in mind. Like Moses, we have been commanded to alter our diet."

"Moses?" Laman scoffed. "*Moses?* Moses ate manna, not *raw meat.*" He spat on the ground. "Next, we'll be striking rocks for water."

Nephi felt the hairs on the back of his neck rise as Laman mocked his father's words.

"Silence," Lehi finally demanded. "The Lord has said that if we cease to make fire, He will make our food sweet. The Lord will be our light in the wilderness." His gaze met Laman's. "God has promised that if we keep His commandments, we will be led toward the promised land. Once we reach the promised land, we will know that it was He who delivered us from destruction."

Laman strode away, his face red with indignation. The other family members continued to grumble at Lehi's words, but no more outbursts were heard. And by the midday meal, hunger was prevalent enough that the first bites of the raw meat were taken. When it was Nephi's turn, his eyes watered in response to the anticipation, but he was surprised that the meat was sweet enough to swallow without his stomach's rejection.

As the day softened into night, the complaints lessened. Nephi found Isaabel in their tent, already asleep. Just as he felt himself fading, he thought he smelled smoke.

Smoke. He sat up, sniffing at the air. "Isa," he said, nudging her form beside him. "Can you smell that?"

A mumble came from Isaabel, then she shifted her position. "No . . ."

Nephi fell silent for a moment, then rose and peered out of the tent. "Isa," he whispered again.

"I'm awake," she said, sitting up. "What is it?"

"Someone is cooking."

"At this time of night?" Isaabel joined him at the tent opening. "Why?"

"Because," Nephi said, "they don't want Father to know about it." He grabbed his robe and pulled it around him, then stepped out into the clear night. "Wait here," he told Isaabel.

Now the scent was stronger. He walked away from his tent and through the sleeping camp. The smell grew pungent as he crested the rise of a low sand dune. Nephi crouched to the ground as he spotted the source of the smoke. Three figures grouped around a small fire several paces away. Nephi's stomach knotted. Laman, Lemuel, and Raamah were deliberately defying the Lord's commandment. It took him only a second to decide what to do next.

Nephi strode toward the men. Almost immediately, they heard him approach and turned. Laman kicked sand over the fire and crossed his arms over his chest. Lemuel looked sheepishly at Nephi, but Raamah's gaze was insolent.

Eyes blazing, Nephi asked, "You dare to disregard the Lord's commandment?"

A low, harsh chuckle came from Laman. "We dare to live. And if that means going against Father's ridiculous request, then so be it."

"We are no longer near Jerusalem, where men may hunt for Father," Lemuel added. "There is no reason why we cannot build a fire here to cook our meat."

"The Lord is trying to protect us," Nephi said, his voice rising.

"From what? Scorpions?" Laman sneered.

Nephi let out a hot breath, anger in his chest exploding. "The desert is populated with warring tribes who prey upon small caravans such as ours."

Laman's eyes widened for a moment. "We haven't seen a soul since we left Shabwah."

"That will change if we make fire," Nephi said matter-of-factly. "Now Father will want to move—"

"Don't tell him," Laman's voice cut in, a look of trepidation on his face. "We won't do it again."

Nephi hesitated. "All right," he finally agreed. "Let's go." The men followed Nephi back to camp and separated to their different tents. As Nephi neared his, he saw a figure approach him.

"Nephi?" Zoram whispered in the darkness. "Did you smell something burning?" He stopped in front of Nephi.

Knowing he couldn't conceal what Zoram suspected, Nephi said, "Yes, there was smoke, but it's gone now."

Zoram studied Nephi for a moment in the reflecting moonlight. "You are protecting your brothers, then," he said, disapproval in his voice. "We will all pay for their mistake." Zoram turned and left Nephi staring after him.

60.40% 1-23-05

CHAPTER 18

Therefore we did pour out our souls in prayer to God, that he would strengthen us and deliver us out of the hands of our enemies.
(Alma 58:10)

In his sleep, Nephi felt the coldness touch his neck again and again. Finally, he reached up to brush away the offending object. Something gripped his hand and twisted it behind his back. Before he could react, his other arm was pinned. Nephi opened his eyes and found himself staring into a filthy face with rotted teeth protruding from a gaping mouth, and a stench so foul that the smell of raw meat seemed sweet.

The marauder shouted a commandment.

Not familiar with the word, Nephi assumed it meant *get up* in the man's dialect. He rose painfully, awkwardly, realizing that his arms had been tied behind his back. His gaze flew to where Isaabel slept. Her bedroll was empty.

The man shouted again, shoving Nephi, until he staggered out of the tent.

"Isaabel!" Nephi called with wild desperation.

A fist hit the back of his head, and he pitched forward onto the ground. Sputtering, he spit the sand from his mouth. The sound of high-pitched yelps came from all around him. Then the smell of smoke reached Nephi's nostrils, and he turned his head to see a blazing fire. The tents had been thrown together and lit. Where was his wife? "Isaabel," he shouted again.

Nephi rotated his head, frantically searching for Isaabel. He couldn't seem to make sense out of the confusion playing out before him. He tried to stagger to his feet but was met with a blow across the back. His knees buckled as he cried out in pain.

A marauder caught hold of his arms and dragged him toward the fire.

"No," yelled Nephi. As the heat of the blaze drew closer, he could see family members lined up, all of them bound hand and foot. With relief, Nephi saw Isaabel among them, alive. He ached to reach her side and protect her. But Nephi was shoved next to Zoram, who glanced at him in terror.

Another body was thrust almost on top of him. "Father?" Nephi whispered. Lehi moaned and tried to turn his head to see his son.

"What is happening?" Lehi whispered.

"They are disposing of the evidence of our existence," Zoram hissed. "We're lucky the valuables are buried."

The tribesmen hooted and hollered all around them, throwing their belongings into the fire. Nephi watched as bedrolls, baskets, and goatskin panels joined the flames. Just outside the camp, Nephi could see the marauders gathering their camels.

"Will they leave us with nothing?" Lehi asked, his face perspiring from the closeness of the fire.

"That would be a blessing," Zoram said. "If they wipe out all traces of our caravan, they will not be attacked by other tribes in a blood feud."

Nephi had heard about feuds among tribes. There were two kinds of feuds—the ones who had no blood feud, but took your camels and weapons—and the ones who had a blood feud and, after they stripped you of your camels and weapons, took your life.

"There is no feud between us and any other tribe," Lehi said, desperation in his voice.

"Yes," Zoram said. "But they don't know that."

"Can't we tell them?" Nephi asked.

"It won't make a difference unless we have protection under another tribe," Zoram replied. "And because of our lack of gold, we could not pay for such protection anyway."

The blaze had somewhat lessened, and the noise from the attackers died down. Zoram fell quiet as they watched the warriors approach. They wore remnants of loincloths, long hair falling down their backs, heads uncovered. Their appearances were similar to other tribesmen, heavy eyebrows shading large eyes with long lashes, bell-shaped noses and thin lips. Some had scruffy beards, while others were clean-shaven with mustaches. All had long daggers strapped to their waists.

When the tribal leader spoke, Lehi rose to his feet and, although his hands were lashed behind his back, stood with dignity.

"We would like to ask for your protection," Lehi said in the Minaean dialect.

The raiders stared at him for a moment, then the tribal leader burst into raucous laughter. The other tribesmen joined in the laughter. Nephi noticed that the leader was missing several fingers.

To Nephi's right, Zoram spoke rapidly in a language that Nephi hadn't heard him use before. *His tongue has been loosened,* Nephi realized.

Stepping toward them, Zoram's voice gained strength as he faced the men. The family members stared at him in awe. The leader stopped his laughter and listened to Zoram's words, nodding as he spoke.

When Zoram finished, there was silence, accompanied only by sparks flying from the fire.

The leader spoke to Zoram, who then translated, "His name is Sulaim, and he is the chief of the Al'Abr tribe. He says their protection costs a great deal."

Lehi nodded for Zoram to answer the chief. "We are a poor caravan traveling through this desert," Zoram said.

The dialect Zoram spoke became clear to Nephi, and then he realized the same thing had happened to his father.

Lehi cleared his throat and interrupted. "We have nothing that would be of value to you."

A look of glee crossed Sulaim's face. "Some of my men need wives."

The breath went out of Nephi, and he fought to keep his composure. "Our women already have husbands."

Behind him, Sariah stirred. "Tell him to take this," she said nudging her trinket box forward with her toe. "It's all we have."

Nephi's eyes settled on the ornamented box that had belonged to his grandmother. His heart sank when he thought about his mother losing something she treasured so dearly, but he knew it might be the only way.

All eyes watched as Sulaim picked up the box and turned it over, then glanced at Sariah. Seeing the key hanging from her veil, he crossed over and retrieved it. He unlocked the trinket box and sifted through the contents. After a moment, he raised his head. "All right."

Lehi's shoulders sagged with relief, then he turned to the family and translated.

"We will guide you to the borders of our territory. Thereafter you may claim protection under the Al'Abr tribe." Sulaim walked along the line of family members, studying each person's face. When he reached Isaabel, he stopped. "Is this one married?"

"Yes," Lehi said in a croaking voice.

"How many children?" Sulaim asked, bringing his face close to inspect Isaabel's.

"None," Lehi replied.

Sulaim touched the outline of Isaabel's cheek. "Perhaps she needs a new husband then."

Although Isaabel couldn't understand the words, she shrank in horror at the man's touch.

But Nephi did understand. Anger and disgust filled him. He rose to his feet and headed straight for the chieftain. Immediately he found himself surrounded, daggers pricking his body.

Sulaim snapped his head around and studied Nephi. "So this is the husband." He looked at Lehi. "This woman is my guarantee that your family will comply with my every wish." His arm snaked around Isaabel's waist. "She rides with me."

From that point on, the travel was agonizingly slow. Surrounded by the Al'Abr tribe, the family moved through the desert day after day, heading northeast against their will. Nephi knew they were nearing the border of the High Sands because the land grew more and more desolate. With most of their provisions burned, the family had nothing but a few surviving necessities. The only things of value that remained were the jewelry the women wore and the buried plates of brass, Liahona, and sword of Laban. A gloom had settled over the family as never before. Even the babies were silent. It was as if the life had gone out of them; no one spoke, and no one looked at each other.

Ahead, Nephi could see Isaabel upon Sulaim's camel. The wind, the biting sand, the heat, the hunger, and the thirst were minimal compared to the resentment he held toward Sulaim. If freeing Isaabel took the sacrifice of his own life, Nephi would give it willingly. Defying the glare of the sun, Nephi kept his gaze on Isaabel and her captor.

Around midday, a shout went up among the tribesmen, "Al'Abr oasis!"

Sam, who walked close to Nephi, said in a hoarse voice, "It must be a well. And by the looks of it, we have company."

Nephi squinted against the sun's rays, and sure enough, he saw another caravan at the sparse oasis. "Oh no," Nephi said through cracked lips.

"I wonder if we'll have to battle for water," Sam whispered with effort.

Blood-curdling cries erupted from the tribesmen, and they charged forward on their camels. Nephi shielded his face from flying sand as the Al'Abr men sped past him, daggers raised. The chief gripped Isaabel tighter as he joined his men in the onslaught.

Fierce shouts were exchanged as the Al'Abr men reached the well. The leader of the caravan at the well threw sand in the air. Sulaim and his men slowed, apparently recognizing the other tribe. The other caravan wore head cloths wound tightly about their heads, their robes draped loosely about their shoulders.

Nephi stopped next to Lehi to watch. "They know each other," Lehi said, relief evident in his voice.

Zoram joined them. "If not, we would have seen bloodshed."

"And with our weapons seized, we would have had no defense," Nephi said.

"With or without weapons, we would not have been killed in this sort of raid," Zoram said, "though we may have become their slaves."

Nephi shuddered at the prospect. A few of the tribesmen rode back to usher them toward the well, directing them to couch their camels.

A stone fort stood over the well. Inside the fort, a narrow passage led to a rope ladder that descended into a cave containing placid water. Nephi watched as the tribesmen brought out goatskins heavy with water, then dumped it into leather buckets for the camels. After the camels had drunk their fill, the tribesmen took their turn, then spread rugs on the ground and ate dates from the palms.

Finally, the family members were able to drink the bitter water and pick their own dates.

The time crept by as the two tribes visited with each other. They fell into animated discussion, and many times the men pointed in the women's direction. Laughter could be heard, and Nephi felt his anxiety increase. Perhaps the tribesmen weren't planning on letting Isaabel go after all.

Eventually Sulaim approached Lehi. "Before we let you go, we want the women's jewelry," he said.

"You would take a woman's mohar?" Lehi asked.

"Perhaps your family should keep the bracelets, and we'll keep the woman." Sulaim's eyes flickered toward Isaabel. She sat huddled on a rug off to the side of the tribesmen. "Brides are replaceable."

"You shall have the jewelry," Lehi said. He crossed to his daughters-in-law and spoke quietly to them. Without hesitation, each of them removed their bracelets, anklets, and nose rings. They had been stripped of their visible status, but not of their dignity.

When Lehi returned to Sulaim and presented the jewelry, the chief turned the gold jewelry over in his hands. A couple of his men examined the craftsmanship.

Then the chief looked at Lehi and said, "You have earned protection under our name. Go in peace, my new friend. But remember, no more fires."

A short time later, the men from both tribes abandoned the well site. Isaabel was finally set free, and she flung herself into Nephi's arms. After a long moment, she made her way to her sisters, embracing each one. "Thank you for giving up your mohar," she whispered, her cheeks wet with tears. At last she came to Sariah.

"You have lost everything," Isaabel said.

"Nonsense," Sariah said. "We still have you, and that's what's important. Everything else can be replaced in the promised land."

Isaabel's voice choked with emotion. "Thank you for your sacrifice."

While the family waited at the oasis, Zoram, Sam, and Heth traveled back to the site of the buried valuables. When they reunited, from then on, the family traveled by night, lighting no fire and eating their meat raw. As they skirted the edge of the Sands, the men were able to hunt for ibex and gazelle in the rocky slopes on the south. By day, they set up the two tents that were saved from the fire and slept as best they could in the radiating heat. Their clothes had not been washed for months and had taken on the appearance of brown or faded black.

On the occasions they met other tribesmen, the valuables were immediately buried by Zoram and Sam, with Rebeka and Tamar standing in front of them to shield the flurry of activity from view of the approaching tribesmen. When Lehi threw sand up in the air, signaling peaceful intentions, the tribal leader would move forward. Once it was learned that they were under the protection of the Al'Abr tribe, they were left alone.

* * *

One afternoon, as the family slept through the heat of the afternoon, Elisheba found herself unable to rest. She left her mother's tent and walked several paces from camp. The sand shimmered beneath her feet as the sun beat down upon her head. She squinted north toward the high dunes and could see nothing but sand. Then she looked east and saw a dark shape against the golden landscape. *An oasis,* she realized.

Deciding not to wake the others, she grabbed two goatskins and headed away from camp. It would be a pleasant surprise when everyone woke to find fresh water to drink.

Some time later, Nephi woke up, soaked in sweat. With the dim light, he could tell that the sun had started to sink behind the dunes. Immediately, he sensed that Isaabel had left their tent. He rose and found her sitting just outside the entrance. "Have you been awake long?" he asked.

She shook her head, and Nephi saw the troubled look in her eyes. "What is it, Isa?"

Isaabel sighed with frustration. "My sisters have grown restless and have begun to murmur again."

He settled next to his wife. "My brothers will likely follow suit."

"Does your father know about the fire they started before the Al'Abr tribe captured us?" Isaabel asked.

"From what Sulaim said upon departure, I think he suspects it," Nephi said, then fell silent, thinking about the cycle of murmuring that lead to vocal complaints and usually ended up with a violent confrontation. *When will it change? When we arrive at the promised land?* he wondered. The other members of the family started to stir from their slumber. Anah and Puah exited their tents with their children and waved in their direction.

Then Sariah appeared and walked to where Nephi and Isaabel sat. "Have you seen Elisheba?" she asked.

"No," Isaabel said, standing. "Maybe she's visiting Tamar and playing with the baby."

"Let's check," Sariah said.

Nephi rose and watched the two women make their way to where Tamar and Sam slept. When they exited, Isaabel signaled that Elisheba wasn't in the tent. Scanning the camp, Nephi felt his stomach tighten. He could hear his wife and his mother calling for Elisheba.

Within a few moments, everyone had gathered and stood in a group, discussing the whereabouts of Elisheba.

Laman arched his back and let out a big yawn. "Are you sure she's not still sleeping in your tent, Mother?" He bit down on a dried date.

"Yes. And the goatskin bags are missing," Sariah said.

"What would she want with empty goatskins?" Laman asked. He looked at Nephi, as if he would have an answer.

Isaabel and Nephi traded glances. He motioned for Isaabel to join him. They walked away from the family toward the perimeter of camp. In the distance, Nephi pointed out a dark shape, possibly the faint outline of palms. He took a few steps, then looked down, noticing tracks. Kneeling, Nephi placed his hand on one.

"Are they Elisheba's?" Isaabel asked.

With a curt nod, Nephi said, "Call my parents."

Isaabel hurried back to Lehi and Sariah and brought them to Nephi.

"Look," Nephi said as Sariah and several family members joined him. He pointed at the trail. "I think she went to get water."

Sariah gazed in the direction the trail led, then cried out, "Why would she walk out there by herself?"

"Let's go," Laman said abruptly. He turned back to camp with Nephi close behind. Laman climbed on his camel, and Nephi untied the next fastest camel.

"I'm coming with you," a voice spoke behind them. It was Raamah.

Together, the three men urged their beasts forward, following the faint desert trail.

"Foolish girl," Laman muttered under his breath. "And it will be dark soon."

Nephi's mouth was set in a grim line, and Raamah continued to urge his camel into a quicker pace. As they neared the oasis, Nephi could see how sparse it was. There was probably not even a well—only a few measly palms grouped together.

The wind started to pick up around them as the temperature decreased. "There's no one here," Laman grumbled. "Are you sure those were human tracks and not of a wild camel?"

"Where else could she be?" Nephi asked.

Raamah ordered his camel to its knees, then climbed off. Without a word, he walked around the meager refuge. Then he stopped and bent to scoop something up.

"What is it?" Nephi asked, joining Raamah.

Handing over a piece of cloth to Nephi, Raamah let out a low whistle.

Nephi took one look at the torn linen swatch and knew it was Elisheba's. "She was here."

"So where is she now?" Laman demanded.

Again Raamah stooped, pushing something around with his stick. "Fresh camel droppings," he said in a somber voice. "Wherever she is, she's not alone."

Raamah walked several paces away, studying the ground, then returned to the men. "Here are your sister's footprints heading back toward camp," he said, pointing to the marks in the sand. Then he hesitated. "She was running when they caught up to her."

A shudder ran through Nephi's body. His fifteen-year-old sister had been abducted. "The sooner we tell Father, the better."

Laman nodded, his expression dark. "I'll go. I have the fastest animal." He climbed onto his camel and whipped it into a gallop.

Nephi watched Laman's frenzied pace back to camp, knowing his parents would be heartbroken. He swallowed at the lump in his throat and turned to speak with Raamah. But Raamah had left and walked a short distance away.

Following Raamah, Nephi saw that he walked next to a set of tracks. Several animal prints were visible, but no human tracks. "They carried her away on a horse," Raamah said softly, as if talking to himself. "But they had camels with them too, laden with heavy cargo—probably stolen goods."

"Stolen?" Nephi asked.

"Men who abduct a young girl would think nothing of raiding others for gain." Raamah crouched to the ground, touching several of the markings in the sand. "There were seven of them," he said, his voice grave. "We must hurry since this trail will be gone by morning."

"Then we have no time to lose," Nephi said. "Where's Laman?" He turned and looked impatiently toward camp. From his vantage point, he couldn't tell what activity was going on.

"It's nearly dark anyway," Raamah said. "So we'll have to follow the trail by the moonlight."

Nephi nodded his head. "We can do that, right?"

"It's not the darkness that I'm worried about. It's what will be happening to your sister in the meantime." Raamah lowered his voice. "It may already be too late."

Nephi pulled off his turban and ran his fingers through his hair. He felt nauseated. Elisheba had probably been captured some time ago, as it was. In the distance, he saw darkened silhouettes against the horizon. "Someone's coming," Nephi said.

The figures of Laman, Lehi, and Sam grew closer.

When the men arrived at the oasis, greetings were skipped. "How long?" Lehi asked. His face was bleak, his eyes sober.

Raamah answered. "Since late afternoon, we think."

"Sam," Lehi said, "stay here and wait for the others. Set up camp until our return. You, Heth, Zoram, Raamah, and Lemuel will protect the women and children."

"Of course," Sam said.

Lehi raised his staff into the air and slapped his camel's reins. Nephi and Laman followed behind their father, heading northeast. They spoke no words, each lost in his own thoughts of urgency. A few moments later, Nephi heard a rider coming up from behind. He turned to see Raamah closing in.

"I'm coming with you."

CHAPTER 19

Surely he hath borne our griefs, and carried our sorrows.
(Isaiah 53:4)

How long they had traveled, the men didn't know. Raamah walked in front, leading his camel. In the moonlight, he could see the outline of the trail better if he was close to the ground. The wind had picked up some time ago, but Raamah still insisted he could see the marks.

Nephi hoped the rest of the family would be protected in their absence. He hadn't had a chance to say good-bye to Isaabel. Remembering her words about the possible affection between Raamah and Elisheba, Nephi suspected that was the reason Raamah insisted on coming along.

In the darkness, the sand dunes appeared to stretch endlessly to the north, seemingly growing in height. Throughout the night, the only sound was the swirling wind, the occasional grunt from a camel, and the soft undertone of Lehi's continual prayers. Finally, as night began its slow awakening to day, Raamah stopped and raised his hand. He motioned for the others to climb off their camels and tie them together. When the men reached Raamah, he whispered, "Crouch low as we crest the top of this rise. I think I heard something."

Nephi fell into line behind Raamah, with Lehi and Laman bringing up the rear. The terrain rose, becoming thick with frankincense trees, and as the men neared the top of a cliff, they kept low to the ground. At first, it was difficult to make out the camp below in the early light, but soon the forms took shape. It was unlike anything Nephi had seen before. A village surrounded by palm groves stretched out before him. Cradled in the center was a collection of wells bordered by a large tent structure, royal in stature, with colored panels and an oversized entrance. Just then, the sun crowned the horizon, illuminating the clefts of limestone on the south side of the village. Rows of triliths marked tombs at the base of the limestone quarry. The triliths were composed of three stones that formed triangular pillars. Beyond the settlement, a savannah of green could be seen, dotted by grazing sheep and goats.

The tribesmen living there were not common nomads but men with obvious wealth and power—whether it was from hard work or plunder, Nephi did not know.

"Are you certain Elisheba is down there?" Laman whispered.

Raamah looked from Laman to Lehi. "I am."

Lehi agreed. "We cannot delay another moment."

The men returned to their animals and began the descent into the community.

As they neared the first outcroppings of the village, Nephi felt his heart hammer. *O Lord, please let us find Elisheba unharmed.* He squeezed his eyes shut briefly. *Soften the hearts of the people here so that we might negotiate her return.*

Sooner than Nephi expected, they were surrounded by a dozen men, their daggers glinting in the haze of dawn.

One shouted something in a dialect similar to the Minaeans.

Lehi replied in kind. "We've come for the girl."

"Girl?" the man closest to Nephi said.

"We are her family. She was captured and brought to your settlement," Nephi said in their dialect. The man was so close to Nephi that he could smell the stench of his body.

Rapid conversation exploded around them. Finally, a consensus was made. "We'll take you to our chief." The tribesmen disarmed them, took hold of their animals, and bound their hands.

The tribesmen led them through the settlement, and several curious onlookers appeared. Nephi saw a few figures that he realized were women. They wore dark clothing and head coverings, their faces covered in a dark material with holes cut for eyes.

Nephi saw that they were being led into the center of the village to the vast, royal-looking tent. After a hasty interchange at the entrance, they were led inside, where the guards made them kneel. Nephi glanced about their surroundings. Dried desert roots burned in metal-type bowls. The carcasses of wild animals—leopards, foxes, oryx—which had been preserved and stuffed to look lifelike, were arranged about the tent in formidable poses. The distinct smell of frankincense permeated the air. Stationed along the walls of the great tent were guards—faces unflinching, hands gripping the hilts of their long knives.

Several girls entered the room, and Nephi tried not to stare at them. They wore colorful tunics with chains of silver and shells wrapped about their waists and necks. Their cropped shoulder-length hair was plaited into hundreds of tresses.

Nephi noticed the other men looking in amazement at the girls. They were neither slaves nor concubines, Nephi realized, but the chief's harem. The girls settled onto pillows that surrounded a raised platform, keeping their gazes lowered as they waited.

Then the chief entered, obviously roused from sleep. His expression was sour as he adjusted his turban. With a twinge in his stomach, Nephi was reminded of Laban. The man's large belly hung over his belt, which held an ornamented dagger. His robe had a luxurious sheen, the narrow pinstripe pattern indicating a fine weave. Heavy gold necklaces and armbands adorned the chief's body, and several jewels encrusted his turban.

The chief exchanged harsh words with the men who had brought Nephi and the others to the tent. The leader sat with a grunt, his generous jowls settling against his embroidered collar. His thick eyebrows raised in appraisal as he studied the men kneeling before him.

Finally, Lehi was allowed to speak. "My daughter has been captured by your men at the oasis west of here. We have come to ask for her release," Lehi said, head bowed in respect.

"Your daughter was alone at the oasis?" the chief asked, bringing a jeweled hand to his beard.

"Yes," Lehi said. He raised his head along with his voice. "She wanted to fetch water for the family while we slept."

The chief remained silent for a moment, then instructed one of the girls to bring him wine. After he took a long sip from the silver cup, he said, "I have seen your daughter. She is young and strong and will bring many sons to my family."

Nephi felt a part of him sigh with relief—Elisheba was alive. But in the same instant another part of him filled with dread, the same feeling he had when Isaabel had to ride with Sulaim.

"Please," Lehi raised his watery eyes to meet the chief. "Take our camels and release the girl. You already have many girls to choose from."

The chief scoffed and pushed away one of the girls with his foot. "These are but ornaments. They are nothing to me. Their seed will be but slaves in my tribe." He leaned forward over his belly with effort. "This daughter of yours is Hebrew?"

"Yes," Lehi whispered.

"Speak louder, Hebrew," the chief said.

Lehi straightened his body and rose to his feet. Several of the guards took a step forward, but the chief raised his hand to ward them off.

"We are from the land of Jerusalem and travel through the wilderness under the protection of the Al'Abr tribe," Lehi said, his voice gaining strength. "We will do whatever is asked in return for my daughter, who is to remain unharmed . . . and untouched."

A low chuckle bubbled beneath the chief's abdomen, soon spilling forth into laughter. Then he stopped altogether and set his searing gaze on Lehi's thin figure. "We have a blood feud with the Al'Abr tribe, and the blood of my brother and nephew is on their hands. The Hebrew woman stays with me!" he said. "Take them away."

Immediately, the guards gripped Nephi, Laman, and Raamah. Lehi called out, "Have mercy on a traveling caravan. Allow us to work for her release. We are strong and our women can work like men . . ." Arms encircled his body, and Lehi was dragged to the tent door.

"Wait," the chief said, rising. The guards halted, Lehi still struggling in their grip. "How many in your family?"

"Sixteen adults, plus children," Lehi said, his breathing coming hard.

The chief walked toward Lehi. Then he moved around Nephi, Raamah, and Laman, assessing their physical features. "You Hebrews are large in stature."

"One of us could do the work of ten servants," Nephi said through clenched teeth.

Another belly laugh came from the chief. "I've no doubt a lad such as you could very well replace ten of my men."

Nephi clamped his jaw shut, biting back a retort. The chief walked around the men again. "Sixteen family members, yes?"

Lehi let out a gasping breath. "We have no valuables, but will trade our labor for the return of my daughter."

"You would offer yourselves as slaves?" the chief asked.

"*Servants* who will receive payment at the end of their service," Lehi said.

The chief stopped and eyed Lehi. "The Hebrew girl is worth at least one hundred camels in this land. It will take you many years to work enough to pay such a debt."

Lehi met the leader's gaze. "How many years if we all worked?" he asked.

Placing a hand on the hilt of his dagger, the chief said, "Five."

* * *

Nephi watched as his father was led away, his wrists and ankles tied like a lamb being taken to a sacrifice. "Take me instead," Nephi had told the tribal chief. But the chief had laughed and ordered Lehi to be removed from the tent.

Once again, the chief approached Nephi. "What do you say to this? Should I trade a young girl for an old man—an old man who has nothing to offer?"

Nephi winced at the words but would not let his apprehension show before the chief. "I want to see the girl. If she is alive and well, we'll make the agreement."

The chief hesitated, amusement in his eyes, then roared, "Bring the captive!"

Time crawled as the anticipation in Nephi's chest intensified. Several men left the tent and, what seemed like ages later, reentered. In their clutches, they held Elisheba. Her face was covered with a black cloth, like the women he'd seen on the way through the settlement. But Nephi could see enough of her eyes to know it was his sister.

Nearby, Raamah bolted forward, tearing away from the guards, only to be stopped with a dagger thrust at his throat.

The chief chuckled. "Interesting . . ." he said and crossed to Raamah. "Is she your concubine?"

Apparently, Raamah understood enough of the dialect, for he shook his head, eyes radiating with fury. Then Raamah leaned toward the chief and spat on the ground.

Taking a surprised step backward, the chief's face became serious. "I can see that there is enough desire in this family to have this girl returned to ensure five years of slave labor will be no problem." He turned to the guards. "Take these two men back to their caravan, then escort the entire family back to my settlement, where they will begin their servitude."

Raamah and Laman were hauled away. Nephi watched in stunned silence as they disappeared through the exit. To his left, Elisheba's shoulders sagged. Knowing that his sister couldn't interpret the dialect, Nephi said in Hebrew, "We will work to earn your freedom." Elisheba turned her head in Nephi's direction, nodding her head.

"Silence," the chief said, looking at Nephi. "You will not speak to my property, for until you have served the five years, she remains mine." He turned to the guards. "Throw him in with the old man."

* * *

Laman stopped struggling as the pressure on his neck increased. The two guards on each side of him held the ends of the rope that was tied around his neck. He and Raamah had been placed on horses, hands tied behind their backs, feet lashed to the animals. "You forgot to bind our eyes," Laman shouted, which prompted another painful tug at the rope around his neck.

Undeterred, Laman turned his head to see Raamah, who was traveling in the rear. "Raamah," he called. Another jerk. "How many guards can you fight?" With a sharp cry, Laman moved his head forward. A trickle of moisture traveled along his collarbone. Laman suspected it was blood, not perspiration. The rope's crude bristles chafed his neck with each jolt of the horse's stride. *Someone needs to show these raiders how to plait a decent rope.* In the brief glimpse of Raamah, Laman had counted at least four more guards—six in all.

Sand stinging his eyes, Laman could only see a short distance ahead, but he knew they neared the location where the rest of the family waited. He calculated the number of men, *Sam, Heth, Lemuel, and Zoram.* Along with him, Raamah, and the women, the raiders would be outnumbered. If only he could get a signal to the others before they were captured. Then once they had fought off the tribesmen, they could rescue Elisheba, Nephi, and Father. "Five years!" Laman said, not realizing he had spoken out loud until he felt the painful reminder of the rope. Just then, shouting rose around him. Someone was coming toward them on a camel.

Within a moment, Laman could make out Sam's form, then Heth, Lemuel, and Zoram's. By now, Laman knew, Sam would be able to see the predicament that he and Raamah were in. *They'll turn and flee,* Laman thought.

But Sam stopped and motioned for the others to halt. As the raiding party closed the distance, Sam's gaze remained steady. He tossed a handful of sand in the air, but when the gesture wasn't returned in kind, Sam withdrew his dagger.

With that prompt, a flurry of activity erupted among the raiders. Laman and Raamah were hauled off their horses and thrust to the ground. A sharp blade touched the back of Laman's neck as he struggled to breathe through a nose and mouthful of sand. Threats were issued by the tribesmen, none of which Laman could decipher but Sam seemed to understand.

A consensus appeared to be reached, and Laman and Raamah were pulled to their feet and forced to walk, following Sam and the others. At one point, Laman called to Sam, "They have imprisoned Nephi and Father too." The rope pulled at his neck.

As they approached the camp, Sam called out to the women, "Come out of your hiding places. We must cooperate with the raiders." Slowly, the women and children emerged from beneath rugs and tent panels, partially covered with sand. When Anah saw Laman, she cried out and started running toward him until Lemuel jumped in her path and restrained her. After a few harsh words, Anah retreated with the other women and followed the men's orders to pack their few belongings.

When the family was ready to depart, Laman and Raamah were loaded onto the horses once again. The rest of the family had to wear camel hobbles. The children rode upon the camels, though only Tamar was allowed to carry her child.

From his position, Laman could see the women as they endured the long march with awkward steps. The hours passed, and Laman found himself nodding off, only to be awakened by a sharp tug around his neck. No stops were made for food or drink. The raiders pressed on through the heat of the day until they eventually reached the settlement in the late afternoon.

Instead of an audience before the chieftain, the men were separated from the women and children. Laman strained against his ropes when Anah's cries sailed above the rest as they were led away. At that moment, fear replaced Laman's indignation as he wondered whether or not he'd see his wife again.

* * *

Landing on her back with a thud, Elisheba moaned, then drew her knees to her chest. The darkness closed in, pressing against her face. Where she'd been left, she wasn't sure. The ground was cold, damp, and smelly. Elisheba let out the breath she held and opened her eyes. *A cave.* No, she realized, it wasn't a cave, but a hole in the ground. And above her—she raised her eyes upward and noticed a sliver of light—a roof of some sort, probably palm fronds and caked mud, covered the opening.

A shiver coursed through her body. *Stand up,* she commanded herself, but her limbs refused to cooperate. A tear fell.

No. Don't pity yourself. Feeling disgust with her emotions, Elisheba forced her legs straight and sat up. "Nothing's broken," she said aloud, wiping at the falling tears. She pushed herself to her feet and stretched toward the opening of the hole. The palm fronds were out of reach. With her eyes adjusted to the dimness, she scoured the crude walls for something to support her climb. It was apparent that many had tried before her. Randomly dug holes had caved in, creating large gouges, useless for climbing leverage.

What if I dig earth from the walls and create a slope to climb out on? Elisheba thought desperately. Even as the idea entered her mind, she knew it would take time and tools, neither of which she had. She sank to the ground and lowered her head.

Suddenly the hole was filled with blinding light. Elisheba looked up just as two guards landed next to her. They tied a rope around her arms and waist and hauled her upward. Then the guards half-dragged her to a hut where they made her kneel.

A shrouded woman stepped forward, holding a dagger, and grabbed Elisheba's hair.

"Please spare my life," Elisheba cried out.

The woman brought the blade toward her and, with swift precision, lopped off a chunk of hair. Long, dark hair littered the ground as the woman sliced Elisheba's locks again and again until nothing was left save patches of stubble.

A sharp order issued by the woman sent the guards out of the hut. Stunned, Elisheba raised her hands to her head and felt the grizzled mess. Another shout from the woman made her drop her hands as the woman grabbed her elbow and forced her to stand. Two other veiled women entered, and they surrounded Elisheba, pulling at her clothes. With little effort, Elisheba understood that they wanted her to change into a coarse robe they had brought.

Moments later, hairless and dressed in the garments of a slave, Elisheba stepped out of the hut. The women escorted her through the village.

I'm still alive, Elisheba marveled. She tried to commit the passing landmarks to memory, but there were too many. Out of the corner of her eye, she scanned the men. None looked familiar. No one seemed to pay attention to her. Perhaps newly inducted slaves were a common occurrence in this region.

The women leading her stopped and shoved her through a low-hanging entrance. Elisheba straightened on the other side and saw that she was in a tent that far exceeded any luxuries she'd seen in the wilderness—and in Jerusalem. Carved ivory pieces adorned tables that were inlaid with jewels. Soft music wafted from a curtained section of the tent, accompanied by the strong odor of frankincense.

A woman stepped from behind a drape and approached Elisheba. The woman was dressed in fine linen, dyed a deep purple, and her wrists and exposed ankles displayed several gold bracelets. But it was the color of her skin that amazed Elisheba—it was as pale as butter. As the woman drew closer, Elisheba could see the moisture beaded upon her forehead.

"Hadi," the woman said in a soft voice touching her chest, then pointed to Elisheba.

"Eli-she-ba," Elisheba said slowly.

The woman called Hadi wrinkled her nose. She walked around Elisheba, touching the coarse garment. "Aqal." The woman stopped in front of Elisheba and touched her shoulder. "Aqal," she said again.

Elisheba nodded, understanding. She'd just been given a new name.

Hadi touched Elisheba's cheeks and bent her head forward. She gazed at the shorn hair for a moment then dropped her hands. "Minaean?"

Shaking her head, Elisheba said, "Hebrew."

Repeating the word with a frown, Hadi took a step back. She turned to the women who had brought Elisheba and ordered them out of the tent. Then Hadi led her to a curtained-off room.

The section was no wider than Elisheba's height. A mat and a rug were on the floor. With a few words and a lot of gesturing from Hadi, Elisheba realized that it was to be her sleeping place.

Hadi took her arm and led her throughout the rest of the rooms, motioning to Elisheba the chores that would be hers.

That night, as Elisheba lay in relative comfort on her mat, she prayed for her family, that they might be living in similar circumstances and spared cruelty. She prayed for their deliverance to be swift. Then she prayed that she might learn to understand her new mistress and would be treated with kindness. Her heart twisted as she paused, thinking of what might happen to a young girl who caught the eye of the chieftain. *Please, O Lord, protect my virtue so that I may be pure upon my day of marriage.* As her mind finally drifted into sleep, the last image she saw was of Raamah being hauled out of the chief's tent.

* * *

Isaabel crouched at the entrance of the small structure. The women had been cordoned off into a hut of some sort. The walls were made of stone and the roof of palm fronds and baked mud that kept out the worst of the heat. Because of the size of the room, there was not enough space for everyone to leave their bedrolls spread out during the day. This morning, Tamar and Zillah had the duty of rolling and stacking all the sleeping mats to make room for the children to play.

Each of them had been assigned different tasks. Sariah and Bashemath were put in charge of tending to the children and carrying water. It proved a dubious task to accomplish both, so Sariah and Bashemath traded off between the morning and afternoon. So far their taskmaster hadn't complained.

Anah, Puah, and Rebeka worked in the chief's cooking rooms. Before the sun rose, they had to begin preparing food for the chief and his household. Since they were not allowed to eat the food they prepared, they returned long after dark, weary and hungry. Sariah saved a portion of the other women's allotment each day for them.

Isaabel pulled her mantle about her while she watched the activities outside; it was not the mantle that she had arrived in, but one made of coarse, black cloth—a slave's garment. After Anah's first day in the cooking room, she had told her sisters to wear the black mask for their own protection. The chief was known to add a slave or two to his harem for short periods.

The information proved to be crucial since a few weeks after arriving at the Mudhail settlement, Isaabel and Tamar were reassigned from collecting camel dung to work in the weaver's hut. At first, Isaabel thought she and Tamar were fortunate in their new chore. But working all day with boiling water and burning dyes, then weaving under the intense heat of the fires among throngs of flies soon destroyed the savor.

Dinah, Tiras, and Jochebed were given the task of collecting the dried camel dung to be used for fire fuel.

"Have the men passed by?" Tamar asked, joining Isaabel at the hut entrance.

"Not yet," Isaabel whispered. Lehi would not be among his sons or the other men when they passed by the women's hut on their way to work. Since his first encounter with Chief bin Kabina, Lehi had remained imprisoned. Rebeka had once taken food to the prisoners and had seen him, but no other contact had been made. None of them had seen Elisheba. With each passing day, Isaabel could see the toll it took on Sariah's demeanor. And each hour, the term of five years seem to stretch endlessly before her.

"They're coming," Tamar said.

Isaabel followed her sister's glance and saw the dark forms approaching. There would be no time for them to stop. All of their movements were watched by the guards stationed throughout the slave quarters. Isaabel was able to pick out Nephi fairly easily among the men. She saw him shift his position in line so that he would be able to pass close by.

Just as Nephi approached, Isaabel slipped out to meet him. "Is everyone well?" he asked.

Nodding, Isaabel said, "Yes, but I am sick."

Nephi kept his gaze forward as Isaabel walked alongside him. "What's wrong?"

"Every morning I lose my breakfast."

He looked sharply at her. "Your . . ." Nephi grinned. "Are you sure?"

"Of course," Isaabel said, smiling back. "I suspected before we were brought to Mudhail, but now I am sure of it."

Nephi picked her up and spun her around.

"Move, Nephi," Lemuel said behind them. "The guard will see us."

"Go!" Laman shoved Nephi forward.

Isaabel scampered back to the hut where Tamar was keeping a lookout. "Are you crazy?" Tamar asked.

"If being with child means I am crazy, then, yes."

Tamar's eyes widened, but Isaabel didn't give her time to respond. She hurried into the hut to get ready for a day of dyeing cloth.

* * *

Elisheba watched Raamah from the market stall as she went through the motions of selecting vegetables. For the past several weeks, Raamah and the other men had been constructing a tower near the marketplace. The work was grueling underneath the brilliant sun, compounded by the taskmasters who often shouted threats. From her vantage point, Elisheba could see no reason for Raamah to suffer reprimand, although every few days, she witnessed Laman erupt into a scuffle with one of the other slaves.

But it was Raamah whom she watched, wondering what his thoughts were and how he felt about serving as a slave because of her. Did he think it was worth it? The first day she had spied the men, she withdrew quickly so that she wouldn't be recognized. On subsequent visits to the market, she wore a veil. Out of habit, she reached up to touch her short hair. *Why don't I want them to recognize me?* She felt her eyes smart. The pain and guilt ran deep, and she couldn't bear the thought of seeing it reflected in her family's eyes.

"Aqal!" a voice called. Elisheba turned in the direction of the sound and saw Hadi motioning to her. She chose vegetables from the meager supply and hurried to her mistress's side. Resisting the urge to take a final backward glance toward the tower, Elisheba followed Hadi home.

The remainder of the afternoon, Elisheba went about her usual chores of cleaning the tent floor, cultivating the garden of herbs that Hadi kept, and preparing meals. As the sun began its descent, she made her final trip of the day to fetch water. On her way to the well, she noticed a group of women hurrying away. They called out something to her, but she didn't understand their words.

As Elisheba lowered the goatskin into the deserted well, someone grabbed her from behind. A firm hand clamped over her mouth, preventing her from screaming.

"Quiet," came a gruff voice. The man dragged her to a clump of palms and turned her to face him.

"Laman," she cried.

"Shh," he said.

Another figure emerged. Raamah. If Elisheba's heart hadn't pounded before, it did now, and if Raamah was startled at her change in appearance, his expression gave no indication.

"Why are you here?" Elisheba asked as soon as she caught her breath.

"We are stealing you back," Laman said in a harsh whisper.

Elisheba glanced at Raamah, who met her gaze with confidence. "But how did you find me?"

"Even your veil couldn't conceal your identity," Raamah said. He took a step forward. "We followed you from the marketplace."

"We must make haste," Laman interrupted, looking from one to the other.

"Wait," Elisheba said as Laman grabbed her arm. "What about the others?"

"When they see that we've rescued you, they'll follow," Laman said. He glanced at Raamah. "Do you see anyone out there?"

Raamah moved away, then came back, shaking his head. "No one."

Elisheba pulled away from Laman. "And Father? He's still imprisoned."

With a sigh, Laman said, "Do you want to be freed or not? Don't tell me you like being a slave."

"No, I—" Elisheba dropped her gaze. "We can't leave Father behind . . . He refused to leave me."

Laman's jaw worked in frustration. "Father has lived many years," he began, then seemed to change his mind. "Once we are clear of the settlement, Raamah and I will return and collect Father. It will be dangerous, but I know we'll be successful." He tugged at Elisheba's arm again. "We must leave. *Now.*"

"I can't," Elisheba said, her voice quavering. In her heart, she couldn't believe her brother's words. "The risk is too great. You and Raamah leave if you must." She looked at Raamah, his gaze seemed to penetrate through her. "I can't let everyone take such a chance for me."

Fists clenched, Laman spoke. "It's not just for *you,* sister, it's for *us.* Shopping at the market each day is something that you might enjoy, but for the rest of us," he paused, "we aren't living in a nice tent with privileges from the chief."

"I don't have privileges," Elisheba said. "I work from dawn to—"

"Perhaps if you gave the chief what he wanted, *Father* would be released, and we could all go free," Laman said.

Elisheba's mouth dropped open. Laman's words stung her very soul. She felt the tears brimming. "How can you make such a request?"

Laman took a step forward and brought his face close to hers. "You are selfish and ungrateful—"

Stepping between them, Raamah blocked Laman. "She's right. Slavery may be degrading, but I will not stand for Elisheba to submit herself to the chief's will." Raamah stared at him until Laman's shoulders dropped. Raamah turned and touched Elisheba's sleeve. "You have humbled me, unlike any period of bondage could." He gazed into her eyes for a moment, then turned and strode away.

Please don't leave, Elisheba thought. But how could she ask him to stay? They would be caught and punished. Laman reached for a low-hanging branch and tore it down, throwing one last glare at his sister.

As her throat constricted, Elisheba turned and ran away from the palms, past the well, until she reached Hadi's tent. It was all she could do to keep from sobbing before reaching her bedroll.

CHAPTER 20

Yea, though I walk through the valley of the shadow of death, I will fear no evil: for thou art with me.
(PSALM 23:4)

"Thank you," Isaabel told the young slave girl who had brought the desert shrub, the juice of which made the russet-brown dye. The girl's skin was the color of frankincense, and she didn't speak any form of the Mudhail dialect, a language that Isaabel was trying to learn herself. Isaabel put the shrub into a woven basket lined up next to the others. Plants and roots such as henna and saffron that were used to produce different colors of dye filled the baskets.

From across the room, she could see Tamar stoking the fire with the snakelike roots of heliotrope kindling. Tamar raised her head and met Isaabel's gaze. Even through the eyeholes of her face covering, Isaabel could tell Tamar smiled at her.

Perhaps they would be able to exchange a few whispered words while they worked. They were not allowed to speak to each other, and it was difficult to do so since a guard watched them as they worked. Isaabel glanced at the guard, who sat on a stool made of woven palms and covered with animal hide. Hanging from his wide waistband was a curved dagger that he continually kept his hand on. Perspiration coated his face and body, which caused the indigo dye from his clothing to stain his arms and chest. But his one good eye was closed.

With the guard asleep, Isaabel made her way to where Tamar crouched before the fire. "How are you feeling?" Tamar asked.

Isaabel's eyes flitted toward the guard before she answered. "Today is a good day, but last night I felt the sickness." As if on cue, nausea welled up from her stomach. "Like now." She brought a hand to her mouth.

Tamar placed a hand on her arm. "Take deep breaths. It will pass."

Looking at Tamar's hand, Isaabel felt her heart sink. Her sister's arm was covered with a fitted black cloth that extended to her hands, so that only the tips of her fingers showed. It had been Anah's recommendation that they cover their arms and hands too so that the guards wouldn't be able to tell how old they were. Isaabel was grateful for the looseness of the tunic she wore that would hide her full belly. The men and women slaves were not allowed to interact with each other, and if a guard noticed she was with child, she would be punished. Worry rose within Isaabel as she wondered how Tamar would be able to cover her absence when the baby was born.

A commotion arose outside, and shouts reverberated into the hut. Isaabel moved away from Tamar immediately. The guard's eye flew open, and he stumbled to the entrance, joining in the yelling. The only word that Isaabel could make out was "scorpion."

Isaabel made her way to the door just as two tribesmen carrying a lifeless body passed by. With a quickening pulse, she realized it was Sariah. "Tamar," she whispered. When Tamar reached her side, she said, "Sariah has been stung by a scorpion. We must go to her."

The two women slipped out of the hut and, from a distance, followed the men who carried their mother-in-law. With the added commotion, they were not stopped or questioned. They waited as the guards placed her inside the hut, and instantly they heard a wail come from Bashemath within the mud walls. When the tribesmen left, Isaabel and Tamar went inside.

"Sariah's dead," Bashemath said, her voice hysterical, when she saw her daughters.

Isaabel knelt by Sariah's side and listened for breathing. "She's alive."

With a cry, Bashemath said, "Praise God." She reached for Tamar, clinging to her. "Do you think she will survive?"

Tamar wrapped an arm about her mother. "I don't know."

"Sariah," Isaabel whispered close to her ear. "Can you hear me?"

A slight move of her head gave Isaabel hope. "Can you speak? Tell me what color the scorpion was."

The movement on Sariah's lips was barely imperceptible. But Isaabel heard the word she spoke.

Bashemath leaned over to Isaabel, "You'd better tell Lehi."

With a nod, Isaabel left Bashemath and stepped out of the hut where Sariah lay. Tell Lehi? *Impossible.* As a female slave, she would not be allowed to approach the chief, let alone expect him to release Lehi at her request. But she had seen Sariah's pale face, still body, and shallow breaths. She had to find where the men worked. Some days the men spent hunting and others they labored constructing shelters. One of them might be able to gain an audience with the chief. Isaabel knew that she couldn't dodge the guards, so she decided to walk straight through the slave quarters as if she were on an errand.

In her heart, she prayed for Sariah, then for Lehi, then for herself. As she neared the gates that exited the slave quarters, she slowed. The guards would never let her through, even if they could understand her stilted attempt at their dialect. To her right, several goats grazed on a few clumps of grass between two huts. She grabbed one and ushered it along with a stick. When she reached the gates, she said, "Cooking Room."

One of the guards nodded and let her through. She walked as quickly as possible without drawing attention and soon found herself outside the walls of the slave quarters. The sight before her was refreshing. Graceful palms lined the dusty streets as a few stray goats ran freely. Women, covered from head to toe, hurried along in their errands. Children ran about, chasing the animals and playing games with sticks and rocks. Isaabel continued prodding the goat as her eyes strained for any sign of her brothers or brothers-in-law.

Eventually she arrived at the immense cooking rooms where Anah, Puah, and Rebeka worked. She hoped that Anah might have a plan to get the message to the men.

"What are you doing here?" a voice spoke behind her.

Isaabel turned to see a willowy figure and narrow eyes—unmistakably Rebeka's. Suddenly the emotion welled up inside her. "It's Sariah," Isaabel said. "She's been stung by a scorpion."

With a gasp, Rebeka grabbed her arm. "How bad is it?"

"She's barely breathing," Isaabel said.

"Wait here," Rebeka said. "I'll tell the others."

Seconds later, Isaabel was surrounded by her sisters, who were quickly donning their veils.

"Was it poisonous?" Anah asked.

"Yes," Isaabel said, lifting her face covering. "Mother told me to tell Lehi."

Puah covered her mouth. "Lehi? How are we to get him out of confinement?"

"That's why I came here. I need to find our husbands," Isaabel whispered.

Another slave came out of the cooking room. Anah bent over the goat, pretending to inspect it. Puah spoke loudly. "This one looks too lean for the chief."

When the slave was out of earshot, Anah said, "They are in the quarry."

"Where is that?" Isaabel asked.

"On the south side," Anah said. "Take the goat and you'll be fine."

"Wait," Rebeka said. She disappeared into the cooking room, then returned with a loaf of bread. "Take this to them."

Without further delay, Isaabel left her sisters and headed south, urging the goat to move faster. The bread was still hot, and she felt its warmth hidden beneath her arm. She could be punished just for having the bread, let alone abandoning the weaving room. No other women were in the streets, and she heard several men hiss at her. Each time it made her skin crawl. Married or not, in this place, she was not protected by the Law of Moses.

Isaabel reached the marketplace, and seeing no way to go around it, she headed through the center. She felt very conspicuous, but no one seemed to pay any special attention to her. Women dressed in fine linen browsed through the wares while their slaves carried the purchases in baskets. Isaabel was shocked to see the display of jewelry that the women wore, with their hair cropped short, braided, and adorned with silken threads. She recognized some of the cloth that she and Tamar had dyed themselves. The slaves were young girls, heads uncovered, wearing russet-colored tunics. The colors of their skin ranged from fair to dark as the night sky.

A hand touched her arm, but Isaabel brushed past it. Again the pressure came. Isaabel turned. She stared at the person before her—it was Elisheba. Her long dark hair had been cut short and plaited. She wore a slave's tunic and carried a woven basket laden with assorted roots. But it was her eyes that had changed the most. The lighthearted innocence was subdued, replaced by trepidation and remorse.

"Elishe—" Isaabel began.

Elisheba brought her finger to her lips. "My woman will notice." She motioned with her head to a woman who was bartering several paces away with a perfume merchant.

"Your mother has been stung by a scorpion," Isaabel blurted out, then covered her mouth.

Shock registered on Elisheba's face. "Is she all right?"

When Isaabel shook her head, Elisheba's eyes welled with tears. "I must find a way to help her. It's my fault she has suffered this affliction." She bit her lower lip.

"Aqal," a voice commanded.

Elisheba spun on her heels and disappeared before Isaabel could answer.

Continuing through the marketplace, Isaabel tried to see if she could spot Elisheba once again. But when she reached the outskirts of the settlement, she gave up hope of trying to discover where Elisheba could possibly be.

Isaabel arrived at the quarry, and from a distance, she watched the men as they worked, cutting limestone and hauling it down a slope. They were heavily guarded since they worked out in the open and had a greater chance of fleeing. If only she could get Nephi's or Sam's attention. Just then, one of the guards shouted for water. Out of a hut made from grass mats, a female slave hurried forward with a goatskin. She offered the guards a drink, then left it in the sand for the slaves to fight over.

When the work commenced, Isaabel made her way to the hut. Inside, it was cool and dark, but a dank smell rose to her nostrils. Isaabel ignored the stench and smiled at the girl. The female slave drew back in the corner, her eyes wide with fear.

Isaabel held out the loaf of bread and took a slow step toward her. The girl watched her for a moment, then moved slightly forward. Isaabel could almost hear the girl's desire for the bread. The girl took another hesitant step, then snatched the bread, biting into it eagerly. The gnawing in Isaabel's stomach grew as she watched the slave eat.

Not long after, another shout was heard for water. Isaabel held out her hand, indicating that she would take the water. Head down, she exited the hut, goatskin in tow. After serving the guards, she waited for the slaves to approach. Nephi was among them. "Sariah has been stung by a scorpion," Isaabel whispered.

Nephi looked at her, stunned. "Isaabel?" After he recovered from his surprise, he asked, "Was the scorpion poisonous?"

"Yes, and my mother said to bring Lehi," Isaabel said.

The expression on Nephi's face tightened. "Return to the grass hut without stopping," he said.

Isaabel turned away, obeying Nephi's words, and walked toward the hut. Before she reached it, she heard shouts go up around her. She looked over her shoulder and saw Nephi wrestled to the ground by several guards. Then he was dragged from the quarry.

* * *

Nephi felt his face plow into the ground as something struck him from behind. He was thankful that a rug covered the dirt and rocks, but the pain was severe nevertheless. Chief bin Kabina had been laughing at something when the guards entered his tent, but he stopped when he saw the blood-streaked face of the Hebrew.

"What is this?" the chief demanded.

"An escapee," one of the guards replied.

"No," Nephi said in a strangled voice. "I just wanted an audience with you." He rose to all fours. "And this was the only way."

The chief stared at him, then started to chuckle, his great belly vibrating. "Because of your obstinance, I will listen to what you have to say . . . Hebrew."

"My mother has been stung by a poisonous scorpion," Nephi began.

The chief's expression was blank.

"Because her life is in danger, I would like to request that my father be allowed to visit her bedside."

"Your father? You mean the old man?" bin Kabina asked. He waved away the cup of wine offered by one of his concubines. "This is a great favor you ask."

"We have fulfilled our duties without complaint for many weeks now," Nephi said, keeping his gaze lowered. "And . . ." He paused. "If you release him, he could work with the rest of us."

The chief stroked his beard, his jeweled hands glittering in the light. "You are a young man of intelligence and . . . persuasion." His smile was condescending. "I could use someone to herd the camels." He bellowed another round of laughter.

The joke fell flat with Nephi. He knew that desert camels didn't need a herdsman, since they were hobbled day and night unless working. Holding his breath, Nephi silently pled with the Lord to soften the chief's heart.

"Perhaps you would be willing to take his place," bin Kabina said, studying Nephi.

Without hesitation, Nephi said, "I will."

The chief waved his hand. "Release him and the old man. Let them say their good-byes to the unfortunate woman. I don't have time to deal with insignificant slaves today." He leaned back into the cushions. "Bring me a fresh cup of wine."

The guards jumped into action and led Nephi outside. Soon Lehi was brought to where Nephi waited, and the two men embraced. Lehi's face had grown gaunt in the past weeks, and his beard was snarled. His thin frame looked as if it could break. It pained Nephi to see his father in such a condition.

"It's a miracle," Lehi said, his cheeks wet with tears.

"It's Mother," Nephi said. "She's been stung by a scorpion."

Lehi brought his hand to his heart. "No."

The guards prodded Lehi and Nephi forward. Father and son gripped each other's arms as they hurried to the slave quarters. Once they entered the gate, Lehi drew in a breath. "This is where you've been living?"

"I'm sure it's better than your conditions," Nephi said.

With a shake of his head, Lehi said, "Not much."

When they reached the women's hut, Nephi called into the dark entrance.

Bashemath appeared. Upon seeing the arrivals, her wailing started again. The men followed her inside, and Lehi sank to the floor next to his wife. Nephi's eyes met Isaabel's, and in an instant, he took her into his arms. Then he too knelt by his mother's side.

"Sariah," Lehi said.

"It's no use," Bashemath cried. "She won't open her eyes."

Isaabel left her husband and took Bashemath's arm, gently leading her outside.

With trembling fingers, Lehi placed his hands on his wife's head. "O Lord," he said. "Spare this righteous woman from the poison which has entered her veins." His voice broke as he tried to catch his breath. "She is the soul of our family. Without her, our hearts would be destitute. O Lord, sustain her, place Thy blessing upon her. Salvation belongeth unto Thee. Amen."

Nephi took his mother's hand, which was cold and limp. Someone entered the room behind them, and Nephi turned, expecting to see Isaabel.

A petite woman stood in the doorway. She was veiled, and her fine clothing betrayed her status—she was one of the chief's wives.

The woman drew forward and introduced herself. "I am Hadi, and I've come to help the sick one." She removed a pouch from her waist and knelt beside Sariah. "Where was she stung?"

"Her foot," Lehi replied in Hadi's language. "Did the chief send you?"

"No, my Hebrew slave told me." She gently applied a sour-odored salve to Sariah's foot. A moan came from Sariah's lips, but she didn't open her eyes.

"Elisheba?" Lehi asked.

The woman continued rubbing Sariah's foot, with each stroke deepening the massage. "I call her Aqal."

Lehi rocked back on his heels and looked at Nephi, his eyes incredulous.

"Elisheba . . . Aqal . . . is well?" Nephi asked.

"She works hard and is loyal, and for that reason I agreed to help her mother." Hadi replaced the medicine into her pouch. "The salve I put on her is ground from the flower and fruit of the rubus plant." She stood and removed a small leather bag from her pouch. "This is an ointment made from the resin of the storax tree. Rub it onto her foot and ankle several times a day. In one day's time, the swelling should lessen, and she will be coherent. She is lucky she was stung in the thick part of her heel. Less poison was able to enter."

Hadi walked to the door, stopped, and looked around. "This hut is deplorable."

Nephi rose to follow her. "This is the women and children's hut, and they have little room to move." He paused. "My wife is with child and sleeps among filth not fit for a goat."

Hadi turned and looked at Nephi. "Aqal must be of great worth to your family."

Lowering his voice, Nephi said, "She is my sister."

* * *

Lehi stayed by his wife's side throughout the first night. With the visit of Hadi, over the next days, their status in the slave quarters was elevated. Each day, boiled barley and fresh goat's milk was brought to the hut. At first, Lehi could only coax Sariah to drink goat's milk, but with the passing time, she grew stronger and was able to eat. Additional huts were assigned to their family, and the husbands and wives were able to live together. Grass mats were given to them for their doorways so that the goats stopped wandering in and out. This relieved them of the many bites they had endured from the ticks the goats carried in their hair.

Several days later, Hadi paid another visit. She once again applied the rubus salve and massaged Sariah's foot. This time Sariah was coherent enough to thank the woman. "My daughter is well?" Sariah asked.

Nodding, Hadi said, "She is sorry that you have chosen to work for her freedom."

"We would do the same for any of our children," Sariah said quietly.

"You have many sons, and yet you value this daughter of yours," Hadi said. "Chief bin Kabina is very curious about your Hebrew customs. He asks me why you travel in this desert, why you leave your home."

From the corner where he sat, Lehi cleared his throat. "Tell your noble chief that if he wishes to know more, I will teach him."

* * *

Isaabel lay awake in the darkness. Her feet were cold, but that was not why she couldn't sleep. A deep persistent ache in her back kept her alert. Nephi slept next to her, exhausted from his days filled with hard labor, followed by discussions of Hebrew traditions with Lehi and Chief bin Kabina. Nephi had told her how interesting the chief thought their beliefs were, to sacrifice animals according to the Law of Moses and to only marry one woman with no concubines. The chief was also fascinated with the imminent destruction of Jerusalem, something he would enjoy participating in himself.

The chief did not think the Hebrews in Jerusalem seemed very wicked. "In a land of one government, there is bound to be unrest," bin Kabina told Nephi. "In our land, where everyone answers to their own tribal leader, there is peace." And when

Lehi told him about the promised land, the chief had decided that he too would like to travel to the promised land.

"Is he sincere?" Isabel asked Nephi.

"I think if he were, we would not still be slaves," Nephi had said.

My child will be born into slavery, Isaabel thought with a grimace. She rolled onto her back with a groan, but her discomfort increased with the new position. She moved to her side again and placed her hand on her belly, receiving a sound kick in return from the infant within. Over the past few months, her workload had been reduced a bit, and for that she was grateful, knowing it was due to Hadi's request. She was required to weave only, something she could do while sitting.

The deep ache returned, this time intensifying until she felt like crying out. Involuntarily she reached for Nephi's arm.

His eyes flew open. "What is it?"

"I don't know," she whispered. "I'm feeling pain."

Nephi placed his hand on Isaabel's belly as she squeezed her eyes shut.

After several deep breaths, Isaabel said, "I think you should fetch your mother."

Nephi rose in the darkness, careful not to wake the others in the hut, and disappeared through the door.

When Nephi left, Isaabel closed her eyes and began to pray. She was dimly aware that Sariah and Bashemath had arrived and attended her as she fought through each wave of pain and nausea. That was what surprised her most, the nausea. *Wasn't the pain of the cramping enough?*

With each ebbing, Isaabel sighed with relief as she had a few moments to regain her strength and focus. It was like climbing a mountain, she decided. The deep ache built until it reached its peak, then descended and became bearable again. With each pain, she squeezed her eyes shut. Above her, Sariah hummed and applied compresses on her forehead. Her mother rubbed her legs and massaged her back.

I will soon see my child, Isaabel realized. The thought kept her sane during the next several cycles. Then no intelligible thought could infiltrate through Isaabel's haze of agony. She had no control over her body and the descending baby. Isaabel was not herself, but an instrument bringing forth life, even if it meant her death. As she succumbed heart and soul to the excruciating ordeal of bearing down, her mind crossed the threshold into another world.

It was as if she were present during another woman's birth. Obediently, her body followed Sariah's instructions, her mind not comprehending. She was not the one crouched, clawing at the ground, shouting those words. And only when she heard the cry of an infant did the surrealness pass, and in its place came total euphoria.

* * *

"Isa," Nephi whispered.

Opening her eyes, Isaabel took a moment to focus on her husband and remember. Then she rewarded him with a smile.

"He is beautiful, like his mother," Nephi said.

Lifting her head, Isaabel looked at the tiny babe in Nephi's arms.

Nephi leaned over and kissed her cheek. "Thank you for having a short labor. I didn't have to worry so long."

Isaabel scrunched her nose. "Every moment was like an eternity."

"For me too." Nephi looked at her with tenderness. "Mother says you should rest as much as possible. So close your eyes, and I'll hold the baby."

Not needing further encouragement, Isaabel fell into an easy slumber, her dreams light and peaceful. The burden of her belly was gone, and the afterbirth pains insignificant.

The next few days, Nephi stayed by her side, caring for the baby, annoying Bashemath and Sariah. Isaabel was surprised that he hadn't been ordered back to work.

"That husband of yours has found favor with the chief," Bashemath told Isaabel. "Why, I asked, why can't he reduce our years of service?"

"Lehi gave the chief our word," Sariah said from the other side of the room where she fed Jacob. "At least he's allowing us to perform our religious sacrifices now."

Nephi rose and smiled at Bashemath. "The Lord is mindful of us and has made us strong enough to bear our burdens. If the Lord sees fit to soften bin Kabina's heart to reduce our servitude, then so be it. But, until then, I rejoice in having a new son and a healthy wife." He strode out of the hut.

Bashemath clucked her tongue at his departure. "He's just like his father," she said with amusement. She looked at Isaabel. "We have been blessed, daughter. You should be grateful for a husband such as Nephi."

"I am," Isaabel said softly. "Believe me, I am."

CHAPTER 21

Stand fast therefore in the liberty wherewith Christ hath made us free, and be not entangled again with the yoke of bondage.
(GALATIANS 5:1)

The five years at the Mudhail settlement elapsed gradually, yet near the end, it seemed that they had passed swiftly. Lehi spent one of the last afternoons in the presence of Chief bin Kabina.

"You have served your time well," the chief said. He took Lehi into his confidence more often than some of his advisors. "One more year of work, and I will give you a place in the community."

Lehi had often been challenged in his conversations with the chief, who was eager to learn and quick to argue. "And you are welcome to join us on our journey to the promised land."

"Yes, this promised land of yours that you speak of—a land of inheritance for your sons." The chief stroked his beard. "I would like to see your grandson again before you leave."

"Of course," Lehi said, knowing he referred to Nephi's four-year-old, Aaron. His posterity continued to grow as Rebeka gave birth to a daughter, Deborah, two years before, and Anah and Puah had young babies, Canaan and Delilah, with Tamar newly expecting. And Sariah was with child again.

"We'll have the camels returned to you in three days. On the morning of the fourth, your daughter will be returned." Bin Kabina paused. "The belongings you arrived with have not been touched. And," the chief continued, "you will find gifts of date palm wine, nuts, spices, and a variety of herbs. And, a sheep— for your next Passover."

Lehi bowed his head, emotion overcoming him. "We are grateful for your kindness."

Chief bin Kabina rose and moved to Lehi's side, placing a hand on Lehi's shoulder. The guards around the room stiffened at the sight of contact between their master and a slave. But the chief ignored them. He kissed Lehi on each cheek and said, "Peace be upon you."

"On you be peace," Lehi replied. He drew back in respect and bowed his head.

"Bring the Hebrew girl," the chief commanded.

Lehi snapped his head up, his gaze focused on the curtain behind the chief. Soon a woman entered the room. Her head uncovered, hair short and plaited. A multicolored tunic was wrapped about her body, and a single gold bracelet adorned her arm.

"Father," Elisheba said.

Not daring to believe that this mature woman was his daughter, Lehi stood in place and stared. But her voice was unmistakable. "You are well," Lehi said, his voice cracking.

"And you," Elisheba said. Without waiting another instant, she ran to him and threw her arms around his neck. "I've missed you."

Lehi wrapped his trembling arms about her and wept.

* * *

Time in the desert is measured neither by day nor week. For Isaabel, it was simply one season or the next: summer or winter.

There was really little difference to the untrained Hebrew eye, but to the Bedouin, winter meant wind from the northeast, and summer meant wind from the southwest. And the family of Lehi had become experienced Bedu.

After returning to the site just outside of Mudhail where the family had buried the brass plates and other valuables five years before, the family traveled in an easterly direction. No longer did they press through the wilderness with impatience; their hearts and bodies had been broken, humbled, and uplifted. They were at one with each other, with God, and with the earth. Each bush, each tree, and each well was cherished. Their camels' every need was met, for camels were the only way to survive in the desert.

With vitality and vigor, Isabel walked next to her favorite camel—it was the color of honey, matching the surrounding terrain. She moved with confidence as she watched her young son thrive and grow. Her heart was at peace. Each day she thanked the Lord for giving her such a strong son and for being able to endure the birthing process. And she knew that if she was faced with it a second time, she would do so without fear. The land had become part of her and part of her young son, who was nearly five. He followed his uncle, Jacob, like a lamb to its shepherd.

Jacob and Aaron walked next to her, their sun-browned hands in hers. Isaabel gazed at the two boys with a smile. Jacob reminded Isaabel so much of Sam—the familiar curly mop of hair, round face, and wide-set eyes. Jacob had taken a liking to the camels, and often his older brothers called him "camel boy." His nature was complacent, opposite of Aaron's unreserved personality. But Jacob was kind to his younger nieces and nephews, especially Aaron.

Isaabel sometimes worried that Jacob's laughter was rare. But Nephi reminded her that he had been reared in a harsh environment, his young years spent within the bonds of slavery. When Lehi was allowed to live among the family members again, he began teaching Jacob to read. The young boy often questioned

Nephi about the brass plates. Several times, Sariah had let Jacob join in with Lehi and Nephi's early-morning discussions.

A sigh escaped Isaabel as she wished Aaron would be a little more studious like his young uncle, but perhaps that would come in time.

"Isa," called Elisheba, joining Isaabel.

Turning, Isaabel was struck again with the woman Elisheba had become. The years in servitude had matured the other family members, but most noticeably Elisheba, who was now a budding twenty-year-old.

"What will we do for Passover?" Elisheba asked.

Isaabel smiled since Elisheba had asked this question the day before. This year was different because her sister-in-law was with the family again. In a few days, it would be Passover, and Isaabel wondered under what conditions the family would celebrate it this time.

"Is that what we are saving the sheep for?" Dinah asked, catching up to them. Her eyes danced with anticipation. At seventeen now, she had also matured but somehow managed to keep her exuberant innocence about her.

"Yes," Isaabel said.

"Tell us again what Passover was like in Jerusalem," Jacob piped in, his open face turned upward.

"All right," Isaabel said, glancing down at Jacob, knowing he had heard the story many times from his mother. "We spent all week cleaning the house and getting rid of leaven or foods containing leaven. Just before sundown, the family gathered together, and my father told us about the traditional meal."

"Is that the one with the different foods?" Jacob asked.

Isaabel nodded. "The roasted lamb, unleavened bread, and bitter herbs."

"Why do the herbs have to be bitter?" asked Jacob.

"The herbs, dipped in salt water, remind us of the tears the Hebrew slaves shed," Elisheba said.

"*We* were slaves," Jacob said.

Isaabel squeezed Aaron and Jacob's hands gently. "But now we are free, just like the Hebrews who fled Egypt with Moses."

"Are Father and Grandfather prophets like Moses?" Aaron asked.

"Yes," Isaabel said smiling.

"And that's why we're going to the promised land," Jacob said with authority. "Because prophets lead their people across the wilderness."

Dinah laughed, then covered her mouth when she saw the hurt on Jacob's face. "I wasn't laughing at you, little brother. Not every prophet takes their people through deserts. Some just preach."

Isaabel looked ahead of them at the endless stretches of sand and rocks. It had been seven years since she'd seen her homeland, yet it was nothing compared to Moses' forty. *Yes,* she thought, *the Lord operates on His own time.*

"Then," Jacob said, interrupting her thoughts, "that's the kind of prophet I'll be."

Offering a rare smile, Elisheba linked arms with Dinah. "If Dinah and I have to wait forty years before finding a husband, we'll be gray when we bear children."

Dinah nudged her sister. "There's always Raamah," she teased. "If you start being nice to him, he might propose."

Isaabel saw the interchange between the two sisters. She threw a stern glance in Dinah's direction, hoping she would not make further comments about Raamah—a subject that obviously distressed Elisheba. Isaabel missed the closeness she used to share with Elisheba, but she also knew that the past five years had changed everyone.

*　*　*

A wild goat jumped out from a cluster of qassis plants. Sam spotted it and stunned the animal with a stick. Just the thought of eating meat again made his stomach grumble. Though the animal was small, it might suffice for a stew. He took the limp beast to his father.

"Should we save it for Passover?" he asked, holding it up for Lehi to see.

Lehi looked at the catch. The family had gone several days without meat, living on dried dates and camel's milk. Anytime they came across a well, they would first water the camels, then for themselves they mixed the camel's milk with the bitter water. A goat would be a welcome change. It had been difficult enough to save the sheep that bin Kabina had given them for Passover.

"We'll eat it now," Lehi said. He brought his camel to a halt, then drove his staff into the earth, signifying that the caravan was to stop. "Unload the camels and let them graze."

Sam analyzed their surroundings. A few abal shrubs were clumped together, and usually the fragile branches had fluffy yellow balls, but these branches were bare. A rather lean-looking acacia tree provided the only shade. One of the camels sniffed it, then walked away. Jacob joined Sam as he prepared the goat's carcass.

"Did you shoot it with an arrow?" Jacob asked, looking for the evidence on the goat.

"No," Sam said with a smile. "It jumped out in front of me too fast, so I hit it with my stick."

"Really?" Jacob's eyes widened with awe. "Nephi's right. He said you're the best hunter in the family."

Again, Sam smiled at his younger brother's comment. "He's being modest." Sam glanced about them and lowered his voice. "Can you keep a confidence?"

Jacob nodded anxiously.

"Soon you'll be old enough to hunt, and I think you'll become the best in the family," Sam said.

A slight smile spread to Jacob's lips, and his eyes brightened. "Can you teach me?"

A shadow fell over Sam and Jacob, and they looked up to see Sariah standing over them. "Teach you what?"

Jacob lowered his head. "Nothing."

Sariah chuckled and crouched to meet Jacob's gaze. "Bring a goatskin of water, so I may start the stew."

Her youngest son bounded away on the errand.

Sam looked at Sariah and noticed the dark circles under her eyes. "How are you feeling, Mother?"

Sariah brought her hand to her belly for an instant. "He keeps me awake at night, but I feel strong nevertheless."

Once the cold stew was prepared, the men gathered to eat, followed by the women and children. Even with the meat, it did little to stay the hunger pains. And some of their precious water had to be used. The family still did not light fire for fear of attracting a hostile tribe.

When the meal was finished, Lehi said, "We will stay here for the evening, rest the camels, and leave in the coolness of the morning." The family members didn't bother to set up the tents received from Chief bin Kabina, but slept under their rugs beneath the open sky.

As the sun disappeared behind the dunes, Sam settled next to Tamar and Govad. Just as his eyes grew heavy, a scream startled him to his senses. "What's that?" he asked.

Tamar sat up beside him. "It sounded like Isaabel."

Sam sprang from his bedroll and rushed in the direction of the sound. Then he came to a hasty stop. Nephi's son, Aaron, was lying on top of a bedroll, his body stiff, eyes round. Creeping around him were three hairy spiders with reddish legs—each as big as the palm of Sam's hand.

Several paces away, Isaabel clung to Nephi, her mouth covered with her hand. When they saw Sam, they motioned for him to keep still.

Hardly daring to breathe, Sam stared at his frightened nephew. He knew it was only a matter of time before the child's fear would rule his actions. It took every bit of willpower that Sam had not to dive for Aaron and pull him free. Sam's gaze met Nephi's, and they seemed to read each other's mind. Together, they began slow movements forward, trying not to alert the spiders and, at the same time, not to cause Aaron any greater distress.

Zoram arrived on the scene and quickly assessed the situation. "There must be a nest under the sand," he whispered. "Once we're close enough to grab Aaron, we'll have to be careful, in case there are more."

"Are they poisonous?" Sam paused in midstride, speaking to Zoram, but keeping his gaze focused on his nephew. He saw Aaron's eyes well with tears as he began to tremble.

"Yes," Nephi and Zoram answered together.

Nephi, who was the closest to his son, whispered, "Hold as still as possible, Aaron."

A hand touched Nephi's shoulder. He flinched and turned to see Isaabel keeping pace. "Stay back," he whispered, and Isaabel nodded fervently.

Nephi spoke to the others. "If each of us can kill a spider at the same time—"

"That won't be necessary," said a hushed voice behind Sam. It was Lehi. He stepped forward and raised his hand, speaking loudly. "In the name of the Lord God, I command these creatures to leave in peace."

Sam's breath caught in his throat. A single bite from one of the spiders could kill his nephew. A shuffling sound to his right caused him to turn and see Laman and Lemuel arrive.

It seemed everyone held their breaths, waiting to see what happened. One spider moved close to Aaron's face. With a lurch, Nephi moved forward, but was restrained by his father's hand.

"It's moving on," Lehi whispered.

In amazement, the family members watched the three spiders scuttle away from the young boy and disappear into the darkness beyond.

Nephi scooped his son into his arms and carried him a short distance away where Isaabel joined them. Sam and Zoram gingerly lifted the bedroll, checking for any other spiders, then shook out the rugs.

"A fire would keep them away," Laman said to no one in particular. "But it might attract raiders, and then we'd spend another five years in bondage."

Lemuel scoffed. "Fire or no fire, I'm not staying here tonight."

"You are right, Lemuel," Lehi replied, ignoring Laman's cynical remark. "We should move on. We don't know if there are more nests."

Isaabel pulled away from Nephi and her son. She crossed to Lehi. "Thank you, Father," she said, kissing his cheek.

Lehi patted her shoulder and smiled, relief evident in his features. "Thank the Lord."

* * *

Elisheba never wandered from the others. In fact, she rarely left her mother or sister's presence. But, inside, her thoughts were often far away. She spent her spare moments repairing tent panels, brooding about her life in Mudhail. The woman whom she served had been kind enough and had even taught her new uses of herbs and plants. And Elisheba was indebted to her family for slaving in order to earn her freedom. Thus, a heavy burden of responsibility weighed on her shoulders.

A thousand times a thousand she had scolded herself. If only she hadn't left camp to walk to the oasis that day so many years ago. If only she hadn't strayed from the family, perhaps they would have reached the promised land by now and she would have been married . . . to Raamah. *No,* she chided herself. She couldn't go back and change anything now. And what must Raamah think of her now? A foolish girl, that's what.

I did it for recognition, she thought. *I wanted the family to wake up and have water. I wanted Raamah to see how resourceful I was.* But it had the opposite effect. *And when he and Laman came to rescue me and I refused to leave . . .* If only she could talk to Raamah and make him understand.

Perhaps if she told Raamah of her continual nightmares, he would understand that she had been helpless from the moment the raiders from Mudhail had spotted her. She shuddered as the familiar wave of fear coursed throughout her body.

The image of the first raider who had reached her made her stomach twist with nausea. She could still smell his rancid breath and see his oily skin framed by wiry hair that smelled of dung. As she had neared the oasis on that horrible afternoon, she hadn't noticed the sleeping figures right away. Only when one of them stirred did she realize the danger. Immediately, she turned and began to run toward her family's camp. She didn't pause to throw sand in the air, signaling peaceful intentions, for she knew that, female or not, she was outnumbered.

Within seconds, Elisheba had discarded the goatskins to lighten her load. But it wasn't enough. The raiders didn't even use their beasts to close the distance, and with swift force, they had captured her and tied her arms and legs with rope. The journey to the Mudhail settlement was perhaps the worst of it—not only the physical pain of being thrown over a camel, but the fear of the unknown, not knowing whether she would live or die. Or, even worse, if she would be defiled and discarded.

Although she knew she'd disappointed the Lord, through His mercy her virtue remained intact. Elisheba shuddered to think what would have happened if her father hadn't arrived and begged for her release.

"Daydreaming again?" Dinah stood over Elisheba, jarring her back to the present.

Elisheba shook her head, feeling a dull ache behind her temples.

"I need help spreading the rugs for Passover," Dinah said.

Rising to follow her sister, Elisheba wished they could have stopped at an oasis for the Passover celebration, but her father thought there would be a risk of meeting hostile tribesmen. They reached Lehi and Sariah's tent and went inside, working together in silence.

"If you don't talk to him, I'll do it for you," Dinah said, breaking into Elisheba's thoughts again.

"Talk to whom?" Elisheba asked as she pulled a corner of the rug straight, her gaze avoiding her sister's.

"Raamah."

Elisheba felt her pulse quicken. *Why did Dinah keep interfering?* "What would I want to talk to him about?"

Dinah rolled her eyes. "Exasperating. That's what you are, Elisheba. Exasperating." She rose and crossed to the exit. "You're going to lose him if you don't."

"I made a mistake, and now I must suffer the consequences. I'm not a young girl anymore, hoping for a smile or a few exchanged words. If Raamah had *any* intentions, which I am convinced he does not, he would have to make the offer, not me," Elisheba said.

"We are beyond those formalities," Dinah said. "We've been in the wilderness with him for seven years."

"And five of those were spent in servitude because of me," Elisheba said, her voice bitter. She pounded a crease in the rug, trying to flatten it.

Dinah stared at her sister as Elisheba beat the rug with her fist. "It wasn't your fault," she said.

Elisheba let her hand drop and hung her head. "It *was* my fault," she whispered. "We could have been in the promised land by now."

With a sigh, Dinah moved to Elisheba and knelt beside her. "I'm younger than you, yet I know that we're not still in the wilderness because of anything you've done."

"Then why?" Elisheba said, remorse haunting her eyes. "Why are we still scraping by in this desert like desperate nomads?"

Dinah placed a hand about her older sister's shoulders. "Only the Lord knows."

Brushing at an angry tear, Elisheba sighed. "When Ishmael died, I still had faith that everything would' be all right. And when Sam was captured, I thought we were being protected. But to have to descend into slavery, being shackled with chains in my bed every night . . ." She paused. "And now Passover in the desert . . . again. I don't think I can stand another day."

With a squeeze, Dinah said, "You definitely need to get married. And the sooner, the better."

The corners of Elisheba's mouth turned up into a slight but puzzled smile. Finally her face erupted into a grin. She threw her arms around her sister's neck with a mixture of laughing and sobbing.

* * *

The family gathered inside of Lehi's tent and sat on rugs, leaning against bedrolls. The sun had nearly set, and the final touches had been made on the preparations for Passover. In the center of the room, a rudimentary table constructed out of acacia poles and rugs held the traditional meal. Three pieces of unleavened Bedu bread were placed on the cover in the center of the table, next to the chopped dates, ôrôt, spices and nuts from Mudhail; roasted lamb; and bowl of bitter herbs—soaked in date vinegar.

Lehi held up his hand for attention, then removed the middle piece of bread and tore it in half. He replaced one-half in the center of the table and gave the other half to Sam to hide.

"Close your eyes," Sam said to the children, who watched the proceedings with eagerness. The children giggled as they closed their eyes. They would be the ones who would hunt for it after the meal. Sam hid the bread, then resumed his place.

Sariah handed Lehi a goatskin with precious date palm wine, a gift from Chief bin Kabina. He took the wine and poured it into four silver teacups. "This wine represents the exodus of Moses and the children of Israel. The first cup represents their freedom, the second, deliverance, the third, redemption, and the fourth, release." His gaze scanned the family members, and Sariah smiled as it landed on her.

During Lehi's instructions, Jacob waited patiently. Tonight he would be the one to answer the Passover questions. He had rehearsed them with his mother several times.

Finally, Lehi looked at his youngest son and motioned for Jacob to rise. "Why do we eat only unleavened bread on Pesach?"

Jacob cleared his throat. "When the children of Israel left Egypt, they had no time to bake bread. They took raw dough on their journey and baked it in the hot desert sun into hard crackers called mazzah." He glanced at his mother, who smiled her approval. "On all other nights, we can eat many kinds of vegetables and herbs."

"Very good, Jacob," Lehi said. "Now, why do we eat bitter herbs, or maror, at our meal?"

Another quick glance at Sariah, and Jacob began. "Maror reminds us of the cruel way Pharaoh treated the Hebrews when they were in Egypt. On other nights we don't dip one food into another—only at Passover we dip the greens in salt water and the bitter herbs in vinegar."

"You are right," Lehi said, smiling. "And why do we dip our foods twice tonight?"

Jacob took a deep breath. "Because the vinegar reminds us how hard the Hebrew slaves worked in Egypt. The chopped nuts and dates look like the clay they used for their bricks. And," he paused, his brow furrowed in concentration, "we dip greens, or the ôrôt, in salt water because the ôrôt is like new life in the spring, and . . . the salt water reminds us of the tears of the children of Israel."

"Correct," Lehi said softly. "Now tell us why we are leaning instead of sitting straight up to eat."

With a memorized tone, Jacob said, "Leaning on the rugs reminds us that we are comfortable and free now, for once we were slaves." His gaze met his father's. "We were slaves just like the Hebrews of Egypt."

"Yes," Lehi said. The other family members sat in silence, each lost in his or her own thoughts. Several of them sniffled. Lehi crossed and put his hand on Jacob's shoulder. "We rejoice tonight in the company of our daughter Elisheba. We are free from the bonds of slavery and have shaken off the chains of captivity. We have been delivered from our enemies and saved from destruction. Tonight is truly a time to remember the slaves who were led out of Egypt by Moses and our own freedom from bondage."

Murmurs of consent were heard throughout the assembled family members.

"Now," Lehi said, his voice tremulous. "Let us pray."

Following the prayer, Lehi took the first bite, then the rest of the family began to eat the shared meal.

The children finished first and anxiously waited for the adults. Sam was the last to finish. He took his time chewing the remaining morsels of food, not because he enjoyed the meal of dates and greens, but because all of the children watched him. Slowly, he took the last bite, his expression light with amusement.

"Hurry, brother," Jacob whispered.

Sam held up a finger as he took one final drink, then let out a contented sigh.

Lehi chuckled as he watched the children fidget with impatience. "Is anyone else still hungry?" He was answered by several groans from the children. "No? All right, then. The children may search for the hidden bread."

A flurry of arms and legs scrambled about the tent. Some of the mothers helped with the youngest ones. "I found it!" five-year-old Govad shouted, holding up the broken half of bread. The adults clapped with laughter.

The children gathered around Govad, and she regally tore off pieces and passed them out. After everyone had eaten, they gathered in a circle, some holding hands, and began to sing.

Avadim hayinu, hayinu
Ata b'nei chorin, b'nei chorin.
Avadim hayinu, hayinu
Ata b'nei chorin, b'nei chorin.
Once we were slaves.
Today we are free people.

With each verse, their voices grew stronger, and soon many eyes were moist. Sariah linked her arm through Lehi's, with Elisheba on her other side. Passover had begun.

CHAPTER 22

The Lord redeemeth the soul of his servants: and none of them that trust in him shall be desolate.

(PSALM 34:22)

  Elisheba walked by Curly, her favorite camel, which Isaabel had named after a pet donkey left behind in Jerusalem. She patted the camel's heaving sides from time to time as the animal stumbled against the black stones that littered the ground. Elisheba encouraged Curly to feed off any shrub or grass the family came upon, though many times the camel would only sniff the dried branches, too thirsty to eat.
  Elisheba scratched the camel's light orange fur. It was rubbed off in several places where the camel had gnawed at insect bites. If it weren't for the camel's milk and dried dates, the family would have nothing to eat in the desolate stretch where they traveled. Sometimes she felt the animals were easier to talk to than her family. Since leaving the Mudhail settlement, Elisheba continued to experience disturbing dreams about being captured over and over, and she woke from them perspiring with cold fear.
  Suddenly the camel halted, a loud groaning noise escaping its throat. In the camel's path slithered a large horned viper. Elisheba took the camel's reins and tried to calm the beast. "Steady, Curly," she said.

Elisheba took a deep breath. She knew the snake was venomous, but that didn't scare her. She glanced quickly around and saw that she had drifted to the back of the group. There was no one to help.

"Whoa, girl," Elisheba said as she grabbed the neck of the camel. She knew to remain calm and not to prod the snake.

Curly's legs trembled as the viper moved in a side-winding motion. Elisheba knew that the camel could lose its balance under the weight of its baggage, and injure itself. Then the snake began to rub its scales together, creating a rattling sound.

"Easy," Elisheba called, stroking the camel's neck, hoping to convince it to listen to her and hold still. But the camel shifted forward, then took an unsteady step. The snake struck.

With a jerk, the camel balked, then started to lope with Elisheba's arms still wrapped around its neck. Elisheba was dragged alongside the animal, her arm twisted in its reins. She called for help until she realized it probably spurred the camel on faster. Elisheba squeezed her eyes shut as her head bobbed against the animal's body. With each second, her grip loosened, and her arm felt as if it would break.

Through the pounding of her head, Elisheba became aware that someone was galloping next to her. It was Laman's camel. "Laman," she cried out.

His arm wrapped around Elisheba, and in a swift movement, he sliced the strap she was tangled in. "Let go," he commanded.

With a scream, Elisheba let go of the camel's neck and latched onto Laman's camel. As the animal slowed, she looked up at her brother. It was not Laman who rescued her. "Oh Raamah, it's you," she said, gasping for breath.

"You could have been killed," Raamah said. He brought the camel to a halt and climbed off, helping her down. "Are you hurt?"

"I don't think so," Elisheba said with a wince, rotating her arm gingerly. It throbbed and was quickly swelling, but not broken. And her ribs felt as though they were on fire. "Curly," she said, searching for the direction it went. "He was bitten by a horned viper."

"Let the camel go," Raamah said. "We'll find it soon enough, although there's probably nothing any of us can do for it."

Feeling like her chest would burst, Elisheba looked at Raamah. "I'm sorry," she whispered.

Raamah kept his gaze toward the dune where the camel had disappeared. His breathing was labored and his face covered in perspiration. "I'm lucky I saw you while I was grazing Laman's camel."

She nodded, glancing at the ground. Drops of blood landed near her feet. "You're injured," she said.

Turning over his hand, Raamah examined the deep gouge the camel's reins had cut. He removed his head covering and tore a strip from it, winding it awkwardly around his palm.

"Let me tie it," Elisheba said. She sensed Raamah's hesitation, but he stretched out his hand anyway. She carefully secured a double knot, noticing that the blood had already soaked through the bandage.

"Thank you," Raamah said, turning his hand over. He stepped away from her. "We'd better catch up with the caravan before your mother starts to worry."

"All right," Elisheba said. She turned and started to walk.

Raamah caught up with her. "I'll take you back on the camel. It will be faster."

Elisheba stopped. "Do you think we should try to find Curly first?"

"No," Raamah said. "I'll return with Laman later. Besides, I don't want your parents to think you're missing again."

Cringing at the words, Elisheba felt guilt and embarrassment descend upon her. "I seem to create more trouble than good."

"I won't argue with that," Raamah said. He helped her up onto the camel, then climbed on himself. "Aiyah," he said, slapping the camel's backside.

Elisheba held on tightly with her one strong hand. She felt her cheeks flame and a lump form in her throat. *Don't cry in front of him,* she reprimanded herself. She was grateful that Raamah couldn't see her face.

With each passing moment, Elisheba felt like she was crumbling on the inside. If they couldn't help the camel, then the family would lose the animal's milk and labor, not to mention a friend. And this was her fault. She should have tried to scare the snake away before it struck.

"There's only one way to keep a woman like you out of trouble," Raamah said.

His voice startled Elisheba, and she didn't know how to respond. After a long pause, she said, "What way is that?"

"If you married, you would be too busy raising babies, and you wouldn't have time to wander off in search of water or to chase camels."

Elisheba didn't know whether to smile or weep. Was Raamah mocking her?

He brought the camel to a stop. "What do you think?" Raamah asked.

"Perhaps you're right," Elisheba said with a sigh. "Although the desert holds few eligible men."

"You only need one," Raamah said.

Elisheba felt her pulse quicken, wondering why Raamah didn't urge the camel forward. "My father would have to pay someone a great amount of silver and gold to take me."

Raamah chuckled, and Elisheba brought her head up in surprise.

"A girl who caused a whole family to work as slaves for five years," she said. "What man would marry a girl like that?"

"A man who had slaved for her freedom," Raamah said, pausing, "without regret."

Breathing in sharply, Elisheba's heart pounded. Was it possible, she wondered, that Raamah held no resentment toward her? If that were true, then what he said about marriage might mean—

"Elisheba," Raamah said. "Look at me."

She turned her head slowly and met his gaze. Just looking at him made her feel dizzy.

"Marry me."

The breath went out of Elisheba's chest, and her voice caught. But Raamah didn't seem to notice. He gazed at her, forgiveness and love in his eyes. "I know I'm not much to look at, and I have nothing to offer. Except I'll kill snakes for you and keep the scorpions away."

A small smile grew on Elisheba's face.

"The misery, the heat, and the sand will continue as before, but you'll have someone other than your mother and sister to complain to." He furrowed his brow. "Your daily tasks will be the same, though you'll be expected to cook for me, set up my tent, and soothe our fussing babies in the middle of the night."

Elisheba started to relax. "I already cook for you, and I haven't seen you set up a tent since the Valley of Lemuel. As for the babies . . ." Her neck grew warm, and she was sure her face was scarlet. "We'll have to negotiate." She stopped, suddenly feeling self-conscious.

"I'm willing to negotiate," Raamah said. His expression sobered. "I'll ask your father tonight." He wrapped an arm about her waist as he whipped the camel into a gallop.

Elisheba's heart pounded in tandem with the thundering hooves. Raamah wanted to marry her. She squeezed her eyes shut, silently thanking the Lord. A short time ago, she thought she was about to perish on a runaway camel, and now she was alive and practically betrothed.

Soon the caravan came into view, and as expected, everyone had stopped. A few shouts went up when they were spotted.

Sariah rushed forward, her lumbering form awkwardly crossing the sand. "What happened? Where did you go?

Where's the camel?" she asked breathlessly when she reached them.

Elisheba dismounted with the help of her mother and Raamah. The sight of her mother and the recent development with Raamah caused her heart to fill with jubilation. She embraced Sariah with one arm.

"The camel was bitten by a snake and bolted," Raamah explained. "Elisheba was caught in the reins and dragged."

Sariah caressed her daughter's face, then examined Elisheba's arm. "Poor dear." She noticed Raamah's blood-soaked wrap. "Both of you, come with me. Laman and the others can track the camel."

* * *

Laman spotted the camel's tracks almost immediately. "The camel can't be too far," he said to Lemuel. The two brothers walked alongside the footprints, their robes sticking to their sweaty backs. Once, Laman had shed all his clothing but his loincloth in order to travel like the natives of the desert, but Lehi had sharply reprimanded him. A smirk crossed Laman's face at the memory. The tribes throughout the desert were distinguishable by their clothing and head coverings. Sometimes just the way a man secured his dagger about his waist was clue enough to tell which tribe he belonged to. No one would ever mistake where *his* family came from—they looked like foolish Hebrews who expected to encounter the cool breezes of the Red Sea at any moment.

"There it is," Lemuel said. "Do you think it'll run when it sees us?"

"No," Laman said, hoisting the goatskin he carried to his other shoulder. "Stay back while I try to approach it." The camel was several dozen paces away, sitting in the shade against the side of a dune. Panels of a tent were scattered about, fallen from the load that was still partially on the animal's back.

From a distance, Laman could see the camel's rapid, shallow breathing. "It's going down, fast," he said. Leaving his brother behind, Laman walked slowly toward the beast. When it turned its head, Laman called softly, "Steady. Easy girl."

The camel bellowed in pain. Its mouth foamed, dripping suds onto the parched ground. Laman increased his pace and spoke soothing words to the animal. When he reached it, he said, "It's all right; I've brought water."

The camel's eyes rolled back as Laman touched its head. "Here," he said gently. "Drink." He maneuvered the camel's head until its lips met the water.

The camel's lips touched the brackish liquid and recoiled.

"I know it's bitter, but it might save your life," Laman said.

The animal turned away, its breathing strenuous.

"Drink!" Laman demanded. He moved around the camel and forced the goatskin toward the camel's head. But he only succeeded in getting the animal's nostrils wet. The camel sputtered and bellowed again.

Lemuel reached the scene, staring at the suffering camel. "It won't drink?" He sighed. "Perhaps the water's too rancid."

"Of course it's rancid," Laman shouted with frustration. "The camel needs to get it through its thick head that if it ignores its palate, its life will be saved."

"Let me try," Lemuel said, reaching for the goatskin.

But Laman brushed him off. "Look for the snake wound."

Lemuel examined the legs and feet of the camel. On the front left leg, he found the festering wound. "I'm surprised the camel made it this far," he whispered. "Look."

Abandoning the goatskin, Laman crouched and looked at the snakebite. The camel moaned in protest. "We're too late," Laman said, his expression grim.

"Can't we drain the poison?" Lemuel asked.

Laman rocked back on his heels. "The camel was foaming when I arrived. Look at its eyes."

Only the whites of the camel's eyes were visible under its heavy lashes. Laman rose and kicked the sand in frustration. "What next?"

Rising, Lemuel said nothing, but stared at the dying camel. With the animal's final breaths, it felt as if his own life were seeping away.

"O Lord," Laman said, "are You mocking us?" He shook his fist at the indifferent sky. "Wasn't five years in bondage enough?" He grabbed the goatskin and poured the water onto the thirsty ground. "If this camel can't save itself, then no one will drink this water."

"We needed that," Lemuel said.

"We needed the camel too," Laman replied, dropping the skin on the ground and stalking away.

* * *

As soon as she spied her brothers returning, Elisheba joined them. "Where is Curly?" she asked. Laman avoided her eyes and continued on, but Lemuel stopped.

"The poison had spread too far to do anything," Lemuel said.

Elisheba stood still, letting the information sink in. "Curly's dead?"

"Yes," Lemuel said, more gently this time. "I'm sorry." He touched his sister's shoulder briefly then left.

"No," Elisheba moaned as hot tears trickled down her cheeks—another failure to add to her haunting collection. She sank to the ground and wrapped her arms about her torso. Guilt consumed her as she thought of the poor animal suffering. How confused it must have been. And now, the family would struggle more than ever with one less beast. Once the family learned about the camel's fate, they would be devastated. She could see the disappointment on her father's face already. And her mother would suffer more in her condition. Her heart sank as another thought entered her mind—surely Raamah would change his mind about marrying her.

A hand touched her shoulder. "It's dead," Elisheba said without looking up.

"I know." It was Raamah. He settled into the sand next to her and waited a few moments.

Finally Elisheba looked at him. "Everything's ruined, and it's my fault."

"Nothing's ruined," Raamah said. "And it's not your fault."

"I was the one—"

"Elisheba," Raamah said sternly. "Do you think the earth is centered on what you do or don't do?"

She stared at him. "What do you mean?"

"Every time something bad happens in the family you think it's your fault." Raamah paused. "Does God plan the day according to your deeds?"

"But if I hadn't—" Elisheba began.

"If the snake hadn't crossed in front of the camel, then none of this would've happened. Do you think you have the power to dictate a snake's path?"

Elisheba lowered her head. "Of course not."

"No one is angry with you," Raamah said, his voice gentle. "We will mourn the loss of the camel, yes, but we are in a harsh land where the challenges are many."

Raising her head slightly, she looked at Raamah. "You don't blame me?"

"Like I said, you'd stay out of mischief if you were married," he said.

"A man's answer to everything," Elisheba said, the burden on her shoulders lifting. "Perhaps you're right."

"I know I'm right." Raamah rose and held out his good hand. "Come, you should be resting."

Elisheba reached for his hand, and he pulled her up. Her face grew warm as Raamah's hand lingered. "Thank you," she whispered.

Raamah held her gaze for a moment. "I'll speak to your father tonight."

Elisheba couldn't contain the smile that lit her face as she watched him walk away.

* * *

When the rest of the family had retired for the night, Raamah approached Lehi, who was tending to the camels.

"Father Lehi," Raamah said. "With Elisheba's consent, I have come to ask your permission to marry her."

Turning, Lehi looked at Raamah and, for a moment, didn't answer. He thought about the hardships his daughter had endured during her captivity. Although the other family members had suffered under the slavery conditions, Elisheba had been separated from her family the entire five years. Lehi knew his daughter was vulnerable and experienced nightmares. He studied Raamah's face in the moonlight. He was not surprised at the man's request and planned to grant Raamah's wish. But first, some things needed to be discussed. Lehi motioned for Raamah to follow him several paces from the camels where they could sit facing each other.

Once situated, Raamah continued, "Because I have no bride price to offer, I am willing to wait until we reach the promised land. I feel eventually I shall be able to acquire the appropriate mohar through hard work." He paused at the sight of reservation on Lehi's features. "I will protect her with my life."

"I know you will," Lehi said. "And you have before, but my daughter needs more than physical protection."

Raamah furrowed a brow. "If you are referring to the camel that was bitten, we have already discussed it."

"Oh?" Lehi asked, surprised. "What did she say?"

Shifting his position, Raamah said, "She feels responsible, of course. And my answer was that . . . she should marry—me."

With a chuckle, Lehi asked, "I can imagine what her response was to that."

"I know she is fearful," Raamah said. "She's as skittish as a goat. That's why I tend to keep an eye on her—and I saw her dragged by the camel and rescued her."

"Yes," Lehi agreed. "You are a capable man, and I appreciate the protection you have already provided." He hesitated, a distant look coming into his eyes. "You have been forgiven of your trespasses against Nephi and me."

Raamah visibly stiffened.

"The Lord has also forgiven you, and perhaps I need to look deeper into my own heart and remove all seeds of mistrust," Lehi said. It pained him to admit his reservations about Raamah. "In Nahom, I saw you change from murderous intentions to defending my life in an instant."

Lowering his head, Raamah stared at the ground as his face reddened. "I was wrong to disobey the Lord's commandments." He raised his gaze to meet Lehi's. "I committed a grievous sin in plotting against your life. But that was a long time ago."

"I would rather have my daughters not marry than be led against the Lord's will by their husbands," Lehi said. "I am not looking for a bride price to compensate me for the loss of a daughter." He hesitated. "What I am looking for is an oath."

"I understand," Raamah said, eagerness in his voice. "As the Lord liveth, I will betroth her unto me forever in righteousness, and in judgment, and in loving-kindness. Elisheba will be protected both physically and spiritually. You will not lose your daughter, but will gain a son. And by the life of God, I promise to respect your leadership and follow God's commandments." He paused. "Like Jacob of old, I have no bride price to offer you, but I promise to serve your family."

Satisfied, Lehi nodded. "We have nothing to write the contract on, thus the sand will be the record of the betrothal." He took a stick and wrote a few words in the soft ground. "Though the winds may erase these words, their essence will remain. Write your name here, and the earth will sanction the agreement."

In the sand, Raamah wrote the Hebrew letters of his name. Then he grasped Lehi's arm.

Lehi embraced him. "Welcome to the family."

* * *

That night, Elisheba sought Isaabel after the children had gone to bed and asked her sister-in-law about bridal attire.

Smiling, Isaabel said, "It would be an honor to have you wear my dress. And I won't have to wear it under my tunic any longer. It will bring good luck right at the start of your marriage."

Elisheba traced the worn lines of the linen dress. She glanced at Isaabel. "Are you sure you won't mind me wearing your bridal dress?"

"Of course not," Isaabel said.

A smile eased onto Elisheba's face. "I can't believe I'm finally marrying Raamah. After all this time and after all that's happened."

"What other outcome could there be?" Isaabel asked. "You were meant for each other, you just took longer than most to realize it." She placed a hand on Elisheba's shoulder. "What's wrong? You seem tired."

"I have trouble sleeping at night," Elisheba confessed.

A knowing look crossed Isaabel's face. "Nephi told me."

Elisheba arched her eyebrows in surprise. "Nephi knows?"

"Your mother told him. And . . . he prays for you each night."

Elisheba felt her eyes smarting. "My brother always puts others first," she said. "I wish I were more considerate like Nephi."

"We all do," Isaabel said. "But we must remember that Nephi's strength doesn't come from within, it comes from the Lord."

"Oh, Isa," Elisheba said, her voice tremulous. "At times I feel so distant from the Lord. My prayers were not answered in the way I hoped while we lived in Mudhail. To be isolated from the family and knowing Father was imprisoned—there's so much I don't understand."

Isaabel remained silent for a moment. "I once felt that way. And it was your mother who taught me I must trust in the Lord." She reached for Elisheba's hand. "We may never know the answers to all our questions, but we can have faith."

Nodding slowly, Elisheba said, "When we began this journey so long ago, I thought it was a great adventure and looked forward to meeting other children to play with. I never worried about food or water, although I did miss the variety of foods back home." Her voice faltered. "But now, every day I wake up wondering if I'll eat, if I'll drink, and if I'll live to see the sun rise again."

"That is part of submitting our will to the Lord's," Isaabel said, her voice catching. "When I first learned we would be following your family into the wilderness, I was very hesitant. The possibility of marrying Nephi made it bearable at the time."

"Perhaps my marriage to Raamah will add some joy to this wilderness."

Isaabel said, "Marriage might make the journey easier." She lowered her voice. "Though bearing children will make it more difficult."

"But—" Elisheba interrupted. "I won't give birth in the wilderness. It can't be much longer until we reach the promised land."

"I don't know about that, Elisheba," Isaabel said in a whisper. "Sometimes I think we have to find the promised land within our hearts. And only then will we discover what the Lord has in store for us."

85.23% 11-24-05

CHAPTER 23

*And I, the Lord God, said . . . that it was not good
that the man should be alone.*
(MOSES 3:18)

Lehi took Elisheba's arm and led her through the surrounding family, halting in front of the groom. Raamah offered a broad grin, and Elisheba returned it, all hunger and suffering forgotten for the day. A makeshift huppah had been erected out of acacia branches, and garlands of leaves decorated the wedding site. They had stopped at the oasis Shahr near the base of the Mahra Region, shaded by several acacia trees and providing a decent place of rest. Family members looked neater than usual, although not much cleaner. Most had shaken out sand from clothing, and a few had washed their faces in the bitter water.

Elisheba was grateful her father hadn't made them wait until arriving at the promised land to marry. Typically, they would have been betrothed for a year, but because of the circumstances, they only waited a week before the marriage date. With Raamah facing her, she was struck by the gentleness she saw in his expression. She was a woman now, different from the girl she once was, yet her pulse still quickened when she was near Raamah. She lowered her eyes, knowing Raamah wished that he could give her a clean home surrounded by fruit trees, such as he had provided his first wife, Leah. But Elisheba knew those times were far removed from the realities of desert living.

The man she was about to marry loved her, a fact she knew. Although Raamah had not spoken those actual words, she felt them in her heart by a mere glance or simple touch. For that reason alone, this marriage would be far different than anything she'd ever experienced. And she hoped to bear him children with strength and health. The soft strains of singing brought Elisheba's thoughts to the present.

Lehi stood before them and began the kiddushin, speaking the ceremonial words slowly.

"Raamah, will you take Elisheba to wife according to the Law of Moses and of Israel?"

"Yes," Raamah said, his voice thick.

"My daughter, Elisheba," Lehi said, his own tone husky. "Will you take Raamah as your husband according to the law of Moses and of Israel?"

Elisheba raised her eyes to meet Raamah's. "Yes." A surreal sensation spread through her. During their years of servitude, she had almost given up hope that this day would ever come.

Dinah held out the cup of date-palm wine. Raamah took a small sip from the precious liquid, then passed it to Elisheba.

The ceremonial ring had been bartered for barley in Mudhail, but in its place, Lehi presented a small circle made out of woven threads.

Raamah took it and gently placed it on Elisheba's finger, being careful not to break any strands. "Behold, thou art consecrated unto me with this ring according to the Law of Moses," Raamah said.

A single tear slipped down Elisheba's cheek as her father spoke the next words. "From the beginning, God created male and female."

As Elisheba circled Raamah, she remembered watching her sisters-in-law marry several years ago. Elisheba let out a low breath and stopped. Raamah lifted her veil and placed its hem on his shoulder. Then he arranged the corners of his prayer shawl on Elisheba's shoulders.

Lehi cleared his throat. "What God hath joined together, let no man put asunder."

Sariah stepped forward and placed a dried garland on Elisheba's and Raamah's heads, then held out a bowl of blessed water into which they dipped their hands.

"O Lord," Lehi said. "Please bless them with the fruit of the vine, which brings joy and sanctification. O God, we praise Thee, who created our earth, and we are grateful for human life." He raised his voice. "O Lord, we ask Thy blessing on this bride and groom. We ask Thy blessing of children born to this union, and the blessing of companionship and joy. We praise thee, O Lord, our God. Amen."

"Amen," echoed the family members.

Raamah leaned down and kissed her. Cheers went up around them, masking Elisheba's pounding heart, and the dancing began.

* * *

Murmuring sounds woke Nephi. Though he wasn't sure if he had been sleeping deeply, he was surprised that he'd heard anything at all. He sat up, careful not to disturb Isaabel or Aaron. The rise and fall of the gentle breeze muffled the sounds at intervals. Human voices, he realized, too soft to decipher. Something told him to investigate.

All was still about the camp as Nephi crept past the sleeping forms. The sounds grew faint, then definite as the wind shifted. He headed north toward a massive dune reaching at least six hundred feet in height. The family had camped along the edge the Mahra Plateau since the marriage the week before. The ground beneath Nephi was covered in stones that had been laid bare by the driving winds. As long as sand ran in rivulets along the ground, the gravel plains were easier to travel for the camels than the towering dunes that formed long rows, which were soft and high. Although the stony ground held risk for the soft feet of the camels, it took less time to cross. Nephi maneuvered his way through the rocks, being careful not to send any skipping.

Pausing at the base of the dune, Nephi strained to hear. The night had fallen silent, but he was sure the voices would come again. *At least I don't smell smoke,* he thought with a grimace.

Nephi crouched low to the ground. In the moonlight, the sand beneath him was strangely dark—the color of baked bricks—intermingled with a pale orange color. The sound came again, and this time Nephi could tell that the voices were arguing. He silently skirted the south end of the dune, knowing that his presence could be detected any moment. When the words became decipherable, he paused, listening as the deep voices chimed clear.

"How many more years do you have left in you? Another five?" It was Laman.

Heth responded. "I don't think I have even one more week left. Zillah cries all night and spends the days asleep. Our children's stomachs are bloated with malnourishment."

"We were better off at Mudhail," Lemuel's voice interrupted. "As slaves."

"How can you argue that, Raamah?" Laman asked.

Nephi stiffened. He had not expected Raamah to be collaborating with Laman again, not after the oath he gave to Lehi and his subsequent marriage to Elisheba. Since the death of the camel, Nephi had sensed Laman's general sullenness turning into resentment. Though the Liahona continued to guide them from well to well, complaints escalated among several of the family members; the desert diet of camel's milk and dates had taken its toll.

"And what is your solution, Laman?" Raamah nearly shouted. He was met with severe shushing, but he went on. "Return to Jerusalem? Traverse the one thousand and some odd miles back over the desert?"

"No," Laman said. "If you'll keep quiet, I'll tell you the plan."

"I'm leaving," Raamah said, his voice angry. "Out of respect to your father—something none of you have—I'm taking myself out of this discussion."

Nephi rose to his feet, heart pounding. Raamah would round the edge of the dune any moment and discover him.

"Wait, Raamah. I know you think you have all the answers, but hear me out. And if you don't agree, then we'll leave you alone," Laman said.

Nephi held his breath until he heard his brother's voice again. Apparently, Raamah had decided to listen to what Laman had to say.

"There's no reason we couldn't have our own tribe," Laman said. "Just as the raiders and marauders live off the desert, so could we."

"You must enjoy this wasteland more than I thought," Raamah said.

"Let me finish," Laman said. With silence commanded, he continued. "We couldn't overtake a large community such as Mudhail. There are too many tribesmen loyal to Chief bin Kabina. But we can start out small—raiding a few scattered groups, building up our own herd of camels and procuring loyal followers from small clans to build our forces. In the Mudhail settlement, we learned the dialect well enough to pass for a ferocious tribe."

Lemuel laughed. "I am Chief bin Laman of the Dunes of Lemuel. Hand over your valuables or die."

Snorting laughter erupted. Nephi cringed.

"As the chief, I'll fight with you, but I will also expect a luxurious lifestyle, complete with guards, delectable foods, and concubines. And, of course, as my brothers and brothers-in-law, you'll enjoy all the same pleasures." Laman paused. "In a couple years, we'll have our lands of inheritance, fought for by our own might."

"You would become like the raiders who have terrorized our family?" Raamah asked.

"I'd rather fight for property than wander from oasis to oasis, hoping that someday we'll find a place with something other than brackish water to drink." Laman's voice rose. "Once again, I ask you the question. How many years are you willing to waste? Seven . . . eight more? In seven years' time we could be living like sultans if we start raiding now."

"I'm in," Lemuel said. A whack resonated, and Lemuel groaned. "What was that for?"

"Of course *you're* in," Laman said with a sneer. "But it won't work unless Heth and Raamah come too, since you wouldn't be able to fight off a tribesman half your size."

"That's what you think," Lemuel sputtered. Scuffling sounds could be heard, followed by a few grunts.

"Enough!" Raamah said. "I've had enough of this."

"Go back to your bride and act the part of the dutiful son-in-law," Laman mocked.

Before Nephi could escape, Raamah appeared. He stopped cold when he saw Nephi. Raamah opened his mouth, as if he were about to say something, then shook his head and continued past Nephi.

"Raamah," Nephi whispered, running to catch up with him.

Keeping his gaze straight ahead, Raamah kept walking. "I need to speak with your father right away."

"All right," Nephi said. "I'll come too. We have to put a stop to Laman's plans."

Raamah threw a glare in Nephi's direction. "That's not what I meant." He hurried away, Nephi moving quickly to keep up.

As Raamah neared Lehi's tent, Nephi took a detour and woke Zoram from sleep. "Relocate the valuables. *Now*," Nephi whispered.

* * *

"I want a timeline," Raamah said, his arms folded across his chest.

Lehi glanced at Nephi, who simply shrugged. Lehi's mind was still fuzzy with sleep. When Raamah and Nephi had awakened him, he had led them to the outskirts of camp to talk. "A timeline?"

"How long," Raamah asked slowly, emphasizing each word, "will it take to reach the promised land?"

Lehi's shoulders felt heavy as he crouched on his heels. "I don't know."

A sigh of frustration came from Raamah. "*No* idea? What did the Liahona say this morning?"

"The same thing as yesterday," Nephi replied.

"Which was?" Raamah prompted.

"It gave the direction that we should be traveling," Lehi said, looking at Raamah. "What is bothering you, son?"

The endearment softened Raamah's demeanor. "I gave you my word. And now I need to know how much longer we are expected to live under these conditions. Are we going to be forced into slavery again?" he asked.

"The Lord has made the women strong, and they are able to nurse their babies," Lehi said. "And he has sweetened the raw meat."

"Meat?" Raamah asked. "We haven't had meat in weeks. Why won't you answer the question?"

"Because he doesn't know the answer," Nephi interjected. "None of us does."

"Yet you've *seen* this promised land?" Raamah asked.

"Yes, in a vision, I was shown the promised land—" Nephi said.

"Did you see *me?*" Raamah pressed.

Nephi looked at him, startled.

"Was I stooped and gray? Was Elisheba an old woman?"

"No," Nephi began. "The vision wasn't like that."

Raamah rose, bitterness in his expression. "Maybe you should think about what you *did* see, Nephi. Then look beyond us and decide if anything in sight you see resembles the promised land. Perhaps it's the next wadi or the next row of dunes." He stopped to catch his breath. "I made an oath to your father, and I will keep it until one of us dies. But until then, I suggest you do some more praying and find out how to deliver our family from this misery on earth." His chest heaved in anger. "Or there will be no family left to see your promised land."

Turning, Raamah strode away, leaving Nephi and Lehi astounded.

After a moment of silence, Lehi said, "It is as I have feared. Laman and Lemuel have started the restlessness." He rose to his feet, his body vibrating in wrath. "They shall answer for their transgressions."

"Father," Nephi said, placing a hand on Lehi's sleeve. "I overheard them planning to leave the family."

"And return to Jerusalem?" Lehi asked.

"They want to take on the mantle of raiders and plunder for a living until they can build their own kingdom."

"Have mercy," Lehi cried out. "Our souls will be dragged into eternal misery." He began to walk in the direction Raamah had gone.

Nephi caught up with him and gripped his father's arm. "Father, perhaps you should wait until morning," he said.

"No," Lehi said with vehemence. "I will not have my sons rebel and commit all manner of wickedness. I will go to them at once and remind them of their duty."

Dropping his hand, Nephi acquiesced. "I'll show you where they are."

In the desert moonlight, they picked their way to the dune where Nephi had overheard their plan. As they rounded the base, Raamah came running toward them. "They're gone," he said, panting from exertion. "I've checked the entire area. Laman's camel is gone, along with one of the other camels."

Lehi reached out, grasping in midair. "No," he said as his legs crumpled beneath him.

Raamah and Nephi grabbed Lehi just before his head hit the ground.

* * *

It had been several days since Laman, Lemuel, and Heth deserted. The days were filled with confusion, anger, and growing hunger. Anah, Puah, and Zillah grieved loudly at first, then fell silent, their souls broken.

Lehi spent morning, afternoon, and night in prayer and supplication. Sariah, her own heart devastated, tried to force Lehi to eat, but he would have nothing to do with food. When Lehi was too faint to kneel, he lay on his side, his lips murmuring prayers.

Nephi desperately tried to talk his father out of his brokenhearted ruminating. His pleadings turned to arguing, which eventually turned to Lehi becoming inconsolable again.

"Father," Nephi said on the fourth morning, "Sam and I are going to track them down. But you must eat something before I leave so I'll have a father to return to."

Lehi's half-closed eyelids flickered. His words were barely audible. "I can't . . . Don't you see? They will perish on their own. God will surely punish them for abandoning their families." Lehi licked his lips. "Without the protection of the Lord, they will die."

"Drink," Nephi said, pressing a waterskin to Lehi's lips.

Lehi turned his head away, squeezing his eyes shut. "How can I bear reaching the promised land without all of my children?"

Suppressing his own trepidation, Nephi said, "If you don't drink, none of us will reach the promised land. Please, Father. Do it for the welfare of the women. Think of Mother, of Bashemath and the wives." He dripped the water onto Lehi's lips, then watched as it dribbled down his father's chin. Nephi felt what little stamina he had drain from his body. His father had become the epitome of all that Nephi felt. It would be easier to give up, to lie down and die, than to continue on year after year, living as scavengers. The look on his father's face was pitiful, full of pain and mourning. Lehi had descended into the depths of deepest agony.

Nephi closed his eyes and thought about his wife and son, his mother, his brothers, and his sisters. *His father.* Nothing on earth was more dear to him than their lives. If something happened to Isaabel or Aaron, he didn't know if he would fare better than his father.

Leaning back on his elbows to recline next to his father's prostrated form, Nephi thought back to the vision he'd seen in the Valley of Lemuel. He had seen the Savior lifted up upon a cross and slain for the sins of the world. The Savior followed God's commandments, even if it meant paying the price with an ultimate sacrifice.

Am I above the Savior? Was more expected of him than the Redeemer Himself? *No.* With an aching heart, Nephi knew what he must do. First, he must ask for forgiveness, then he must convince his father to live.

Nephi touched his father's shoulder, rousing Lehi from an exhausted stupor. "The Lord has not forgotten us." He spoke louder. "And the Lord has not forgotten Laman and Lemuel."

Turning his head slowly in the direction of Nephi's voice, Lehi opened his eyes a slit. "Will they return?" he whispered.

"We'll find them, I know it." Nephi took his father's hand. "This is like the tree of life. We are journeying toward the promised land, or the tree of life, but Laman and Lemuel have taken a forbidden path." He squeezed Lehi's shoulder. "Don't you see?" Nephi prodded. "We must stay on the straight and narrow path in order to reach the promised land. By staying *here*, we are stuck in the depths of the fountain, wallowing in self-pity."

Lehi's eyes opened. His gaze struggled to focus on Nephi.

"The Liahona is like the man in the white robe, and we must follow him." Nephi paused. "The Lord knew this would happen from the beginning. Laman and Lemuel are out wandering on strange roads. But in your vision, you saw the rest of us hold onto the iron rod and partake of the fruit."

"Yes," Lehi said, his expression lightening. "But how do we get them to find the straight and narrow path?"

"First," Nephi said, supporting his father's weight until he was in a sitting position, "You must eat of this fruit." He placed a small piece of date in Lehi's mouth. Then another. "Next, we must follow the direction of the Liahona. God will bring your sons back to you."

* * *

Another day survived, another night to get through, Isabel thought as she stared at the numberless stars above, thinking over the past few weeks. They had stopped at an oasis. With its thick grove of date palms, they were provided with some shelter and relief. But the days were indistinguishable from each other. Isabel knew that time had moved simply because Sariah's belly continued to grow. With Lehi coherent again, her mother-in-law never let a moment pass without thanking the Lord. Isabel knew that the desertion of Sariah's two sons had pierced her heart, but the loss of her husband would have bled it dry.

Isaabel had worn herself out trying to console Bashemath, Anah, Puah, and Zillah. If the men didn't return, their wives would be forever disgraced. *And their parents.* According to traditional law, Laman, Lemuel, and Heth had committed a crime against their parents and could be put to death by stoning or hanging.

She frequently heard Raamah and Nephi arguing about the law, then Zoram and Sam would step in, and the disagreements would escalate. She knew that the contention was upsetting to Elisheba and the other women.

But out of the women, it was her mother who worried Isaabel most. Bashemath had lost her husband, and now her son had rejected the family, abandoning his wife and child in the process. *Laman,* Isaabel thought with angst, *what have you finally done to us?* Her throat swelled with emotion. Perhaps the five years spent in slavery had shattered their loyalty. Patience had run out. It had been difficult and degrading for all of them. How could she blame the men for losing faith?

She had overheard Sariah pleading with the Lord. "What happened to my dear firstborn, the son who used to give me such joy? The young, handsome boy with his wavy curls and merry eyes? How did you become so full of hatred and disrespect that you would forsake your own parents who love you as no other?" Raising her fist to her mouth, Sariah had bit down on her knuckles to quell her rising sobs. "O Lord," she had prayed, "bring them back. Protect them, and bring them safely to us."

Exhausted, Isaabel turned to her side, she watched Nephi's deep breathing on the bedroll next to her. At least he slept peacefully tonight. Most of the time, he was tormented with restlessness. Nephi spent many hours with his father, trying to get him to eat and consoling him in his grief. He had been able to get Lehi to eat a little more each day.

O Lord, Thou art the only with whom I can share my sorrow. Then, beyond the pain of her bruised heart, Isaabel felt warmth and knew it could only come from God. *Thank Thee.*

With a sigh, Isaabel rolled onto her back as fresh tears pricked her eyes. She thought about the babe that Sariah was soon to bring forth. *Another child born in the wilderness.* And this child would be born to parents who were drowning in the depths of sorrow.

CHAPTER 24

*A foolish son is a grief to his father, and bitterness
to her that bare him.*
(Proverbs 17:25)

The days passed in sullen travel, days of wading through hot sand. It had been nearly two months since the family's departure from the Mudhail settlement. On a particularly hot day, the family spotted another oasis, as directed by the Liahona. Lehi stopped and raised his hand to shield his eyes, then pushed his staff into the soft sand. Letting go, his myrtle stick fell to the earth. Behind him, Nephi picked up the staff and handed it back. Overwhelmed with hopelessness, Lehi couldn't even bring himself to utter a thank you.

Nephi blinked his eyes against the dry heat. Up ahead, date palms were moving. "Did you see that, Father?" When he received no reply, he said, "It's another tribe, and they've beat us to the oasis." He took a few steps forward and tossed a handful of sand into the air.

From the short distance, Nephi could see their gesture returned in kind. "Let's go meet the peace-bearing men."

"Go ahead," Lehi said, remaining where he stood.

Nephi hesitated, glancing where Zoram and Sam were quickly burying the valuables, their wives blocking the view.

After Sam marked the area with a grouping of dead roots, Nephi moved forward to greet the leader of the tribe alone, reminding himself to be grateful that his father was well enough to travel.

When Nephi reached the leader of the tribe, he offered a broad smile. "We come in peace."

The leader returned the smile. "Welcome. I am Amair of the Mahra tribe."

Nephi bowed his head slightly. "I am Nephi, son of Lehi. We would like permission to share the oasis."

"As you wish. There is enough room at Shisur for both of us." The tribesman spread out his hands. "Do you have any meat?"

"No," Nephi said.

"Then join us for our meal. We will share the meat that we have."

* * *

The days spent at Shisur turned into weeks. Structures made of uncut stone and mortar had been erected in the dry wadi bed by some earlier people, generations before. The tribesmen and Lehi's family divided up the standing buildings among themselves. And for the first time in months, Elisheba slept with a palm frond roof over her head. Her parents had been pleased when one of the tribesmen told them that Shisur was an oasis known to all desert people.

Each morning, Elisheba and the women drew and hauled the water for the camels and for other uses. She and Isaabel took it upon themselves to wash everyone's clothing. The women wore veils while outside to deter the curious eyes of the tribesmen. But their meals were shared with the tribesmen and often other wandering camel herders or travelers.

One evening, about two months after their arrival in Shisur, Elisheba went to sleep feeling ill. During the night, she woke, pain throbbing through her back and abdomen. With a groan, she rose to sitting position. Next to her, Raamah was sleeping deeply. Not wanting to disturb him, she left the shelter and walked a short distance, trying to ease the ache. It was then that she saw a silhouette in the moonlight some distance away, crouched on the ground. In an instant, fear flooded through her. Was it a raider stalking their camp? she wondered. Although her reason told her to return and alert Raamah, her instinct drew her closer. Soft cries came from the figure, and Elisheba began to run toward the person.

"Mother," she said when she recognized the shrouded woman.

Sariah lifted her head, and Elisheba saw immediately that her mother was in great pain.

"The babe . . . is coming . . . now," Sariah managed to say through gasping breaths. Clutching her stomach, she tried to rise but staggered backward.

Elisheba took her mother's shoulders and held her firmly, recognizing the signs of the imminent birth. There was no time for a birthing tent, soothing herbs, or the aid of another.

"Bashemath—" Sariah said.

"By the time I fetch her, it will be too late, Mother," Elisheba said. "I will help you."

"No," Sariah began. "You haven't the skill."

"I have," Elisheba said, "I helped Hadi with her babe while in captivity. Besides, you are in no position to deny my offer." She looked into Sariah's eyes. "I am a woman now. Please have faith."

Sariah seemed to relax with her daughter's words. Elisheba spread her mantle on the ground to receive the infant, then placed her dagger on top of the cloth, within reach, to cut the cord of life. The rest period between the persistent pains shortened until Elisheba couldn't determine when one ended and the next began.

"O Lord," Sariah pled, "Give me Thy strength to deliver this child."

Elisheba sensed delirium had descended upon her mother as Sariah's eyes lost all focus and her grip tightened. Elisheba began to say her own prayers as she tried to support Sariah's desperate hold.

As the two women prayed, crouched in the sand, Sariah bore another son in the wilderness.

* * *

When the members of the Mahra tribe learned that a male child had been born, they insisted on holding a celebration. Date palm wine appeared, and dried dates were passed around. Nephi felt pleased to see his father accept congratulations with humbleness. For the moment, his grief had eased.

Jacob couldn't contain his delight at becoming an older brother. Over and over he told the Mahra tribesmen the story of their names and how Jacob's son Joseph was sold into Egypt.

As the evening drew late and the celebrating ended with snoring, intoxicated tribesmen scattered about, Nephi went to speak with Lehi. "How is Mother?"

"She's remarkably well, considering the manner of delivery. Your wife is keeping a faithful vigil," Lehi said. He was leaning against the sides of the building that he and Sariah shared.

"Mother is recovering fine?" Nephi asked. He squatted next to his father.

"Your mother is stronger than I've ever seen her after such an ordeal."

Nephi fell into silence, thinking, then said, "We have been greatly blessed. Experiencing the things we have and still being strong and healthy."

"Yes, you are right. And just as Joseph of Egypt, our little Joseph has been born into a family with many older brothers."

Lehi's voice filled with emotion. "Older brothers whom I pray will return to our fold."

Nodding, Nephi stayed by his father for a long time until they both dozed.

Some time later, Nephi felt something on his foot. He jerked back, thinking a scorpion had stung him. But when he opened his eyes, he realized that he was in much more danger. A firm hand clamped over his mouth, and several other hands restrained his body. He looked around for his father, but Lehi was nowhere in sight.

The men who dragged him across the ground were unlike any he'd ever seen. They wore only loincloths, and their bodies were painted in lines with some sort of dye. In the moonlight, he could see that it was still wet. Their heads were uncovered, and long wiry hair protruded from all angles.

Nephi felt himself lifted into the air, then dropped. With a thud, he landed on top of another body. The first thought that came to his mind was Isaabel and Aaron; the second, his mother and his new baby brother, Joseph. Where were they?

Struggling, Nephi tried to see what was going on. His hands and feet were bound, as were the other captives' who surrounded him. "Isaabel!" Nephi cried out. Other shouts came, but none distinguishable. The human pile which Nephi had been thrown on top of writhed with arms and legs, all trying to escape. The confused voices rose up around him, and in the midst of them, Nephi heard Hebrew.

They were voices that he hadn't heard for some time—Laman and Lemuel.

"Laman," Nephi shouted frantically. "Where are you?" He paused, trying to hear above the chaos. "Lemuel?"

No one responded that he could distinguish. "It's Nephi," he yelled, hoping to make himself heard. Moments passed, the mayhem continuing. "O Lord," he said, "protect our family from these marauders."

Nephi felt a swift elbow in his stomach that almost knocked the breath out of him. More jabs came his way until he began to feel dizzy.

"Is that you, Nephi?"

Hearing his name, Nephi struggled to raise his head. "Heth?" He couldn't see the person standing above him, but the voice was unmistakable.

"I'll be right back," Heth said.

"No, wait," Nephi called, but Heth was already gone. With relief, Nephi closed his eyes. He hoped that having his brothers and Heth among the group of marauders was a good thing.

"Where is he?" asked a rough voice.

Nephi heard the words and knew they belonged to Laman.

"Over here somewhere," came Heth's reply.

Suddenly, Nephi was jerked from underneath the person who was half sprawled on top of him. With a thump, he landed on the hard ground and found himself staring up at the painted face of Laman.

"I don't believe it," Laman said, his grin showing a broken tooth. "I was ready to order Heth's hand removed for lying to me."

Next to him, Heth's face went pale. "The others must be somewhere in the pile too."

"I should have known we'd run into you at some point," Laman said. A couple of marauders approached Laman, who fired commands and ordered them away. Laman's gaze settled again on Nephi. "Don't worry, you'll be treated like next of kin," he sneered.

Laman turned away and shouted more orders at the scurrying tribesmen. Apparently he was in a position of power, perhaps the leader.

"Please," Nephi began. "Mother just gave birth."

With a glare, Laman looked at Nephi. "I'm not a barbarian, little brother. There's nothing wrong with a little scare to establish my place in the family."

Inside, Nephi's heart leaped with hope. "Then call off the raid. That is, if you have the authority."

Laman's eyes narrowed. "Untie him," he said to Heth, who immediately obliged.

With effort, Nephi rose to his feet, rubbing his wrists. He met Laman's gaze with a challenging look.

Raising his hand in the air, Laman shouted. "Stenna! Stop!"

The commotion began to die down as a few of the marauders stopped and stared at Laman.

"Stenna!" Laman commanded again, then looked at Nephi. "Are the Mahra your friends?"

Nephi nodded, and Laman issued orders for all to be lined up.

Near the fire, Lehi's family and the Mahra tribesmen were placed at attention, guarded by knifepoint. All their weapons had been confiscated and piled on the other side of the fire. Finally, Nephi saw his wife and son. They were together and Isaabel was bound, but appeared unharmed. He moved in their direction, only to be stopped by one of Laman's men.

Nephi opened his palms to indicate that he held no weapon.

Seeing the interchange, Laman said, "Let him join the woman."

Nephi moved past and joined Isaabel's side. Quickly he unloosed her ropes, then picked up Aaron.

"Is that Laman?" Isaabel whispered, her eyes incredulous. With his loin-clad body, uncovered head and painted skin, he looked like a fierce desert raider.

"Lemuel and Heth are with him too," Nephi said, drawing Isaabel close. He looked for his mother, who stood next to Lehi. In her arms, she held a bundle—baby Joseph. Sariah hummed quietly to her baby, with lowered eyes. But Lehi studied the scene, his jaw set firm. Nephi knew it wouldn't be long before his father recognized the leader.

With relief, Nephi saw Jacob gripping Lehi's robe. A quick survey told him all the other family members were present and appeared unharmed.

"Laman?" Lehi's voice cried out. "Son?"

A couple of the raiders moved menacingly toward Lehi, but he ignored their drawn daggers.

Stepping forward, Lehi opened his arms wide. "I thought you had perished."

Laman froze where he stood, his back toward them. Lehi took another step, and two marauders seized him.

Slowly, Laman turned around, his lean and muscular figure intimidating in the firelight. The perspiration on his skin blended with the painted dye, creating rivulets of color. His chest heaved with exertion and, by the look on his face, fury.

Nephi wondered if Laman was enraged because his Hebrew identity had been revealed to his followers or because he had been caught in a disobedient act by his father.

"Father?" It was Lemuel's voice. He appeared from down the line, where the Mahra tribesmen stood. "Mother?"

"You're alive," Lehi said, struggling against the guards.

"Let him go," Lemuel commanded, and Lehi was released immediately.

Lehi's tears flowed freely as he embraced his son. "I thought you lost forever." He clung to Lemuel, dye smearing on his robe.

Sariah walked toward the two men, holding the baby, with Jacob in tow. She joined their embrace, wetting Lemuel with her tears. Then Lemuel knelt to receive Jacob. Unreserved, Jacob embraced his bother. Lemuel tousled his hair and squeezed him tight.

Close by, some of the women broke out in sobs.

Heth joined the family, embracing his weeping mother and wife. In turn, he greeted his sisters.

"Silence!" Laman bellowed.

All eyes turned from the poignant reunion to Laman, who stared past the emotional meeting and locked eyes with Raamah.

"Quite the *occasion,* eh, Laman?" Raamah said. "You've abandoned your parents, your wife, your children . . . and now you've surprised us all with a violent reunion." He spread his arms wide. "What will you do now? Murder and plunder innocent women and children—your own kin?" Raamah stepped forward, his face twisted with antagonism. "Where are your riches? The delectable food? The concubines? All I see are a few scraggly raiders who could possibly pass as guards . . . for a poor nomad who thinks himself a powerful chief." His voice rose, mocking. "Look at the Sultan in his fine robes and precious jewelry."

Another step. "A loin cloth?" Raamah continued with a scoff. "Is that what you traded for your family?" He pointed to Anah, who clutched little Canaan, then gestured toward Shem. "Your sons—will inherit your lands?"

Laman's jaw worked in hostility, his expression incensed.

Nephi knew that Laman's next decision would determine the future of the family. Would he choose the marauding party he led, or would he relinquish his authority and rejoin the family under the domain of Lehi?

"Father," a child's voice said. Shem, Laman's oldest son, broke free and ran toward him. The guards made no attempt to stop the youth. He flung himself at Laman's bare legs and held fast.

Anah stumbled forward and sank to her knees as she cried out, "Have mercy, husband, and return to your family."

Everyone waited for Laman's reaction, knowing their lives were in his hands. He stood like a statue, ignoring the child who clung to him, and stared past his weeping wife.

The surrounding guards looked confused, not understanding the language. Nephi put his arm around Isaabel and gripped Aaron tighter. He knew very well that mayhem could break out. Now that Laman's identity had been revealed, Raamah wouldn't let him leave again without a fight. Nephi glanced toward the stacked weapons. Only two guards stood near them. His eyes met Sam's and saw that his brother was thinking the same thing.

With rising dread, Nephi wondered if somehow the events in his vision were about to start prematurely.

He saw an army forming. The warriors had dark skin, shaved heads, and painted faces. They advanced city by city, slaughtering men, women, and children. Another army rose, and another.

Nephi's stomach churned at the memory. *O, Lord,* he pled with all his might. *Deliver us this night from the darkness of evil. Soften Laman's heart and spare our lives.*

A nudge from Isaabel alerted him. Nephi looked at Laman, whose hand had settled onto Shem's thin shoulder.

CHAPTER 25

*Execute true judgment, and shew mercy and
compassions every man to his brother.*
(Zechariah 7:9)

It was the touch of his son that melted Laman's heart. As he lowered his hand to Shem's brown shoulder, Laman felt a shiver travel from his fingertips throughout his entire body. His heart had been closed for some time, and now, like a bursting spark, it reopened. Laman sank to his knees and took his son into his trembling arms.

Then he wept.

Indescribable agony filled his core as he poured out his soul to God. Around him, all fell to their knees. They openly shed tears as Laman supplicated the Lord for forgiveness. Time could not be calculated. But when Laman finished, he rose to his feet, his arm encircling his son, and crossed to his parents. He leaned toward little Joseph and took the baby's hand. Tears dripped down his cheeks as he tenderly kissed his new brother. Then he embraced Sariah and Lehi. The anger, bitterness, and hurt fled in that moment—and the healing began.

Slowly, Laman pulled away from his parents and moved to Anah. He grasped her arm and lifted her gently to her feet. For several moments, they clung to each other.

Next to Nephi, Isaabel wiped her eyes. Nearby, the tribesmen grinned, not fully understanding what was happening, but rejoicing in the family's happiness and apparent newfound freedom.

Laman released Anah, one arm still about her, and spoke to the gaping marauders. "Your work is done. Please go in peace."

A few of the raiders stared at him in disbelief, while others located their camels or horses and left in haste.

"This is my family," Laman explained to the remaining men. "And I will be traveling with them from here."

When the last raider had left Shisur, the tribesmen approached Laman one by one, thanking him profusely. Laman waved away their gratitude and begged for their forgiveness.

Finally, Raamah walked to Laman. For a long moment, they stood facing each other, each man regretting what had happened between them. They embraced heartily, then kissed each other's cheeks.

The tribesmen eventually returned to their sleeping quarters, everyone feeling the exhaustion of the terrifying events.

When just the family members surrounded the dwindling campfire, Laman stood before the group. "According to the Law of Moses, Father has every right to put me to death." He lowered his gaze and knelt. "I kneel here, at the mercy of my father, ready to receive just punishment."

Lehi moved forward and placed a hand on Laman's shoulder. "You may rise, my son. There will be no stoning tonight." His voice fell to a whisper. "I forgive you."

His grip firm on Laman, Lehi faced the family and said in a trembling voice, "Our prayers have been answered. Our sons have returned to us safely. Mother has delivered a healthy baby, and our lives have been spared once again from marauders. In place of the penalty of death, we will exercise repentance and forgiveness. Tomorrow we shall present a sin offering for the complete cleansing of Laman, Lemuel, and Heth."

Lehi turned his gaze to meet Nephi's. "I must ask forgiveness for myself. For some time, I have failed as the patriarch of our family. I spent every waking moment in sorrow for the loss of my eldest sons and have neglected my duties. But, as Nephi reminded me, the Lord was mindful of my sons and did not forget." He scanned the other family members. "As we keep the commandments, God will nourish us, strengthen us, and provide the means whereby we can accomplish His will. We have sojourned in this wilderness for nearly eight years," Lehi continued. "I know that we are eager to reach the promised land—a place that is not only in our dreams, but is as real and tangible as the earth beneath our feet. I ask for your diligence, patience, and faith. If we work together, we'll reach the new land of our inheritance." His voice cracked. "My heart . . . has been broken . . . by the actions of my sons." His eyes settled on Lemuel. "But I know the Lord will be merciful to them if they but hearken unto Him."

Lehi bowed his head and began to pray. "O Lord, have mercy on our souls. Cleanse us from our pride and shame. Our distress has turned to rejoicing, O God. We rejoice in Thee. Thou hast put gladness in our hearts. Bless us this night as we lay down in peace and sleep that we may dwell in safety." He paused. "Our voices shalt Thou hear in the morning, O Lord, as we direct our prayers unto Thee. Sustain us in our journey, for we know Thou wilt bless Thy children. Amen."

"Amen," Laman said. He moved forward to embrace his brothers again. Then he put his arm around his father's bony shoulder. A few white streaks in Lehi's beard had surfaced since Laman last saw him, as well as some lines in his face. But tonight, Lehi's expression was radiant.

* * *

Isaabel walked alongside Elisheba. Their silence was companionable, but Isaabel waited patiently for Elisheba to say what troubled her. Isaabel couldn't see her expression because both of them were swathed in full head wraps with only their noses, eyes, and lips exposed to the harsh sun. They had left Shisur the previous morning and made their way south. At each outcropping of vegetation they came across, they stopped and let the camels graze. Two horses had been added to the caravan, each procured by Laman in his travels. Whether they were stolen or traded, no one asked.

"I know about Raamah's meeting with Laman and Lemuel the night they disappeared," Elisheba said.

Isaabel waited for her to continue.

"Since Laman's return, I've felt sick at heart, wondering what would have happened if he had chosen to go with them," Elisheba said.

Placing her hand on her sister-in-law's arm, Isaabel answered, "But he didn't. And I'm sure it had to do with his feelings for you. He's an honorable man and won't break an oath."

Elisheba sighed. "Perhaps. But he wants to know *when* we'll reach the promised land."

"We all do," Isaabel said. "We have to continue in patience, no matter how frustrating it may be."

Shaking her head, Elisheba said, "I know on the outside, Raamah is following my father's lead, but on the inside, it's as if a pot of water is beginning to boil." She pulled her mantle about her tighter as the wind picked up. "I don't know how to help him when he broods."

"Do nothing," Isaabel advised. "He will have to learn on his own. You can't change the way he feels about things. All you can do is pray and have faith."

A tear escaped Elisheba's eye, absorbed by her headdress. "That's what I was afraid of."

The sky grew dark above them, and the women glanced upward. Heavy, low clouds had seemingly appeared out of nowhere, racing northward. Forked lightning split the sky, and the sound of muted thunder rolled through the heavens. The entire family came to a stop, staring at the approaching storm in wonder. The camels raised their noses upward, their massive lips quivering, as if they could smell the coming moisture.

The word *rain* rippled like a wave through the family members, and they spread their arms wide, welcoming the storm.

And rain it did.

Isaabel and Elisheba began to giggle when the first drops hit their cheeks and noses. As the rain fell faster and faster, pelting the ground in a frenzy, the women danced in the gathering puddles, the rain drenching their clothing and hair.

Almost as quickly as it appeared, the thunderstorm moved on. The ground had absorbed the moisture within seconds, leaving sodden sand. Unbidden, the camels made their way over the next rise to where there was a stony outcrop. The family followed their beasts and saw the rain puddled on the rocky floor. The animals bent their necks and drank the fresh water. Soon the family members joined their beasts, kneeling and drinking the sweet rain.

After everyone had drunk their fill, they scooped water by the handfuls into their goatskins. For the next several miles, the family encountered rain puddles, which they used to add water to the skins.

Elisheba caught up with Isaabel and squeezed her arm. "Raamah can't complain about this," she said, elation in her voice. "Surely there is more to come."

But Isaabel shook her head slowly. "Summer is not yet over. We're in for more dry than wet."

The next day, Isaabel watched the sky with hope but grew disappointed as a cloud passed without any evidence of promising rain. Wilted vegetation lay in the dry streambeds where the rain had evaporated. Only the hardiest trees and tufts of grass survived. Every so often, they would come across a grouping of frankincense trees. The thick stems of the shrub miraculously sprouted from the dry earth, topped off with spindly branches.

With Elisheba's knowledge gained from Hadi, they had made it a practice to gather the aromatic gum residue from the frankincense tree. The sap had oozed and dried from previous incisions cut into the bark by other nomads. After Isaabel and Elisheba made their collections, they added more incisions to be ready for the next person. Then they further dried the harvested frankincense, preserving it for the time when it could be of value to the family.

* * *

Nephi heard voices in the still of the night. Remembering the time before when Raamah had been arguing with the others, Nephi felt panic set in. His pulse quickened as he strained to hear the intonation of the conversation. It didn't sound angry, he thought.

Curiosity overcoming him, Nephi rose and crept around the sleeping family members. Most of them slept in the open, covered with their rugs. Others slept under a shrub, hoping to gain a little protection from the blowing sand. A short distance from camp, four men sat, deep in conversation. Nephi could make out the forms of Raamah, Laman, Lemuel. Dread filled his heart. *Not again.* But then the fourth form came into view—Sam.

Just then, Sam spotted Nephi approaching and waved him over. "Couldn't sleep?" he asked amiably.

Nephi felt his body relax, knowing that nothing was being plotted. He joined the men and glanced at Laman.

Laman smiled pleasantly. "Come to hear the story?"

"A story of what?" Nephi asked, glancing at Sam.

"Tell him," Sam prompted Laman. "Tell him how great your reign as a chief marauder really was."

Laman chortled. "Most ludicrous thing I've ever done."

Nephi joined in the laughter. Warmth enveloped him, hearing his brother speak about his foolish actions in such a way.

"And what's even more absurd is that Lemuel and Heth went along with it," Laman said.

Lemuel's jaw dropped opened. "What?" He threw a blind punch in Laman's direction, who deftly avoided it.

"Oh, we were full of anger and venom at the beginning. But soon we realized that we had brought no food, and the water was almost gone." Laman swatted at an insect, then scratched his nose. "And without Father's ball—"

"Liahona," Sam interrupted.

"—whatever, we didn't know where to find the next well," Laman said.

Nephi leaned back on his elbows.

Laman glared at Lemuel and said, "Then our irrational brother had the great idea that we should start digging."

"Just trying to help," Lemuel said in defense. He looked at the others. "What's wrong with that?"

"We dug," Laman said with a scoff. "And we dug . . . about three paces down we found . . . rock."

Sam burst out laughing, joined by Raamah and Nephi.

"Tell them what happened next," Lemuel pressed.

"Go ahead," Laman said nonchalantly. "This is too painful to talk about."

Lemuel leaned forward eagerly, gleaning off the captivated audience. "We were captured!" He let the words sink in, then continued. "By *real* marauders. They stole our camels and stripped us of everything . . . except a little clothing. So we had nothing and wandered for weeks—"

"Days," Laman said. "We wandered for a few days."

"But we were starving, and there was nothing . . . unless you like to eat sand," Lemuel continued. "Then, a miracle happened."

Nephi looked at Lemuel in surprise.

"We found a wild camel," Lemuel said.

A pit formed in Nephi's stomach at the thought of his brothers having to resort to eating an unclean beast to survive.

Laman met Nephi's gaze. "Don't worry, we didn't eat it."

"No," Lemuel said, "but we stuck a stick down its throat to bring up the stomach contents."

"Ohhh!" Raamah groaned, clutching his middle in revulsion.

Sam and Nephi exchanged looks of abhorrence.

"Pretty awful, eh?" Lemuel said, his expression enthusiastic. "Makes eating a few locusts seem like nothing."

"Who said there's something wrong with eating locusts?" Laman asked.

"So," Raamah said, "how did you arrive in Shisur leading a group of raiders with horses?"

Laman's face turned grim. "We tracked those marauders who plundered from us and attacked them in the middle of the night." He paused, rubbing his arm as if it were still sore from fighting. "We ended up better than when we first started out."

"But not much better," Lemuel said quietly.

The men fell silent as each contemplated the events leading up to Shisur.

* * *

Another slow day of travel, and the family stopped for a few days at the Ma Shadid oasis, where they were able to water their camels and fill goatskins. The camels were noticeably more content since the rain had stirred a little plant growth. More greenery could be found, and the animals grazed at their leisure.

On the third morning, Nephi felt rather than heard a rumbling in the air, and he searched the horizon on all sides for any sign of storm clouds. One by one, other members of the family began to notice the sound too.

Finally Sam pointed toward the south. "Look, I can see a dark cloud, and it's moving fast."

Nephi followed Sam's direction. "And it's changing shape rapidly," he said. The noise grew louder, though it was not the sound of crackling thunder, but of a humming drone. Nephi abandoned his task of plugging the waterskin leaks with splinters of wood and stood still, watching.

Isaabel joined him. "Is it another rainstorm?" she asked, hope in her voice. "Or smoke?"

"No," Nephi said, putting a hand on her arm. "Smoke doesn't make that sound." Then, with horror, he realized what the dark cloud was. Swarms of desert locusts rolled across the ground directly toward them. Their massed bodies spanned several miles wide and probably hundreds of paces deep, creating an ominous front of destruction.

Isaabel gasped, understanding in the same moment. "Locusts?"

A cry went up among the family members, and everyone looked at the dark horizon. In awed fascination, they stood rooted in place, unable to take their eyes from the approaching swarm.

"Hobble the camels!" someone shouted.

The daze was broken. Everyone rushed into action. Women collected their children, making them lie down on the ground and covering them with rugs. The men tied the camels and forced them to kneel.

Nephi grabbed Aaron and covered him with his own body, Isaabel burrowing in next to them. A few screams sounded as the droning closed in, eventually drowning out all other sounds.

The first flutter made Nephi recoil. A few large hoppers landed on his body for a short time, only to take off in their winged flight. They alighted by the dozens—then by the hundreds. Beneath him, he could feel Aaron's trembling body. Nephi raised his head, keeping his nose and mouth covered with the flaps of his turban. The sight before him was astonishing—

thousands, if not tens of thousands, of long-legged creatures had settled on the palm trees, breaking branches with their weight. The green growth from the rain the week before had been stripped bare.

The camels bawled out in complaint. They tried to rise but couldn't because of their hobbled knees. Nephi saw a young child standing in the middle of the flurry, hands shielding his face just before he was grabbed by one of the adults and covered with a rug. Isaabel shifted next to him. She raised her face for a moment, taking in the scene, then buried it again with a moan.

After what seemed like a long time later, but was only a few moments, the locusts moved on. In their wake, they left a decimated oasis. Palm branches had been broken and stripped bare. The brush that grew near the well opening had been reduced to a few exposed roots. Even the flies that continually barraged the camels had vanished.

Nephi rose to his hands and knees, brushing a lame grasshopper from his sleeve. Scattered throughout the area were some straggling locusts, either injured or still feeding on plant stubble.

"Get! Get!"

Nephi turned to see Dinah running about, swatting the locusts with a stick. Soon the other children rose from their places and joined in the action. They were laughing together until Sariah reprimanded them.

"Stop scaring them away. We will capture the remaining insects and dry them for food," Sariah said.

"We're going to eat locusts?" Aaron asked Nephi, a look of disgust on his face. He had stayed by his parents instead of running with the children.

Nephi chuckled. "Dried locusts are a delicacy in the desert, son." He put his arm about Aaron's shoulders and squeezed. "There was a time when it was all we had to eat." Then Nephi reached out to Isaabel and helped her to her feet.

"You tend to feel differently when they arrive in a swarm," Isabel said, wrinkling her nose. She took Aaron's hand. "Come on, let's help the others."

"All right," Aaron said, "but that doesn't mean I have to eat them."

Nephi smiled after his wife and son, watching them join in the chase. Then worry creased his brow. With the locusts devouring everything as they moved north and the family traveling south, what little vegetation there had been might be gone.

Seeing Lehi move among the family members, asking them to catch any remaining locusts, Nephi knew that his father shared the same concern. When Lehi reached Nephi's side, he clapped Nephi on the shoulder. "Are you all right?"

"Yes," Nephi said. "How widespread do you think the destruction is?"

Lehi let out a heavy sigh and rubbed his beard. "I don't know, but the Liahona continues to point in a southerly direction. Let's pray our camels will continue to find fodder."

Just as Nephi anticipated, the desert foliage had been ravished by the swarming locusts. Every possible green outcropping had been devoured, leaving nothing for the camels to eat. As the day passed, their pace slowed even more. No one rode upon the animals, trying to preserve any potential scrap of strength.

Strewn about the desert floor were carcasses, animals dead from starvation. Yet they provided no food. The Hebrew dietary laws dictated they could not eat an animal that had perished of natural causes.

Collected locusts from the swarm became the family's evening meal and helped reduce their hunger pangs. But their thirst was unquenchable. The weakened camels produced less and less milk, so that only the children were allowed to drink it. Sariah kept a strict guard over the water and rationed it to the adults. Although the family members' bags were filled with dates, they felt too thirsty to eat.

That night, as the family met in prayer, Lehi pleaded with the Lord that they would be delivered from their hunger . . . once again. When the family dispersed for the evening, no complaints were heard among the adults. As Nephi went to sleep, he added his pleas to his father's and asked for deliverance, and when he drifted into sleep, he wondered if the same dreary wilderness would spread out before them the next morning, with no beginning and seemingly no end.

CHAPTER 26

*Trust in the Lord with all thine heart; and lean
not unto thine own understanding.*
(Proverbs 3:5)

The following morning, Nephi woke to a rusty-colored dawn. He rubbed his eyes and looked at the horizon again. Hues of red painted the eastern sky where the sun was about to crest over a mountain enshrouded with mist. *A mountain.* His first thought was that the family would have to coerce the camels to travel uphill in their weakened condition. His second thought filled his heart with gladness. The promise of vegetation, water, and meat was too joyful not to share immediately.

"Isa," he whispered, careful not to wake Aaron, "look."

Isaabel sat up next to her husband and looked in the direction he pointed. "A mountain!" She clapped her hands together.

Nephi chuckled softly and placed his hands over hers. "Yes, the Lord has heard our prayers." He wrapped an arm about his wife and kissed her.

As the other family members roused from sleep, excited murmuring surrounded them. It hadn't taken long to see the rising mountain in the distance.

Throughout the remainder of the day, though progress continued to be tedious, hope burned bright in Nephi's bosom.

With each stride, the mount grew closer, increasing the anticipation of nourishment.

Lehi joined Nephi's side. "I hope there will still be vegetation at the base. If not, we will have to find a pass."

"If it takes climbing the slopes to find fodder for the camels, I will do it," Nephi said.

A faint smile pushed back the weathered creases on Lehi's face. "You'll be next in line after the camels. Let's hope they hold out. We might have to remove the cargo from their backs."

Nephi looked at the camel that plodded next to him. It trembled with each step, saliva foaming at its mouth. He placed a hand on the animal's side and felt the protruding ribs heave with each labored breath. "Come on, girl," he said gently. "By nightfall, you'll be eating."

As they neared the base of the mountain, Nephi was surprised to see the rising slope bare of vegetation. In the evening light, he squinted upward, trying to make out where the line of greenery began. He couldn't see one.

"It must be out of sight," Nephi said out loud to himself.

Sam overheard the comment. "I think it's more than out of sight," he said, shaking his head in disappointment as he crossed toward Nephi. He crouched and fingered the broken branches of a dead shrub. "The locusts were here."

Nephi sighed, his shoulders drooping. "Didn't they leave anything?" He turned as he heard his father approach. "What is it?" he asked.

Coming to a stop, Lehi craned his neck upward, then brought his gaze to meet Nephi's. "Since there's no vegetation in view, we might as well settle down for the night. In the morning we'll travel through the pass, and perhaps there will be something on the other side."

"We need more than *something*, Father," Laman said, joining the group. "Two of the camels are lying on their sides and refuse to move. Tomorrow might be too late for them, and the children cried themselves to sleep last night with empty stomachs."

Lehi spread his hands. "We have done all we can, son. It's up to the Lord now."

Laman shook his head and walked away.

* * *

Nephi woke in the early morning feeling something wet on his cheek and raised his hand to wipe it away. His eyes opened, and he stared at the water on his fingers. *Dew.* He licked the moisture off his hand, his parched tongue feeling like sand granules on his skin. Looking about the camp, he saw that everything was covered with a fine mist. *Where had it come from?* He wondered.

Isaabel stirred next to him. "Why am I wet?" she asked in a drowsy voice. Her eyes flew open, and she sat up. "Did it rain?"

"No," Nephi said. "It's dew."

As the family awoke, they were delighted with the bit of moisture that had formed. It gave everyone a small supply of energy with which to face the day. After they received their minute ration of food and water, they formed into their procession behind Lehi and Nephi, who had scouted a pass that cut through the mountain. When they reached the narrow opening, they walked single file. The air was cool and misty—refreshing after the months spent under the penetrating sun.

Second in line behind his father, Nephi tilted his head back, looking up at the towering cliffs through which they passed. The white limestone of the mountain contrasted with the brilliant blueness of the sky. His skin felt moist in the humid air as he stumbled along the rocky path that they walked. With ginger steps, the camels picked their way through the protruding stones.

At midday, Sariah called the family to stop for a meal. Although the nourishment was scant—a few dates and a small portion of water for each person—it helped reinvigorate them. As they rested, Isaabel collected some tufts of grass that had pushed through the rocky ground and fed it to the camels. A couple of the camels merely sniffed the grass and turned away.

As the family prepared to walk again, Nephi moved to his father's side and said, "Let me travel ahead, Father, to see if I can find any water."

"No," Lehi said. "We must stay together."

"There's no place to get lost," Nephi said.

Lehi, eyes bright, looked at Nephi. "Does this mist remind you of something? A mist of darkness. We don't know who or what might be around the next bend."

Nephi nodded. "Let's get started then." He offered a hand and pulled his father to his feet, and they continued the slow, measured march until they reached the end of the narrow passage.

It was sudden. So sudden that Lehi and Nephi stopped and stared, disbelieving their eyes. Then they moved aside so that the other family members could see the spectacular view.

They stood upon a precipice overlooking a sloping valley of leafy green. The waving trees below them were thick like a jungle, rolling down to a pool of blue water. Beyond, shimmering in the afternoon sun, white beaches bordered a sapphire sea.

Nephi felt tears well in his eyes. Inhaling, he breathed in the fragrant, moist air. It was like a balm covering his sore, aching limbs, a tender caress to his face and hands.

The family stood together in silence—even the children were in awe—as they stared at the backdrop of what could have passed for the Garden of Eden. Most of them had never seen a sea before, let alone a lush jungle.

Lehi gripped his staff and sank to his knees, tears streaming down his face in joy. Soon he was followed by Nephi, then the rest of the family.

"O Lord," Lehi said, raising his voice to the heavens. "We thank Thee for this paradise." His voice broke.

"Heaven be thanked," Sariah cried out. Her words were echoed by several others.

Humble silence followed as each person soaked in the sight of yellow-flowered meadows surrounded by white and black cliffs, the leafy forest of trees, pure sandy beaches, and the brilliant sea.

The tranquility of the moment was broken by the uproar of the camels. They had smelled water. The revitalized beasts pushed ahead, eager to fill their reservoirs. The family members laughed in delight. Then they embraced each other, crying with elation.

The camels jogged forward, the family encouraging them and keeping pace. Sariah stared at the variety of foliage they passed, verbally calculating the medicinal herbs she would be able to concoct. Herons flew away before her feet, startled at the new guests. Through the tall sycamore and tamarind trees of the escarpment, the family traveled until they reached a pool in the bottom of the wadi. The camels plunged into the water, bending their necks to drink. The children followed the animals and drank their fill.

Isaabel walked into the lagoon, soaking her clothing, then drank and laughed as others followed suit. Nephi joined his wife, basking in the cool water. He crossed to Elisheba and grinned at the joy he saw in her eyes.

"Now I understand, Nephi," Elisheba said in a soft voice. "The Lord has a reason for all things . . . our bondage, our sufferings, the hunger, the thirst." She paused. "I see He was guiding us all along, preparing us for His deliverance, for this place. He *wants* to bless us."

Nephi took his sister's hand and kissed her cheek. "As long as we keep the Lord's commandments, He will continue to provide for us."

"The reward is sweeter than I could have ever imagined," Elisheba said, embracing him. Releasing him, she let out a happy yell and bounded away.

Smiling, Nephi watched her go, reminded of a much younger Elisheba.

From his position, Nephi could see trees with reddish bark bearing a golden orange fruit. He waded through the lagoon to reach the other side and plucked a fruit from the tree. The sweet juice exploded onto his tongue. Nephi chewed the luscious flesh, then swallowed. He was in paradise.

He gathered several fruits and called out to Isaabel. She joined him, and soon they carried a bundle to the family. After passing out the fruit to the others, Nephi noticed that his father wasn't among the celebrators. He turned and scanned the region, then finally saw a lone figure on the beach below. Standing next to Nephi, Isaabel followed his gaze.

"Go to him," she said quietly.

Nephi swallowed at the lump in his throat, feeling as if his heart would burst with joy. He kissed his wife and left the gaiety.

* * *

Lehi knelt on the sandy surface, staring at the hard, incoming waves. "O Lord," he whispered, "we are grateful to Thee for this land which Thou hast prepared for us."

A single tear slipped down his cheek. The family had traveled so far, waded through much affliction, descended into such great depths of sorrow, that sometimes he'd wondered if they would have been better off dying. *But now,* he thought, *we have finally arrived in the land of much fruit. Praise the Lord.*

He stared at the sea of many waters before him. *Irreantum.*

The rhythm of the rolling waves mesmerized him as they thundered onto the shoreline. He sensed footsteps approaching behind him, but he did not turn. He knew it was Nephi.

"Father," Nephi said, "I've brought some food." He knelt in the sand next to Lehi and placed the fruit in his father's hands.

Slowly, Lehi turned over the golden fruit, then brought it to his nose and inhaled the fragrance. Closing his eyes, he sighed. "A land of much fruit."

"And honey," Nephi said. "I passed a cave filled with bees."

"Bountiful," Lehi said quietly. "We shall call this place of much fruit and wild honey the land of Bountiful." After a pause he bit into the fruit, savoring the taste as it played in his mouth and slipped down his throat. Pleasure crept to his face. "It's good."

"Anything is better than dates and bitter water," Nephi said with a chuckle. "Here we will have plenty of food and water." He glanced up and down the beach. "Where will we set up our tents?"

"Right by the seashore," Lehi said. "After so many years in the desert, it will be a pleasure to wake to the sound of the surf each morning." He used his staff to stand up. "I'll inform the others of our new campsite. And," he paused, noticing smoke coming from the next hillside. "I need to tell Sam and Zoram to bury the valuables. It looks like we will have neighbors." Lehi looked down at Nephi. "Thank you for the fruit."

* * *

When his father left, Nephi drew his knees to his chest and wrapped his arms around himself. Entranced by the incoming tide and the scampering white crabs, he felt his skin prickle as the sea breeze blew across his face. *Bountiful.* The name appealed to his senses. *A land of plenty.* Nephi picked up another piece of fruit and took a bite. Juice ran down the sides of his mouth, and he happily licked it away.

"Father!" a young voice shouted. Nephi turned to see his son, Aaron, running toward him. "It's the sea!" Aaron ran toward the line where the water met the land and watched in amazement. He skipped along the shoreline for a few moments, then suddenly noticing the crabs, he crouched and laughed in delight as they scurried on the wet sand. Aaron raced back to where Nephi sat, his eyes dancing, his voice breathless, then he ran away again to chase the crabs.

A hand touched Nephi's shoulder, and he looked up and saw Isaabel. She smiled and settled next to him, her clothing still wet and drops of water trickling down her forehead from her hairline. They watched their son play in peaceful silence.

"Father," Aaron called as he neared them. "What is this place called?"

"Bountiful," Nephi said with a smile. "Grandfather calls it Bountiful."

Next to him Isaabel placed her hand in Nephi's. "Bountiful. I like that name."

"It's fitting for a place such as this," Nephi agreed. Aaron had gone back to dodging the ripples of waves. "And the sea we shall call Irreantum—because of the many waters."

Isaabel squeezed his hand and sighed. "It's like a dream." She turned and looked at Nephi. "Are we really here?"

Nephi wrapped his arms around his wife, squeezing her tight. "This is the best dream I've ever had." His words brushed her ear. "I hope we never wake up."

Isaabel relaxed into his embrace.

Soon, Aaron abandoned his play and ran to his parents, squeezing between them. Together, they watched the swells of the sea, rising and falling, in a pattern of perpetuity. Aaron's eyes grew heavy and his breathing relaxed until it deepened and he drifted off to sleep.

CHAPTER NOTES

CHAPTER 1

Scripture referenced: 1 Nephi 16:14

In 1 Nephi 16:14, it is documented that Lehi's family continued in the same direction as before (south southeast), "keeping in the most fertile parts of the wilderness, which were in the borders near the Red Sea."

It is reasonable to assume that the prayers of Lehi or Nephi, along with other family members, would have been similar to those found in Psalms 4 and 5. With careful study, a pattern emerges, such as the opening address "O God," or "O Lord." Questions were then asked and praises given to the Lord. Love and gratitude were also expressed.

In Genesis 48:14–15, "Israel stretched out his right hand, . . . laid it upon Ephraim's head," and blessed him. Another example is found in the Dead Sea Scrolls. "The Genesis Apocryphon" documents that Abraham placed his hands on Pharaoh's head and blessed him. Thus we may expect that Lehi, too, likely gave "blessings" in this manner to members of the family.

Authors George Potter and Richard Wellington theorize that the Camp of the Broken Bow is in the vicinity of the oasis Bishah for several reasons. Bishah is a generally accessible oasis on the incense trail and is in close proximity to the mountains. Also, two wadis pass through or near Bishah, creating a natural path to the mountains. In addition, Potter and Wellington observe that the atim olive tree grew in the area, providing the necessary wood characteristics needed for making a good bow (*Lehi in the Wilderness* [Springville, UT: Cedar Fort, 2003], 95–98).

Hugh Nibley points out that in a Bedouin society, the women do the bulk of the work. He quotes Antonin Jaussen, "The Arab talks in his tent, cares for the animals, or goes hunting, while the women do all the work." In Nibley's observations, Laman and Lemuel seem to have adapted quite naturally to this lifestyle (*An Approach to the Book of Mormon*, 250). In the article "Desert Epiphany: Sariah and the Women in 1 Nephi," Camille Fronk outlines the desert woman's duties: "They collected water, gathered firewood, churned butter, guarded flocks, prepared meals, spun yarn from which mantles were woven to keep the family warm, braided palm matting that covered tent floors, and wove and repaired cords used to secure the tents" (*Journal of Book of Mormon Studies* 9, no. 2 [2000]: 13). In addition, the women were in charge of loading and unloading tents and supplies, and setting up camp once a new site was reached (13).

CHAPTER 2

One type of tea common in Yemen is made from the leaves of the shrub *catha edulis*.

We can assume that most of the women of Lehi and Ishmael's families gave birth at least once during the eight-year journey through the wilderness (see 1 Ne. 17:1; 18:7). Doughty describes the primitive conditions that a nomad woman would have to give birth in. The older women would likely assist the mother, taking her away from camp, "apart in the wilderness," to give birth. The birthing place would consist of "a mantle or tent-cloth spread upon the earth." If a birthing chair was not available, the laboring mother would kneel or sit on her heels. Doughty states, "The woman's sex is despised by the old nomad and divine law in Moses; for a female birth the days of her purification are doubled, also the estimation of her babe shall be at the half" (*Travels in Arabia Deserta* [New York: Random House, 1936], 1:280).

In this volume, Sariah says, "Thy will be done," during childbirth. While we don't know her exact words, I thought it fitting for her to acknowledge her subservience and dependence on the Lord in her time of utter helplessness. Notably, it was said by Lehi on his deathbed (see 2 Ne. 1:19) and later by Jacob (see Jacob 7:14).

Washing or cleansing rituals may have been a part of the afterbirth process and later in the purification sacrifice. Jacob Milgrom notes that "both mother and child had to be purified from the pollution of birth" and "both underwent a ritual bath" (*Leviticus 1–16: A New Translation with Introduction and Commentary, The Anchor Bible,* [New York: Doubleday, 1991], 762). It is also important to understand that the birthing mother has only suffered "physical impurity" and has "committed no moral wrong that requires divine forgiveness" (760, emphasis in original).

Of interest, Sariah would have been considered the head of the household among the women, since she would have important influence and supervision over her new daughters-in-law. According to Israelite culture, when a daughter marries, she becomes a part of her new husband's household (Fronk, 12).

Chapter 3

Scriptures referenced: Genesis 25:23; 26–27; Leviticus 12:2

Deuteronomy 12 outlines the laws of sacrifice according to the Mosaic law, which indicates that sacrifices be made at the altar of the temple. David Rolph Seely explains that Lehi was allowed to build altars and offer sacrifices because according to the Mosaic requirement, "the offering of sacrifice [was] allowed only outside of the radius of a three days' journey from the temple in Jerusalem" ("Lehi's Altar and Sacrifice in the Wilderness," *Journal of Book of Mormon Studies* 10, no.1 [2001], 69).

Nibley informs us that Lehi's sacrifices in the desert were common among the Semitic people. Many stone altars are still seen throughout the desert region (*Lehi in the Desert*, 62–63). Authors John A. Tvedtnes and Matthew Roper note that "during the 1970s, archaeologists uncovered Israelite temples and sacrificial altars at the ancient sites of Arad, Beer-Sheba, and Dan, all of which were contemporaries of Solomon's temple" (*Animals and the Law of Moses*, unpublished manuscript).

The peace offering is discussed in Brown's book, *From Jerusalem to Zarahemla*. Brown points out the three reasons for a peace offering included an offering for well-being (safety in traveling), thanksgiving, or rejoicing (2). Lehi may have directed a peace offering to the Lord in order to express his gratitude for the safe arrival of his son's birth. Details of the events surrounding a peace offering are outlined in Leviticus 3. Brown notes that the sacrifice itself was either a male or female animal (Lev. 3:1, 6, 12) that was to be eaten the same day (Lev. 7:15) in conjunction with unleavened foods (2). According to the Bible Dictionary, sacrifices "were accompanied by prayer, devotion, and dedication" ("Sacrifices," 766).

Throughout the ancient world, women were considered unclean during childbirth and/or menses. "In Babylonia, the menstruant was not only impure herself; she also contaminated others, even those in her proximity. In ancient Persia, parturients [babies] and menstruants [mothers] were routinely quarantined" (Milgrom, 763).

The Bedu use sand to scrub their hands after eating and taking care of toiletry matters if they are not by a well with water available (Wilfred Thesiger, *Arabian Sands* [New York: E.P. Dutton, 1959], 48).

Chapter 4

Scriptures referenced: 1 Nephi 16:16; Leviticus 12:3, 6–8

Thesiger points out that the Arabs he traveled with wore "socks knitted from coarse black hair"—whether it was in the summer or winter—to protect their feet from the heat or the cold temperature of the sand (122).

George Potter and Richard Wellington observe that Tathlith and Najran oases may have been those encountered by Lehi's family on their way to Nahom (107).

Under the law, Sariah would have made a burnt offering and a sin offering—an atonement—to "cleanse" her after childbirth (see Lev. 12:6–8). Jacob Milgrom states that both sacrifices were expiatory in function, and two birds were used so that "the priest benefits from the meat of the purification offering, the burnt offering is added to provide a decent contribution to the altar, that is, to God" (763).

One of the main dangers in traveling in the Arabian wilderness is raiders. Nibley informs us that, "Once [raiders] have spotted a caravan they follow it all day, keeping just out of sight, 'and in the night they silently fall upon the camp, and carry off one part of it before the rest are got under arms.' And so it was in Lehi's day" (*An Approach to the Book of Mormon*, 243). This observation was also made by Thomas in his explorations: "Many had been (and will be) the bloody conflicts upon this road along the southern borderlands, for waterless no-man's-lands as they are, yet they are the fairway between water-holes which are used only and inevitably by raiders on murder and plunder bent" (*Arabia Felix: Across the "Empty Quarter" of Arabia* [New York: Charles Scribner's Sons, 1932], 149).

Chapter 5

According to the Prophet Joseph Smith, the intermarriage of Lehi and Ishmael's families (descendents of Manasseh and Ephraim respectively) fulfilled the words spoken by Jacob when he blesses his two grandsons that their lineage will be conjoined (*Encyclopedia of Mormonism*, 5 vols. [New York: Macmillan, 1992], 400–401).

While the scriptures say Lehi left all of his valuables, it may be theorized that Sariah brought along her inherited jewelry or trinkets—something with great meaning. The gifts from a woman's family that she receives upon her marriage remain her own property (Ephraim Neufeld, *Ancient Hebrew Marriage Laws* [New York: Longmans, Green, 1944], 239).

Among the tribes of ancient Arabia, "All the men are warriors of equal rank; half naked, clad in coloured cloaks down to the waist, overrunning different countries, with the aid of swift and active horses and speedy camels, alike in times of peace and war. Nor does any member of their tribe ever take plough in hand or cultivate a tree, or seek food by the tillage of the land; but they are perpetually wandering over various and extensive districts, having no home, no fixed abode or laws; nor can they endure to remain long in the same climate, no one district or country pleasing them for a continuance" (Ammianus Marcellinus, *The Roman History* [London: George Bell and Sons, 1902], Book XIV.iv.3).

Chapter 6

Scripture referenced: Genesis 48:16

Lehi's walking stick or staff could have been made of myrtle wood. Myrtle grows in Israel and is a symbol of peace and divine blessing (*The Anchor Bible Dictionary*, David Noel Freedman, et al. ed. [New York: Doubleday, 1992], 2:807).

Scholars believe the location of Nahom, or Nehem, probably lay on the south side of Wadi Jawf, a valley situated in northwest Yemen, almost fourteen hundred miles south-southeast of Jerusalem (Warren P. Aston and Michaela Knoth Aston, *In the Footsteps of Lehi* [Salt Lake City: Deseret Book, 1994], 21; Potter and Wellington, 113; Brown, "New Light from Arabia on Lehi's Trail," *Echoes and Evidences of the Book of Mormon*, Donald W. Parry, Daniel C. Peterson, John W. Welch, ed. [Provo, UT: FARMS, 2002], 81–82).

In addition, Nahom seems to be the actual name used by local people, not a site named by Lehi (Lynn M. Hilton and Hope A. Hilton, *Discovering Lehi* [Springville, UT: Cedar Fort, 1996], 127). The Astons point out that because of the wording found in 1 Nephi 16:34, "'the place which *was called Nahom*,' indicates that *Nahom* was an already existing, locally known name" (10; emphasis in original).

Potter and Wellington describe the Wadi Jawf as being populated with Minaean people. They believe there was an abundance of pastures and farmlands that the Minaeans irrigated with rainwater (Potter and Wellington, 113). Thesiger confirms that "the Minaeans had developed a civilization as early as 1000 B.C. in the north-eastern part of the Yemen" (30). The Astons theorize that the family may have stayed in Nahom long enough to grow crops before their eastward departure (21). They quote Philby, who observed that "the evidence of more plentiful water in these parts in ancient times argues the presence of a large agricultural and pastoral community in those days" (21). Connecting with this point of view, Brian Doe remarked, "Now dry and arid, such settlements could have only occurred under milder and wetter conditions. This was probably at least before the III millennium B.C. and even earlier" (qtd. in Aston and Aston, *In Lehi's Footsteps,* 21).

Brown also suspects that the first children of the daughters of Ishmael were likely born in Nahom, since it can be assumed the family stayed there for some time ("'The Place That Was Called Nahom': New Light from Ancient Yemen," *Journal of Book of Mormon Studies* 8, no. 1 [1999]: 66–67).

Chapter 7

Scriptures referenced: 1 Nephi 16:34–35

Men are not included in the mourning rites. Among the Syrian Bedouins, or Bedus, the mourning begins immediately at death and continues for seven days for a few hours each day. The wives, daughters, and female relations all join together in cries of lamentation that are repeated over and over (Nibley, *An Approach to the Book of Mormon,* 251).

In the Old Testament, when Abraham negotiated with Heth for the purchase of a burial place for Sarah, Ephron set the price, and Abraham agreed to it (Gen. 23). The Old Testament also mentions that psalteries, or dulcimers, musical instruments with strings, were typical instruments played during this time.

In the Book of Mormon, we read that Ishmael "was buried in the place which was called Nahom" (1 Ne. 16:34). The Astons state, "There is no reason why the local people [Minaeans] would not have allowed a Hebrew burial on their sacred ground." A French archaeological team discovered an ancient burial ground in the hills of Nehem. These tombs were circular in fashion and built according to Arabian tradition (Aston and Aston, 19).

Mohar (or *moher*) is the custom of the groom giving his future parents-in-law a present or bride price (*Encyclopedia Judaica,* 185). Gifts of mohar may include jewels of silver and gold for the bride and precious things or money for the parents (see Gen. 24:53). We can safely assume that the daughters of Ishmael had received gifts of jewelry for their wedding day, such as gold necklaces, silver anklets, gold earrings, bracelets, and a nose ring (John G. Kennedy, ed., "Changes in Nubian Wedding Ceremonials," *Nubian Ceremonial Life: Studies in Islamic Syncretism and Cultural Change* [Cairo & Berkeley: American University in Cairo Press and University of California Press, 1978], 180).

Many of the Arabian names and descriptions of clothing throughout this volume are based on names and descriptions outlined by Thesiger (picture of a woman of the Harasis, 193; a girl from the Saar, 190; names and details, 31, 97–98, 100, 160).

CHAPTER 8

Scriptures referenced: 1 Nephi 16:35–36; 18:6, 24

It is probable that Lehi's family did not plant the seeds they brought from Jerusalem until they reached the Promised Land (see 1 Ne. 18:6, 24).

Barley and millet were already growing in Nahom, as well as dates. The Minaeans were also wealthy in flocks and timber (Hilton and Hilton, 113). The Astons suggest that there is ample evidence to support the idea of "extensive vegetation with streams and herds of wild animals" existing in Nahom. Scholars believe that major changes have occurred in the climate over the past few thousand years. Specifically, since a.d. 300, a continual drought has contributed to the decline of the incense trade (20).

CHAPTER 9

Scripture referenced: 1 Nephi 16:37–38

CHAPTER 11

Scripture referenced: 1 Nephi 2:20

Nibley explains that Laman and Lemuel could never carry through their threats and return to Jerusalem because of the fear of being "cut off" from their people. If they were found to be without tribe or identity, they would forfeit their own identity (*Lehi in the Desert*, 71). In addition, they would have been chief suspects in the death of Laban. It may have been possible though, that Laman and Lemuel attempted to break from the family to form their own tribe.

Thomas informs us that in a desert environment, "physical fitness, brute strength, and an aggressive character are qualities which Nature demands and rewards." And for some tribes, the beating of women was a common and accepted occurrence (271). Although one may not be able to discern whether or not Laman or one of his brothers made it a practice to abuse his wife, it certainly wouldn't have been unlikely.

Chapter 12

Scriptures referenced: 1 Nephi 1:13; 16:39

It is interesting to compare the experience of Laman and Lemuel to that of Alma the Younger when each of them were chastised by the Lord. "The voice of the Lord came and did speak many words unto [Laman and Lemuel], and did chasten them exceedingly; . . . they did turn away their anger, and did repent of their sins" (1 Ne. 16:39). Yet, when the family reached the Land of Bountiful and Nephi was commanded to build a ship, Laman and Lemuel murmured (1 Ne. 17:17) and then tried to kill Nephi (17:48). In contrast, when Alma the Younger was chastised by the Lord, following his repentance he also found "peace to [his] soul" (Alma 38:7–8). Alma the Younger changed his life and followed the Lord from that point on, bringing numerous souls to Christ.

Chapter 13

Halômut leaves, or mallow, are from an annual herb in which the fruit, leaf, and seed were used for food and the leaves for a demulcent and laxative (Freedman, 2:812).

Limestone is found throughout southern Arabia. In his article, "Newly Found Altars from Nahom," Warren Aston discusses the limestone altars in the area of Nahom that were locally quarried (*Journal of Book of Mormon Studies* 10, no. 2 [2001], 58).

Chapter 14

Scriptures referenced: 1 Nephi 15:24, 34; 16:2

I based the description of the tribal group that captured Sam on the armies of Giddianhi described in 3 Nephi 4:7. I thought it was interesting that the Giddianhi armies are compared to "robbers"—which reminded me of the raiders that Lehi and Nephi could have encountered. Perhaps the stories of the family's wilderness encounters were handed down throughout the generations and influenced their descendents in more ways than one.

In the first century a.d., a merchant who sailed along the coast of India claims to have encountered "barbarous tribes, among which are the Kirradai with squeezed noses, and savage." Also observed was "another tribe, that of the Bargusoi, and that of the Hippioprosopoi who are said to be cannibals," a characteristic borrowed for the purposes of the story (G. W. B. Huntingford (tr. & ed.), *The Periplus of the Erythraean Sea: Travel and Trade in the Indian Ocean by a Merchant of the First Century:* London: The Hakluyt Society [1980], 55).

Chapter 15

Scriptures referenced: Genesis 46:29–30; 48:21; 50:2, 13

Perhaps Ishmael's wife, and later Sariah or Lehi, experienced what President Gordon B. Hinckley expressed after the passing of his beloved Marjorie: "Only those who have passed through this dark valley know its utter desolation. To lose one's much-loved partner with whom one has long walked through sunshine and shadow is absolutely devastating. There is a consuming loneliness that increases in intensity. It painfully gnaws at one's very soul" (Marjorie Pay Hinckley, *Letters* [Salt Lake City: Deseret Book, 2004], 264).

Chapter 16

Scripture referenced: 1 Nephi 17:1

Marib was the site of a great dam that was in working order until about A.D. 570 (Aston and Aston, 20). Constructed in about 685 B.C., it is interesting to note the parallelism to Lehi's "Tree of Life" dream. Lehi saw a cultivated area with "a large and spacious field" and "a river of water" running near the tree (1 Ne. 8:9, 13). Brown suggests that perhaps Lehi saw places in his dream that he would later encounter in the wilderness—such as Marib and Timna—where the water systems were meant to capture and store rainfall and could be channeled to water their crops (*Voices from the Dust*, 40–41).

Barley has been present since 5,000 B.C. in Egypt, and by biblical times, it was also important in Israel. Among grains, barley can best survive heat and drought. The grain was not commonly used in breads; instead it was mixed with spelt, millet, or pea meal. Barley has a shorter harvesting season than wheat and can be used medicinally for a poultice or demulcent. Egyptians used barley in many other ways, including regnancy tests. A record of barley used for a sacrificial ritual can be found in Numbers 5:15 (Freedman, 2:808–809).

In the *Anchor Bible Dictionary*, we learn that juniper had many uses: the wood for construction, the berries for flavoring, hair dye, as an expectorant, stimulant, and poultice (2:805).

The Hebrew word for wind is *ruach*, meaning wind, breath, or Spirit. I had Sam use the Persian translation *govad* instead because the Hebrew one could have interchanged with divinity. Sam would have been exposed to international languages in Jerusalem, not only because Jerusalem was an international center, but also because Lehi would have known several languages through his occupation as a trader and merchant.

Chapter 17

Scriptures referenced: Exodus 16:15; 17:6; Isaiah 48:21; 49:15–16; 1 Ne. 8:9, 13, 26; 17:2, 12–14

In 1 Nephi, Nephi quotes Isaiah extensively (1 Ne. 20–21). Presumably, Nephi was familiar with the text to the extent of having memorized portions of it. It is likely that during the years in the wilderness, he and his father spent a great deal of time reading and discussing Isaiah's words on the brass plates.

According to Brown, Shabwah, one of the last places of civilization that Lehi likely passed through before reaching Bountiful, may have been another place Lehi saw in his dream. The "great and spacious building" could be compared to the multistory architecture of cities such as Shabwah. Approaching the area at night, the buildings may have appeared "high above the earth" (1 Ne. 8:26) with light emitting from the top windows. In *Voices from the Dust,* Brown notes that even before reaching Nahom, Lehi and his party would have passed through the region of Najran, where they would have seen large buildings and temple structures (38).

In a similar thread, Nephi explained that the river of water which Lehi had seen in the dream was "filthiness" (1 Ne. 15:27). Brown notes that when it rains in the desert, the water that runs out of the wadis or valleys are filled with dirt and debris (*Voices from the Dust,* 40).

The acacia tree comes in several varieties. It is native to the Mediterranean but is also found throughout Arabia. Its wood was used for tent poles, furniture, fuel, and tools. The bark was used for tanning leather, and its fiber was used for making rope. The fruit and flowers were used for animal fodder (Freedman, 2:804).

It is important to note that the law of Moses prohibits any consumption of blood. In Genesis 9 and Deuteronomy 12, it explains that blood must be drained from the meat before eating (Tvedtnes and Roper).

Thesiger notes that the tribes he encountered in Southern Arabia spoke different dialects of common origin. He quotes Thomas, who had studied the dialects and concluded that they were "closely related to the ancient Semitic languages of the Minaeans, Sabeans, and Himyarites" (33).

Chapter 18

Thomas explains the law of the blood feud as follows: "The party numerically stronger, better mounted and better armed must prevail, . . . but if one of the attackers has been killed, the law of the blood-feud must operate and his life be forfeit. Thus raiding parties are of two kinds, that whose tribe and yours have no blood-feud, that where the blood-feud exists. Both want your camels and arms, the second your life as well" (173–74).

Traveling nearly eastward from Nahom, the family may have passed through Marib, "then bent southeast to the city of Timna before turning northeast to Shabwah, the main center for gathering incense before shipping it more than 1,500 miles to the Mediterranean" (Brown, *Voices from the Dust,* 43). From there, Brown suggests that the party may have moved "as far north as al-'Abr, turning eastward would have brought them into a desolate corridor where they could walk between the high dunes of the Empty Quarter on their north and the fractured tableland to their south"

("Refining the Spotlight on Lehi and Sariah," unpublished manuscript). Perhaps they observed the same sites found in Thesiger's description of the high dunes, "It is this blending of two colours which gives such depth and richness to the Sands: gold with silver, orange with cream, brick-red with white, burnt-brown with pink, yellow with grey—they have an infinite variety of shades and colours" (105).

Brown also observes that "it is now known that the tribes in the region east of Shabwah were in a constant state of tension with one another and that a person could not cross tribal boundaries without having to negotiate afresh the terms of safe conduct. Such negotiations could and often did lead to temporary servility for the traveler among local tribes." In addition, "agriculture was little practiced" (*Echoes and Evidences of the Book of Mormon*, 90).

Thesiger informs us that the Bedu were able to decipher camel tracks and figure out what area the camel came from, whether it was ridden or free, and from which tribe it was from. Also, "from looking at their droppings they could often deduce where a camel had been grazing, and they could certainly tell when it had last been watered [and where]," (Thesiger, 52). The Bedu could also distinguish from the tracks which camel was the best (208).

Chapter 19

The settlement of Mudhail in this volume is based in part on the description of Liwa—"an oasis with palm groves and villages which extended for two days' camel journey" (Thesiger, 101). David Roberts discusses the legendary region of Ubar, "a vanished civilization—one that in ancient times ranked among the most prosperous and influential in the world" ("On the Frankincense Trail," *Smithsonian Magazine* [Oct. 1998], 124). This region may have included eight oases, among them Shisur, Jurub and Damqut, Habrut, and Sarif (126). Juris Zarins notes that "the region reportedly was well irrigated, forested, and had many fortresses and palaces" (*The Oxford Encyclopedia of Archaeology in the Near East* [New York: Oxford University Press, 1997], 5:252). The description of Sarif caught my attention with its crystalline pools, limestone precipice, giant figs and palms (Roberts, 134). It may be possible that Lehi's family encountered a civilization like Ubar that had been cultivated, such as the research of Roman geographers, Christian prophets, Herodotus, and the Koran indicate (123–124).

As introduced in the preface of this volume, Brown presents a theory that "Nephi's use of the verb *to sojourn* points to one or more periods of servility" (*From Jerusalem to Zarahemla*, 56). Brown makes a strong case supporting the idea that the families of Lehi and Ishmael were faced with "living in a condition of dependency, even subjugation or slavery" during their journey in the wilderness (60). In further exploration, Brown suggests when Lehi blessed Jacob and Joseph, he indicated that their journey in the wilderness "was the worst of times" ("A Case for Lehi's Bondage," *Journal of Book of Mormon Studies 6,* no. 2 [1997]: 210). Knowing that Lehi was prepared to live in the wilderness and was experienced in traveling, "there must have been an event—or series or events—that had soured him" (210).

Thesiger described the colors of the clothing found in Southern Arabia and from whose roots and plants the dyes were derived in his *Arabian Sands.* The juice of a desert shrub, such as the abal bush, made a russet-brown color (53, 66). Indigo was another color Thesiger saw throughout the region (31). Thomas also noted the common appearance of the "usual indigo mantle" (53).

According to Thesiger, firewood was easily located. Dead shrubs were abundant, and the local tribesmen would gather them and burn the roots (123). Also, flint was plentiful in the desert, and when combined with the steel blade of a dagger, the making of fire was relatively effortless (47). Apparently, the Lord didn't forbid the building of fires for Lehi due to the lack of fuel or flint.

Chapter 20

Scorpions were plentiful in the desert wherever there was any vegetation. Other common creatures included horned vipers and large spiders that "were as much as three inches across, with hairy, reddish legs, and pendulous bodies" (Thesiger, 108).

The bramble, or the blackberry, was used for the treatment of dysentery. The leaf could be chewed to treat bleeding gums and as a salve for burns. "The flower and fruit were considered a remedy for venomous bites" (Freedman, 2:805). The peel of the citron was also used for the treatment of snakebite (807). Storax could be used to make an ointment to reduce swelling (806).

In his travels, Thesiger visited a family's cave in which the floor was covered with goat-droppings. The leathery ticks came from the goats housed within the caves during the rainy season. The bites created painful lumps and sometimes caused fever (67).

Chapter 21

Scripture referenced: Exodus 12

The question may arise within this chapter: Why would the Lord allow Lehi and his family to live in bondage? If Lehi and his family lived as slaves during their stay in the wilderness, it wouldn't have been the first nor the last time the Lord allowed His people to live in such a way. The story of Moses and the Hebrew slaves is well known, but the experience of Lehi may have been reiterated much later in time, namely, when Alma (the Elder) and his people were persecuted and held captive by Amulon. The Lord did not deliver the people of Alma immediately but strengthened them so that they could bear their burdens with patience (see Mosiah 24:14–15). And when the people of Alma *were* delivered, it was by the hand of the Lord (24:21). Perhaps the Lord allows His people to labor in bondage from time to time so that He can deliver them.

In Hebrew and Egyptian tradition, a master presents gifts to his servant upon dismissal (Brown, *From Jerusalem to Zarahemla,* 61; Deut. 15:13–15). The Israelite slaves received the gift of redemption when they left Egypt, in addition to other goods such as flocks and herds. David Daube notes that it was natural when Pharaoh allowed the Israelites to leave with cattle and valuables: "Pharaoh is requested to behave as a decent master should" (*The Exodus Pattern in the Bible* [London: Faber and Faber, 1963], 51). Perhaps something similar happened when Lehi and his party took leave of a settlement in which they served.

Andrew C. Skinner explains that Passover commemorates "the night in Egypt when the angel of death, sent by Jehovah, passed over the homes of the children of Israel and spared the lives of their firstborn, providing they had sacrificed an unblemished male lamb, eaten the roasted meat, and daubed the blood of the lamb on the lintel and doorposts of their houses" (*Gethsemane* [Salt Lake City: Deseret Book, 2002], 28).

Skinner discusses the changes to Passover between the time of Moses and twelve hundred years later when Jesus came (29–31). Lehi's family would have celebrated Passover similar to traditions during the time of Moses found in Exodus 12. The elements of Lehi's Passover celebration would have included (or been modified depending on their circumstances) a male lamb that was slain as a sacrifice, blood placed on the doorpost, followed by the consumption of the lamb. This represented the future atonement of Jesus Christ. The unleavened bread—representing the children of Israel leaving Egypt in haste—would have been eaten at the Passover meal and for the following seven days. The bitter herbs would have also been consumed in memory of the bitterness of the slavery endured by the people of Moses (30).

Plants that grow in the sands include the tribulus, the heliotrope, abal, and the salt bush, which provided much needed fodder for camels (Thesiger, 115).

Thesiger remarks on the characteristics of the Bedu people in Arabia, who were always hungry but never turned away a guest unfed (50). The Bedu lived mainly on camel's milk, thus they usually only rode females (42). Thesiger discusses their love for conversation, their style of sitting—squatting, their soles hard from walking barefoot, and how they used sand to scrub their hands clean (48). The Bedu live in a tribal society, and Thesiger remarks that "there is no security in the desert for an individual outside the framework of his tribe" (79). Ironically, the tribal laws work best in anarchy but break down when peace is imposed (80).

The Bedu sleep under an open sky, using trees or rocks for shelter. Tents are used by those who live in the sands (73). Many of the wells contain bitter water, which is unpalatable, but the Arabians mix the water with camel's milk so that it is possible to drink (122). Some of their daily activities include repairing clothing, plaiting ropes, shaping camel-sticks, and gathering roots for fire (108).

Chapter 22

Scriptures referenced: Genesis 29:18; Hosea 2:19–20

Camels are able to travel unloaded up to twenty days without water, but only if they are able to find grazing (Thesiger, 103).

Ze'ev W. Falk explains that Samson made the offer of marriage to the woman of his choice, and then arranged the wedding festivities, just as Ishmael's son may have done *(Hebrew Law in Biblical Times* [Provo, UT: Brigham Young University Press, and Winona Lake, IN: Eisenbrauns, 2001], 125–126; see also Judges 14–15).

According to Falk, "biblical law distinguished between the two stages of the marriage relation: the betrothal and the nuptials" (145). The main purpose of the betrothal was centered on the mohar. Ezekiel 16:8 indicates that an oath or a covenant was also required (146). Nibley informs us that an oath made among desert people is considered sacred. In order to be binding, "an oath should be by the *life* of something" (*Lehi in the Desert,*

103). If the mohar wasn't available, "the bride-price was satisfied in the form of service to the father-in-law" (Falk, 147), something that may have happened if one of Ishmael's sons married one of Lehi's daughters in the wilderness.

Written marriage contracts existed in Babylonian society and are found on the Aramaic papyri. Among the Samaritans and the Jews of the first century B.C., marriage deeds were used. Falk theorizes that oral marriage contracts may have been sufficient during biblical times (149–50).

Chapter 23

Scriptures referenced: Deuteronomy 21:18–21; Matthew 19:6; 1 Nephi 8:5, 17–18, 28, 32; 11:33; Bible Dictionary, "Marriage"

Thesiger and his party rode along the gravel plains, parallel to the sands, because the traveling was easier on their camels (94). Brown theorizes that Lehi's party may have traveled with the same precautions if they went as far north as al-'Abr and turned eastward where they walked "between the sands of the 'Empty Quarter' on the north and the craggy landscape on the south" (*Echoes and Evidences of the Book of Mormon*, 90).

Roberts describes the Habrut oasis, which is thirty-five miles southwest of Shisur, where "a thick stand of date palms proclaimed the hidden spring that had made this oasis habitable for more than 3,000 years" (134). The characteristics at Habrut would have typified the oases that Lehi and his family would have encountered.

Chapter 24

Scripture referenced: 2 Nephi 3:1

According to Thesiger, with a "desert [that] was empty and full of fear," throwing up sand into the air when herdsmen were spotted was an accepted sign of peaceful intentions (57). Also, Thomas noted that "An approaching party may be friend, but is always assumed to be foe" (172).

Shisur is an oasis in Oman that has ruins existing from the Iron Age and later (1200 B.C.–A.D. 500). It was known as one of the eight oases in the legendary region of Ubar (Roberts, 124). Thesiger described Shisur as a well that is marked by the ruins of a stone fort—"the only permanent water in the central steppes." He remarked that the site was a place known for its many fierce fights between desert raiders. Thesiger's party spent two hours digging out the drifted sand in order to reach the bitter water (86).

Chapter 25

Scripture referenced: 1 Nephi 17:3.

According to Falk, a rebellious son could be put to death. The mistreatment of or rebellion against parents was considered a serious crime, and as outlined in Deuteronomy 21:18–21 and Exodus 21:15, 17, the rebellious son could be stoned to death (71).

Thomas described a desert thunderstorm as follows: "The low, rumbling thunder was like music to our ears. The sky grew dark, the lightning nearer, and the thunder-claps more violent; our camels shared the excitement" (151). He also describes the benefits of the head wraps his companions wore as they journeyed into the sun's glare: "The sun turned my face first lobster colour, then blistering raw; but now I had learnt the secret of swathing my head in the full wraps of an Arab head-dress" (155).

Frankincense was harvested by cutting incisions in the branches, through which the aromatic gum oozed (Freedman, 2:812). Roberts informs us that "even today, bedouins perfume their hair with frankincense, and Yemeni women ward off evil spirits by burning it as they celebrate the birth of a child" (130).

According to Gene Schramm, *kasrut* or *kashruth* (kosher law meaning "correctness"), it would have been considered unclean for Lehi's family to eat the meat of a camel (Freedman, 4:648). In Leviticus 11:4 it reads, "as the camel, because he cheweth the cud, but divideth not the hoof; he is unclean unto you." Schramm informs us that keeping kashruth is important for sanctification purposes, and physical health is considered an added benefit. In addition, practicing the law sets the Jewish people apart from the rest of the world (4:650).

A map of wells appears at the back of Thesiger's book, *Arabian Sands*, outlining possible oases where Lehi's party may have stopped. If traveling from Shisur to the Dhofar region (possible location for Bountiful), the family could have encountered the oasis Ma Shadid, then Aiyun, and/or Kismim.

Fish and locusts are the only exceptions to the requirement of ritual slaughter in which the blood is drained and the tallow removed (Freedman,

4:649). The habits of locusts are outlined in Thesiger's account where he observed "packed bands of hoppers extending over a front of several miles and with a depth of a hundred yards or more," which were considered small bands (28). Swarms bred in India during the monsoon, then moved to southern Persia or Arabia where they bred again, then passed on to East Africa or the Sudan. Then, inevitably disease riddled them and they would disappear as quickly as they appeared. The region of Dhofar was considered an outbreak center during the monsoon season (27–29).

Chapter 26

Scripture referenced: 1 Nephi 17:5–6

The Nephites and Lamanites observed the Law of Moses until the coming of Christ. Therefore, the family wouldn't have been able to eat certain animals in the wilderness (Tvedtnes and Roper). A list of kosher animals can be found in Leviticus 11. If Lehi's family encountered dead animal carcasses, they would not have been able to eat them. According to Jewish meal customs, animals that had died of natural causes were forbidden as food (Freedman, 4:649).

Possible locations for Bountiful have been researched by many scholars. According to Brown, without a doubt, Lehi's family "emerged from the desert at some point along the south coast of modern Oman. The one-hundred-mile long maritime plain is the only region in southern Arabia that fits Nephi's portrait of 'much fruit,' 'wild honey,' and 'timbers.' The summer monsoon rains turn the area into a garden of Eden, enlivening an isolated ecosystem that is bounded on the north by the desert and on the south by the sea" ("Refining the Spotlight on Lehi and Sariah").

Thomas discusses the presence of dew in the Qara region (52), a possible candidate for the land of Bountiful. Nibley quotes Thomas's experience when he first saw this stretch of coast: "What a glorious place! Mountains three thousand feet high basking above a tropical ocean, their seaward slopes velvety with waving jungle, their roofs fragrant with rolling yellow meadows, beyond which the mountains slope northwards to a red sandstone steppe" (*Lehi in the Desert,* 110).

Aston outlines the criteria that Bountiful needed in order to fit Nephi's description: "'nearly eastward' from Nahom, overland access possible from the interior desert, fertile land, area surrounding Bountiful was probably fertile, suitable for a long encampment and for shipbuilding, available timber, year-round supply of freshwater, a prominent mountain, cliffs overlooking the ocean, a source of ore, and suitable winds and currents to carry the ship out into the Arabian Sea and eventually into the Indian Ocean" ("The Arabian Bountiful Discovered? Evidence for Nephi's Bountiful," *Journal of Book of Mormon Studies* 7, no. 1, [1998], 7–11).

Ziziphus, or *zéd,* was a source of nourishment in the Dhofar region of Oman. The yellow fruit grows sweeter and softer with age and tastes similar to an apple. Ziziphus also provided fodder for grazing livestock in drier seasons, its flowers provided bee forage, and the leaves were used as a cleansing agent for the hair and scalp (Anthony G. Miller and Miranda Morris, *Plants of Dhofar: The Southern Region of Oman Traditional, Economic and Medicinal Uses,* [Prepared and Published by the Office of the Adviser for Conservation of the Environment, Diwan of Royal Court Sultinate of Oman, 1988], 242, 329).

In Nephi's vision, he saw a water barrier between his descendants and the later explorers, but he wouldn't have known enough about geography to have any idea of where the land of promise was (see 1 Ne. 13:10, 12). It is possible that when the family reached their Bountiful, many or all of them thought they had arrived in the promised land. I suspect that although Lehi and Nephi were grateful to be in such a beautiful place, it didn't take long before they realized they hadn't arrived at their final destination.

In poignant reflection, President Joseph F. Smith said, "I have learned that there are a great many things which are far worse than death. I would far rather follow every child I have to the grave in their innocence and purity, than to see them grow up to man and womanhood and degrade themselves by the pernicious practices of the world, forget the Gospel, forget God and the plan of life and salvation, and turn away from the only hope of eternal reward and exaltation in the world to come" (*Teachings of the Presidents of the Church: Joseph F. Smith* [Salt Lake City: The Church of Jesus Christ of Latter-day Saints, 1998], 133). We know that Laman and Lemuel complained, "Our women have toiled, . . . and they have . . . suffered all things, save it were death; and it would have been better that they had died." (1 Ne. 17:20). And Lehi spoke these words concerning his youngest son, Joseph, "Thou wast born in the wilderness of mine afflictions; yea, in the days of my greatest sorrow did thy mother bear thee" (2 Ne. 3:1). Like President Smith, perhaps Lehi knew there were worse things than death, and he and his family had experienced them.

As a final note, in Thesiger's timeless words, "A cloud gathers, the rain falls, men live; the cloud disperses without rain, and men and animals die. In the deserts of southern Arabia there is no rhythm of the seasons, no rise and fall of sap, but empty wastes where only the changing temperature marks the passage of the years. It is a bitter, desiccated land which knows nothing of gentleness or ease" (1).

Lehi and his family—strangers in Arabia—survived this wilderness that Thesiger speaks of, their lives dependent on the mercy of God.

SELECTED BIBLIOGRAPHY

Aston, Warren P., and Michaela Knoth Aston. *In the Footsteps of Lehi.* Salt Lake City: Deseret Book, 1994.

Brown, S. Kent. *From Jerusalem to Zarehemla.* Salt Lake City: Bookcraft, and Provo, UT: Religious Studies Center, Brigham Young University, 1998.

———. *Voices from the Dust.* American Fork, UT: Covenant Communications, 2004.

Doughty, Charles. *Travels in Arabia Deserta.* 2 vols. New York: Random House, 1936.

Hilton, Lynn M., and Hope A. Hilton. *Discovering Lehi.* Springville, UT: Cedar Fort, 1996.

Nibley, Hugh. *An Approach to the Book of Mormon.* The Collected Works of Hugh Nibley 6. Salt Lake City: Deseret Book, and Provo, UT: FARMS, 1988.

———. *Lehi in the Desert.* The Collected Works of Hugh Nibley 5. Salt Lake City: Deseret Book, and Provo, UT: FARMS, 1988.

Potter, George, and Richard Wellington. *Lehi in the Wilderness.* Springville, UT: Cedar Fort, 2003.

Thesiger, Wilfred. *Arabian Sands.* New York: E. P. Dutton, 1959.

Thomas, Bertram. *Arabia Felix.* New York: Charles Scribner's Sons, 1932.